Angels
And
Demons
by
Michael Porter

Copyright © 2023 Michael Porter
All rights reserved.
ISBN: **9798866500017**

DEDICATION

Thanks to Lloyd R. Martin, a fellow wordsmith for encouragement and the exact opposite on occasion.

Thanks to John Kenny, songsmith and guitarist, whose lyrics appear occasionally throughout this volume.

Special thanks to my wife Jackie, who appears twice in this novel. A cancer survivor.

For Chris Greenwood, guitarist and perfectionist, he appears as Nutter, sorry Chris I didn't have a place for a guitarist. Gone far too soon, taken by cancer. Rest in Peace.

For Dave "The Squirrel" Littlewood, a great keyboard player, another taken from us by cancer, Rest in Peace.

Remember no matter how evil may assail you,

There is still love in this world.

Chapter 1: The Axe and Cleaver

The Axe and Cleaver is a quiet country pub at the only crossroads in a small village in Lincolnshire, very few who have never been there even know of its existence. The place is called North Somercotes, see, I told you you'd never heard of it. Karen the landlady called into the almost empty lounge bar.

"You guys want more beer?"

"That'd be great," said Roaddog. Jackie turned and smiled at Karen.

"Do we really need to?" asked Jackie, her voice low enough so that no one else in the bar could hear her.

"We were making an awful lot of money," he replied just as quietly. They both paused while Karen dropped their beers on the table and removed the empty plates.

"That trade destroyed the Dragonriders," said Jackie as soon as Karen was out of earshot, he nodded slowly, she was in many respects right, it was a war with drug dealers that got most of the Dragonriders killed. "How are the miners doing?" she asked.

"Great, we're making a lot of money there, and with the power being free, those solar panels are so much more efficient than my old ones, the batteries are huge, we can probably run all the lights off the batteries as well as the miners."

"Let's not be too greedy, we need to be running somethings off the grid, then the electric company won't want to visit."

"You could be right there, though there is nothing that they can say about our power systems. I'll go settle up." He stood up and walked over to the bar. Jackie watched as he walked away, 'Damn, he looks fine in those tight jeans,' she thought, smiling to herself. Roaddog presented his card to Karen, who was watching Jackie as he was coming towards her, thinking much the same. She also thought that Jackie looked far too young for him. 'Not that it is any of my business.' she admonished herself silently before his card payment was cleared.

"How's things going?" she asked.

"We're doing okay, it's going to be tight to get things completed before the opening day, but we should make it."

"When's that going to be?"

"First week august, I'm hoping to build something up before the bank holiday. We'll see. I have an idea though."

"Go on," Karen said inquisitively.

"I'm not going to attempt a beer licence, so what if I send the thirsty ones here, you sell them beer in plastic glasses, and I bring them back when I collect them?"

"That sounds okay, but you're going to be selling food as well."

"I'm going to be offering bacon butties and burgers from a roadside van, nothing like as good as the food you serve here. I don't believe we'll be stealing any of your trade, you might even find the more discerning customers coming here to eat anyway. How much is a case of plastic glasses?"

"Forty quid, I think."

Roaddog pulled two twenties from his wallet and passed them to Karen.

"We're going to be selling burned meat between bits of bread and sauce that comes in two colours, your burgers are something special. I've eaten enough of them," he laughed.

"That's for certain," smiled Karen.

"See ya later," said Roaddog turning away.

When he got back to the table Jackie was just standing up.

"What was the cash for?" she asked, "services rendered?"

"Behave, she's a happily married woman," he pulled her close and kissed her firmly.

"Let's go home," she whispered pushing him away.

"Fine," he muttered, keeping one arm on her waist, and moving them both towards the door.

"See ya Karen," called Jackie as they neared the door, Karen waved, and they were out into the night. In a moment the soft rumble of the Victory filled the quiet of the village as they pulled out onto the main street. The roads were empty even though the night was only young, the track to the place they were staying was potholed and rough, the unlit lane was in a real state, but he knew where the major holes were and avoided them with relative ease. When they arrived at the static caravan they were staying in, Jackie jumped off and helped pull the heavy bike backwards over the rough gravel, the kickstand dropped onto the two-foot square paving stone, the only one on the path. The pair had some practise at this manoeuvre over the last two months. In only minutes they were in bed, but sleep was about an hour away, it had been a terribly busy day.

Roaddog woke to the sound of birds scampering on the roof, he rolled slowly out of bed and went into the living room, pausing to put the kettle on, he reached up and opened the front curtains, out of the window he saw the row of caravans parked across the gravelled road, and beyond them the lake. The sun was just up above the horizon and the ripples on the lake scattered flashing red light in his eyes.

"Put some clothes on, you'll frighten the natives," said Jackie from behind him.

"There's no one up this time of day," he replied smiling. "Look at that view, it's just so lovely here."

"It's that," she answered coming to the front of the van to stand beside him, equally scary for the natives. "Should we stay here when the workshop is finished?" she asked.

"I'd like to, but I'd worry about all the hardware we have in that place."

"We can beef the alarms and the doors and windows," she whispered, as a passing fisherman waved to them both, on his way to his early morning set up.

"You'd like to live here rather than in the village?" he asked.

"Wouldn't you?"

"I'm not sure how the locals would like us living here full time."

"They'll learn to deal with it, they can always shut their eyes," she laughed, turning towards the kitchen, she slapped him on the ass and went to make their morning coffee.

"Damn, bitch, when did your hands get so hard?"

"When some bastard put me to work building walls and rooms, plumbing is fun, electric wiring is great as well. So, I've now got hands like a navvy, and muscles like a weightlifter."

"Well, at least you're having a good time," laughed Roaddog.

"Good time, my ass," she smiled, returning to the sunlit front window with a cup for him and one for herself. They stood side by side watching the sun climb slowly higher.

"Come on," he said, "we got shit to do today. Let's get moving."

"So, what's the plan?" she asked moving away from the window. They went into the bedroom and started getting dressed, t-shirts and jeans the order of the day.

"If we can get the partition walls erected and the painting finished that should be enough for today."

"Have we got enough plasterboard?" she asked, "I think we're a few sheets short."

"I'll check when we get there, I can get more delivered before lunch. What about the supplies for the burger van."

"We got enough to start with, I don't expect that we'll need too much until the bank holiday weekend."

"Tonight, we'll go to that bike meet in Horncastle, should be a nice ride-out and there should be at least three or four clubs there."

"So, a hot sweaty day labouring and then off to press the flesh with some bikers. Sounds like heaven."

"We'll come back here for a shower then."

"Deal. Get dressed." In only minutes they were on the road back to the new garage.

They pulled up outside the big shutter doors. Jackie got off and inserted her key into the control box, slowly with some grinding noises the shutter rose, once it was high enough Roaddog rolled his bike inside. After a few seconds he rolled the beaten-up transit van out onto the forecourt. The building was a strange shape, a huge arched corrugated iron roof ran the full length but, in the front, were two huge doors big enough for double decker buses to pass through without any problem. This was an old bus garage, surrounded with more than enough space for fifty buses to park, or there used to be, much of the space was now scrubland and brambles. The rear one third of the roof was covered with the new solar panels, maybe not the most efficient arrangement but the sheer square meterage was enough for a large business, and this was going to be that. With a quick count Roaddog realised that Jackie was correct, a phone call left a message on an answering machine, Roaddog knew that his supplier wouldn't let him down, ten more sheets on the way. Maybe it was a bit early to be ringing businesses. Jackie started the bacon butties while he checked on the success of the miners.

"Wow," he called once the figures where in.

"What you get?" she shouted back from the kitchen area.

"Four hits, total about two K. Switching it all now, shit, I hope we get some sun, those miners got hungry in the dark," he laughed loudly.

"Will they get hungry during the day?"

"Maybe, we'll just have to see, but even at those rates we can afford to feed them from the grid."

"How are they for temperature?"

"Not good, we might have to put in more coolers."

"If they're going to make us that much, we can afford some, but it was real warm last night."

"You certainly got hot," he smiled walking over and taking a sandwich in one hand and her waist in the other, a smouldering kiss was exchanged before they stepped apart to eat breakfast. The coffee machine kicked out two cups as they started work. It was indeed sweaty labour, lifting heavy sheets of plasterboard into place and fixing them to the stud work they had been building for the last few days. Before they stopped for lunch a flatbed truck rolled up and dropped them the sheets that they needed. As soon as they were moved inside, Jackie called lunch.

"Let's go the pub," she said, "come get washed up a bit, ya know Karen doesn't like workmen in her place." They spent a few minutes blowing the dust from their clothes and then they washed the worst off their hands. Roaddog put the transit back inside and Jackie started the door closing, he had to duck quite low by the time he got there, he smiled as he took her hand and together, they walked towards the Axe.

"You two timed it perfectly," said Karen as she opened the door to them.

"We know what time you open," said Roaddog, "Citra for me, lager for Jackie, we'll have two of your lovely burgers and we'll sit in the pool room, you know, in case some of your posh customers come in."

"You're all heart," laughed Karen, stepping aside so they could walk in, the two turned left into the pool room. Just as Karen was bringing their beers over Roaddog's phone rang, he looked at it for a moment or two before he answered it.

"Hello," he said.

"Roaddog?" asked the voice.

"Maybe."

"It's Wolf, you're a hard man to get hold of."

"I plan to keep it that way."

"I don't blame ya, have you any idea how much of a shit storm you set off?"

"Not really, the guys tell me the cops are real pissed, but they got no proof."

"Oh, they got tons of proof, just none of it points to you."

"That's just the way I like it. You guys taking some heat or something?" he asked.

"You could say that, by the time the cops turned up at that place in Hyde the vultures had already descended. There were kids running around with kilo bags of coke, it went nuts. They came round to our clubhouse mob handed and loaded for bear. They took so many of us in, but we'd cleared the gear out. It was very close though; the couriers were only minutes down the road when the vans came in."

"Sorry about that man, but I wasn't leaving the girls to those bastards."

"Oh, we fully understand what went down, they were looking for shotguns, lots of them."

"Let them keep looking, you didn't have any did ya?"

"No, they thought that there must have been five guns at least, but none that match the ones they recovered."

"Yes, they got a pump and a sawn-off double."

"They made a big thing about the two machine guns they captured."

"So, they missed one."

"What do you mean?"

"We left three behind."

"You just left them?"

"Yes, I don't need them, and they are damned thirsty."

"I saw the pics on the news, were all three the same?"

"Yep."

"So, who got number three?"

"One of the vultures?" laughed Roaddog.

"You mean there's some kid running around my city with a fucking mac 10?" demanded Wolf.

"Unless one of the cops wanted a trophy, I wouldn't worry about it though, first time some kid fires the thing, he'll be dry in two seconds, then he'll piss in his pants."

"But how many can he kill in that time?"

"Some if he does it right, but I'm betting he's already emptied it, showing off to his mates, keep your ears open for someone after forty-five bullets, they'll want a lot as well," he paused before continuing. "When did you meet Slowball?"

"I bumped into him at a Chorley Centurions rock night, he sent me your number."

"I know that, he asked permission first."

"That Man-Dare was real pissed you know?"

"Yes, she has mentioned it a time or two."

"One of those assholes gave her crabs," laughed Wolf.

"She doing okay now?"

"Yes, she's still with Billy, and settled in with the new crowd, Billy is doing okay as well, she's not actually killed anyone yet."

"Billy's the one that'll have a heart attack."

"At least he'll die happy," said Wolf, "anyway enough chit chat, you want some goods sending over, our supplier seems to have lost one of his major customers."

"Sorry man, not interested, I'm making enough money from other sources, and I don't want that sort of shit happening again, hell there's only me and Jackie here."

"Wherever here is?"

"I'll invite you to the opening of the new place but be prepared for a good ride."

"Yes, I hear that you are a long ways off."

"I gotta be careful in case the cops are still sniffing around ya know."

"I understand, well it's been great talking to ya."

"No sweat man," said Roaddog, "I'll try and get some camp site cleared out if you and some of the guys want to come down, you know for a weekend."

"That'd be good. Catch ya sometime." Wolf hung up.

"Wolf okay?" asked Jackie.

"Yes, getting some heat from the cops, and has excess product to move."

"But you turned him down."

"I did, you heard me. That was not easy."

"We don't need that anymore, once we get the garage up and running, we'll be making more than enough," her smile made him happy. Karen turned up from the kitchen and put their meals on the table.

"Everything okay?" she asked.

"Everything is fine, some friends from back home are having a hard time with the cops for some reason, but they're much too far away for us to be able to help. You might even get to meet some of them if they come over for the opening day."

"That would be nice," said Karen, "it's always nice to make new friends."

"It is," laughed Jackie. She watched as Karen walked away.

"She'd keep a body warm on a winters night," she whispered to Roaddog.

"Behave," he muttered, "she's married, and this is a rural area, almost every guy has at least one shotgun."

"And most of the girls," she laughed loudly, then reached across running her hand up his thigh, "I prefer your gun any day."

"Damn it girl, you're crazy."

"I wasn't until I met you."

"Eat, woman," he said, smiling still.

They focused on the meals in front of them, silence descended on the pool room. Karen came to the bar and looked at the two of them, but she didn't interrupt, they were too engrossed in the food. She smiled as someone came into the other bar; she went to serve them.

By the time Roaddog and Jackie had finished eating the place was starting to get quite busy, but still Karen brought them each a beer, as this was their normal lunch time method, food and beer, then beer.

"If we can get the boards up and the edges taped, we'll call that it for today, I'll set up the sprayer and do the painting tomorrow," said Roaddog.

"I'll check out the burger bar, make sure everything is clean and ready, we might even make our own lunch," Jackie laughed.

"I heard that," said Karen from the bar.

"Just as an experiment," laughed Roaddog, "we've still got too much to do to be making our own meals. Anyway, it's much nicer to come here for lunch."

"You smooth talking devil," Karen laughed as she went back into the other bar.

"So, once we get the painting done, there's not a lot left," said Jackie.

"Oh, there's still some to do, there's a bar to set up, music systems, work benches, we've got more than enough to keep us going for a few weeks."

"We don't have a few weeks," said Jackie.

"We have enough time, but I need to find some furniture, we need a couple of couches and some good chairs."

"You planning on making this place just like the old one?"

"Why not? We had plenty of good times there."

"And some bad ones."

"Some," he whispered. Jackie reached out and took his hand, she saw the tears in his eyes as the memories came flooding back.

"You did everything that anyone could have expected."

"Except keep them all alive," he said, his voice hoarse in his throat.

"If you'd been there, we'd all have died."

"I know, but I'd have preferred that none of us had been killed."

"We'll not get involved in anything like that again, you've already turned Wolf down."

"I know, we'll keep things as straight as we can," he smiled, "well, nearly."

"Come on," she said, "pay Karen then we can get back to work."

They walked down to the garage and set to, they almost didn't need to talk at all, they had so much practise working together that each knew what the other was doing and anticipated their every move. Taping up the edges to hide the joints and the screws took only another hour, by four o-clock they were ready to leave.

"Van or bike?" asked Jackie.

"If we go in the van the bikers will think we are out to steal bikes, bike of course."

"Just thought I'd check. Home first for a shower or pub for tea?"

"There's bound to be a burger van there tonight, so we'll have a burger and see if we can get a flyer up in their van."

"I'm getting sick of burgers, come weekend you are taking me out for a real meal, get it?"

"I understand, we've been working so hard that you deserve something real nice, I'll ask Karen where I should take you for a special treat."

"You know she's going to say the axe," she slapped him on the arm and went to get her lid.

"Damn bitch, that hurt," he smiled at her.

"What do you expect, you've turned me into a labourer?"

"I'm sorry about that, but fuck do I love those muscles."

"You like that my arms look like a muscle mans'?" she asked, flexing her right bicep, which was indeed quite impressive for a woman.

"No," laughed Roaddog, "I was thinking more about those muscles in the core that make your whole body shake at those special moments." The sparkle in his eyes made her shake her head and walk out of the front door. He fired the Victory and rolled out of the main door; her key caused the door to grind downwards in its tracks. Then she swung her leg over the bike and settled into the rear seat. When her knees gripped his hips, he threw out the clutch and set off for their current home. As she pulled the bike backwards into its parking space she called above the noise of the exhaust.

"Is the bike sounding a bit rough?"

"Yes, she needs a run, and she's going to get one."

"Sounds great to me. Let's get cleaned up first."

They climbed the steps to the decking and then in through the front door. Before Jackie had walked through the kitchen she was naked, she stepped into the bathroom, and fired up the shower, she looked at Roaddog and grinned as she stepped into the tiny shower cubicle and closed the door.

"Fuck we gotta get a bigger shower or better still a bath," snarled Roaddog, as he moved into the small bathroom to watch.

By the time he had watched Jackie get herself clean he was really excited. Jackie stepped out of the shower and grinned up at him reaching out to grip the most excited part of him.

"Get clean," she said, "we have a long way to go before we can go to bed."

"You know you can be a real bitch," he said as she pulled him towards the shower cubicle and walked into the bedroom to get dressed.

By the time he came out of the shower she was drying her hair and smiling at him.

"You could have put some clothes on," he said. She was sitting on the bed with the hair dryer in her right hand and a brush in her left. She spread her legs wide to give him a better view. He moved in close with a growl. Her legs snapped shut and she pushed him away with the spiky hairbrush.

"Later," she whispered.

"Bitch," he muttered moving over to the chest of drawers that contained, well his drawers. He pulled up the bikini briefs and dropped a t-shirt over his head before he turned to see that she was already wearing her panties and t-shirt, she was pulling on her jeans.

"Damn it girl, you got some gorgeous tits," he said admiring the way they moved without a bra.

"You're not so bad yourself," she said grabbing the bulge in his underpants. "How long to Hornycastle?" she asked, stroking him slowly.

"That's Horncastle, and about forty-five minutes."

"Well, we need to hit the road," she laughed.

"You do know that you can be a complete bitch, don't you?" he said as she moved away from him.

"Of course I do," she grinned, "maybe we'll have some fun later." She hitched her jeans up and went into the living room, leaving him to his own devices.

He followed her in a minute or two, she smiled at him and started fastening her boots, he stopped to watch the action going on under her t-shirt as every buckle snapped shut.

"Stop gawking," she said without looking up, "get dressed, it's been far too long since we had a real ride."

"I can't help it, I'm enjoying the view, damn it girl you're gorgeous."

"You just like the tits," she grinned up at him.

"You're not wrong."

"Jane didn't have much in the way of tits."

"But she was beautiful anyway, I wonder if she'll ever come back to us?"

"I hope so, she was wonderful, I really miss her." Jackie's voice gradually faded away and sadness filled her eyes.

"So do I," he whispered, taking her in his arms and kissing her softly.

"Come on," she said pushing him away, "let's hit the road." He followed her outside and together they set off around the site roads and down the lane to the main road. Soon the Victory was singing its characteristic song as he snapped up and down the gearbox. Jackie was leaning back against the backrest, feeling the road beneath her, and the heavy beat of the engine, simply enjoying the freedom of the open road, her thoughts turned inwards as her body flowed along with the motorcycle. She thought of Jane again, how much she missed her presence and her touch, her smell and her taste.

"Damn it," she whispered to herself, "she has to come back to us." She leaned forwards and pressed her body against Roaddog, then snapped her knees against his hips. She could feel his whole body smile as the power rolled on through the heavy frame and the bike leapt forwards, he knew what she wanted, and he was going to do his very best to deliver. As she rested against him the bike accelerated into the bends and then even harder out, on the straights his wheels were dodging from one side of the centre line to the other, depending on which side the cars where on. The Cadwell park motorcycle racing track flew past on their left at more than one hundred miles an hour, a distance further on, but not very much in time at all they encountered that most unusual of situations in Lincolnshire, there were some steep hills, some rapid curves on a downhill followed by the same climbing out of the valley. Another hill without any curves and then some more flats without bends, only a tiny village that flashed past in an instant. Leaving behind the blare of angry horns and the twin flash of a speed camera. Roaddog laughed aloud and kept pouring on the power, wondering for the briefest of moments who was going to get that ticket. He shut the throttle down as he went past the metallic giraffes just outside Horncastle. Jackie looked up as the speed fell rapidly, the steady rumble of the v-twin made her smile, she squeezed Roaddog and settled back in the seat again. Through the middle of the town he went at the speed limit, when he pulled up at the red traffic light the motorcyclists that he'd passed along the road started to catch up. When the lights turned to green the bikes all set off, in a polite and orderly manner, something to do with the police car parked on the other side of the junction. It was not too much of a surprise for Roaddog, as he knew that the meeting place was only a hundred yards up the road, he pulled off into the Black Swan car park, which was already busy with bikes. He rolled backwards into an empty slot and killed the motor. Jackie dismounted and stood beside him for a moment as the bike settled onto its stand. He stood up and turned to Jackie, "What's wrong?" he asked, barely loud enough to be heard over the noise of motorcycle engines.

"I was thinking of Jane, I miss her."

"Me too, talk to her and let her know how you feel, perhaps she'll come over for a visit."

"If she comes for a weekend," laughed Jackie, "she ain't ever going home." He joined her in the laughter then asked.

"Beer or food?"

"Beer," she replied.

She followed him as he made his way into the pub, the bar was packed, he joined the crush as Jackie stepped back and made her way outside, the queue at the burger van was not much better, but she decided not to join it, food could wait. She wandered slowly around the car park, checking out the bikes, there were a lot of good looking motorcycles there and more than one or two really tatty looking ones, 'rat bikes' she thought remembering something that Roaddog had told her. She had a rough count and came to a hundred or so motorcycles already, and it was still early. She returned to the bar and found Roaddog coming towards the door with four pints in his hands, she snatched the palest two and smiled at him. Together they walked around the back of the pub, there were even more bikes on that side, and a gate into the field behind was open, already being used as overflow parking.

"Well, that blows my estimate away," said Jackie,

"There's a real crowd here," he said.

"We may not have enough flyers."

"We don't want too many turning up on opening day, but if we pass out enough flyers, we might just get enough interest."

"The more the merrier," laughed Jackie, putting down her now empty first pint.

"Damn girl, you've turned into a serious drinker."

"You've turned me into a serious labourer, so I deserve a beer."

"Me too," he laughed, dropping his glass inside hers on the corner of a table. He glanced at the people around the table and handed a flyer to two of them.

"New shop and workshop opening for the bank holiday weekend, there'll be food available, plenty of parking and music, come on down, it'll be a blast," he said.

"Maybe," said one of the guys, "we'll be up that neck of the woods that weekend, there's a rally nearby."

"Where at?" asked Jackie.

"Marshchapel," said the man. Jackie looked at Roaddog.

"It's about two villages north on the coast road," he turned to the man, "who's running that one?"

"It's one of the Grimsby clubs, so it's sure to be on. There's a car show and a bike show, and an outside stage for the bands."

"Sounds like a good do," said Roaddog, "perhaps we'll see you that weekend."

"Perhaps," said the man smiling. Roaddog nodded and walked away. Jackie followed him, this conversation was repeated many times as they wandered around the crowd of bikers passing out flyers and talking to everyone that showed even the slightest of interest, in this respect Jackie's lack of a bra was helping enormously.

"I need another beer," she said, steering them towards the bar. Inside he got them more beer and handed out a few more flyers, Jackie had found an empty table in a corner, it wasn't quiet, but she was at least able to make a telephone call. He sat beside her only getting one half of the conversation, but he soon realised that she was talking to Jane. Eventually the talk ran down and Jackie hung up.

"Is she going to come?" he asked.

"Maybe, that's the best I could get out of her, maybe."

"How are things back home?"

"She's doing okay, still working at the club, still meeting with the bands and the bikers, and the rugby crowd, but she's bored."

"She'd not be bored if she came here."

"I've told her, but she still scared."

"She still won't talk to me," his voice trailed off as he spoke.

"She's frightened of you and everything."

"I hope she comes round, she's a lovely girl, and we all fit together so well."

"I miss her too." Jackie frowned as the conversation turned back to the thoughts she had on the way to the Black Swan.

"I have an idea," smiled Roaddog, "you know that tatty trike frame I picked up a couple of weeks ago?"

"Yes, what about it?"

"I've got an old sportster motor in one of those crates, I can put the thing together and offer it to Jane, maybe she'll feel more at home here if she wasn't stuck with that car of hers."

"Ya can give it a try; we could both share it."

"Now that's an even better idea."

"Of course it is, come on I've had enough of this place, I wanna feel the road under me again," she finished her pint in a heartbeat and dragged him to his feet. Moments later they were climbing aboard his motorcycle and setting off towards home, the roads were now dark and the streetlights few and far between once they were out of the small villages, the ride home was a little more relaxed than the ride out had been, but not by so much. It was quite late when they pulled up outside the caravan.

Chapter 2: Opening day.

It was still full dark when Roaddog got out of bed, not that he had slept much, the worry about the day ahead had filled his mind all night. August bank holiday is on Monday and today is Saturday, the weathermen were saying it was going to be a fine day, he snorted to himself as he read the latest from the met office. He was staring out of the front window waiting for the sun to rise, when he heard the button on the kettle click down. He turned to watch as Jackie walked towards him.

"Can't sleep?" she asked.

"You too?"

"I slept okay, but it got cold when you left."

"The weathermen say it's going to be a good day."

"What do they know?" she smiled, "it's going to be a great day."

"It's going to be hard work."

"It's been that already," she laughed, flexing her right arm and showing the increased muscle mass caused by the hard work they had both been doing.

"Shop's ready to go, workshop is ready to go, stores are built and stocked, still some work to do on the living quarters, but no real rush for that, not while we've got this place. It's just a shame that we didn't get it all ready earlier, I suppose the Saturday of a bank holiday weekend is as good a time as any to be opening." Behind him the kettle clicked, and the sound of coffee being made added to the noise of his words. The lightening of the sky foretold sunrise, he smiled at the peace all around. Jackie came to the front of the van, put his cup on the table and bent over to kiss him. As she stood up, an old man came out of the van between theirs and the lake, he waved at the pair, and they waved back. The man came down his steps and picked up his rods and his trolley and set off around the lake, a big smile on his face.

"His wife collared me yesterday," Roaddog said quietly.

"And?" Jackie asked sitting down facing Roaddog.

"He's mentioned seeing us naked in the mornings."

"And?"

"She's sad that we've gone to work before she gets up, but she's happy about the increase in other things, it's like someone has taken ten years off his age, her words."

"That's so nice," said Jackie.

"And unusual in people of her age, she must be in her seventies."

"That means they grew up in the sixties, wild flower power hippies, perhaps they remember running around naked and having fun."

"Maybe, perhaps they're just randy old people." The door on the other van opened and a woman walked out, she turned towards them. Roaddog stood up so that he was clearly visible to her and lifted his cup, in his right hand, then beckoned her with his left. She stood very still for a few seconds then started towards them.

"Put the kettle on, we have a visitor coming," he said to Jackie.

"Clothes?" she asked.

"Nah, she already knows we're naked." The woman checked carefully before she crossed the road, not so much for traffic, more to see if any of the neighbours were awake and watching. She almost ran across the road and up the steps to the front door. Roaddog opened the door and waved her in.

"Damn you're gorgeous," she said as she went past.

"Tea, coffee," asked Roaddog, "bourbon, vodka?"

"No vodka, I finished that last night," said Jackie.

"Okay," said Roaddog, "Tea, coffee or bourbon?"

"Too early for spirits I think," said the old woman, "Coffee if you please my dear, you are beautiful too."

"Coffee it is," smiled Jackie waving towards a seat at the front of the van.

"My name is Gladys, by the way," she said taking the seat the Jackie had just vacated.

"I'm Roaddog, and that beautiful girl is Jackie."

"Please to meet you, I'm sure," said Gladys.

"The weathermen say it's going to be another nice day," said Roaddog as Jackie handed Gladys a steaming mug and sat down next to him.

"I didn't come here to talk about the weather," she said.

"What would you like to talk about?" asked Roaddog.

"You and your naked antics."

"You want us to stop?"

"Hell no, I'm getting far more sex now than I was last year."

"So, you're worried we'll steal your man away."

"Hell no again, we were together before the commune in Kent, and we were married soon after we left it. He'll not leave me."

"So what are you worried about?"

"Right now the old fool is probably round the other side of the lake, under his big brolly, jacking off, thinking about that naked pussy of yours," she nodded at Jackie, "I'm frightened he'll give himself a heart attack."

"That'd be a headline and a half," laughed Roaddog.

"Won't it," agreed Gladys, "Did he come before he went?" she laughed.

"So what can we do to help?" asked Jackie.

"Well," said Gladys, "I do have a question."

"Ask," said Roaddog.

"I can see, quite clearly see, that both of you are shaved, why?"

"Who likes a mouthful of pubic hair?" he asked.

"There are some that do," said Jackie, "heard of a woman in the papers last year, she had surgery to remove a massive hairball from her stomach."

"That's plain sick," said Roaddog. They both looked at Gladys who was sitting with her mouth hanging open. After a short pause, "What's wrong Gladys?" he asked.

"Sort of stunned," she whispered.

"By what?"

"Well, you actually do the mouth thing, and some people eat pubic hair, that's a lot to take in."

"Oh, it can be," laughed Jackie.

"My husband is not exactly small," Gladys said, "if you know what I mean."

"Oh, I understand," said Jackie, "but we know a girl that can eat a foot long hotdog without biting it," her and Roaddog laughed at the size of Gladys's eyes.

"You're joking surely?" she asked, shakily.

"No," said Jackie, "Cherie has a certain oral talent, but she's not without challengers."

"I've always thought that oral was sort of dirty."

"It can be, that's part of the fun, I do prefer my dick nice and clean from the shower, but there are times when sweaty and straight from the jeans, stuffed down the throat is the only way to go."

"And you," said Gladys looking into Roaddog's eyes and then down at Jackie's crotch and back.

"Oh yes, I love the taste of pussy, clean from the shower, chlorinated from the swimming pool, or hot tangy and sweaty from a night of drinking and dancing. Can't be beat. You've never done it?"

"What with a woman?" asked Gladys, even more shocked than ever.

"Oh, you should try that," said Jackie, "it's really different."

"You people are crazy," said Gladys, looking down at Roaddog, "Oh my, do you want me to leave?" she asked quietly.

"Of course not," said Jackie, "we're talking about sex and he's not dead, what did you expect to happen?" She reached across and took Roaddog in hand slowly stroking.

"Crazy, you're crazy," whispered Gladys, unable to remove her eyes from Roaddog's penis.

"You were curious about shaving?" asked Jackie, shaking Gladys back to eye contact.

"Yes, other than the pubic hair in the mouth, why?"

"It feels smooth and clean, but it itches like a bastard when it starts to grow back."

"High maintenance then?"

"Only if you have to do it yourself, if you get a friend to do it, then that's a whole new kettle of fish," smiled Jackie.

"He shaves you?"

"And I him, occasionally. That really is scary, scrotum the only thing that bleeds worse than a head wound," she smiled.

"I can't ask him to do it, I'd planned it as a surprise."

"Get a girl friend to do it."

"I don't have that sort of girlfriend," said Gladys.

"Nor do I anymore," said Jackie looking down, her hand stopped. For a short while silence descended on the caravan, eventually Roaddog's cock twitched in Jackie's hand, it was unhappy at the lack of motion. She looked up at him, her eyes narrowed, then flashed in the direction of Gladys, and back again. A question in them. Roaddog shook his head, it moved no more than a hairs breadth, but she could see it. Her eyes flashed again, and this time her left hand tensed, harshly. Roaddog's eyes opened wide, again the shake of the head. Jackie's eyes narrowed and flashed towards Gladys, her left hand clenched. Roaddog swallowed loudly.

"Gladys, would you like me to shave you? I have to ask, or she's going to squeeze my cock so hard the end will drop off."

"You people are crazy, just crazy," muttered Gladys, shaking her head.

"She's not running away," said Jackie moving her hand away from Roaddog.

"No she's not," said Roaddog, "but I think you've broken me." Looking down at a seriously deflated dick.

"Don't worry, I'll kiss it better later," she turned to Gladys, "yes or no?"

"Damn it yes, how do we do this and do it quick before I change my mind?" Jackie jumped to her feet and ran into the bathroom, seconds later she returned with towel, shaving foam, and two disposable razors, a quick stop in the kitchen to pick up the scissors and back to the front of the van.

"Hitch down on the seat, sit on the towel, pants off and spread 'em," laughed Jackie.

"No one has seen me naked since I married John," mumbled Gladys.

"No one other than the team in the delivery room," laughed Jackie.

"A woman is not at her best in those circumstances," said Gladys, "what with the blood and the sweat and the screaming."

"There's that," laughed Jackie.

"And the puking and the fainting, but that was down to John, the midwife just rolled him into a corner and ignored him, I laughed so much I pissed myself, and the midwife."

"I'd prefer it if you didn't get that excited," said Roaddog.

"I'll try," said Gladys. The moment of no return was upon her, and she had to follow through or run away. She took a deep breath and the heavy blue dressing gown fell open, and dropped to the couch behind her, the cotton nightie, with its picture of tweety-pie was pulled up and dropped on top of the gown, the white cotton knickers fell to the ground, to be kicked into a corner. She sat on the towel as instructed and spread her legs. She closed her eyes and held her breath. Jackie reached over and took her hand.

"You okay?" she asked softly.

"I don't know, I'm so old and ugly."

"Old you may be, this body has lived, loved, laughed and cried, old yes, ugly never," said Roaddog. He paused for a moment or two. "Are you sure Gladys, the only place you see a bush like this is in nineteen seventies Danish porn, this is a treasure from the past, for those of us that grew up in the eighties and nineties."

"Given the way John raves about shaved pussy, your shaved pussy bitch," laughed Gladys, "get the strimmer on it." The scissors went to work with a will, and Jackie leaned in close.

"Make me a promise," she said.

"What?" asked Gladys opening her eyes.

"Make sure he licks your pussy, tell him how to do it right, then tell him you're not going to suck his cock unless he lets you shave him," she smiled.

"That's wicked," laughed Gladys, she giggled even more as the cold shaving gel hit her shorn mound.

"Do it," insisted Jackie, "it'll be worth it. Some guys just need training."

"Did yours?"

"Hell no, he came pre-trained, and Jane is simply amazing with her tongue." Jackie shivered with the memories.

"Crazy, you're all crazy," mumbled Gladys, as the razor started its work, and tough work it was.

"Hint for ya," said Jackie.

"Go on."

"Don't buy the pink razors, they're expensive and nowhere near as good as the guy's razors."

"Thanks, I'll just use his."

"It's better if you use them and throw them away, if he tries to shave his face after you've used one there's going to be claret everywhere. Which is okay if he's pissed you off."

"You really are a bitch, aren't you?"

"You should see it when me and Jane work him over, it's awesome."

"That very much depends on your point of view," said Roaddog.

"You never complain," said Jackie.

"What have you got when you've got one green ball in one hand and one green ball in the other?" he asked.

"I don't know," said Gladys.

"The undivided attention of the jolly green giant. That's how those two make me feel sometimes," he said.

"And you love it," said Jackie.

"Most certainly," replied Roaddog, he tossed the first razor aside and clicked the cover off a new one. Gladys' hand tensed in Jackie's and her eyes locked hard on the younger woman's. Jackie leaned closer.

"God he's turning me on," she whispered hoping that Roaddog couldn't hear her.

"You want me to tell him to get you off?" whispered Jackie. Gladys eyes opened wide as saucers.

"I tell him and he's straight in there, foam, fur, stubble and all, he loves a good pussy."

"No, I'll wait until John can do it for me," she whispered.

"Only if you're sure," said Roaddog, laughing.

"Bastard," said Gladys, "I'm so turned on now, god do I want it."

"Nearly done," said Roaddog, a few more swipes of the razor and he picked up the corner of the towel and wiped all around, clearing the foam and debris. Slowly he leaned down and kissed the top of her naked slit, after a second her hands grabbed the hair on his head and pulled him away. He smiled and licked his lips, after a few seconds she pushed him away and sat up.

"You are a bad man, and thank you, I think. You two nutters have given me a lot to think about, I get the feeling I have missed out on some things in my life."

"You've loved and lived, what more can a person want?" asked Jackie, she looked out of the window, the sun was well above the trees. "When do we need to get to the shop?" she asked.

"It's getting close," said Roaddog, "Time for some bacon butties first though, it's going to be a damned long day."

"Stay for breakfast?" asked Jackie looking at Gladys.

"I don't mind if I do," she smiled.

"Great," said Jackie, she turned to Roaddog, "coffee's as well," as she took a seat opposite Gladys.

"Am I cooking?" asked Roaddog, the look told him everything he needed to know, he went into the kitchen and took the grill pan out, then over to the fridge to get the bacon. Once the grill was hot, he put the bacon in to cook, and started the kettle. Returning to the front lounge area he collected the cups.

"Hey girl," he said to Jackie, "you made a promise earlier."

"Get the brews made and then come back."

Roaddog went into the kitchen and made the coffees, then he bent over the grill to check on the bacon.

"Isn't that the best view in town?" asked Jackie.

"Your man certainly has a good-looking ass, far better than John."

"He'll get there if he lives long enough," laughed Jackie.

Roaddog returned from the kitchen and dropped the cups on the table. He stepped up to Jackie, who immediately started to give Gladys a demonstration of fellatio techniques, including a commentary, which sort of destroyed the flow. She broke off and said, "Go check the bacon."

He snarled but did as he was bid, turning the bacon and coming back to Jackie.

"I saw you turn the grill down," she said, going on with her demonstration.

Roaddog's phone started to make a noise, first it buzzed for a few seconds then the unmistakeable riff from smoke on the water sounded.

"What the fuck does he want?" snarled Roaddog, clicking the button to accept the call and then putting it on loudspeaker.

"Hey bro," he said, "what's happening?"

"Well," replied Slowball, "we found the shop but it seems that no one is at home, where the fuck are ya?"

"We'll be there in about half an hour," said Roaddog groaning.

"Gladys can you check on the bacon?" asked Jackie loudly, before returning to her task. Gladys was laughing quietly as she went into the kitchen.

"Hey Bug," came Slowballs voice from the phone, "sounds like Gladys is checking the bacon and Dog is getting a blowjob. Roaddog where are ya man? The curtains are getting awful twitchy round here."

"Fine," said Roaddog, "Out of the shop turn left, then left at the axe."

"Got it," laughed Slowball, the sound of engines came from the speaker as Roaddog grabbed Jackie's head and pulled her in tight, groaning as he spent in her mouth.

"Bastards," muttered Roaddog. He released Jackie's head when he heard the sound of the engines that told him they had made the left at the pub.

"You're looking for a tiny left turn, it looks like a farm track," he gave Slowball the name of the street, and they listened for a while until the turn was made.

"Right bastards," said Roaddog, "keep the fucking noise down, and tell that ass Bug to keep that pipe closed. At the white house turn right, follow the track, through the gate. After the track turns left, third van up on the right is us, don't block the fucking road, and be quiet." The soft rumble of the VW was unmistakeable, but he could hear nothing of Bug's raucous honda.

While the bikes were getting nearer Gladys was talking to Jackie.

"Should I get dressed?"

"Up to you, these guys won't mind."

"I'm not likely to get raped by a group of hairy bikers, am I?"

"Only if you want it, if you ask nicely they'll make you airtight." Jackie smiled.

"I don't understand," said Gladys.

"I'll explain later, they're here," she mimicked the voice of the little girl in the film Poltergeist. The rumble of engines fell silent, the van shook, a dark shape occluded the glass front door, Roaddog opened the door. Slowball stepped in and hugged his friend, with absolutely no thought for his nudity, he stepped aside, and the much smaller Bug did the same, followed by Cherie and Sylvia.

"Trust you, you bastard," snapped Slowball, "here you are with two naked chicks, and bacon on the go, what more does a guy need?"

"This guy needs a pee," snapped Cherie, her head tipped to one side the question hung in the air.

"That way first door on the left," said Jackie, pointing the way.

"Sounds like a plan," said Slowball.

"I'm next, asshole", said Sylvia, following Cherie.

"Ah," said Slowball, he turned to the front door, and stepped through.

"Don't frighten the natives," called Roaddog softly. Bug followed Slowball. Roaddog knew they were bound for the hedge at the back of the van.

"Are these people your friends?" asked Gladys.

"More than friends," said Jackie, "these guys saved my life."

"Are they dangerous?"

"Oh yes, in ways you won't believe, but you are safe amongst friends here."

"What ways?"

"Pray you never find out." whispered Jackie directly into her ear. Then she kissed the lobe of that ear. Gladys jumped and giggled.

"You people are crazy," she said.

"You having fun?" asked Jackie.

"More than I have had in years, maybe I'm crazy too. Is this Alzheimer's?"

"No but it's fun, I just wish that Jane was here to share in this," Jackie's face dropped at the thought of her friend.

"Come on girl," laughed Gladys, "we got hungry bikers to feed, get some more bacon cooking, or they'll be eating us."

"Turn the fucking grill off, I'm horny as hell."

"Crazy and fun," laughed Gladys as Cherie came into view. Bug came in through the front door, Slowball on his heels.

"That feels much better," said Slowball.

"Hey Bug, what happened to the little Honda?" asked Roaddog.

"Had to sell it, had to get something bigger, no space on the Honda for a fat bitch," said Bug. Cherie turned to him and swung in low a wide right hand that took him low in the ribs and almost knocked him over.

"I'm not fat, you bastard, I'm pregnant, and you did it," she snarled.

"And you're sure it was him?" asked Roaddog, grinning.

Cherie turned on him, this time a left came howling into his gut, but he was ready, he rode it out and engulfed her in his arms, hugging her and kissing her.

"How you been love?" he asked, once her anger had abated some.

"How do you think, lonely, bored and shagging the short guy."

"Hey," said Bug, a little upset.

"How's it been at home?" asked Roaddog.

"Damned cops have been buzzing around like flies on shit, but they got nothing."

"What about the clubhouse?"

"Fuck man," said Slowball. "Fire bobbies tried for hours to make it go out, they gave up, and just kept everything around wet, it was a joy to watch."

"And?"

"And nothing, just ash, that's all they found, ash, they couldn't even be sure what sort of ash it was." Slowball looked at Gladys for an instant, Roaddog knew there was more to tell, but he wasn't going to push right now.

"What the fuck are you lot doing here anyway?" asked Roaddog.

"Opening day," said Sylvia, "you think we'd miss that?"

"Great, I could use all the help I can get, it could get crazy."

"Oh, it could do that," said Slowball with a grin.

"You know something bastard," snapped Roaddog.

"Saying fuck all," replied Slowball with a grin, "I like my balls where they are," he reached down to check the location of said artifacts, presence confirmed he released them with the characteristic Michael Jackson "Oh".

"I've talked to Wolf, the cops recovered two Mac tens, know anything about the third?" asked Roaddog. Slowball said nothing but his eyes flashed onto Bug. Roaddog turned that way.

"How full?" he whispered.

"Half," replied Bug.

"Keep it hid," whispered Roaddog.

"How's Vera?" asked Slowball.

"She's fine, but resting, in the left-hand pannier," laughed Roaddog.

"Good to know," laughed Slowball.

"That's guy talk we shouldn't be hearing?" asked Gladys of Jackie.

"Correct."

"What are they talking about?"

"You don't want to know, believe me."

"Mac ten means something I just can't quite remember," whispered Gladys. Jackie caught Sylvia's eyes and looked at the grill, got a nod, then she grabbed Gladys's arm and dragged her into the bedroom. Closing the door softly.

"These are good men, they were put into a bad position by some very bad people, they came to rescue me and Cherie and two other girls, we would have been killed, or worse. They came and were outnumbered, they faced machine guns, and still they came, please don't make their lives any more difficult."

"My father was awarded the Military Cross for taking out machine gun nests on the beaches at Normandy, I know who heroes are. Have no fear."

"You sure?" asked Jackie.

"The heroes of today's generation are footballers, reality TV stars, and Influencers, whatever the hell they are, the human race is doomed until it finds real heroes again."

"I pray that it never needs them."

"So do I my dear, so do I." Gladys opened her arms, and Jackie stepped inside, they hugged for a long time. "You got things to do today," whispered Gladys.

"We do. Thanks for understanding."

"No sweat, are the cops likely to show up here?"

"Nah, we're all dead."

"How the fuck did you manage that?" said Gladys, then her hand slapped over her mouth.

"Again, you don't want to know," smiled Jackie.

"They're going to be getting tense out there, aren't they?"

"Probably."

"Let's see what we can do about that shall we? Before we do, airtight?"

"You really want to know?"

"I've missed out on somethings; I want to know."

"Three guys, one in your pussy, one in your mouth, and one in your ass."

Gladys's jaw dropped open for a moment.

"That's gotta hurt," she whispered.

"Some like it."

"I don't think I'll try it," smiled Gladys, "let's go meet the guys."

"After you," said Jackie more than a little uncertainly. Gladys smiled. She opened the bedroom door, the tension in the room was positively palpable, she walked straight up to Roaddog, threw her arms around his neck and kissed him, as the kiss rolled on, she hitched up on her tip toes and pressed herself against him. She wriggled a little from side to side, feeling him starting to swell. She broke the kiss and moved her head back.

"Damn that does feel different," she smiled, "I'm told you are a hero, that is good enough for me." He smiled nervously back. "This is a rural community," she continued, "we have many ways of getting rid of people we don't want around anymore," she whispered directly into his ear, "especially dead people." She pulled his head down again and kissed him some more.

"Judas kissed the one he loved," said Roaddog as the kiss broke.

"No Judases round here," her reply as she moved on to Slowball. She was hanging from his shoulders as she kissed him, before dropping to the floor and moving over to Bug. Bug's hand grabbed her ass, but she didn't shy away, she broke the kiss and leaned in to whisper in his ear.

"I'm old enough to be your mother."

"Mother never had an ass like that," he smiled as she picked up her clothes. Tweety dropped over her body and the blue dressing gown tied over the top.

"I think I'm going to go and give my man a surprise," she said as she walked out of the door. She turned on the step outside. "I'll see you all later. I have just got to see what all the fuss is about."

"That's one crazy mama," said Bug as he watched her walk down the road in the same direction her husband had taken.

"A mama that left her knickers behind," laughed Jackie.

Chapter 3: Opening day, later.

The two bikes and Slowball's VW set off from the caravan and progressed slowly along the track. Roaddog pulled over in front of the white house and the others followed suit. Roaddog went to talk to the guy sitting in a lawn chair by the back door to his house.

"Hi Leo," he said.

"Hi Roaddog," Leo smiled.

"As you can see, I have a few friends, this isn't going to be an issue?" asked Roaddog.

"No worries, just keep the noise down, the locals are mainly old folks, and they get nervous when it gets loud."

"No problem, I did think that Bug would be a problem, but he's had to change the NC30 for a Pan-Euro, his birds up the duff," Roaddog laughed.

"Shit and happens," laughed Leo.

"We'll definitely keep the noise down, but I don't believe that Gladys is ever going to complain," replied Roaddog.

"Why not?" asked Leo.

"I really can't say," said Roaddog, a huge smile on his face.

"Is it opening day?" asked Leo.

"Yes, you coming up later? I can guarantee some burgers and some music, the rest depends on other people."

"We'll swing by for a bit later, don't know when," said Leo.

"Great, we'll see ya," Roaddog turned, walked towards his bike and mounted up, the three set off along the lane at a very sedate pace. In less than three minutes they were pulling up outside the shop, Jackie jumped off and opened the main shutter door, Roaddog rolled in and turned his bike around, and parked up against one wall, Bug rolled in next to him, and finally Slowball reversed into the space that was left.

"What's the plan then?" asked Bug.

"Well," said Roaddog, "I wasn't actually planning on having so many people here, how about Jackie and Sylvia work the burger van, Cherie, you can run the coffee machine, me and the guys will sell parts and bikes."

"Sounds to me like you three are going to be sitting round while the three of us girls are going to be running around like fools," said Jackie.

"Well," smiled Roaddog, "you could always quote for repair jobs and parts."

"You know damned well we can't do that," laughed Jackie.

"Actually they can't do that either," grinned Roaddog.

"What do you mean?" asked Slowball.

"Well, if you remember the sort of costings we used to use, then add between thirty and fifty percent, you'll still be thirty percent below the local competition."

"You're kidding," laughed Bug, "what a bunch of rip off merchants."

"Even the independents are only about five percent lower than the main dealers."

"So how much work can you deal with?" asked Slowball.

"That very much depends on how many hands I have," replied Roaddog softly.

"You offering us jobs?" demanded Bug.

"If you want them, accommodations will be friendly until we can get this place sorted out, I'm planning on five bedrooms, and the usual bunk room, if things go well, I should be able to employ the girls as well. You know the burger van will need manning, and there could be admin as well, the other business is doing really well just now."

"What other business?" asked Bug nervously.

"I'm mining bitcoin and doing okay," replied Roaddog.

"That's what all those solar panels are for," laughed Slowball.

"Yep," said Roaddog, "the power is free, and the returns are currently high. I could actually live on the successes, but not too well."

"And with nothing to do you'd spend everything on beer and petrol," laughed Jackie.

"That's for sure," said Bug with a smile on his face.

"Great," said Roaddog, "we all know what we are doing, so get with it, we open in an hour and I want to be ready."

Long before the hour had elapsed everything was prepared, the burger van was ready, bacon and burgers sitting in the warmers, onions on the griddles, fridges full of cold cans. Cherie presented coffees for all as they sat around awaiting customers.

"I hate this bit," snarled Roaddog, "the waiting is just horrible."

"What's that line?" laughed Bug, "If you build it, they will come."

"That's some movie or other," said Sylvia.

"Not helping," said Roaddog, he was looking longingly at the bar in the corner, but he knew that if he started drinking now it would not end well. Conversation was slow but they talked for the best part of an hour before they heard the first motorcycle, it slowed down and turned into the front of the shop. The lone motorcyclist looked round undecided as to where he should park, eventually he simply stopped where he was and dropped the bike over onto its side stand. He strolled slowly over to them and smiled.

"Morning," he said.

"Morning," said Roaddog, "What are you looking for?"

"Just looking really, it's not often that a new bike place opens up round here, and they don't seem to last long."

"Why is that?"

"They always seem to be way too expensive; service is crap, they just fold after a while."

"My name is Roaddog, I have no intention of shutting up any time soon."

"They call me Vince, how much for a service on my Harley?"

"Slowball what you reckon?"

Slowball looked at the Harley in question, thought for a moment.

"Short service fifty, full service one hundred and twenty. Plus parts of course."

"Then there's VAT," snapped Vince.

"That depends very much on the method of payment," laughed Roaddog.

"I like the way you think," said Vince, "Parts, what sort?"

"You get to choose, nice Harley original parts, or cheaper none Harley parts."

"What about brakes?"

"They're a known bone of contention, if your bike does seven thousand miles a year, which many don't, then your brakes should last three years, even for a heavy dyna like yours. It may surprise you to know that even the Harley service manual says change brake pads if necessary."

"The club has a requirement of ten thousand a year for your primary ride, and Harley dealers, twelve months and they'll change the brakes every time."

"It's necessary for their profits. I don't work that way; I will give you three choices when it comes time to change the discs. Original Harley, cheap pattern, or expensive pattern, the expensive patterns are still twenty five percent less than Harley, I have no idea what motor manufacturers have done with their brake discs, but they don't seem to last any time at all, my expensive discs will outlast your bike."

"I thought they were supposed to wear?" asked Vince.

"Excellent training, originally discs used to last the life of the vehicle, unless it's a heavy van at the hundred-thousand-mile mark."

"How much heavier are your discs?"

"Good question, they are about five percent heavier, more chromium in them, but it's the heat treatment that gives them their wear resistance."

"Sounds like you know your shit," said Vince.

"He does," said Slowball, "he knows all about shit."

"Nice collection in your garage," said Vince. Looking at the trike and the two motorcycles.

"Those aren't for sale, the ones for sale are on the other side." said Bug.

"What about that ratty looking trike at the back?"

"Not for sale, I have plans for that one," said Roaddog smiling at Jackie, his grin was returned.

"What about custom parts?" asked Vince.

"I don't have much in the way of stock at the moment, but the catalogues are over there," he waved in the direction of the showroom area, "find the part you need, and I can get it in a couple of weeks."

"Payment in advance?"

"Fifty percent refundable deposit, in case the supplier fails to deliver."

"If you can keep your promises, you should do okay, when's the bacon butties ready?"

"Now," replied Jackie, "you hungry?"

"Not really, but I do know a few that should be by now," he pulled his phone from his inside pocket and punched a speed-dial. They all listened to one side of the conversation.

"This place in Somercotes looks good."

"Guy knows his stuff."

"Burger van is far better than the one we have, and the serving girls are far prettier."

"No beer, so bring some." He hung up and turned to Roaddog.

"There's going to be a few coming this way, it's less than ten minutes from Marshchapel. Does the pub do good food?"

"Oh yes, the food in the Axe is great, but it doesn't open until twelve."

"That'll be good for the run back, the food at our place is not good and far too expensive, I think they are taking the piss."

"Wouldn't be unusual, I know what rally venues are like," smiled Roaddog.

"These guys are charging more than a tenner for bangers and mash."

"Go to the Axe, tell Karen I sent you."

"What good will that do?"

"May get me a discount next time I go in," laughed Roaddog.

"Thanks friend," laughed Vince, "will she be able to cope with fifty hungry bikers?"

"Certainly not, but she'll give it a good try, you can be certain that she'll not make promises she can't keep."

"That's good to know," Vince paused for a moment, "I think I'll pop up as soon as they open and get myself a table arranged."

"How soon before your guys get here?" asked Jackie.

"Could be half an hour or so, some of them were pretty wasted last night, there'll be a run out to Mablethorpe to fill up on booze at some point today, cheap beer and bourbon there."

"You've got time for breakfast on the house then," she said going into the van, "red or brown?" she called, looking through the window at Vince.

"Just a bit of butter for me," he replied.

In only moments she returned with a barmcake full of bacon wrapped in a serviette. "Check out the side panels," she said, "that's the menu for the Axe."

"I'll give them a look over," Vince smiled at her, "I'm going to check out your catalogues," he said wandering over to the bench that was covered in the heavy books.

"Could be a good start," said Slowball, softly.

"Depends how many are going to drop in, and how much money they are going to spend. His club is local-ish, Grimsby based," said Roaddog. "Hey Vince," he called, "where did you hear about us?"

"I got a flyer from someone who'd been to the bike night in Horncastle, and another from a guy outside the motorcycle shop in Louth, the one near the bus station."

"Unusual a bike shop advertising its rivals?"

"Not the bike shop, some guy, seems his bike is still in their shop, and they haven't fixed it in five weeks, every time they fuck with the engine management it gets worse."

"You get a name?"

"Nah, but he'll most likely turn up today, he said he'd seen you and your girl passing out flyers all over the place, the ones he was giving out he'd printed himself."

"Must be pissed at the shop."

"Pissed not the word, they'd had him arrested for disturbing the peace, would you believe it?"

"Well if you see him, send him my way, I'll have his bike back on the road in a couple of days at worst."

"I'll do that," replied Vince, "these foot boards how quick can you get them?"

"What's the name on the catalogue?"

"Jersey."

"About ten days, Jersey can be a problem sometimes, but ten days is usually right."

"I'll have front and rears, they'll look real good." Roaddog walked over to where Vince was and glanced at the catalogue.

"Call it twenty quid a pair, so twenty quid deposit okay?"

"No problem." Vince took out his wallet and handed over a twenty.

Roaddog stuffed the note in his back pocket and smiled, he turned to Bug.

"Bug, order us some of those skull foot boards for a Dyna-glide, front and rear." He turned back to Vince, "you got contact details?"

Vince took a card from his wallet and passed it to Roaddog, who smiled.

"How come your cut doesn't say President?"

"Everyone knows me, how come your cut says that you used to be a member of a club?"

"The club died," whispered Roaddog.

"It's sad when clubs fade away," said Vince.

"No, the club was killed."

"Ah, and the killers?"

"All dead," snarled Roaddog.

"Bar one," said Slowball.

"If that cunt's got the balls to come looking for us, I'll kill his ass as well."

"How come you left a survivor?" asked Vince.

"I don't raid hospitals to kill off a dick head."

"Ha," laughed Cherie.

"Child molesters are different, they have nowhere to Hyde."

Bug came out of the office.

"Jersey have promised despatch today, should be here Thursday or Friday."

"Thanks Bug," said Roaddog, turning back to Vince. "I'll call you when they're in, and you can bring the bike here, we'll fit them."

"What's this we?" asked Slowball, "we're going home Monday."

"Wanna bet?" asked Cherie. Her voice was almost drowned by the sound of approaching motorcycles. Ten bikes turned into the forecourt and arrayed themselves either side of Vince's. Nine of them male riders with women on the pillion seat, one, the one that took pride of place next to Vince's bike, a black Triumph Rocket Three, with a rider that dwarfed it.

"Fuck that guy is huge, he's nearly as tall as Lurch," said Slowball.

"And he's a damned sight wider," said Roaddog.

"He's beautiful, isn't he?" said Vince, "Give him a harness and he can pick that bike up, look at those muscles." The tall man's badges said Horse, and Master at Arms. Vince walked towards the new arrivals.

"Master at Arms it says, and look at those arms," whispered Slowball.

"Scary dude," laughed Roaddog, as the pair listen to Vince.

"Listen up people," said Vince loudly, "boss man is Roaddog, he knows his stuff, he can get all sorts of parts from all over the world, I got new footboards on the way already, he deals in cash. Anyone got a bike due service?"

"My Slim needs one in six hundred miles, I'm saving money for it, still a little short."

Vince turned and shouted. "Can you service a Slim?"

"Small service no issue, I'm not sure I've got the right tranny oil for a major service."

"I only need an interim," said the voice from the back.

"We can do that," laughed Roaddog.

"Now?" asked Vince.

"Pushy bastard ain't ya?" said Roaddog, Vince only nodded.

"Slowball, Bug," said Roaddog, "get that thing serviced."

"We're here as visitors, not labour," said Bug.
"Wanna bet?" laughed Cherie, "get on with it."
"Fuck Dog," said Slowball, "the damned things hot."
"Try not to burn yourselves."
"I hate you sometimes," said Slowball, gathering Bug with his eyes, and walking over to where the Slim was parked, the guy passed them the keys, and they rolled the bike slowly into the workshop area. As they passed Vince, Vince threw an arm around Horses waist and reached up to kiss him. Slowball almost tripped over the rear foot peg of the bike he was pushing.
"Don't drop the fucking thing," muttered Bug.
"Er." mumbled Slowball.
"Shut your mouth and keep walking," smiled Bug.
Horse and Vince walked over to where Roaddog was watching his friends trying not to drop the slim.
"Not something you see every day," he said.
"You can imagine how difficult it was to gain acceptance," said Horse, his voice soft and high, nothing like the gravel that used to be Lurch's sound.
"We did try one of the gay biker clubs in Lincoln, but I hate to say this, they were just too gay," said Vince.
"Yeah," laughed Horse.
"So we tagged onto this group," said Vince, "the old pres was really stuck in the sixties, so he had to go, I took him out in personal combat, while Horse held his lieutenants in check."
"For check, read hospital," laughed Horse.
"Sometimes he forgets how strong he is," smiled Vince.
"How's the club doing?" asked Roaddog.
"Strength to strength, membership is up two hundred percent, profit up four hundred, we're doing okay."
More motorcycles started to arrive, these guys didn't have club insignia, but followed the lines of the bikes already parked up.
"I'll check on the service," said Roaddog, as he walked away.
"How's it going?" he asked as Bug was pulling a spark plug from the Slim.
"Simple stuff, other than the motor being fucking hot. Warm is better you know that."
"Yes I know but, we gotta look good for these guys."
"Guys?" snorted Slowball.
"Problem?" asked Roaddog.

"They're gay, what if they fancy me?"

"Come on, they're in a stable relationship, long term, they're not even looking."

"But what if they are?"

"Their gaydar is far better than yours, they wouldn't waste their time on you."

"What do you mean?"

"Did you see that Vince was gay?"

"No."

"I did, not instantly, but it did become obvious in a short time."

"How? He looks just like an ordinary guy."

"He is an ordinary guy, but he likes guys, not girls."

"How can you tell?"

"Remember when Jackie gave him a free bacon butty?"

"Yes."

"He said thank you to her eyes, not her tits."

"I never noticed."

"I did and so did she, you two both look at her tits at every opportunity that presents itself."

"That and her ass," said Bug.

"So what if he's looking at my ass like that?" asked Slowball.

"You'll never know so stop worrying about it."

"How do you know all this stuff?" asked Slowball.

"There are things about my past that you don't want to know. Anyway service?"

"I've checked the map on this thing, and someone has fucked it up royally," said Slowball, turning a laptop so that Roaddog could see.

"Someone has definitely screwed that one up." Roaddog walked away, he found Vince in a moment.

"Hey Vince, who does that Slim belong to?"

"Jack," shouted Vince, "get your ass over here." Jack came over.

"What's up?" asked Jack.

"Who mapped your Slim?" asked Roaddog.

"Some guy in Cleethorpes, a Harley specialist."

"I don't know what his speciality is, but Harleys it ain't." said Roaddog, "it pops and bangs on the over run?"

"Yes, sounds great."

"It's costing you fuel and power. I have heard it said that Harleys turn petrol into noise without the dreadful by product of horsepower, do you follow this opinion?"

"Of course not. What are you saying?"

"Idiot mapped it to sound good, you get some torque, but not much, and it's costing you a fortune in fuel, just looking at the curve I reckon you're down to about thirty-five to the gallon."

"I get thirty-seven."

"You want sixty?"

"You can do that?"

"Yes, it won't pop, it won't bang, the torque will come in earlier, and the peak power later, but you'll get more than seventy-five fucking miles on a tank."

"How much will that cost?" asked Jack.

"Call it opening day special offer, one remap for free." Jack's jaw fell open.

"Thanks man," said Vince. Roaddog shook his head and went back into the workshop. He walked over to Slowball.

"Give it a standard curve then push the torque a touch early and the power curve a little late and high," he said.

"Easy peasy," said Slowball.

"I got people to meet, thanks guys," said Roaddog walking away to talk to people around the bench where the catalogues were. The burger van was doing a roaring trade, the queue was quite long, but moving slowly as it should be. Jackie and Sylvia were working well as a team, even within the confined space. Jackie spotted him as he passed.

"Dog," she yelled, he turned. "Get us a pack of burgers and bacon from the freezer." He nodded and set off into the back of the workshop. Jackie set to, creating a cheeseburger for a guy with a huge beard when a small voice called out.

"Hey Jackie, where's Roaddog." Jackie looked up, her mouth fell open for a moment then she dropped the burger she was making and ran out of the door at the end of the van, she jumped down the three steps and ran to the woman standing in front of the van. She engulfed her in her arms and kissed her thoroughly. The kiss broke, Jackie threw her head back and screamed. "Roaddog," then straight back to the kissing. Roaddog heard the urgency of her call and dropped what he was carrying, sprinting out to the front of the building he saw the two, and immediately joined in the hugging and kissing. Almost a minute later a bearded man tapped Jackie on the shoulder.

"What about my burger?" he asked. The tension in the group changed and the two girls released their grips on each other, they separated, leaving Roaddog between them, Roaddog felt hands on the back of his belt, then the girls turned to the man, each with a black stiletto.

"This is a family reunion; you really want to get in the way?" asked Jackie quietly.

"Think carefully man," said Roaddog, "I have a friend in Saltfleet who really doesn't care what he uses as bait in his lobster pots." People were moving all around them, mainly away. Two people were moving towards the conflict, Vince and Horse stood behind Roaddog. Sylvia came out of the van and stuffed a burger in the man's hand.

"You're served, fuck off," she said, turning on a heel and going back into the van. The man backed away slowly then turned to where his friends were waiting nervously.

"I have a question," said Vince. Roaddog and the girls turned towards him.

"Ask," smiled Roaddog.

"It's not about these two lovely girls, though how they associate with you is beyond me. Their movements were effective and practiced, but my question is not about them, it's about those two," he nodded in the direction of the building, "What are they waiting for?" Slowball and Bug were standing beside motorcycles. "I can't believe they are planning on running."

"They are awaiting a stand down." Roaddog nodded to the pair and they went back to working on the Slim. Vince and Horse exchanged looks, Horse nodded.

"I know that you have your family thing to sort out," said Vince, "we have a great band on tomorrow night, you and yours are welcome to come, we will have things to talk about as well. Horse ticket them." Horse reached inside his jacket and brought out a bunch of cards, he gave three to Roaddog. Jackie turned to Jane and kissed her firmly, "I got work to do," she said softly, "please hang around?"

"I'll be here," replied Jane. Jackie smiled and went back to the burger van, the queue was starting to reform, though the people in it seemed more than a little subdued, if not actually scared.

Roaddog took Jane by the hand and pulled her slowly into the office.

"How you been?" he asked.

"Bored as fuck," she answered.

"Problems with the cops?"

"Some, that bastard Hopkins keeps buzzing around, but he had nothing, your fire wiped out almost everything, they were trying to piece together who was there from the rivets in their jeans. There was an awful lot of lead in the bottom of that container. The cops reckon three machine guns each firing off about a hundred and fifty rounds."

"You should know, you were there."

"I remember, I still get nightmares. I still see Lurch in that doorway, torn to pieces by those guns."

"He was a good man," said Roaddog, "he died well."

"Is there a good way to die?"

"There are worse ways than defending your friends."

"I'm not sure about that," her voice quaked with emotion.

"Better to die like Lurch than like the two rapists that Jackie finished off."

"I'm sure she had other plans for them, but we were pushed for time."

"I am certain that Jackie can be as imaginative as Bandit Queen, if she tries."

"She does have a mean streak," Jane smiled.

"You going to stay with us a while, or you going back home?"

"Home is boring as hell, all the bikers just seem to be posers, and the rugby players are just pissed up posers, every time that fucker Hopkins shows up, they run away."

"Won't that ass let go?"

"No, he keeps parading the guy with the busted leg, last time I saw him he had one of those big plastic boots on, seems Jackie smashed him up good."

"More like the drugs he was doing fucked up his healing."

"Well Hopkins is looking for you."

"Why?"

"He doesn't believe that you are dead."

"He wasn't ever going to, I knew that, but he'll struggle to find me."

"I wouldn't bet on that, he's real good at his job."

"I'll worry about that when he shows up, more important things to talk about, are you planning on staying?"

"For the weekend at least, if you'll have me."

"Shit girl, we've done nothing else but talk about trying to get you to come over, and hopefully stay."

"You've done a lot more than nothing, just look at this place."

"I'm hoping it will do well, first day is beginning to look promising."

"You still doing the drugs?" Her look told him how important this question was to her.

"No, Wolf offered me some at a good discount, but I turned him down."

"Why?"

"We don't need it, if this place bombs we'll just sit around all day drinking beer and laughing, if it goes well, that's just gravy."

"How come?"

"I've got four times the miners and eight times the solar panels, far more than I had at the house. We're doing quite well with those right now."

"It seems like a lot of work just to stop you being bored?"

"Maybe but it's what I like to do, and Jackie's been a wonder."

"I'm sorry," Jane looked down.

"Hey girl, not a dig, you had things to deal with, new shit for you."

"It was new to Jackie as well."

"She's seen more of the world; it wasn't quite so much of a shock to her."

"I'm still not sure if I'm going to stay more than the weekend."

"The choice my love is always yours," he smiled and kissed her.

"You feel up to doing something useful?" he asked, gently.

"What do you have in mind?"

"Could you go help Jackie? Give Sylvia a chance to get out of the van for a bit."

"Hell of a way to spend my weekend off, three-hour drive then back in the kitchen," she laughed, kissed him and went to do just as he had asked. Roaddog went to check on the people that were around, Bug and Slowball had long finished the service on the Slim, Slowball handed Roaddog the cash they had got from the rider and smiled.

"You're buying supper," he said.

"No worries," laughed Roaddog, hoping that Karen could fit them all in.

The burger van did a good steady trade all day, the pub was doing well, judging by the number of plastic glasses Roaddog had collected. Leo and his son Edward turned up for a visit, as did Gladys and John. Her kiss for Roaddog got more than a few looks, but only a grin from John. Roaddog was just considering shutting up shop, there hadn't been any customers for the best part of an hour, when he heard the approach of many motorcycles. Vince and his whole group pulled up onto the forecourt. The motorcyclists arranged themselves in a line facing the building, Horse raised his left arm, all the engines started to rev loudly, the noise was deafening, Horse's arm dropped, and the silence was even more deafening as all the motors stilled at once.

"Hey Vince," said Roaddog, nodding to Horse at Vince's side.

"Hey Roaddog, gone a little quiet?" smiled Vince.

"Yes, it has now, but it's been a good day."

"Just came by to remind you to come for the show tomorrow night, it's going to be a good time."

"We'll be there, you want burgers or something?"

"Nah, we'd better get back, see ya tomorrow."

"No worries." Roaddog was a little surprised as the group fired up and rode away, not a single rider dismounted.

"That was strange," said Slowball.

"He's desperate for us to go to their rally tomorrow, he's after something and I have an idea what. We'll go early, maybe get home before midnight."

"Who you kidding?" laughed Bug.

"Right," called Roaddog loudly, "let's pack it up, and go get some supper."

Chapter 4: Opening day over and local troubles.

It took them a short while to get everything shut down and packed away, but they left the bikes where they were and walked up the street to the pub. It was half past six when they walked in.

"I almost thought you weren't going to bother," said Karen.

"Like we would do that to you, but there are a few more than originally planned."

"Not a problem, you can have the big table, I don't need it until after eight."

"You're a star," said Roaddog handing her a box full of plastic glasses. "You sold quite a bit of beer today."

"I did, thanks to you and your shop, also had more than a few come in for lunch."

"Were they all well behaved?"

"I was a little worried when two of them came in, their jackets said Vince and Horse, damn that Horse is a big guy."

"Most likely in more ways than one, you don't get a name like horse from bikers unless you really deserve it."

"Seems like a waste, him being gay."

"Vince appears to be happy with the situation."

"I know, but those muscles," Karen grinned as she escorted them to the biggest table in the place.

"You're a married woman," laughed Roaddog.

"A girl's allowed a fantasy," she laughed, "I'll send someone to get your drink orders." They had barely sorted out their seating around the table when a young serving girl came over, she dropped menus in front of each and smiled.

"Hi Liz," said Roaddog.

"Hello Roaddog," she grinned as she spoke, "Jackie, nice to see you again, I don't know the rest of you yet."

"Well, next to Jackie is Sylvia, then Slowball, then Bug, and Cherie, and finally next to me is Jane." Liz smiled at each in turn, then spoke their names softly, as if to herself. Her smile for Jane lasted longer than the others, eye contact flashed between them for a long moment or two. Finally, Liz snatched a lung full of air, she hadn't realised that she was holding her breath.

"What can I get you to drink?" she asked. Orders were given and she turned to walk away. Many eyes followed her as she weaved between the tables.

"Damn she's pretty," whispered Jane.

"You fancy her?" asked Roaddog.

"I'm not dead," said Jane, "but she's too young."

"Is there such a thing?" asked Bug.

"Definitely, watch who brings the drinks," Jane laughed at Bug's confused look. Sure enough one of the older members of staff brought out their tray full of drinks.

"Thanks Mandy," said Roaddog, "give us a few minutes to make up our minds." Mandy smiled and wandered back to the bar.

"I don't get it," said Bug.

"Liz is old enough to take orders for drink, but not old enough to serve them," laughed Jane, "She's only sixteen."

"She could be seventeen," observed Sylvia.

"No," said Jane, "she's sixteen and gay."

"How do you know?" asked Sylvia.

"It's just so obvious," laughed Jane.

"Go on," said Sylvia.

"The eye contact, it was far more than simple serving girl and punter," said Jane.

"You'll have to explain that to us mere mortals," said Slowball.

"Let me," laughed Roaddog, he turned to Slowball, "when we talk to people we generally look them in the eye, it's the polite thing to do, though guys often look at tits, it's in the genes," he laughed.

"No, jeans is something else," giggled Jackie.

"Shush," laughed Roaddog, "well, look at me." Slowball did as he was requested. "People look into each other's eyes, it's just what they do, now if someone's eyes crinkle, smile without bringing along the rest of the face, see what I mean?" Slowball nodded. "Then the chin lifts and comes forward, the head tips a little to one side. Bang." The last word snapped. "You looked away, the contact was getting too personal, you could feel it and turned away. If there is any interest there, then you wouldn't have looked away."

"Damn, man," said Jane. "Guys aren't supposed to know about this stuff."

"Call it experience."

"Where you learn this?"

"Some other time."

"Anyway, Liz, her breathing stalled, and her heart rate was climbing, her pupils dilated, there is no missing those signs," said Jane. "Damn she's hot."

"I'm not sure she'd be into a four way," laughed Jackie.

"I'm certain she wouldn't be," agreed Jane, she looked up as Liz walked towards them, her pad held nervously in her left hand. Jane and Jackie both leaned against Roaddog and placed a hand on his thigh, so high that they were actually touching. His arms reached around both girls and pulled them in tight. Jane smiled up at Liz and watched Liz's face fall.

"Sorry Liz," she whispered, "taken, both of us." Liz nodded, glanced at the ground while she got her thoughts together, she looked up and smiled.

"What can I get for you tonight?" she asked, the smile solid and plastic at the same time.

It only took a few minutes for orders to be placed and for Liz to go into the kitchen.

"She was devastated for almost a whole second," said Jackie.

"Yes," replied Jane, "excellent recovery, she'll cry later, perhaps I shouldn't have led her on so much. I was just so surprised by the intensity of her eyes, what colour are they?"

"Grey," said Roaddog.

"Blue," said Slowball.

"Hazel," said Jackie.

"Thirty-four C," said Bug, getting a slap from Cherie, he smiled and kissed her.

"Her eyes are almost violet, more amethyst, like Elizabeth Taylor," said Jane. "You people need to pay more attention." Conversation turned to the events of the day and the money that had come in through the parts sales and the burger van. Seems the van was way ahead. Jackie was smiling at the contribution she was making to the business. The food arrived delivered by both Liz and Mandy. More beers were ordered and delivered; conversation stopped. It had been a long day and they were all hungry, Liz watched them from the kitchen door, a single tear fell as she thought of Jane. She turned away and disappeared into the dark. Jane felt the eyes break away and turned to the kitchen door briefly. She glanced at Roaddog, then at the door, she dropped her cutlery on her plate and stood up. She smiled down at Roaddog putting one hand on his shoulder, simply to keep him in his place. Jane walked across the bar and into the kitchen, she found Liz standing by a sink.

"Hey," said Mandy, "you're not supposed to be in here." Jane looked her hard in the eyes, until Mandy backed down and went to find something else to do.

"Liz," said Jane. Liz didn't turn to look at her, just stared down into the dirty dishes in the sink.

"Liz, I'm sorry, your eyes are too lovely to ignore, but I am involved with Roaddog. If I were a few years younger, then I would be after you in a flash, you're gorgeous. Do you understand?"

"Not really, I thought for a moment then we had a connection," Liz whispered.

"I would so love to have a connection with you," replied Jane, "but I am already involved in a complex situation, something that you wouldn't want to join in with."

"I could, to be with you."

"That's where you are wrong, you shouldn't do something like that for someone else, you should do it for you."

"You did it."

"I'm different, I'm involved with those two for the craziest of reasons, we've been through so much together. You need to find someone your own age to take up with, someone a little like yourself, but not too much."

"In this god forsaken bastard village," yelled Liz. Jane stepped up and threw her arms around Liz, pulling her in tight and pressing her head against the younger girls.

"Keep looking, there are more people out there, many more like us than many see. You'll find someone, watch for the eyes, they'll hit you all the time."

"Normally it's just guys like Bug."

"He has a thing for tits, it's a guy thing, so do I, but eyes are what count, watch for the eyes."

"There was a girl in here last week, her eyes followed me all over the place, I got more than a little nervous, it was creepy."

"Why was it creepy?"

"She was one of those goths, all in black and white face, black lipstick, a real Mortitia." Liz pulled back a little so she could look into Jane's eyes again. Jane laughed. "What's funny?" asked Liz.

"Oh girl, she's gone goth to make herself different from all the others, you might have missed a chance there."

"She's a local, but she's weird."

"Says the girl crying into a sink full of dirty dishes because some strange girl turned her down?"

"So, what should I do?" asked Liz.

"Next time she's in, hit her with those gorgeous eyes," Jane pulled back and looked straight into the eyes in question. "Catch her as she comes out of the ladies and kiss her." Jane moved slowly forwards and pressed her lips against Liz's softly at first, then more firmly. She pulled back again. "If she slaps ya, you were wrong. If not, goth's not a bad look, if it makes her happy, and you make her happy then you've got a future, with me you've got no future, I'm not even sure I'm going to be here after Monday."

"What about your friends?"

"I'm not sure, things to sort out, you know past and future, it's all a huge mess."

"Dog and Jackie have been coming in here for months, always as a couple, and now you turn up."

"I know, it's strange, but that does seem to be our speciality, your problems are simple compared to ours."

"Are you happy?"

"You have no idea how happy I was to see them both again, and to be accepted, and within two minutes there was a knife fight in the offing. Scary, mad, exciting, all these things and more. Shit I've been so bored away from them."

"But happy now you're back?"

"Oh yes."

"Then go to your friends before they think you've deserted them for me."

"They'd never think that; they might think that you had kidnapped me."

"I could do that."

"Big mistake, that's been tried. Roaddog is coming for me and you have no idea what sort of hell rides with him."

"That sounds like an interesting tale."

"One I'll never tell. Go find your goth and make her yours." Jane leaned in slowly and kissed Liz softly, then stepped away, smiled and walked out of the kitchen.

When she got back to the table and took her seat Roaddog looked at her and asked, "Everything OK?"

"Should be now," smiled Jane, "the kid's less confused, and has a target, hope I've not led her astray." She picked up her knife and fork and set about catching up with the others who had almost finished. The general hubbub of the place suddenly stopped. A silence fell over the entire room.

"Jake." Karen's voice was heard over the nothing that filled the air. "You be nice."

"Right," said a low voice. Heavy boots tramped across the floor to where Roaddog was sitting with his friends. "You're those damned hells angels, you've started all this crap, now my cows are dying, and people are going to be next."

"Sorry Roaddog," said Karen. Roaddog looked at her for a moment and smiled.

"So, Jake," he said, "what's your problem?" Roaddog took in the older man facing him, he looked to be mid-fourties, only five feet ten inches tall but stocky with it, his movements suggested a hidden strength.

"Not mine, everyone's. Your foolishness has allowed the demons to appear, they've been killing my cows and it's your fault."

"I know nothing about demons or dead cows, what are you talking about old man?"

"You've been messing with powers that should be left alone, you've drawn witch circles in the old church and let the monsters out. Once they've had their fill of cows, they'll be smothering people with bay leaves and sending them to hell."

"Jake, we know nothing of witch circles, or old churches."

"You summoned the creature, and his face is clear on the wall of the church, a face surrounded by leaves, a green face."

"We know nothing of a green face, or an old church." Roaddog was starting to get angry.

"The old church, Saint Botolph's at Skidbrooke," said Jake.

"Skidbrooke, I've never heard of and Boltoffs, what the fuck is that?"

"Skidbrooke is a village, and Saint Botolph's is an old church there, do you people know nothing?" Jake shrugged and turned away, stumping his way out of the pub, the crowd opened before him, then closed after he had passed.

"Crazy old man," said Roaddog.

"Perhaps not so crazy," whispered Jane.

"What do you mean?"

"The green man," she muttered.

"Go on."

"It's an old tale from Germany I think, a devil collecting souls, smothers people with laurel leaves, he's made of laurel leaves."

"And where did you hear this?"

"That's the thing, I'm not sure, it's just something that I remember from being a small child, 'watch out for Jack in the green, he'll take you to hell', that's what they say."

"That's what who say?"

"I've no idea."

"Karen," called Roaddog, "Skidbrooke and Boltoffs. You know them?"

"Of course, everyone does, Skidbrooke, village three miles away at most. and Saint Botolph's, not boltoff, Botolph's, is an old, ruined church, not used anymore though the graveyard still gets some new residents occasionally. It's a nice place when the sun is shining, not so much in the dark."

"Fine, how do we find it?"

"Easy, rather than turning into the lane to go home, you carry on straight, follow the road, it's a little twisty, but follow it, Botolph's is a left turn and signed. Just don't go in the dark, it's not a place to be when the sun has gone down." She glanced over to the door where a group of people had just walked in. Roaddog followed her look and then glanced round the table. Everyone had finished eating.

"Right people pick up your drinks we'll move to the other bar, Karen needs this table," he said, standing up slowly, he nodded to Jackie to lead the way, he was last to leave the table.

"Thanks Roaddog," whispered Karen as he leaned in close.

"No problem, thanks for putting up with us," he kissed her on the cheek and started to walk away.

"You are right," she whispered.

"About what?"

"Horse, he's huge," she looked at the ground for a moment before catching his eyes again.

"Jake, where does he live?"

"South farm, it's on a right-hand bend as you get close to Botolph's."

"I'll check in with him after I take a look at the creepy church, tomorrow."

Karen smiled widely as he turned to follow the others into the pool room, she waved Liz and Mandy to come and clear the table for the next group who were ordering drinks at the bar.

By the time he got to the other bar everyone was seated and more drinks were on the table. He sat between Jackie and Jane again, smiled at each and kissed them both.

"So, what do you really know about this green man thing?" he asked.

"Not much," replied Jane, "it's an old fairy tale, I don't know when I heard it, but it sort of stuck with me, there was a green man pub nearby and I thought the face on the sign looked more than a little scary."

"Was the pub haunted?" asked Sylvia.

"I don't know I was very young when we moved to Leyland."

"We'll go and have a look at this church," said Roaddog, "then see if we can find out what Jake is actually bitching about."

"He's probably just some crazy old geezer," said Slowball.

"I hope so," said Roaddog. "If he's right and there is some monster killing his cows, we may have to try to help him."

"Why us?" asked Bug.

"You saw the people in the bar," he paused while Bug nodded his agreement, "They believe that something strange is killing his cows, but they're not sure if we are to blame. We have to try to fit in here, we will need their support if we are going to make a go of things in this village."

"Agreed," smiled Bug, "but I think that whatever is killing his cows is more likely to be someone he has pissed off, not a spook, one of his neighbours, that is not going to go down well with the rest of them."

"Yeah," said Roaddog slowly, "we do what we can to come out smelling of roses, see how things turn out. It's one of the problems of small rural towns, everyone knows everyone and outsiders like us are usually to blame for anything that goes wrong."

"So, feeding the bad guy to the lobsters is not a viable option," laughed Bug.

"Only if nothing else works," said Roaddog.

"So, we're not ruling out disappearing a few people?" asked Slowball.

"It is one of the things we do best, and in a rural community like this there are just so many opportunities."

"It is a centre of pig rearing," laughed Slowball, "famous across the world are Lincolnshire sausages."

"Great," said Roaddog smiling, "lobsters, pigs, and I have heard a rumour that some of the cess pits around here are without bottoms."

"So many options," smiled Bug.

"I feel a need for some sleep," said Roaddog, "let's drink up and get out of here."

"Agreed," said Jackie, picking up her drink and emptying it. Roaddog stood up taking his beer to the bar, he signalled to Karen. She came over.

"Can I settle up?" he asked.

"Of course," Karen presented him with his bill and took his card as a payment. In only a minute they were all walking back down the street towards the workshop. Once the doors were up Roaddog spoke up.

"When we get to the caravan, Jane you reverse in first, all the way to the hedge, Slowball next, and we'll stick the bikes wherever we can." Things went exactly to his plan, and they were inside the caravan, sitting down. The coffee was being made and the bourbon bottle was making the rounds.

Roaddog passed the bottle of Western Gold round the group again, once it came back to him he scowled at it.

"Slowball, you're going to have to go the Lidl in Mablethorpe tomorrow, I don't have enough of this to last the weekend."

"No problem," laughed Slowball.

"Perhaps you should take the van?" suggested Jackie.

"Van's not big enough," laughed Jane.

"Someone's going to have to go every day at this rate," laughed Bug.

"Don't forget the coke for the pregnant girl," said Cherie.

"Here's to a great opening day," said Roaddog, raising his glass. Everyone joined in with the toast.

"I need a shower," said Jackie, "I stink of fast food and bacon butties."

"I knew there was something around here worth eating," laughed Roaddog.

There was a moment or two of silence, then Slowball spoke up.

"I gotta know," he said, "I just gotta know."

"Are you sure?" asked Roaddog. His big friend only nodded.

"What's going on?" asked Bug.

"Well," replied Roaddog, "Slowball got a bit antsy earlier today when he saw two guys dressed in leather," he paused.

"It's a biker shop, of course guys are going to be wearing leather," said Bug more than a little confused.

"Yes, but these two guys were walking around holding hands," smiled Roaddog.

"And?" demanded Bug.

"We had a brief discussion about gay bikers and things, in the end I told him there were things that he didn't want to know."

"You are a bad man," laughed Sylvia, "he's nosier than the worst of neighbours."

"I knew it would drive him crazy," he turned to Slowball, "once you know about my past it could change our friendship forever."

"Come on man, we've done everything together, we've fucked the same girls, we've killed guys together, we've disposed of bodies together, what more can there be?"

"Fine, I'll tell you about my younger years," he paused for a moment, just to be sure he had their attention, "I was gay." He stopped and let that statement sink in for a few breaths. Slowball's mouth fell open and he stared.

"There's more," whispered Slowball.

"Much more, you want to know?" he asked, Slowball nodded.

"I was gay, it wasn't my choice, but everyone said I was gay."

"They all say that nowadays," said Bug, "it's not a choice they make its who they are."

"No, it really wasn't my choice." said Roaddog slowly. "I was thirteen at the time, it was a very confusing time for me, but I did eventually get things straight in my head. The guy with his dick up my ass, he wasn't gay, his two friends holding me down, they weren't gay, I worked out that they couldn't be gay because they were rugby players and rugby players can't be gay." He looked around at his friends, shocked stares from the two guys, concern from the girls, Jackie and Cherie had tears running down their faces.

"Fuck," whispered Slowball.

"Yeah," said Roaddog, "anyway I was gay, everyone knew it, and I was beaten and spat on and all the other things that boys do to boys. Did you know that stimulation of the prostate can cause both erection and orgasm? I had my first ever orgasm face down in the changing room showers," he stopped and looked down, as if afraid to look into his friend's eyes. Both Jackie and Jane took his hands and held them tight.

"Shit," said Slowball, "you've got more reason to hate gays than I have."

"I suppose, but that's not the way I see it, I can't waste a perfectly good hate on an amorphous faceless mass, that's not how hate works, hate needs a real target, I know it's an unfashionable way to think about things, but it is the only way I can see it."

"So, you can hate those three guys?" asked Slowball, his hands clenching, large fists forming waiting for something to punch.

"Sadly no, again it's a very unfashionable way to think these days, but I see nothing to be gained from hating the dead. They really don't give a fuck anymore, hating them achieves nothing. Not fashionable I know."

"How much older than you were they?" asked Bug.

"A couple of years, why?"

"Three young men all died before their time, what are the odds?" Bug asked.

"Did you kill 'em Dog?" asked Slowball.

"I read the newspaper reports, one jumped off a tower block in Manchester stoned out of his mind on acid, one was mugged in London, lone white guy in Lambeth, and the last one was run over by a German army truck in Dusseldorf, I think, not sure where now."

"I reckon he killed 'em." said Slowball to Bug.

"Probably," replied Bug, "but the local plod aren't going to make any connections between deaths so far apart."

"Shit man," said Slowball, "I'd never have guessed."

"Almost no one knows, and I'd like it to stay that way."

"No sweat." said Slowball, Bug nodded, then spoke slowly, "I thought you learned karate while you were at school?"

"I did," smiled Roaddog, "I got damned good, and did it real fast. Before long I'd taken out each of those guys singly, and once as a threesome, they left me alone after that."

"Good man," said Slowball.

"I managed to reduce their predations more than a little, word got round and younger boys turned to me for help. Things were so much nicer once they'd moved on to university." There was a long pause.

"I think it's bedtime," said Roaddog smiling at Jackie and Jane. "Those two couches pull out into almost double beds, so you lot should be OK," he said to the others as he went towards the bedroom at the back of the van.

"Damn this bed's a bit small," said Jane, as she closed the door behind herself.

"What do you expect in a static caravan?" asked Jackie, "wait until you see the shower."

"That'll be about now," laughed Jane, "I gotta pee." When she returned she was laughing.

"What's funny?" asked Roaddog.

"I just thought about Slowball in that shower, if he drops the soap, he's going to have to get someone else to get it, cos he can't bend over in there without getting jammed between the walls."

"It is tight," said Roaddog, "definitely not big enough for two."

"Not even two our size," said Jackie looking straight at Jane.

"I don't know," replied Jane, "could be fun."

"Certainly a spectator sport," laughed Roaddog.

"Pervert," said Jane grinning. "How big is the bathroom above the shop?"

"Not finished yet," said Jackie, "but it should be big enough for three at least."

"That sounds better than this place."

"Could be fun, if you choose to stay," Jackie stepped in close and hugged Jane, "please stay, we've both missed you so much."

"Not enough to come home."

"You know we can't do that," whispered Roaddog, joining in the hug, "that asshole Hopkins is still sniffing around."

"He has been more than a bit of a pain," admitted Jane. Jackie started to remove Janes clothing, t-shirt went first, Jane lifting her arms to help out. Jackie's shirt went next, then there was a frenzy of belt buckles and jeans, very soon all three were naked, mouths and hands roaming all around, Roaddog pulled them towards the bed, they fell into a heap and the action became more intense. Jane was certainly the centre of attention, Jackie was licking her pussy and Roaddog was focused on her small breasts. Jane's first orgasm caught her a little by surprise, she grunted loudly and writhed around the bed. As the pleasure subsided, she spun around and latched hard onto Jackie who took Roaddog straight into her throat. The re-union proceeded much as all had hoped.

It was utterly dark when Jane opened her eyes, and completely silent. She felt the naked pressure of Jackie against her and was reassured, but still a little nervous. Jane squeezed Jackie gently, until she felt the sudden intake of breath that told her that Jackie was now awake.

"What's up?" whispered Jackie.

"It's so dark and quiet, is it always like this?"

"Oh it's always this dark, you should see the stars when there is no cloud, it's really beautiful. Occasionally it gets noisy, you can hear deer calling, and foxes hunting, the occasional scream of a rat taken by an owl."

"It's just so quiet."

"I love it," whispered Jackie, "no traffic noise, no sirens, no people in the street. Just the occasional boy racer on the road, but even that's a long way away." Jackie pulled Jane even tighter against her back. "Go to sleep, things start early around here." Jane's eyes were starting to pick out shapes in the darkness, but nothing that made too much in the way of sense. She pushed her head down into the pillow and held on to Jackie, sleep took her in a few minutes.

Chapter 5: Sunday morning time for church.

Jane woke to feel soft lips on hers, she returned the kiss and opened her eyes. There was some light coming through the skylight, but it was definitely not sunny out there.

"Come on sleepy head," said Jackie, "it's time to get up."

"What time is it?"

"Nearly sunrise," laughed Jackie softly.

"You gotta be kidding?"

"No, I said early."

"This isn't early it's insane."

"Maybe, but it's worth it." The gurgling of the cistern told her that the bathroom was going to be free in a moment, so she rolled to her feet and left the room, leaving Jane alone. Jane looked at the open door and considered going back to sleep. She decided to find out what all the interest in sunrise was, she walked slowly into the main room, where Roaddog was opening the curtains. Slowball looked up from the pull-out bed he was sharing with Sylvia.

"Shit Dog," he said, "that's not a sight one expects at this time in the morning, put some fucking clothes on."

"No," said Roaddog quietly, "wake up, sunrise is coming."

"I've heard of this sunrise thing," muttered Sylvia, "but never had the incentive to actually get out of bed at stupid o'clock to catch it." Jackie came out of the bathroom and put the kettle on as she passed through the kitchen area, she went to the front window and put an arm around Roaddog's waist.

"Now that's a better sight," said Slowball, earning himself a heavy nudge from Sylvia. Cherie groaned and rolled quickly out of the other bed, and almost ran to the bathroom. Bug grunted as he woke.

"What's happening?" he asked.

"Sunrise," said Jackie, as Jane stood alongside Roaddog and snaked her arm along Jackie's round his back, her head propped against Roaddog's upper arm.

"Fuck that," snarled Bug, pulling the covers up over his head.

The rapidly lightening sky behind the trees on the other side of the lake told that sunrise was very close. For Roaddog and Jackie this was one of their favourite moments of the day, the black birds in the hedge behind the van started up their own greeting for the sun, the geese on the lake honking gently to one another, as if making plans for the day ahead. A flash of red light leapt through the trees and illuminated the faces of the three standing in the window. Quickly the red light travelled down their bodies as the sun crawled its way upwards. By the time that the click of the kettle sounded they were lit by reflections off the ripples in the lake. Suddenly something spooked the geese, and they took flight, skipping across the surface of the lake, shattering the reflections, their honking and the whistling of their wings filled the air. They circled once and then set off towards the sun.

"We will ride on the wings of heaven," sang Roaddog softly.

"It's really beautiful," said Jane, "but I'm not sure about being out of bed at this time on a damned Sunday."

"I'm with you on that," said Cherie crawling back into bed alongside Bug, her head disappeared under the covers. Silence returned as the geese flew away, to be replaced by the small sounds of birds, they had been driven into hiding by the noise of the geese.

"Damn this place is so different from home," mumbled Slowball, "it's just so peaceful."

"Yeah," replied Roaddog, "I love it, I just hope it stays peaceful."

"It'll be fine once we get Jake sorted out, he really can't believe we are responsible for his dead cows," said Jackie.

"Cows are important to farmers; we'll have a look at that church later and go and talk to Jake. After breakfast."

"You damned men can cook breakfast, I was at it all day yesterday and no doubt will be doing the same thing again today," said Jackie.

"No worries," said Roaddog, he noticed that John came out of the caravan opposite, "I don't think John is going fishing today," he whispered. Jackie looked at John who was standing on his decking looking around, almost guiltily. He was wearing a dressing gown with his bare legs visible below, his feet stuffed into slippers. John looked at Roaddog, Jackie, and Jane standing in the sunlit front window. John dropped his dressing gown and was revealed to be wearing only his slippers, he threw the trio a quick salute and turned to go back inside, pausing for a moment to pick up his discarded dressing gown.

"Well," said Roaddog, "looks like he's found something other than fishing to do this morning," chuckling softly.

"Gladys seems to have been at work with the razor as well," laughed Jackie.

"For an old guy he's not exactly small," laughed Jane, "what the fuck have you lot been up to with your elderly neighbours?"

"Gladys was here yesterday morning having her pussy shaved," laughed Slowball, "your man did an excellent job." Jane turned to Roaddog.

"A man of hidden talents," she laughed.

"I'm going to have a shower," said Jackie, "I stink of burgers still, I don't think I'll ever get my hair clean."

"Don't take too long," said Roaddog, "there's far too many people here today."

"If your shower was bigger, we could do two at once," she giggled, slapping him gently on the ass.

"That would take three times as long, and do you have any idea of the price of bottled gas to run that thing," he returned the slap with interest, "hurry along." He went into the kitchen area as Jackie went into the bathroom, coffee first, then bacon for breakfast. By the time Jackie came out of the bathroom, which was immediately taken over by Jane, breakfast barmcakes were waiting for her, she smiled at Roaddog and the rest of the guests, who were at least partially dressed by now. Beds had been folded away and tables erected. It was almost back to normal, well normal for them, Roaddog standing at the cooker frying bacon wearing only his cooking apron.

"What's the plan for today?" asked Slowball.

"We'll go and check out the church, sounds like it might be interesting, and then we'll have a chat with Jake. I want to have the workshop open by eleven, we can have tea at the axe, then off to see Vince and his group at Marshchapel. A night of rock music and beer."

"Going to be a busy day then," said Slowball. "Shop opening Monday?" he asked.

"Maybe," laughed Roaddog, "depends what time, or if we get back from Marshchapel."

"So, I suppose we better get moving then," said Bug, heading for the bathroom.

"I'll ride with Slowball," said Jane, "it'll cut down the number of vehicles." She knew that none of the bikes would be left behind, but her car was just an encumbrance in too many ways.

"That's great," said Roaddog hugging her. It was after eight o'clock by the time they were ready to go, as they went outside and Roaddog was locking the door, John came out of the caravan opposite, dressed for fishing this time.

"Hey John," called Roaddog softly, "how's it hanging?"

"Fucked is the word," laughed John, "she's snoring so I thought I'd go and catch some smaller fish."

"Good idea, you have a good day."

"How can it go wrong now?" laughed John, picking up his trolley and setting off along the road to the back of the lake.

"If he gets struck by lightning, he'll die a happy man," laughed Slowball.

"Nothing wrong with that," said Sylvia.

"Okay people," called Roaddog, slipping his leg over his saddle, "let's go to church." Jackie stepped up behind him, as the big motor barked into life, Bugs Honda was almost silent by comparison, the same could not be said for the VW. In only five minutes they were turning off the road into the driveway of the church, it was long and straight, between two fields, to the left barley and the right six-foot-high corn. They rolled through the gap in the hedges and parked on a grass area outside the lynch gate. Even the noise of the motorcycles failed to frighten off the collection of birds on the roof of the gate.

"What the fuck are those birds?" demanded Bug.

"No idea," said Sylvia, "they look like big fat soft grey pigeons."

"They look hungry," said Bug.

"What do you mean?" asked Roaddog.

"They are looking at me like I am breakfast."

"Frightened?" asked Jane.

"Spooky old church, creepy birds staring, you've seen the damned movie." muttered Bug, he picked up a fallen twig and threw it at the birds on the roof. They all took wing, not with the clatter of pigeons, or the whirl of pheasants, but with a soft blurred sound, like the beating of owl's wings. Unlike frightened pigeons they didn't fly so far away, they scattered amongst the headstones of the graves in the yard all around. By the time the people had walked through the gate the roof was covered again, only with wings so quiet they didn't even notice until Bug looked back and muttered, "Fuck." The birds stood silently on the roof, just looking at the people. From the gate the path was only short, it passed between two huge yew trees, each at least thirty feet high. They walked into the church through the south doorway, any door long gone. Two rows of heavy columns supported the roof over the nave, the floor was covered in interlocking tiles, and three gravestones, each carved with barely discernible writing. To their left was an uneven hole in the ground, where a font had most likely been removed. In the centre of the nave was an area of tiles that looked like it had been disturbed, spread around this area were some burned out tea lights.

"Someone has been here in the dark," said Sylvia. "See that faint white line?"

"What of it?" asked Jane, the broad line was very faint, and described a circle around the place they were standing.

"It's salt, as a form of occult protection."

"You mean witches and that?" laughed Bug.

"Some believe," smiled Sylvia. The main entrance to the church was the west door, this had long been boarded up with heavy wooden panels, much weathered by the elements. Just about head height in the centre panel was what looked at first to be a dark stain. Roaddog went over for a closer look, Jackie and Jane went the other way to look at the place where the altar used to be, the windows as simple holes in the wall shed plenty of light for them to see, the same not true for Roaddog. The tower above his head and the complete lack of windows in the lower section of the tower made it quite dark. In a moment his phone turned into a torch and illuminated the dark patch, little showed until he moved the light to the side and then it picked out the pattern far better.

"Shit," he called, "look at this."

"I can see it from here," replied Jackie loudly. "It's the green man."

"That's for sure," said Bug. "It's the sign hanging outside every one of those pubs in the country."

"That looks weird," said Jane, "how's it been painted?"

"That's the strange thing," replied Roaddog, "it's not paint, and it's not carved, it looks like it's embossed into the surface of the wood, that's why it shows up when lit from the side."

"How can it be green? Something weird is definitely going on here," said Slowball.

"Yes," agreed Roaddog, "let's go and talk to Jake, see what else he can tell us."

They all left the church and followed the path to the gate, every gravestone along the way had a grey bird perched on it, and the roof of the lynch gate was covered.

"I hate birds," muttered Bug.

"I'm beginning to be a little concerned," said Roaddog, smiling at his friend. Roaddog had a hand on one of is knives as they walked through the gate, the birds made no aggressive moves, but equally they didn't move away. They only took fright when Roaddog gunned the big engine of the victory, they took to the air and circled the tower before settling on the roof of the church. The trip to south farm only took a few seconds because it was very close to the church. Roaddog walked up to the front door and knocked loudly. After a moment there were heavy footsteps inside, and the door opened. A large woman in her late forties stood there, the door was resting against her right shoulder and her whole right arm was hidden behind it.

"Yes," she sounded a little disturbed to have visitors.

"Hi, I'm looking for Jake, he came to the pub to talk to us last night, is he around?" asked Roaddog.

"This time of day he should be in the milking parlour, cleaning down."

Before Roaddog could ask anything further there was the unmistakeable report of a shotgun emptying both barrels. The woman yanked the door open, and her right hand was holding a shotgun, she barged passed Roaddog and set off along the side of the house. Roaddog ran to his bike, and Bug to his. In moments they were both following the woman, while assembling their own guns. As the woman approached a large shed like structure the shotgun boomed again, another two shots. A voice could be heard screaming inside the building. The woman opened the door, her gun snapped to her shoulder and cracked twice, as she lowered it, she broke it, and two spent cases flew free, she set about reloading. Roaddog stepped around her with Bug close on his heels. To their left Jake was standing with his back to the wall, his shotgun snapped closed and fired both barrels from the hip, it broke again in a heartbeat, as Jake fumbled in his pocket for more cartridges. Roaddog saw what Jake was shooting at and his jaw dropped open for a moment, it was a vaguely man shaped figure, that appeared to be a spinning bush, a bush of bright green leaves, the dark rich glossy green of rhododendrons. The woman's gun closed with a snap and fired again, almost as one. Two plumes of leaves separated from the figure, spun around and returned to the roiling mass.

"The face," yelled Jake, "shoot the face." His own gun fired again, and two jets of shattered leaves left the mass, falling smoking to the floor. Roaddog pulled the bolt on the Thompson and raised it to his shoulder, the staccato roar of the machine gun filled the barn, dead leaves scattering all around the thing as it moved away from Jake towards its new target, Roaddog. The thing was struggling as if wading against a fast-flowing river, only this was a river of pellets. Suddenly there was silence, the Thompson jammed. The woman's shotgun sounded briefly, then Bug stepped up, a stream of forty-five calibre slugs tore through the face and a plume of dead leaves fluttered to the floor, Jake's shotgun fired again, then he threw it to the ground. The only sound of the mac 10 was the clicking of the bolt as it moved backwards and forwards, that and the tinkling of falling brass cases. As the mac-10 ran out of bullets the Thompson started to roar again, the blockage cleared, every shot scattered more of the walking bush, until it faded away into nothing, as the last of its leaves fell dead to the ground the face vanished. Jake ran to the woman and hugged her tightly in his arms.

"Damn it Mary," he said softly, "how many times, home defence guns use swan shot, not birdshot." He kissed her and looked around the parlour, then he turned to Roaddog.

"Thanks man."

"No worries, I'd like to inform you that we had absolutely nothing to do with that thing at all, other than assisting in its demise."

"I only hope that it is gone," said Jake, looking around again, this time checking out the damage that had been done. "I can see where my shotgun has torn holes in the wall, Mary's birdshot barely makes a mark, the stream of bullets from that machine gun have torn chunks from some pipework, but I can see no damage from your tommy gun, it is a tommy gun, isn't it?"

"It is, but heavily modified, and I'm using softer shot, I don't want ricochets when there are friendlies around."

"Well, I'm sure it's illegal, you need help reloading?"

"You got the gear, I had to leave mine behind?"

"Of course I have, most of us around here load our own, no point in letting the cops know what you are shooting now is there, let's go into the house, I'll fix up the damage in here later, I think I need a drink." He took Mary's hand and led them to the back door of the house, they walked into the kitchen, Roaddog looked around and was a little surprised, it must have shown on his face.

"What's wrong?" asked Mary.

"Sorry," replied Roaddog, "it's just not what I expected."

"I know what you mean," Mary laughed, as she stashed her shotgun in the rack by the door. "People like you, from the towns, all expect a farmer's kitchen to be something from your cliché TV shows, big plain wooden table, heavy enough to butcher a cow on, and a coal fired range that takes up one wall." She turned to her husband, and gave him a look, then pointed at her gun in the rack. "What do you tell me?" she asked in a gentle tone but wrapped in barbed wire.

"Fuck," whispered Jake, almost running out of the door.

"Let me guess," said Jane, "he bitches about you leaving your gun somewhere else?"

"All the time," laughed Mary, "but I think I'll take his advice and change my loads."

"Does he really think we caused this monster?" asked Roaddog.

"He sure that someone has, and you are the strangers in town."

"We saw candles and a ring of salt," said Sylvia.

"That's not too unusual, that place has certainly attracted more than its fair share of idiots. Come Halloween the church is packed."

"Judging by what we have just seen there, they may be right," said Roaddog. Jake walked in carrying his shotgun and dropped it in the rack.

"Don't just put it there," snapped Mary, "clean it and do mine while you're at it." He nodded and picked up his gun, taking it over to the extended dining table that looked like it was straight out of Ikea. Mary filled the large kettle and set it to boiling.

"Tea anyone?" she asked, "I don't know about the rest of you, but I need something to take away the taste of all that gunfire." More of the visitors wanted coffee, so cups were set up while the kettle boiled. Mary looked at Jake as he was pulling a rag through a barrel on his shot gun.

"What?" he asked.

"When you've done that, collect all those tiny shotgun cartridges and at least renew the primers."

"If you find the ones that caused the jam," laughed Roaddog, "curse them, stamp on them, and bin the bastards, I never want to see them again."

"When you've done that," said Mary, "you can discuss with," she turned to Roaddog,

"Roaddog," he said, her eyebrows raised a little.

"Roaddog," she said, "pellets and sizes and suppliers."

"Unusual name," she said turning back to Roaddog.

"One I was given," he went on to introduce the others.

"So," said Mary, "all you pretty girls are known by the names your parents gave you, but the guys have new names, strikes me as a little unfair." Sylvia almost spit out her tea.

"I suppose it is," replied Roaddog slowly, "it's the way bike clubs are I'm afraid, the women have to be really special to earn themselves a name." He paused, "that doesn't sound any better, does it?"

"Not much," laughed Mary. "Are you girls happy with the arrangements?"

"I am," said Jackie, "I have no idea how Bandit Queen earned her name, but I was there when Man-Dare was christened, I'm happy to be Jackie."

"I read some books about hells angels when I was younger, it seemed an interesting if dangerous lifestyle," said Mary. Jackie explained to Mary the details of Man-Dare's fight, punishment, and christening. Mary was only a little shocked.

"Every man?" she asked.

"Not everyone, Roaddog didn't because he had his prospective girlfriend on his arm, and Geronimo said she looked too much like his daughter at the time," laughed Jackie.

"Seems I missed much of the fun," said Jane.

"You've had plenty of fun," laughed Jackie, leaning over and kissing Jane.

"Thought that you were Roaddog's girl?" asked Mary.

"We both are," said Jane.

"Both?" whispered Jake.

"Concentrate on your cleaning," said Mary. "I may have missed out on some things in this life."

"Are you happy with the arrangements?" asked Sylvia.

"I am," laughed Mary, "I am, but the occasional dream has to be allowed. Jake, go get a jug, these people deserve a drink, after all they did save your miserable life." Jake looked at her his jaw hanging open.

"Go," snapped Mary with a twitch of the head. Jake stamped off through the house, to return in only a minute with a gallon demi-john full almost to the brim with a light golden liquid, a heavy cork jammed into the neck. Mary picked up the demi-john and with a practised hand rolled it onto her arm, taking glasses from the pine dresser she poured a small measure into each, and passed them out to the guests, then poured a pair of slightly bigger measures for herself and Jake. Roaddog sniffed his glass and his eyes opened wide. Mary laughed.

"Damned yanks think they invented moonshine, they're amateurs compared to us, my family has been making shine for five hundred years. Careful girls, this stuff will put hairs on your chests," she raised her glass slowly and looked directly at Roaddog, "you and your crazy machine gun saved my man's life today, I thank you from the bottom of my heart, cheers," she put her glass to her lips and sipped a healthy portion of the not so healthy potion. The others sipped, there was some choking and some coughing, Roaddog struggled to find his voice.

"Smooth," he stuttered, "mighty smooth."

"I forgot to mention," said Mary, "this one is sixty percent by volume, which is much stronger than you are used to."

"That's the understatement of the year," said Roaddog, feeling his throat burning as the liquid fire spread down into his stomach. He drained his glass with a second sip and put it down on the table. There was a deep rumbling sound and the ground shook beneath their feet.

"Fuck," shouted Jake.

"I did just feel the earth move, didn't I?" asked Slowball.

"Yes, you did," said Jake, "same sound, same shake, two days before the cows started to die."

"I think we'll go back to that damned church and see what has happened," said Roaddog.

"I'll come along, I want to know what is coming next."

"You think there is something more?" asked Roaddog.

"The way my luck is running, there has to be something worse coming," said Jake looking down.

"No worries," said Roaddog, "drink up let's go find out." He turned to Mary, "thank you my dear for such a fine example of the moonshiners art."

"No problem, look after Jake for me."

Roaddog just nodded and led his group out of the back door, by the time they had got to the bikes and stashed the guns away Jake rolled up on a small quad bike. Only seconds later they were rolling down the long driveway towards the church. Parked on the grass was a car that hadn't been there when they left. They strolled into the church, Bug's machine gun stayed in his pannier, it was no use without bullets. Roaddog had his Thompson, as he strode through the south door he spotted three people inside, one a priest, the other two children in their early teens. He nodded to them then walked over to the west door, the face of the green man was gone, it had been replaced by something else, a wide face, with short stubby horns above, and a beard that looked like tentacles, there was a hint of blue about it, though the eyes were a deep red.

"What the fuck is this?" he asked of no one in particular.

"That is Kyronatha," said the priest.

"And what is a Kyronatha?"

"Just a demon, quite a powerful one, but only a demon." The two children were huddled against the priest, obviously frightened.

"Why are you here?" demanded Roaddog.

"I felt something change about half an hour ago, so I came over to see what was happening, found these children here, why are you here?"

"We killed the green man and then felt the ground shake. Jake says that's what happened before the green man appeared."

"Something has definitely happened here, I was just asking these children if they knew anything, when some noisy motorcycles arrived, I am Father Francis."

"Roaddog, well kids, what happened here? Something disturbed the floor, even more now, and something drew this picture on the wall."

"You're frightening them, and the damned machine gun isn't helping," said Father Francis. Roaddog held the gun behind his back.

"Back off Dog," smiled Jane, she moved forwards and sat on the ground next to the children. "He's a tad grumpy today, can you tell me what happened?"

"I don't know," said the girl hiding her face in the priest's long cassock.

"What about you?" asked Jane looking at the boy and reaching for his hand. From his standing position he had an excellent view down the front of Jane's t-shirt, and he was taking advantage of it.

"I think we did something wicked," he whispered.

"How old are you?"

"Fourteen."

"Just how wicked can a fourteen-year-old get?" she smiled, leaning forward a little.

"I don't want to tell," he muttered.

"Did the ground make the same noise as it did today?"

"Yes, and a face appeared on the wall."

"So, what were you doing when this happened?"

"I don't want to say," he mumbled.

"If you don't tell us we won't be able to fix it, tell us, please." Again, she leaned forwards.

"We had sex."

"That's criminal," said Father Francis, loudly.

"You can back off as well," said Jane, her voice calm and level. Francis shrugged but didn't move away, he knew the children would need him.

"You are both a little young for that you know?"

"Yes," whispered the girl, "but all the girls at school ever talk about is sex."

"Most of them will be lying, did it hurt?" Jane whispered.

"Yes, it hurt a lot."

"It can do the first time, especially when you are so young. I'm sure he didn't mean to hurt you."

"I told him to take it out, but he took forever," the girl sobbed.

"I couldn't help it, my body was out of control, I'm sorry," the boy mumbled.

"You brought candles?" asked Jane.

"Yes," said the boy, "mothers pretty red candles, she only had five left, so I took them all, they smelled great."

"So, it was dark?"

"Yes, I had a torch as well, so we didn't need our phones."

"What's the point in that?"

"Phones turned off, no trackers," the boy smiled.

"When you set the candles was there something else here?"

"Yes, a faint white ring, I put the candles around that circle."

"Was there semen?" The boy nodded.

"First time for you as well?" he nodded again. Jane smiled at him, then looked up at Father Francis.

"Salt circle, five candles, cinnamon scented, virgin blood, and virgin semen, would that be enough?" she asked.

"Certainly a very powerful mixture, it could be enough to open the way."

"The way to where?" asked Roaddog.

"Hell, where else?" replied Father Francis.

"Will you be able to close it?"

"We'll give it a good try, but it is by no means certain."

Jane whispered softly to the children, "The words you say when you go into confession speak them now." For a moment the children looked at her then both spoke almost as one.

"Bless me father for I have sinned, it has been a week since my last confession."

Jane looked up at Father Francis and smiled.

"Why did you do that?" asked Father Francis.

"If you tell anyone about what you have heard here, you will be breaking the sanctity of the confessional."

"But I can still share with my colleagues."

"Yes, but not their parents."

The children both hugged Jane.

"Children you are going to have to deal with this, currently only the Father knows, but it won't stay secret for very long, you will have to tell your parents, but it'll be better coming from you rather than him."

"They're not old enough to make these decisions," said Father Francis.

"They are now," smiled Jane, "but their next confession is going to be a doozy."

"We are going straight to the church now, to get that sorted out," said Father Francis.

"Before you go," said Jane, she turned to the girl. "Did he rape you?"

"No, of course not."

"People are going to try to get you to say that he did, you will have to stand up to them, especially your parents, they are going to want to make it all his fault."

"We did it together, we both wanted to try it."

"We did it together," said the boy.

"Well, you'll not be trying it again for a while, you'll not be getting out of the house for a long time," laughed Jane. "You are both going to be under the most intense observation for a long time. All with the best possible intentions of course."

"The road to hell is paved with good intentions," said the boy.

"Ouch," said the priest. "They do listen occasionally."

"I've heard that three or four times a year since I was seven."

"And the no sex before marriage one?" asked Father Francis.

"Oh, a whole lot more," giggled the girl.

"Good intentions have to be trained," said Jane, "sex is built into the basic design."

"Have you any idea when this Kyronatha will appear?" asked Roaddog.

"I have no clue," said Father Francis. "Any way, I have things to do, come on children, I may not be able to tell your parents, but I can at least arrange your penance."

"I'm going to need those cartridges ready today, can you do that?" asked Roaddog of Jake.

"I'll get on them as soon as I get home, I'll have to use the lead I have on hand, but I'll get them back to you this afternoon, I'll bring them up to the bus depot."

"That would be great, not birdshot though, something a little heavier. Come on people we have a store to open." They all left the church and went out to the bikes, while they were loading up and starting the bikes, Father Francis waited with a child in each hand, the path was too narrow to have his car and Slowball's trike on it at the same time. He drove off towards the village once the motorcycles had left.

Chapter 6: Sunday opening.

Roaddog and the others opened the store as they had the day before and waited not so patiently for customers to arrive. Around eleven o'clock Karen and her husband Terry turned up.

"Hi Roaddog," she said, "how's it going?"

"It's a little quiet, but we're doing OK, you two had breakfast?"

"Actually no, I thought we'd come and try your food out, see what the competition is like," laughed Karen, wandering over to the van and talking to Jackie. She came back a few minutes later, with a monster bacon butty for herself, and a burger for Terry. Terry was talking to Roaddog about a very pretty sportster.

"What do you think Karen?" he asked, "I could see me tearing around the fens on one of these."

"You'll be on your own, just make sure the life insurance is up to date," she howled with laughter.

"You don't think he could ride one?" asked Roaddog.

"Come on Dog, he trips over his own feet most of the time."

"The low centre of gravity of these lowriders makes them real easy to ride."

"That'll make no difference to him, anyway, how many barrels of beer can it carry?"

"It's not for carrying beer, it's for cruising," said Terry.

"And when do we have time for that?"

"True I suppose." Terry looked seriously dejected, he had built his hopes up, but logic and Karen had shot him down. Karen turned to Roaddog.

"Your food is really good, and the prices are more than fair, I think we are going to lose a little custom to you."

"Perhaps, but you'll certainly be selling a lot more beer," laughed Roaddog.

"True," said Terry, "and we had more than a few just turn up for lunch yesterday, could be we both make money at this."

"That's the plan," replied Roaddog, "lots of new people stopping by in the village, it can't be bad for the local economy."

"That's very true," said Karen, "we got to go and open up, you have a good day, will you be stopping for food after you close?"

"Yes, we've an invite to a party, so we'll eat first," he laughed.

"I'll hold you a big table until about seven then."

"That would be great."

"See you later," said Karen walking away, pulling Terry with her, his fascination for the Harley held his eyes almost until they were on the road. Roaddog smiled as he remembered the look in his own eyes when he saw the first Harley that he actually wanted. It would have been nice to sell a bike in the first weekend, but he knew that Karen was going to block any expenditure of that size.

Gradually the number of bikes in front of the old bus depot increased, there were many people queueing for food, and plenty talking about the bikes that Roaddog had on sale, it was about one o'clock when Bug's skills finally paid off, he took a deposit payment for the lowrider, a thousand pounds through the till, and a promise of the other four by the end of the week, no finance companies to deal with, a simple sale, the very best kind, or nearly. A suitcase of money the only better option, but that almost never happens these days.

Less than half an hour later the quiet of the village was disturbed by the thunder of many motorcycles, they all appeared to be sticking to the speed limits, but none were running at low revs, Vince and Horse at the front of the cavalcade each raised a fist, then threw a huge rev out, the over run as the throttles closed caused all sorts of pops and bangs, and a plume of flame from the downturned pipes on Vince's Dyna-glide. Roaddog smiled and raised an arm in salute, as each motorcycle did the same thing as they passed the forecourt. Jackie and Jane laughed loudly within the confines of the burger van. 'I wonder where they are off to.' thought Roaddog, 'is the place ready for the invasion?' he chuckled softly to himself. He turned to see a small disturbance in the queue for the ladies toilet, he shouted of Bug. It looked like Cherie was attempting to get to the front of the queue, and a rather formidable looking woman was unhappy about her queue jumping technique, and was holding her by the arm. Cherie looked at the woman for a moment, then bent over and proceeded to deposit the remnants of breakfast over the woman's boots. Bug arrived on the scene.

"Are you okay?" he asked.

"Okay, bastard?" she snarled, "it's supposed to be morning sickness, not middle of the afternoon sickness, I'm gonna cut that dick off." Then she bent over again as the spasms clenched her guts and the pointless heaving took over. The woman's face had gone from utter outrage to total concern in a heartbeat, she glared at Bug, and reached an arm across Cherie's shoulder.

"It'll be okay, my dear, let it out." She looked at Bug again and mouthed a couple of words, might have been russian, ended in off at least. Once the ravages of vomiting had subsided, she took Cherie into the ladies and helped her with the clean-up.

"You my friend are in deep shit," said Slowball to Bug when he returned to the showroom section.

"I know, but what can I do about it?"

"Absolutely cock all," Slowball laughed, and looked up as Cherie and her new friend were walking towards them.

"You better look after this young woman, or I'll find you and make you pay," she said. Bug looked at her and longed for the feeling of the mac-10 in his hand, 'Fuck,' he thought, 'she's bigger than Bandit Queen.'

"You can rest assured that I will do everything that I can to keep her safe and make her life as easy as possible."

"You better young man," she patted Cherie on the arm and turned away.

"That's you fucking told," laughed Cherie.

"Who is she?" asked Bug.

"I've no idea, but I think she's great."

"She's certainly impressive."

"And damned strong, she's got a grip like you won't believe."

"Scary bitch," laughed Bug.

"Oh, she's that," smiled Cherie, as she leaned in to kiss him, "watch your ass", she whispered turning away.

Roaddog was out front when a quad bike that he recognised turned up. Jake dismounted and lifted a heavy bag from the back of his quad.

"Hey man," said Jake, handing over the bag. Roaddog had a quick look inside.

"Thanks Jake," he said.

"No sweat," smiled Jake, "the wife says that I owe you reloads for ever, after this morning's action, and there's a couple of cases in there of new ones, I don't have much use for those small ones, but I bought them when they were on special offer a couple of years ago."

"Will the loads be heavy enough?"

"They will be now," laughed Jake. "There's a lot of people here, so many strangers."

"Yes, and some of them are spending money," replied Roaddog, "and here comes someone even stranger." He nodded in the direction of a black clothed figure.

"Good afternoon gentlemen," said Father Francis.

"What's up?" asked Roaddog.

"Nothing new, I've been by the church and nothing has changed, I've come to tell you that my friends won't be at the church until about nine o'clock, one of them can't get something he needs until Monday morning, and then he's got a long drive from London."

Jane came over from the burger van.

"How are the kids doing? Still saying their 'Hail Mary's'," she asked.

"No, I let them off light," smiled Francis.

"You mean you twisted their arms to make them talk, what was it, one hundred 'our fathers' or five if they told their parents?"

"Actually two hundred and ten, it worked."

"You really are a bastard."

"We can't have secrets getting in the way of closing that portal."

"You know fuck all about secrets," snapped Jane.

"At least the children will be out of the way."

"Dickhead," snarled Jane, "they opened it, what if you need them to close it? Can you see their parents letting them walk into that much danger?"

"When my friends arrive, we'll shut the thing down."

"Sure?"

"Fairly sure, they will be bringing enough faith and power with them."

"What if it's going to take blood to close it? Will theirs do? How many of your holy men are actually virgins?" demanded Jane.

"I really can't answer that."

"Then answer for the only guy who's actually here."

"Sadly, I am no virgin," replied Father Francis.

"So much for your vow of celibacy."

"It was before I took my final vows."

"Just tell me it was a girl," said Jane.

"She was a sister."

"You fucked your sister and then complain about a couple of kids screwing?"

"Not my sister, a sister."

"And that makes things different?" laughed Jane. "Was she a test, and did you pass?"

"I've never thought of it like that," he whispered, "she was shipped out and I never heard from her again." He paused briefly, then continued. "For someone so young, you are quite cynical."

"Especially where organised religion is concerned."

"All this aside, we'll be at Botolph's about nine o'clock. I would personally like your support, as the only people I know who have actually defeated a demon. Please help us."

"We'll be there," said Roaddog.

"You sure about that?" asked Jake.

"No," smiled Roaddog, "but I'll be there."

"Me too," said Jake shaking his head.

"Thank you," said Father Francis as he turned to Jane, "Will you be there to represent the powers of womanhood?"

"No, I'll be there to back my man."

"That will be wonderful, this is going to be exciting," he bowed and turned away.

"Is it just me, or does he seem far too happy that this shit is happening?" asked Jake.

"Yes," whispered Jane, "it almost feels like his life's work is about to be fulfilled."

"He's been stationed here to watch that place," said Jake.

"How do you know?" demanded Roaddog.

"This parish has always been a sort of retirement home for elderly priests, until about fifteen years ago, then up pops a very young Father Francis. Everyone expected him to be gone in a couple of years, but I think the bishop wants him here, maybe this is why."

"So, he's all set up for this?" asked Roaddog.

"Should be," laughed Jake.

"He was surprised by the green man, even frightened," said Jane.

"This is something he has been waiting for and dreading at the same time," said Roaddog.

"Not much more we can do right now," said Jake.

"Okay," said Roaddog.

"Great," said Jake, "I'll see y'all at Botolph's tomorrow." He nodded to both and wandered off to his quad.

"This gets worse," said Jane.

"Could be, but at least I've got a full load for Vera."

"That may help," she said, before kissing him and going back to the van to take over from Jackie for a while.

Roaddog went over to where Bug was in conversation with a tall thin guy.

"Hey Dog," said Bug, "tell this guy about your labour rates, he don't want to believe me."

"Hi man," said Roaddog, "I only charge thirty quid an hour, and most of that is for the rent on this place. I ain't a main dealer."

"Dealers are charging fifty around here."

"I don't do that shit, I want people to come back again."

"The harley dealer always gets people coming back because there's nowhere else to go."

"That is no longer true, I'm a specialist in Harleys and can get parts cheaper than they can."

"That's great news for us Harley owners. I'll put the word out to all the HOG members that I know."

"That would be great," said Roaddog, "I've been spreading flyers at biker meets for the last couple of months."

"That's why I'm here, I picked one up at Horncastle," said the tall guy, Roaddog smiled broadly.

"What's so funny?" asked the tall guy.

"One of my girls calls it Hornycastle."

"Why?" asked the tall guy laughing.

"It's thirty minutes away on a Victory."

"That'll tickle her nicely."

"It was certainly fun when we got home."

"Okay man, I'll catch you around some time." The two shook hands and the tall guy walked away. Bug smiled briefly before speaking.

"You're going to do okay if the stealers are robbing people that much."

"The more mechs I have the more money we'll make," said Roaddog hopefully.

"You know I can't commit to that sort of thing without talking to Cherie, she might not want to move that far from home."

"What home? Dragonriders was her home, and now there's you."

"If she wants to stay in Lancashire then I have to stay too, there's a kid to think about."

"I understand that, talk to her, she may be okay with moving here, we can fix up the back of the shop real quick. Hospitals could be an issue though."

"Why?" asked Bug.

"They're a damned long way away, small one in Louth but the nearest big hospital is Grimsby, a good thirty minutes, I don't know where the nearest maternity unit is."

"These are going to be important to Cherie in the next few months,

I'll talk to her, see how she feels."

"It would be good if you could move over here, I could do with some help, though I don't think the actual work will be that important to us, the miners are doing well."

"We'll see," Bug smiled and walked into the seating area to talk to Cherie. Though as Roaddog watched there was very little verbal communications, he smiled as they kissed and turned to talk to some customer that had just walked up.

At four o'clock Roaddog went round telling customers that they were closing up, there were only a few, Jackie had already shut down the burger van and was sitting with the rest of the girls,

"Shall we go to the Axe for tea?" asked Roaddog.

"That'll make a change," laughed Jackie.

"Is there anywhere else to eat in this village?" asked Sylvia.

"Yes," said Roaddog, "but we don't go there because the food is so much better at the Axe, and the beer is better, and there's that service with a smile thing, the other pub doesn't have any of these."

"Is it that bad?" asked Slowball.

"Yes, and worse on occasion, so we don't bother."

"Axe it is then," said Cherie.

"And it's in walking distance," said Jackie. The last of the punters fired up his motorcycle, and the heavy shutters started to fall. Roaddog went into the back room to check on things, a quick check showed that he had done well during the day, the miners had hit twice, and on both occasions taking a good pay-out. He sold some of the bitcoin and moved it into his current account and moved the rest into the offshore accounts. It took him quite a time, to get the deals moving, so much so that Jackie and Jane came looking for him.

"What's up?" asked Jackie.

"Miners have done well today, but the batteries are almost empty."

"You could turn them off until the batteries are full again," suggested Jane.

"Stuff that," laughed Roaddog, "if we hit some more like today's I'm happy to pay for the juice."

"So, are we going to expand the mining operation?" asked Jane.

"I think so, but where can we put more solar panels?"

"How about a lean to on one side of the building, so that we can park bikes under it, and cover it with panels," said Jackie.

"Now that's an idea," Roaddog smiled, "we'll look into that tomorrow, today I feel the need for beer and food."

"Let's go and see Karen," laughed Jane.

The three went into the main section of the building and gathered up their friends. As usual they walked to the Axe, Karen was happy to see them and still had their table available.

"Mining's been real good today," said Roaddog as they took their seats, "beer and food are on me."

"That's very good of you," laughed Bug, "what we doing later?"

"We'll go to Marshchapel and see what Vince has to say for himself," said Roaddog.

"I wonder what he actually wants?" said Slowball.

"We can worry about that later," said Roaddog, "in the meantime, food and beer." The young waitress came over to take their orders and returned quickly with their drinks.

"What are we going to do about the miners?" asked Jackie.

"I'll get some more, and some battery packs once we have the lean to up and covered with solars," said Roaddog.

"That sounds like a plan," laughed Bug.

"But what about the other issue we currently have?" asked Slowball.

"The damned demons?" asked Roaddog.

"Them's the ones," laughed Jane.

"I don't know, no weapon forged, that's what the priest said, any ideas?" asked Roaddog.

"How about a weapon of the gods?" asked Slowball.

"What do you mean?"

"Fire, stolen from the gods by Prometheus."

"Yeah," said Bug, "burn the bastard."

"Now that does sound good," said Roaddog. "We'll make some napalm in the morning, and some Molotovs. That should keep the bastard dancing."

"We can always hope that the priest and his friends close the portal first," said Sylvia.

"It's good to have a plan B," laughed Roaddog.

"How about plan C?" asked Bug.

"Like what?" asked Jackie.

"Priests are plan A, fire as plan B, but what about another backup."

"Plan C," laughed Roaddog, "hotter fire. Drive the bastard into a house full of propane, not so many round here are on gas mains."

"So, all we need is a house with a full tank of propane and no people," said Slowball.

"How about something smaller, say, a static?" asked Jane.

"Wouldn't work," replied Roaddog, "the dangers of propane are well known and statics have more than enough ventilation to bleed the propane out, it's heavier than air and just falls out the holes in the floors."

"I'm sure we can find somewhere if we really need to," laughed Slowball. At this point the food arrived and everyone went quiet, at least while they were eating.

"When should we set off for Marshchapel?" asked Slowball, once the last chip had been used to scrape up his pepper sauce.

"I'd like to get some sleep before we go to that church in the morning, so I think we should go early, and leave as soon as is politic," said Roaddog.

"Time for another beer then," laughed Slowball, waving at Mandy, who came straight over. Drinks were ordered and delivered before everyone had finished eating.

"What are we going to do at the church tomorrow?" asked Bug.

"Whatever we can, we got to get that gateway closed down," said Roaddog, "god alone knows what's going to crawl out next."

"You'll never guess what all this shit reminds me of," laughed Bug.

"Go on," said Slowball.

"Buffy."

"You could be right," laughed Jane, "some kids opened a hell mouth in Botolph's church."

"Well," laughed Roaddog, "I'll be more than happy for Sarah Michelle Geller to turn up and sort this crap out."

"That's just not going to happen, is it?" asked Jackie.

"No, I really don't need another blonde in my life right now."

"You suddenly chicken or something?" asked Jane.

"No," he laughed, "I just know my limits, you two are more than enough for me."

"Yes, chicken," said Jackie.

"We'll see," said Roaddog, "when all those vampires start crawling through the floor in the church."

"Just think how that priest is going to deal with that," laughed Bug, "he'll shit in his pants."

"Can't have vampires during the day," said Slowball.

"There's always some other sort of demon," said Sylvia, taking Slowball's hand and smiling at him.

"Yes, we got blue face guy to deal with first," said Roaddog, "maybe it'll be vamps next."

"I don't want a next," said Jane, "I want that damned thing closed."

"We can only hope that the clergyman and his friends can do that." Roaddog laughed.

The conversation died for a moment, then Roaddog spoke again,

"Let's go meet with Vince and see what he's after." Roaddog emptied his beer and went to the bar to pay Karen, by the time he returned they were all ready to leave. As the bikes rolled out of the old bus depot Roaddog was surprised to see Jackie climb onto Slowball's trike, and Jane wearing her helmet stood beside his bike. He knew that Jackie had been talking to her as soon as he felt her hands on his shoulders, in seconds he felt the bike settle as she dropped into the pillion seat.

"Go easy on me for a bit, will you?" she asked quietly as the Victory fired up.

"No worries," said Roaddog, sliding the clutch gently and rolling out into the main street. Bug and Slowball followed only a second behind. The roads were quiet, but then they always are in these rural villages. He led the way out of the village and onto the main coast road, it ran between open grassland, with the occasional farm, and more occasional village. They were all enjoying the ride, the roads had short straights and good bends, some tight others wide open, it seemed like no time at all until they were making the S bend into the village of Marshchapel. On the left was the White Horse, they pulled into the carpark and rode up to the entrance to the back field where the rally was being held. Roaddog showed the card Vince had given him to one of the stewards in a florescent jacket, he was told to park the bikes to the right just inside the gate and the other one would go and get Vince. By the time they had the bikes turned around and parked with their tails to the fence Vince was walking towards them.

"Good evening," he called as he approached.

"Hi ya Vince," said Roaddog. "You had a good day?"

"It's been ok, we had a ride out to Sutton on Sea, frightened a few of the natives, then a cruise to Skeggy and back. Nice day. You?"

"Not a bad day, plenty of customers and sold a bike, so a good day really."

"Come with me," said Vince, "let's find somewhere for a chat." They all followed Vince into the centre of the camp site, and met up with Horse, who handed out bottles of beer, and waved for everyone to sit down. Roaddog was a little surprised to see that there were no members of Vince's club anywhere nearby.

"I have a question to ask," said Vince quietly.

"So, ask," smiled Roaddog.

"When there was a chance of a fight yesterday two of your guys were standing by their bikes, I believe they were hoping not to have to pull some important weapons from those bikes, they didn't move away until they got an instruction from you, is my guess right?"

"If it is, what is your interest?"

"I'd like to buy them or even sell you ammunition."

"So, you believe we have some guns."

"Nothing else fits the actions of your crew."

"Fine," Roaddog laughed, "we need 45 calibre bullets in large boxes, can you help?"

"I can meet that, how many?"

"Say five hundred."

"What the fuck you need that many for?"

"Mac-10," smiled Bug.

"I'd like to buy that piece," said Vince.

"I'll sell it to you when we've finished the current shit," laughed Bug, "damned thing makes me nervous just sitting there, and Cherie really doesn't like it."

"How much do you want for it?"

"I've no idea, I got it for nowt."

"How many magazines you got?"

"Three, long ones."

"I'll give you a grand for it, and your first box of ammo included."

"Is that a good price?" asked Roaddog.

"I've no idea," replied Vince, "they just don't come up anywhere. What's this shit you're involved in, maybe we can help?"

"I'm not even sure you'll believe us."

"Try me." Roaddog paused for a while before telling Vince and Horse about their meeting with the Father Francis and with the green man.

"That's some crazy shit," said Vince.

"You believe me?" asked Roaddog.

"Actually it doesn't really surprise me, this whole area is mad."

"That does surprise me, I somehow expected a rural farming community to be the ultimate of level-headed people."

"No," laughed Vince, "they're just as crazy as the rest."

"Will you help us with ammunition?"

"No worries." Vince turned to Horse, "Go get Jingo." Horse went off, and returned in moments with a short biker, who took scruffy to entirely new levels. His t-shirt was holey, his jeans the same, his cut ragged, his hair worse.

"Jingo," said Vince, "go get us a case of 45 rounds, five hundred."

"What, now?" answered the small biker.

"Yes now," snarled Vince.

"I'll be about thirty minutes," said Jingo, turning away slowly.

"What's his problem?" asked Roaddog.

"He's been a bad boy," said Vince, offering no further information. After a moments silence he continued, "Would you like some help from us?"

"I don't think so, we should be able to handle the odd demon or two." Vince looked at him with a wry grin.

"I don't believe I just said that either," laughed Roaddog.

"We'll be here until late tomorrow, just give us a call if you need something."

"We have a few churchmen coming tomorrow, we're only there as back up, they should be dealing with this sort of shit, after all it's their shit."

"Churchmen eh," smiled Vince, "I may be able to help you on that score." He turned towards the rest of the camp and yelled, "Nutter," he turned back to Roaddog, "This guy is real special."

"How special?"

"You'll see." Vince waved to a biker walking slowly toward them, he was difficult to see with the lights of the DJ behind him, as he got nearer it became clear that he was quite old.

"Nutter, sit a spell, these people have some information for you." Nutter lowered himself slowly to the grass and leaned on one arm while looking around the circle.

"What do you know?" he asked, they all shivered as his voice sounded so much like Lurch, deep and gravelly.

Roaddog looked at Vince, who smiled and nodded. Roaddog looked Nutter in the eye and spoke slowly.

"We think a door to hell has opened at a church nearby. We've already killed one demon, and we're expecting another sometime soon." Nutter looked from face to face, waiting for someone to laugh, but none did.

"I can't believe it's finally happened," said the old biker, "after all these damned years, now, I only hope I'm strong enough, I'm with you."

"You actually believe me?" asked Roaddog.

"Yes," Nutter shook his head slowly, then turned to Vince. "I told you, you bastard, I told you."

"I know old friend, I am sorry that we didn't believe you, but these people are so earnest, they're not like you at all."

"He thought I was just some stir crazy fool," said Nutter to Roaddog, "Now he believes. Why couldn't this have happened ten years ago, why now?"

"A couple of randy kids, it seems that's all it took," smiled Roaddog.

"Virgins both," whispered Nutter.

"Right," said Jane, "now they're both scared to death."

"They should be careful because that could be truer than you know." He looked up at the darkening sky, "What are you doing about closing the damned thing."

"That's in the hands of the local priest, a Father Francis," said Roaddog.

"A fucking priest, that's not going to be enough" mumbled Nutter, barely audible over the pounding bass from the DJ's speakers.

"He's got four friends coming in tomorrow morning, they have some sort of plan, they may even have been waiting for this to happen."

"They've known about it for a long time, and Botolph's has been getting more and more jumpy in the last couple of years."

"So, you know where it is?"

"There are a couple of old churches round here, but nothing nearly as active as Botolph's."

"The place is covered in fat grey birds," said Bug.

"No surprise," laughed Nutter, "they are the harbingers, which demon have you killed, and who's next?"

"We killed the green man, and next is," Roaddog paused, "blue guy, short horns, and a squirmy beard, Cerra-something."

"Kyronatha."

"That's the name the priest used."

"Fuck he's gonna be hard, no weapon forged." Nutter shook his head slowly. "I'm too weak for this shit now," he lowered his head, his shoulders shaking as he sobbed.

"Don't worry about it man," said Roaddog, "we'll deal with this asshole, have you any idea how to kill it, we were planning on burning his ass."

"Fuck that," snapped Nutter, "I've been waiting most of my life for this shit to hit the fan, I'm gonna be there to see this through." His eyes held Roaddog's until the younger man looked away. "So, who's this

Francis?"

"Just some local priest, though there is some thought that he was sent to watch the church in question."

"I know him," muttered Nutter, "guy's a pompous ass, which cretin set him to watch this place, the church is full of political fools nowadays."

"You know this priest?" asked Roaddog.

"Does he," laughed Vince.

"I think I'm missing something here," said Roaddog.

"Just a bit." Vince was rocking backwards and forwards he was laughing so much.

"Spill it," snapped Roaddog.

"I can't," replied Vince, "I promised."

"Tell me," snarled Roaddog, looking straight at Nutter.

"Fine, I wasn't always a biker, I used to wear my collar the wrong way round."

"You were a priest?"

"I was, and then I wasn't."

"What the fuck happened?"

"I hope you never find out."

"Is this history going to get in the way of us killing this fucking demon?"

"Definitely not. May make things difficult for Franky boy though." Nutter giggled at the thought.

"Well, if he can't close the thing, we'll block it with their corpses and fill it in with their blood."

"That won't work, but it would be fun to try."

"Sounds to me like tomorrow is going to be quite strenuous." said Roaddog.

"Oh, you're going to have your work cut out for you tomorrow, especially if Kyronatha puts in an appearance."

"Right," Roaddog paused, looking around he saw Jingo coming towards them, "we'll head off, we need to get some firebombs sorted before tomorrow and we need to get some sleep. Thanks, Vince for your help," he turned to Nutter, "I'm assuming we'll see you tomorrow at the church, about nine?"

"I'll be there," mumbled Nutter shaking his head.

"No problem, just let us know how it goes." said Vince, taking a heavy bag from Jingo and passing it to Bug. "I want that chatter gun."

"Once we've got this demon shit sorted you can have it," said Bug.

They all stood and exchanged handshakes, before the Dragonriders set off towards home.

Roaddog decided as they were driving back to the village that he would make the firebombs in the morning; he really couldn't be bothered as it was getting very late. They arrived at the caravan and parked up. Once they were all inside and the kettle was on Roaddog got a bottle of jacks from the cupboard and passed round glasses to all.

"Looks like tomorrow's going to be interesting," he said.

"Could be very dangerous," said Slowball.

"We'll be ready, and those damned clerics should have the thing shut down before Kyron-whatever gets out."

"Kyronatha," laughed Bug, "what do you reckon of that Nutter?"

"Fuck he's old, he's gotta be sixty if he's a day," replied Roaddog.

"He moves like he's real sick," muttered Jane.

"Yes, he's not a healthy person," said Sylvia.

"He's an extra pair of hands if things go wrong," said Roaddog.

"Let's hope things don't go that bad," said Slowball.

"I'm with you," said Roaddog.

Chapter 7: Church again, strangeness abounds.

Roaddog led the small convoy into the long straight driveway that led to Saint Botolph's church. The sun was quite high in the clear blue sky, they were travelling almost directly into it, the entrance to the church shrouded in the glare, a black and intimidating place. As soon as they passed through the gap in the hedges they were bathed in soft green light, filtered by the tall trees. They parked alongside a scout troupe minibus, to Roaddog it seemed somehow completely out of place. Roaddog retrieved Vera from the pannier of the victory and assembled it, Bug did the same with the Mac-10, two long clips stuffed through his belt. Slowball pulled heavy glass bottles from his lock box, passing them to the girls, keeping the heaviest a full gallon of cloudy and strangely viscous liquid to himself. Once everyone was equipped, they walked slowly through the lynch gate, Bug staring at the ground so he couldn't see the birds that covered the gateway completely. They walked in through the south doorway and met a very strange assemblage. Father Francis stood with a child's hand in each of his, facing this small trio were four men, each so different that Roaddog was forced to laugh out loud. The noise caused the children to press against Father Francis.

"Is this the beginning of a very non-PC joke or what?" he paused for a moment, "the Priest, the Rabbi, the Imam, the Bhikkhu, and the, er, Druid? Walked into a church."

"This is in no way funny," said Father Francis, "five out of five, I only know five people who would get all those correct and they're all here, how does someone like you know these things?"

"Classical education, sorry my latin is more than a little rusty. You think that you five can close this damned portal?"

"I can close it forever," said the Druid.

"That's the sort of positivity I want to hear," said Roaddog. "Say on."

"We five form the pentagram and build the cage over the end of the gateway, within the circle the children re-create the act that opened the way, then at the ultimate moment I plunge the staff of yew through their bodies into the ground, the blood of their death seals this place for all eternity." Jackie and Jane gasped, unable to believe what they had heard, Roaddog lowered Vera and pulled the bolt, the metallic clack echoed round the columns of the church, the muzzle of the Thompson pressed against the Druids belly.

"Is there any reason I shouldn't simply cut you in two right now?" he whispered, as he felt two knives leave his belt.

"Relax Roaddog," said Father Francis, "he has already been informed that this is not an acceptable solution."

"That's no reason," the cold voice did nothing to hide the click of the safety coming off, nor the gentle sound of two knives locking open.

"We need five to balance the circle and the pentagram," said Francis loudly, "this magic is too complex for four."

"Stay," said Roaddog, "you get a stay, death sentence still stands, you have to earn your life." He lifted Vera and clicked the safety back on. He caught his two girlfriends with his eyes. "If this turns to shit and he runs, he's yours." Jackie and Jane both smiled. "Father I want your van keys." The priest frowned for only an instant, then tossed the keys to him, he passed them to Cherie.

"Take the children and put them in the van, if this all goes to hell, you get in the van and get all the children out of here, understood?"

Cherie only nodded and took the children out of the church.

"I think you gentlemen should start with your magic, don't you?" asked Roaddog.

"Agreed," replied Francis, he turned and bent over a small suitcase that was behind him on the ground. He took three white containers of table salt and went to the very centre of the nave, and slowly made three wide circles around the disturbed tiles. The Imam and the Rabbi took wide pieces of chalk from the case and constructed a large pentagram and wrote symbols within the circles. The Druid took heavy black candles and placed them at the apexes of the pentagram, the Bhikkhu moved around the symbols playing finger cymbals, and chanting in a language that Roaddog couldn't understand. Then he heard a sound he could understand, the deepthroated roar of a Harley. This one wasn't stopping in the parking area, it rumbled slowly in through the door and stopped well short of the diagrams on the ground. The silence as the motor stopped was almost palpable. Nutter dropped his helmet onto the handlebar as he stepped off his bike.

"Sorry I'm late," he said, his voice harsh and liquid in his throat. "Having a bad day."

"I know you," called Father Francis.

"And I know you," sneered Nutter.

"He can't be here," said Francis to Roaddog, "This is a consecrated place, his presence is a desecration of that sanctity."

"Demons come and go at will, but this man is a desecration, explain," said Roaddog.

"I know his sin."

"You specialise in sin, sort it quick."

"I can't. His sin can't be forgiven."

"Tell him or I will," said Nutter.

"I can't speak of it," said Francis.

"Fine," said Nutter, "I was a priest like him," he waved in the direction of Francis' who had now turned his back, "I caught a cardinal with his dick in a screaming altar boy, so I removed the offending appendage and inserted it in the cardinal. Then watched him bleed to death. The church excommunicated me, and the law locked me up for twenty-five years. While I was inside, I learned that drag queens call it tucking and you don't have to actually cut the penis off," he smiled and chuckled, the laughter turning into a soft coughing fit that left Nutter panting.

"Father," said Roaddog gently, "he stays, deal with it." Nutter nodded and went over to his bike, from a holster on the side that they couldn't see he pulled a pump action twelve bore. With a simple press of the thumb he locked the hammer back, then checked to be sure the safety was on. He smiled at Roaddog and walked over to the diagram on the ground, taking care not to disturb the chalked lines or the salt circles. He studied it for a while then smiled.

"Franky," he said, waiting for the priest to look up from his writing. "You're short something." The priest frowned and shook his head. Nutter smiled, coughed deeply, hawked and spat a large brown gob into the middle of the circle. Francis recoiled in horror.

"By all that is holy," said the Druid, "that's it."

"That's what?" demanded Francis.

"The blood of death." The druid bowed deeply to Nutter.

"Blood of death," whispered Francis. "Brother how can I help you?" he asked of Nutter.

"Brother Roaddog," said Nutter, "I need a favour."

"Name your favour brother," said Roaddog solemnly.

"If this bastard tries to give me last rites, blow his head off, I'm not ending up in his fucking hell."

"My word," said Roaddog.

"Right assholes," called Nutter, "get this shit moving, we ain't got long left, Kyronatha is near." The clerics started to move into position at the apexes of the pentagram.

"Slowball," said Roaddog, "you got the fire, break that jar over his head, the small ones are only ignition, me and Bug will try and keep him distracted with pain, Bug go for the head and the eyes, I'll try and take his feet out from under him. Fuck. This thing is man shape isn't it?"

"Biped," said Francis, "two arms, two horns, two eyes, and no neck."

The five clerics took their places at the apexes of the diagram, three facing east, the Buddhist sitting cross legged facing the centre, the Druid standing, feet slightly spread, staff upright, both hands gripping it below the head. Roaddog paid attention to the staff for the first time, it seemed to be fashioned from a straight, if gnarled, tree branch, but at the head small branches have been formed into a cage to contain a large rose quartz crystal. The man is chanting so quietly that Roaddog can make out no words. The Priest is kneeling his rosary in his hands, he is praying in Latin, though Roaddog's memory is too slow to make out the meanings. The Imam is kneeling with his head to the ground, calling loudly, the only word that Roaddog understands is Allah. The Rabbi is bowing and nodding and chanting in some language that Roaddog can't understand. Sweeping the clerics with his eyes they return to the Druid and his staff, shifting down to the ground Roaddog saw that the tip of the staff is a dark bronze colour, and pointed, not like a spear, but sharp enough to punch a hole in a person with sufficient force behind it. 'Definitely not your typical walking staff.' He thought. The voices of the clerics mingled in a strange pattern and the whole building throbbed with the sound, a deep vibration that made them all uneasy. Trickles of disturbed dust fell from the old timbers of the roof, spiralling as they came, to fall within the circles. Roaddog tracked one of the heavy falls from a capital of one of the columns, the stream of dust spun slowly and fell into the centre of the circles, as he watched all three of the circles flashed with white light, not brilliant, but enough to light up the people within the pentagram. Roaddog watched as the three facing east turned to face the centre, the Imam kneeling on his haunches chanting, the Priest upright on his knees, speaking fast, the rosary flashing through his fingers, the Rabbi nodding and bowing, his curls swinging to and fro, chanting and swaying. The inner circle of white light slowly lifted at one edge and the whole thing started to rotate around an axis that ran north, south across the nave of the church. One half of the circle lifted up and passed over the top, then descended to the ground, as it vanished below ground the opposite edge lifted from the ground and started its journey to follow the other. 'Like the ring of a gimbal.' thought Roaddog, Then the second circle flashed with light and started to turn similarly. The two increased their speed for a number of seconds to be finally joined by the third, now the turning and twisting became too much for the eyes to follow. The speeding circles made a cage of light around the centre, moving too fast to be seen now they blended into three spheres. Within the spheres the centre darkened, it was filled with a deep purple light, or maybe the absence of light, something other than darkness filled it. The stone in the Druids staff burst into brightness, flashing a rosy glow into the spinning circles, it showed a ball of purple within the centre, a writhing mass of light and dark, so distorted that it twists the eyes and the brains of those that see it. Small sparks of lightning crawl across its surface. Two short gnarled horns appear below the purple light, then a blue head as if the body had stepped up a ladder. Another step, more head, face, chin, wide spaced yellow eyes, with vertical slit pupils of the deepest obsidian. The purple light washed down over the head and vanished. Another step up the ladder and wide shoulders came into view, blue shoulders speckled with what looked like barnacles or maybe rocks embedded in the surface. Roaddog flicked the safety off Vera, Bug followed suit, Nutter only an instant behind, none wanted to fire, hoping the cage would hold. Another step, elbows and chest appeared, one studded with huge stone bosses, the other scattered with smaller excrescences. The demon was facing the Druid as it climbed up from below ground. The look in the druid's face could only be described as fear, but his chanting didn't stop, his sweating only got worse, Roaddog spared an instant to check on the other clerics, all were sweating profusely from the effort they were expending to hold the cage against the rising power of Kyronatha. Hips, thighs, knees and finally feet appeared on the ground within the spinning circles. The druid spared a glance and a slight nod for Roaddog.

"Slowball," he yelled, "hit it." Slowball stepped forwards and threw the heavy glass bottle, it fell through the twisting lights, an opening in the cage appeared for an instant then closed as soon as the bottle passed through, it shattered on the horns and a whole gallon of syrupy liquid fell down around the demon. The demon reached out to the bars of light and touched them, there was a flash, and the demon withdrew the hand, checking the fingers for damage.

"Light him up," yelled Roaddog. Jackie and Jane lit their Molotov's and cast them into the twisting cage of light. Each travelled to the target through an opportune opening in the bars of light, each struck true, but their lights were extinguished before contact, no conflagration.

"Fuck," yelled Roaddog. He squeezed the trigger and started

pumping rounds into the cage of light, hoping to strike some sparks from the hard stones in the demon's skin, Bug sprayed a whole clip into the horns and head, with a similar lack of success. Nutter's pump seemed to have more effect, causing the demon to step backwards and recoil from the caging light. Six rounds and Nutter was empty, he threw down his shotgun in disgust, turned to Roaddog.

"Salt and remember," he yelled, then turned to the Druid, snatched the staff and stepped into the cage, he walked into the demons' open arms, these snapped shut and crushed Nutter against the rock studded chest, Nutter turned the staff and brought the crystal down onto Kyronatha's horns. There was a flash as energy jumped from the stone to the horns. Then a thump as the petrol ignited, followed by a roar as the rest was triggered, a concussion knocked the people to the ground, Kyronatha and Nutter were engulfed in a howling column of flame, it burned hot and blue, the demon screamed but Nutter was already dead. The demon fell forwards crushing Nutter's remains beneath his weight, the staff fell from Nutters charred hands and skittered across the floor as the people started to pick themselves up. A column of black oily smoke rose from the remains upon the ground, the clerics were all stunned as they watched the flames burn high, smoke filled the upper reaches of the church, and drifted into the corners, despite it being full daylight the bats left their boxes to find somewhere slightly more pleasant to roost. Hundreds of bats, flying round then out of the upper windows. Roaddog kept Vera targeted on the roaring fire that was once Nutter and Kyronatha. The druid crawled over to where his staff had landed and picked it up, he held the crystal in both hands and pressed it against his forehead, slowly he smiled. Roaddog looked at Francis and got a nod as the priest climbed to his feet. They went around the room getting people to their feet. Cherie was the only one standing on her own, she had been too far from the blast, standing by the door, ready to run. Jackie and Jane ran into Roaddog's arms all three sobbing with relief at still being alive, and sadness for the end of Nutter. Once the echo of the blast had stopped rattling around his head Roaddog heard a new noise.

"What the fuck now?" he shouted, shrugging the girls away and setting Vera to a shoulder. Cherie ran from the doorway into Bug's arms as he snapped another clip into the Mac-10. Two bright headlights came through the south doorway. Just inside both motorcycles stopped and dropped onto their kickstands, the noise outside slowly lessened as more and more of the motorcycles stopped.

"Fuck," yelled Vince, "that crazy old bastard was right."

"What are you on about?" demanded Roaddog, lowering the Thompson.

"No one believed him, I certainly didn't, but he made me promise. His instructions were very precise, we were to wait at south farm until his phone went dark. I assume that our brother is part of that dark mess on the floor."

"He is, we couldn't get the fire to light, he stepped inside and lit it."

"He didn't have long left anyway; cancer was going to get him in a couple of months."

"I need to do something for him," said Father Francis, walking towards the smoking wreckage. Roaddog trained Vera on the priest.

"If your intention is to give him last rites, I promised to kill you first." Francis stopped.

"He was a priest for all that is holy."

"Was," snapped Roaddog, "then you lot turned your backs on him." Francis turned to the other clerics to see if he could help them.

"It's not closed," said the Druid, "it's not too late, we can still close it, that crazy biker didn't drain all my power."

"You were told," snapped Roaddog turning the Thompson to the new target, with a stuttering roar Vera spoke, each boom threw the druid another step backwards, by the time he hit the column he was dead, only the impact of lead was keeping his body upright, but it could only take so much punishment until it fell into two parts. Silence descended.

The silence lasted for almost thirty seconds then a new voice spoke from the north door.

"Hey Roaddog, you okay?" It was Jake, he stepped into view, a double barrelled twelve bore in each hand, and a bandolier across his chest.

"We're fine Jake. You?"

"I'm okay, those assholes blocked me in the farm, I had to go the long way round, you fuckers don't dick about," he said looking at the remains of the druid.

"That ass wanted to kill children, he was warned."

"The rest?" asked Jake looking at the blackened mess in the middle of the church floor.

"Crazy biker and ex-demon, another one done."

"What's next? Damned thing doesn't feel like it's closed."

"Francis, any idea what's next?"

"Not a clue," he pointedly looked at the wooden wall, now without an image upon it.

"You know the guy with the artillery?" asked Vince.

"Yes, friendly. We killed the green man when it was trying to eat him."

"We didn't know, just didn't want civilians involved in this, speaking of which there's some frightened kids in a minibus outside."

"Cherie," called Roaddog, "please bring the kids in, it's safe for them now."

"Define safe?" asked Vince.

"Well, given our extensive experience of these phenomena, when a demon is dead it takes a while to reset for the next one. Last time it was the best part of an hour."

"How many times have you done this?"

"Once," laughed Roaddog.

"You people are definitely crazy," laughed Vince, "Anything we can do to help?"

"Clean up would be good."

"That's one of the reasons we are here, Nutter knew today was one way, we have come to take his bike and his remains." Vince paused and glanced at the remains of the druid. "We can remove that as well."

"That would be good, thanks."

"No problem, we have excellent disposal systems," laughed Vince.

"You can't do that," said Father Francis, "that man was murdered."

"He wanted to kill children to stop this thing, so he died," said Roaddog. "You really want to be involved in a police investigation right now? They'll never believe you, and you'll not be able to do anything about this portal because they'll have you locked up."

"The pigs are hungry, and extra one or four wouldn't be an issue," said Vince quietly.

"Sadly Vince," laughed Roaddog, "we may actually need one or two of these. Their magic was impressive, but ultimately it took a good man's death to stop Kyronatha."

There was a sudden high pitched scream. Cherie had just walked in with the children, the young girl was now pressed against Cherie's chest, her eyes tightly closed, sobbing.

"It's all right," whispered Cherie, stroking her gently. "He can't harm anyone now. He wanted to kill you, Roaddog was very firm when he told him no." The boy didn't take his eyes off the remains of the druid, but he wasn't crying. Cherie walked them slowly over to the priest and handed them over.

"Look after them," she said, "we wouldn't want any more accidents." Father Francis knelt and took the girl in his arms, whispering softly to her.

"Roaddog," said a voice that none had heard before. He turned to the Buddhist monk.

"Yes," replied Roaddog softly.

"You carry a great deal of death with you."

"I can understand that, you're point is?"

"You have much to do to reach enlightenment, nirvana is many lifetimes away for you."

"That my friend is where you are wrong, nirvana is to be found here on earth and in this life, there is no need to wait to die."

"That cannot be."

"Oh, but it is. You will never find it, but it is here."

"Can you show me?"

"It comes simply from acts of human love."

"But those are only momentary, ephemeral."

"Perhaps, but subjectively they last forever."

"The joy of nirvana is eternal."

"To be subsumed within that mass is not joy, it is imprisonment."

"How can you say that?"

"Easy, I am an individual, and I will stay that way as long as I possibly can."

"I feel very sad for you," the Buddhist bowed and turned away, Roaddog shook his head and turned to Jackie and Jane.

"You okay?" he asked.

They nodded and stepped into his arms, he looked up as three of Vince's men were cleaning up the burned-out mess and another two were stuffing the remains of the druid into black garbage bags. A deep resonance filled the air, the whole building started to shake, dust fell from the roof beams, and the capitals of the columns. A heavy ripple passed through the floor making them all stagger. The young girl screamed and clutched at Father Francis again. The low frequency sounds were replaced by the high-pitched raucous noise of motorcycle alarms, both inside and outside the church.

"What the fuck was that?" shouted Vince, reaching into a pocket and turning off the alarm on his motorcycle.

"That was a reset," laughed Roaddog.

"So, who's next to the party?" asked Jake.

Roaddog went to the wooden wall and shone his torch from the side.

"Looks like some sort of minotaur, bull head and sort of man shaped."

"Oh my," said Father Francis, "not Minotaur, that's Melchion."

"And what is a Melchion?" asked Roaddog.

"All I've got is a name, I'll need to check my books."

"You better find out as soon as you can, I am more worried about that," said Roaddog pointing at the centre of the pentagram.

"By Allah," whispered the Imam,

"The lord protect us," called the Rabbi, stepping backwards and looking upwards.

"What's the problem?" asked Vince, "all I see is an old stone floor, it's a bit of a mess, but nothing to be worried about."

Roaddog stared at Vince for a moment, then walked slowly into the centre of the design, being careful to step over the chalk and salt. He looked into Vince's eyes and took a step forwards.

"Fuck," said Vince as Roaddog took another step.

"Fuck, fuck, fuck," whispered Vince.

"Vince," said Roaddog, "tell me what you see."

"Shit," said Vince, "you are buried up to your thighs in the floor, it looks like you are part of the stones that make up the floor."

"What do you see Father Francis?" asked Roaddog.

"You are standing in a narrow stairway, one that Kyronatha walked up earlier."

"Horse," said Roaddog, "Come and stand here in the circle, but be careful of the designs." Horse checked with Vince before he went into the circles, his long legs made stepping over the symbols really easy. Roaddog waved him into position.

"Right," he smiled at Horse, "if you take a step towards me, you will be taking a step down the stairway." Horse paused for a moment before stepping forwards.

"Fuck," said Roaddog, "you're standing on fresh air."

"No," replied Horse, "I'm standing on solid ground." To emphasise this, he stamped a heavy boot, and the sound rang out through the church.

"Great," said Roaddog, "Everyone that sees the stairway raise your hand." A rapid canvas showed that anyone who had witnessed the emergence of Kyronatha could see the stairs, everyone else saw the heavy stones of the church floor, disturbed but solid. "Everyone who was here when the demon died can see the stairway, but it isn't going anywhere near heaven."

"The real question," said Father Francis, "is do we go down?"

"Not a question," said Roaddog, "given that Melchion is going to be coming up and killing people sometime soon, we have no choice."

"We really need to know what we are up against," said Father Francis.

"Go check your books, find out and get back to me as soon as you can."

"I'll do that." Father Francis led the children by the hand and the remaining clerics followed him out of the door. Vince's clean-up crews had just about finished packing up the remains and were carrying the heavy bags out to the trikes they had brought.

"We'll get shut of this," said Vince, "but we are going home to Grimsby today, so all we can do is wish you luck with the trials to come. If you need more ammunition, just call and I'll send some to you, any other clean ups required you will have to see to yourselves."

"Thanks for all your help," said Roaddog, "I'll let you know how things go, so long as we survive."

"No problem brother," said Vince, he turned to the rest of his group. "Let's get the hell out of this place, before hell gets out all around us." He laughed loudly and waved to Roaddog as he mounted and rolled his bike backwards out of the church.

"Right," said Roaddog loudly, "let's get the store opened, there's little we can do until we know what we are dealing with."

"Once I've got my stuff sorted for the day I'll come up and see ya," said Jake turning to leave with a simple wave.

"That damned hole gives me the willies," said Slowball.

"Yeah," replied Roaddog, "but only we can see it, so it's not a problem from this side."

"That doesn't really help much," smiled Slowball.

Together they left the church and walked through the gate, the roof now covered in fat grey birds again. The minibus was still travelling slowly down the drive, it had been held up by the large number of motorcycles from Vince's club.

"You think he'll have anything to tell us?" asked Bug.

"He got a name as soon as he saw the thing, so there must be something in it, how much we'll find out later."

"When though?"

"As soon as he can, stop fretting."

"Not him, that damned demon, when is it going to make an appearance?"

"Who can tell? I just hope we don't have to go down that hole."

"It doesn't look fun," said Slowball, as his VW cracked into life.

"That's for sure," replied Roaddog, firing his Victory and waiting for Jane to drop onto the pillion seat.

Chapter 8: Bank Holiday Monday at the workshop.

Roaddog and his friends pulled up at the shop and opened the main doors, rolling the bikes inside. The time was approaching ten o'clock, so they were a little behind with the opening preparations, but between them they managed to get everything done before the first bike rolled into the forecourt. A young man on a small motorcycle, he parked up then looked around, in less than a minute there were three more, obviously his friends, all three bikes carrying L plates. Bug walked out to talk to them, just to introduce himself and see if he could help them in any way.

"Thanks mate," said the tallest, "just looking, we heard about this new place and decided we had fuck all else to do today, so we came for a look see."

"No worries," said Bug, "burgers from the van, a few bikes for sale, and parts available from the desk over there." He waved in the direction of Slowball who was standing behind a counter.

"Thanks man," replied the youngster as Bug walked back into the shop.

"I'm going to check on the back room," said Roaddog. Bug nodded as Roaddog turned away. The heavy rumble of motorcycle engines made Bug look back out to the road again. Five bikes rolled into the yard and parked up, again Bug went to talk to them. Again more visitors, just come to see what was happening on a boring Bank Holiday

Monday. Bug shook his head as he walked away wishing that his bank holiday was boring, there was already too much excitement for one day. Returning to the workshop he caught Roaddog coming out with a huge grin.

"What's up?" asked Bug.

"We can shut the shop," laughed Roaddog.

"Why?"

"I think some of the big players must have dropped out of the mining circuits, four more big hits over night, and another about ten this morning."

"How much?"

"Twenty thousand."

"Fuck."

"Yeah, fuck indeed," smiled Roaddog. "I'm going to need bank details, so you guys can get your shares."

"That'd be nice," laughed Bug.

"We'll sort it out later." Roaddog strolled out to the van to have a quick word with Jackie and Jane. He opened the door to the little caravan and leaned in.

"How far can we cut prices without actually making a loss?" he asked.

"Half price easy," replied Jackie a question in her raised eyebrows.

"Miners are hitting hard right now, if we sell all the bikes we have today we're still going to make more on the miners. Cut the prices, but limit the numbers, we don't want greedy bastards running us out of stock."

"Done," Jackie laughed and set about changing the prices on the boards.

"Jane," he called to the younger girl who was flipping burgers on the griddle.

"What?" her terse reply.

"Give me your bank card and I'll arrange your wages for this weekend."

"You expect me to trust you with my card?"

"You trust me with your pussy, don't ya?"

"I suppose," she giggled as she reached into her wallet and tossed him her card.

"What about me?" asked Jackie.

"I already got all of your details."

"That's for sure," Jackie smiled and leaned through the door to kiss him gently.

"What's going on?" asked Jane after he had left.

"Miners have been doing well, so he's sharing it out."

"Do for me, I thought I was a volunteer," Jane smiled as she returned to the griddle.

Roaddog similarly collected bank cards from the rest of his friends and returned to the gloom of the back room. While he was sitting in the dark setting up the transfers, he thought about the people who were his truest friends in the world. 'They may not be members of a club, but they certainly qualify as family.' He was just shutting down the international banking program when the room was flooded with light as Bug came in through the door.

"Hey man," said Bug, "you got a safe yet?"

"Why?"

"I get nervous with that damned chatter gun in my panniers."

"Not yet, but really we need to have the firepower at the moment."

"I know, but I really want shut of the thing."

"You could stash it in one of the lockers back here, but you'd have to get it out of the pannier where everyone out there can see it."

"I know, I'm just getting more nervous that some damned busybody copper is going to find it."

"You seen a copper yet?"

"Not one, but ya never can tell."

"Well, if you see one you can be sure he is lost," laughed Roaddog.

"That really doesn't help."

"Once we got this damned hell mouth thing sorted you can give it to Vince, he'll be delirious."

"How much longer is this going to take?"

"I've no idea, we can ask Father Francis when he turns up."

"Fine," Bug turned away and went back out into the daylight, followed in a moment by Roaddog. They were both quite surprised by the number of motorcycles parked in front of the workshop, and the queue in front of the burger van. As they looked around, they saw Jake and his quad roll slowly into the car park, they walked over to talk to him.

"Hi Jake," said Roaddog.

"Hi mate," replied the farmer, "any news from the priest?"

"Nothing yet, anything happening at the church?"

"No, everything is quiet, it's scary."

"I understand." Roaddog looked pointedly at the two shotgun

holsters on the sides of the quad.

"Can I stash my guns somewhere?" asked Jake, softly.

"Follow me," said Roaddog, he turned slowly as Jake pulled the shotguns out and broke each one, dropping the cartridges into his jacket pocket. The two walked into the shop and through the door into the back, many nervous eyes followed them. Roaddog showed Jake which locker to put them in and gave him a key so it could be safely locked.

"What goes on back here?" asked Jake.

"Not much yet, we're going to turn it into living quarters, at the moment it's just for the internet hardware."

"That's no way standard network stuff," laughed Jake.

"You're not wrong," replied Roaddog, offering no further information.

"Fine, let's go back outside, I could do with something to eat." Jake smiled, leading the way. As they passed through the door Roaddog caught Slowball's eye and indicated he should watch the door with a simple glance, he got a nod as a reply. Jake went to join the queue for food and Roaddog went to where Bug was talking to someone near one of the bikes that was for sale. While they were talking about the optional extras already fitted to the dyna-glide a scout minibus rolled slowly into the car park. It manoeuvred carefully around the rows of motorcycles, until it stopped alongside the building. Parking on rough ground that the bikers would prefer not to use. Most of the bikers in the parking area watched as the priest walked slowly around the van and looked around for Roaddog, finally the priest's eyes locked onto the cold blue and he walked towards the workshop. Roaddog stepped into the sunlight and met the cleric.

"We need to talk in private," said Father Francis as quietly as he could. Roaddog nodded and walked back into the shade of the workshop, and through the door into the darkness of the back rooms.

"What do you know?" he asked as the door closed behind the priest.

"This Melchion is going to be a real bitch to kill."

"I wasn't expecting things to get easier."

"Well, the good news is forged weapons will work, the last time Melchion was defeated it took a whole troop of Templars, the stories are a little confused, but it seems that Melchion took many lances to the body and was eventually dispatched by the removal of his head."

"Sounds like it's bad news time."

"Again, the stories are confusing, every time Melchion attacked a person, that person died. One tale says, 'they surrendered their lives to his blade', another says 'Melchion's attacks could not be stopped'. In all the reports, many written years later, there was only one occasion when Melchion's direct attack on a knight was thwarted, a squire got in the way and blocked the blade."

"Were squires armed?"

"No, nor armoured."

"So how did a squire stop a demon's attack?"

"This comes from only one report, written in Arabic, translated to Greek and then into Latin, the original has been lost for hundreds of years, it didn't survive the end of the Templars."

"When was this?" asked Roaddog.

"Thirteenth of November eleven seventy-five."

"You can be that certain of the date?"

"Oh yes, demon appearances are very rare. This one was actually well documented at the time, considering that most people couldn't read or write."

"There were Templars here in Lincolnshire in the eleven hundreds?"

"No, this was in Spain."

"You're kidding?"

"The eleventh of November is the local saints day in a place called Ginestar, something summoned Melchion, no idea what. The local Templar headquarters at Miravet was called and a troop despatched. The knights arrived in Ginestar before noon on the thirteenth, it was a sunny day." Father Francis smiled.

"You know all this?"

"Though many of the knights were barely literate they generally had a scribe or diarist with them."

"Are you sure?"

"Your picture of knights comes from the movies, lances with pennons flying, pretty coloured surcoats, shields and swords, columns of two trotting into battle."

"Yes."

"Well, each knight had three or four horses, one or two squires, and a cleric, not all these people mounted."

"So, they walked to battle?"

"Yes, you can forget your mile long cavalry charge as well, two hundred yards was nearer the mark, the shorter the better, because those heavy horses weren't good for much more than a short run."

"I've never really thought about any of this, so tell me the details of the battle."

"The local clergy had faced the demon and lost, farmers armed with mattocks and scythes were no match, so the demon just wandered around the neighbourhood killing anyone that got in his way. Most of the townsfolk just hid or ran, those running towards the Templars castle slowed the knights down considerably. As the column of knights approached the village one of the squires returned from a scouting patrol to report that the demon was in one of the olive groves, the knights mounted their heavy horse and took lances, leaving the squires to carry sword and axe. When they reached the olive grove, they found that two squires were harassing the demon with arrow fire, they weren't causing much in the way of damage, but they were holding it in place and making it run around. The spacing between the trees was too small for more than one knight to attack at once, the first knight turned to face the demon, his horse balked briefly, the knight's spurs reminded it of its training, together they rode down upon the demon, his lance struck true, and shattered into splinters on the demon's chest, the demon staggered but didn't fall, it made no attempt to stop the knight as he rode passed. The attack continued in a similar manner, most lances shattered, four knights were unhorsed, each killed with a single slash from the demon's broadsword. Five lances penetrated the demon, but they did little to slow it down. The last of the knights decided on a different tactic, rather than going for the heart of the demon, he aimed for its head. Driving the horse faster with his heels he planned to use the whole weight of the horse to knock the demon down, even though he knew that he had little chance of staying in his seat. The heavy steel tip of the lance was running true to its target when the demon's broadsword swung up and across his body, it struck the lance just behind the tip and pushed it to the demons right. The shaft of the lance pushed against the horse's neck forcing the horse to move to its left, the butt of the lance was forced to the knight's right, the lance trapped under the knight's arm gave him no chance to release it, with the horse turning left and the knight moving right a fall from the saddle was inevitable. The heavily armoured knight dropped from the saddle straight into the demon's arms, knocking both to the ground. The knight's momentum was such that he didn't stop, he rolled and slid along the ground, slowed by the roots of the trees, dust blowing in the air as he rolled to a stop. The demon climbed to its feet and walked towards the fallen knight, it raised its sword high as it stood over the fallen knight, a squire ran in from the side and slashed at the demon's legs as he ran past, his short sword struck at the demon where his knees should have been, but the legs were something other than human, the blade opened a large wound but did no serious damage, the dark blood of the demon fell smoking to the ground. The demon plunged its sword straight through the body of the fallen knight, three feet of black steel went through the man's body and armour, the knight twitched and died, his white surcoat catching fire around the demon's weapon. The demon turned to the squire, but he was long gone, mounted knights were now moving in again, snatching great swords from their squires as they came. The first knight back into the fray charged straight at the demon, sword raised ready to strike an overhand blow, the demons head was level with his shoulder, despite the size of the horse under the knight. The horse crashed into the demon, as the demon's sword slashed at the horse's neck, the horse fell kicking its legs and tangled in the demon's arms. The fallen knight swept at the demon's legs; the blow was without any real power but still it cut deep into the demon's shins. The demon turned on the fallen knight and its eyes flashed red, it raised its sword and then slashed down across the knight's body, the knight lifted his sword to block the demon's attack, the demon's heavy sword shattered the knights steel into a shower of sparks and plunged straight through his body, separating him at the waist. The next knight into the fray struck the demon from behind and opened a shallow cut on its back, the demon turned, its eyes flashed, and it struck the knight, the broadsword tore straight through the knight's chain mail and cut deep into his body, the knight's sword arm fell to the ground and blood poured from the severed end. More knights came in to take on the demon, one attacked it head on with an axe, another took the demon from behind with a sweeping blow of a broadsword. As the axe flashed down to strike sparks from the demon's horns, Melchion's sword plunged through the knight's surcoat and heart, the smoking tip protruded briefly from the templar's back, before it was withdrawn as the demon turned to face the knight behind him. The demon swept his sword round he caught the knight's eyes, the knight took the sword blow on his shield, the knight was surprised when his shield held, the blow was enough to make him step back, but not quite enough to knock him over. He swung overhand at the demon as Melchion's eyes flashed in his own, the knight's sword chopped a piece from the demon's right horn, the knight smiled even as the demon's sword plunged through his body and ended his life. As the demon turned to face the next knight it's feet got tangled in the fallen man's surcoat, Melchion staggered to the left, his right arm swinging fast across his body to recover his balance, this left his whole right side open, a heavy axe slashed into the demon's exposed right flank, the impact was enough to make the demon step to the left again, but the damage was minimal, a shallow cut and only a little of the black blood came to the surface. Melchion having recovered his stability swept his sword back to the right, taking the axe wielder in the head with the flat and knocking him to the ground, the knight he had been intending on attacking next plunged his sword into the demon's belly, this strike opened a deep cut in the demon's guts, then the sword flashed across the knight rising from hip to shoulder dividing the knight completely. The demon turned to the fallen axe wielder, its eyes flashed, and its sword fell towards the man's exposed back, a squire dived across the knights back and took the blow for himself, hoping to save the life of his master and friend. He was successful, the blow, though heavy and driven with the full force of demonic strength, struck but didn't cut, the squire was hurt, stunned, but unbloodied. Two more templars moved to the attack, one targeted the demon's sword wrist, the other his left ankle. Both blows struck true, but did little damage, though the impact to the demon's foot did cause it to stagger again. Now two more templars moved in surrounding the demon, each attacking in turn, each attempting to disable the demon, striking at limbs or head, not giving the demon time to attack, it was completely on the defensive. A nearby knight threw down his sword and yelled for his mace, a squire came running in and handed the weapon over before retreating with the knight's sword. The mace wielder barged his way into the melee around the demon, as the demon turned away from him, he struck, the mace swung in around the demon's thighs, the heavy ball flashed around and with a flick of the shaft locked in place, fastening the demon's legs together, the knights pushed the demon over, and two fell on its legs and two more on each arm. An axe wielding knight leaned over the fallen demon looking down into its flashing eyes, then he struck, it took four strikes of the heavy two-handed axe to cut the demons head completely off. Immediately the body started to burn with a hot green light, the flames blew up into the branches of the trees, soon the whole grove was ablaze, and the knights were struggling to get out onto the road. Of the thirty knights that attacked only twelve survived."

"Damn," said Roaddog, "that's some bad ass demon."

"It may interest you to know that there are no records of the green man ever being defeated, he collects his souls and vanishes."

"Well, he's never come up against Vera before," laughed Roaddog.

"That's for sure. Melchion is going to be difficult."

"Have you any sort of restraining magic that could be of use?"

"The one with the most skills in that area fell foul of Vera as well."

"Sorry, dumb bastard just didn't know when to shut the fuck up."

"Agreed, but he was highly skilled."

"I was not prepared to sacrifice the children."

"Nor were we."

"He'd have kept on piling the pressure on, maybe some of the others who didn't actually know the children would have caved in to that pressure."

"Not me," whispered Father Francis.

"What do you get from that report? How reliable is this information?"

"The information is as reliable as it can be, but multiple translations and so many years, who can tell what distortions have accumulated in these words."

"But what do you make of it?"

"The demons flashing eyes are important, but I'm not sure why. Only some can injure the demon, and others aren't injured by it, it's weird."

"Not so much, I see it."

"What?" demanded Father Francis.

"The demons eyes flash to select a target, that target he can kill, his sword cannot be stopped, anyone else he attacks is simply hit by some sort of practise weapon. The squire took a sword stroke to the back and survived, if it had struck the knight he was lying on, the knight would have been killed."

"That sort of makes some sense."

"And only the demons target can cause it damage."

"So, you have to be the target before you can attack it?"

"No, before you can hurt it."

"So, you're going to make yourself its target, then attack it?"

"That's the plan," shrugged Roaddog.

"Risky."

"Yes."

"You're putting a lot of faith in this report."

"There has to be something behind it."

"Yes, but it could be so wrong."

"Gives us somewhere to start, and this demon has never come up against modern fire power. Or has it?"

"No records exist, that I know of. Demon incursions are far less common in the last three hundred years than they were before."

"There's a reason for that," laughed Roaddog.

"I know," replied Father Francis dejectedly.

"Your influence is waning, but I still need your help."

"What do you need?"

"The templars were warrior priests?"

"That is true."

"Their weapons were blessed by the church?"

"Again, true."

"Here," Roaddog removed all four of his stilettos, "Sort these out for me, if Vera can't kill it, we'll have to get in close."

"Watch out for that sword."

"I know, I have a sort of plan, but not sure what yet," laughed Roaddog.

"There may be a clue as to his arrival."

"That would be good."

"It seems the birds are well known as indicators of demonic presence."

"They are?"

"Yes, I was checking up and they are sometimes called 'the harbingers of doom.' They know the portal is open, they are waiting for the demons to give them something to eat, they are the scavengers."

"So how do they tell us that the demon is here?"

"They take to the air; they form a gyre over the demon."

"A what?"

"They circle like the vultures you see in the movies, but lower and much more tightly packed. They are said to take the form of a cone or a column over the demon's head."

"That should give us some clue as to where the damned thing is."

"It won't help if it surfaces at night," observed Father Francis.

"Do the birds still fly at night?"

"These do, or so the tales say."

"Can you bless my blades; the damned thing could pop up anytime?"

"I have everything I need right here," replied Father Francis.

"Do you have a printout of that Templar report?"

"Yes, why?"

"Email it to me, I want to read it for myself," said Roaddog passing Father Francis a business card.

"I'll do that as soon as I get home."

"Can't you do it from your phone?" asked Roaddog.

"Technology not really my thing," laughed Father Francis.

"Fine," smiled Roaddog, "I'll go and talk to the others, bring the knives to me when you're finished." He walked away and opened the door to the showroom, as he pulled the door something large and heavy came with it.

"Woah," said Slowball, releasing the door handle before he was all the way into the back room. "We were beginning to get worried about you," he continued.

"The priest has some information, some really good information, so long as it is true," said Roaddog.

"Will we be able to beat the bastard?"

"There are a few options for us, but yeah, we stand a good chance."

"Good news, any idea when it'll appear?"

"No, but the birds should tell us. Where is Jake?"

"Last seen sitting in the sun, enjoying a bacon butty," laughed Slowball, waving an arm in the general direction of the road. Roaddog laughed as he saw Jake sitting on his quad, just watching the people around him.

"Hey Jake," said Roaddog as he approached the farmer.

"Hi man," was the gentle reply.

"This morning, when you were coming towards the church, the long way round, were the birds up in the air?"

"As a matter of fact they were, but before I got there they were all back on the roofs."

"The priest says that the birds will fly when the demons are about."

"I'll keep an eye on them, and I'll let you know, give me your phone number," said Jake.

Telephone numbers were exchanged and then Jake went into the showroom, as he opened the door to the back room Father Francis walked out, Jake smiled, and Father Francis nodded but said nothing. Father Francis walked up to Roaddog and handed over the four knives, with a smile.

"Thanks, Father," said Roaddog, "you'll e-mail me as soon as you get home?"

"Of course, and I'll find out if there is anything else you need to know before you face Melchion."

"It would be good if there was some simple trick to send the bastard back."

"That's not something that I am aware of," laughed Father Francis.

"I'll let you know how it goes when this one turns up, we'll need your knowledge again if this one isn't the last."

"Oh, he's not the last. There is a saying 'third time's the charm' but not so in these cases. The last time one of these opened there were five demons before it closed."

"Great, you look into other methods of closing it. What I'd like to see is bishops, cardinals, and even the damned pontiff helping out."

"I have news for you on that front."

"Go on."

"The holy father cut short a visit to Spain, and ran for the Vatican City, gates are already closed, or so the bishop told me."

"Great, so they've abandoned you, much as they did Nutter."

"You could look at it that way."

"How does it make you feel?"

"Pretty shitty really, but I'll not shrink from my duty, if I survive, I shall be having some harsh words with a few people."

"I'd record the whole incident and set those documents for release if you don't block the sending in the next twenty-four hours."

"I'm ahead of you there, it's all on paper, and the housekeeper will post them to the newspapers if I die suddenly."

"Call me a cynical bastard if you will, she's employed by the church, can you really trust her?"

"Er," replied Father Francis, pausing to think for a while, before continuing, "maybe not. You are a cynical bastard, but I'll send the stuff by email to someone outside the church, with instructions."

"Good, if we survive, I'll make sure you have an escort for your visit to the bishop." Roaddog reached out a hand to Father Francis. The priest nodded and shook hands briefly, then he turned away towards his minibus.

"That looked intense," said Bug as he walked up.

"Yes," shrugged Roaddog, "he's just realised how much his superiors have set him up."

"Is he going to be useful?"

"Oh, yes. I've promised him escort if some of us survive, make sure it happens."

"No worries. We'll help him. You planning on dying here?"

"No, but better to be prepared, and you got a baby to look after."

"You send me away like you did Cherie, and I'll stick the Thompson up your ass."

"Understood," Roaddog smiled, and slapped Bug on the shoulder.

"Do we have a plan for the next asshole?"

"Sort of, I'm waiting for an e-mail from the priest, once I've read the report, I'll have a clearer idea."

"Do we stand a chance?"

"Yes, quite a good chance, after all thirty Templars took it on and twelve survived," Roaddog smiled broadly.

"So, if we three take it on only one will survive."

"We got far better odds than that, these demons have never come up against our sort of firepower."

"I'd hope so."

"We'll kill this one without too much in the way of problems, but who can tell what's next."

"Does the priest not have a clue?"

"No, he's as much in the dark as we are," laughed Roaddog.

"Well, it'll be different," said Bug. Roaddog turned and walked over to the burger van. He leaned in through the door and smiled at Jackie and Jane.

"How's it going?" he asked.

"Doing well," replied Jackie, "not too many being greedy bastards, we'll need a run to the wholesalers probably by Wednesday."

"Don't forget it'll be a lot quieter tomorrow."

"I know," she replied, "we could do with a rest."

"Damned right," said Jane.

"I'm waiting for information from the priest, we'll talk more about the damned demon over a beer and a burger," grinned Roaddog.

"Right," said Jane, "we're shutting this place down now, once the queue is gone."

"There's one guy waiting, that's all," laughed Jackie, shooing Roaddog away.

Jane gave the last customer the burger he wanted, with a smile. As soon as he walked away Jackie went outside and dropped the serving hatch and locked it into place.

"Right," she said as she returned to the much darker van, "let's get this shut down as quick as we can."

"Yes," replied Jane, "I really wasn't expecting to be working this hard."

"Or involved in all this other stuff?" asked Jackie.

"I'm not sure that I believe in the other stuff," grumbled Jane.

"You can't deny it now, you were there when Nutter died."

"I know, doesn't make it any easier to believe, I still feel like I'm in one of those old Hammer Horror films, I keep looking round for Vincent Price."

"I'm expecting Christopher Lee," laughed Jackie.

"If either of them show up, I'm gonna run for my life," said Jane, scooping the remaining bacon and burgers out onto buns, with onions and cheese. Almost nothing was left for the bins. It took them very little time to clean the place down for the next day, together they walked out into the car park, Jackie locked the door and pulled the power cable, she dropped that into the front locker and closed the padlock on the door. They walked into the showroom and passed out the left-over buns.

"There's an advantage to having your own burger bar," laughed Slowball, taking a huge bite of a cheeseburger, a couple of onions slid from the edge and left a trail of grease down his jacket.

"The dis-advantage is that I smell of burgers and bacon," moaned Jackie.

"I wish your shower was bigger," said Jane taking Jackie's hand and smiling. Jackie looked back, then leaned in close to kiss the younger girl.

"So do I," grinned Slowball, "that'd be fun." Sylvia jabbed him in the back with a rigid finger.

"With you of course dear," he laughed.

"Damned right, and don't you forget it," she laughed and leaned in, tipping her head up so she could kiss him. Roaddog was looking at his phone and pressing the occasional button. Shortly the printer on the counter started slowly spitting out pages. He collected them, and then distributed them amongst the group.

"What's this?" asked Bug.

"The report from the priest, everyone have a read, let me know what you think." He popped the tops from bottles of beer and passed them to each of his friends. "Cherie you better read it to Bug, we don't have all night for him to catch up."

"Bastard," muttered Bug.

"I know you struggle," smiled Roaddog, "no sweat." Silence descended as they all studied the documents. Roaddog flashed through his copy, he already knew what it said, and his impressions were only confirmed. He turned to watch Jackie and Jane as they poured over their shared printout. 'How can one guy be so lucky?' he thought, looking on as they whispered to each other, so close that they were touching. 'When they are so close Jane looks almost fragile, but she's anything but.' He thought back to her reaction to the kidnap, it was only a few months ago. 'She's recovered well from that dreadful experience, she's stronger, and far less brittle.' He nodded and smiled. 'She's tougher, she'll not shatter.' He looked around his friends and gave them time to read the report, before asking a question.

"Any thoughts?"

"Yes," Slowball jumped in quickly, "demon targets with flashing eyes, target can be killed, or can kill him, against others his attacks are weak, as are theirs."

"That's the way I read it," said Bug.

"Reminds me of something I read, many years ago," said Roaddog.

"What?" asked Jackie.

"I can't remember too clearly," smiled Roaddog, "something about the power of three."

"I know what you mean," said Slowball, "one guy gets targeted, and the two others stand in the way."

"Sounds reasonable," replied Roaddog, "its attacks are going to hurt, but not enough to kill."

"If the bastard targets me," said Bug, "I'm gonna rip him a new hole with forty-five slugs."

"And Vera will be more than happy to join the party."

"I'll borrow one of Jake's spares," said Slowball.

"There could be another issue," muttered Roaddog.

"Elucidate," snapped Cherie.

"The Templar weapons are blessed by the church, what if that is what makes them work?"

"Get Father Francis to bless the guns and the bullets," said Jackie.

"That might work, but he's already blessed my blades."

"I don't think blessing the guns or the bullets will help," said Sylvia.

"Why not?" asked Slowball.

"I can't help it, I was brought up a good religious girl, and there is a memory, something about fire burning away any blessing, that's why witches were burned, to remove Satan's blessings from them."

"Where did you hear this sort of thing?" asked Jackie.

"Sunday school."

"You're kidding, they teach this sort of stuff to kids?" asked Jane.

"Well, not generally, but my family did belong to a rather extreme splinter group."

"And you managed to get out?" demanded Roaddog.

"It wasn't easy."

"Do you want to tell us?" whispered Slowball.

"Not really."

"Fine," said Roaddog, "you got out and we are happy about that, glad that you were strong enough to breakout of a tough situation. We could go and explain to them their errors if you wish, when this shit is over."

"Won't do any good," whispered Sylvia, "they're all gone now."

"How?" asked Slowball.

"They hid from the wickedness of the world, and when the world came to ask questions, they all killed themselves."

"That's nuts," whispered Jackie.

"Yes," replied Sylvia, "Father Ezekiel made all the rules, after my family escaped it got worse, the children weren't even allowed to go to school, eventually the local authorities wanted to know that the children were being looked after, when the cops turned up in force they all drank poison. How can mothers do that to their own children?"

"When was this?" snapped Slowball.

"Nineteen eighty-one," whispered Sylvia.

"Fuck," whispered Slowball, taking her hands in his large ones, "it made the national press, there were forty dead, some sort of religious cult, Hampshire I think."

"We got out in seventy-nine, I was ten."

"What made your family break away?" asked Cherie.

"Ezekiel decided that the virginity of all women should be given to god as soon as possible after their menarche."

"How is this accomplished?" asked Cherie.

"God's representative obviously," smiled Sylvia.

"Bastard," whispered Cherie.

"Actually mother called him a pencil dicked bastard."

"Personal experience?" asked Cherie.

"Yes," replied Sylvia looking down, "she thought she was buying a place in heaven for us all."

"But you all got out," said Roaddog.

"Yes, and she explained it all to us, sometimes there was far too much information, I think she just wanted to be sure we wouldn't fall for the same stuff."

"Did it work?" asked Slowball.

"Almost," laughed Sylvia, "I did fall for a different kind of silver-tongued devil."

"Do you mean me?"

"Of course not, that bastard of an ex-husband of mine."

"Is that where your fathers gun collection came from?" asked Roaddog.

"Maybe, if they were going to come and take us back, he was going to put up a fight."

"Good man."

"Anyway," said Sylvia, "all this is not about the damned demons."

"Agreed," said Roaddog, "I'll call Father Francis and ask him about blessing the guns, if he says no, we'll just have to rely on these." Two stilettos snapped into his hands and flashed open. Thinking of that, something I need to do." He went into the back room and fired up the computer. A quick search on one of his favourite sites, a few clicks and a package was on its way.

"Let's shut up shop and go get some real food," he said as he returned to the showroom.

"Oi!" shouted Jackie.

"You know what I mean love," he smiled and pulled her into his arms, his kiss stopped any further discussion, if only for a short time.

"Hey," said Jane, "I cook too." Jackie pushed away from Roaddog, and turned to the smaller girl, Jackie lunged forwards and kissed her firmly, stroking a hand slowly down her back until it cupped her ass cheek.

"Bitch," whispered Jane when the kiss separated.

Roaddog walked to where the last two visitors were looking at the bikes they had for sale, "Sorry guys, we're closing, we need to get some food, and it's been a long day, you understand."

"No problem," said the smaller of the two, "we'll be back at weekend, work tomorrow."

"Thanks guys," said Roaddog as the two walked slowly to their bikes, he started the roller door coming down as soon as they crossed the threshold. Jackie went and checked the security on the burger van, Slowball and Bug were cleaning up the front of the shop as the two visitors fired up their bikes and left.

Chapter 9: Axe and later.

In only minutes the seven were walking towards the Axe, Roaddog took out his phone and selected the number for Father Francis. After only two rings the priest answered.

"Hi Father."

"Hey Roaddog, what's up, demon showed?"

"Not yet, as far as we are aware, I have an unusual question for you."

"Ask."

"Can you bless our guns and bullets?"

"I can, but it will do no good."

"Why?"

"The fire cleanses everything."

"That's what I have already been told, just wanted confirmation from a current priest. What about a rail gun?" laughed Roaddog.

"That's electric, so it would probably work, however the only mobile ones are the size of a ship, you got one?"

"No, just thought I'd ask, how do you know that anyway?"

"Crazy action movie with Arnie, can't remember than name of it now, but lots of bad guys running around with portable rail guns. It was hilarious, but great fun once you accept the premise that a rail gun will eventually be portable."

"Just thought I'd ask," laughed Roaddog, "you want to be called when the demon shows?"

"Of course, I've already talked to Jake, he'll call you then me, I'll bring the guys, we could be of some use, if only as decoys."

"Nice of you to offer, I'll see you when the next battle is joined."

"See you soon. Before you go, I have a question."

"Ask."

"You do know you could just walk away?"

"Yes, but I plan on living around here, can't let all my new neighbours get murdered, now can I?"

"I suppose, just thought I'd ask."

"Fine, I'll make sure you know when Melchion appears."

"Thanks for that, see you soon," said Father Francis before cancelling the call.

"Hey Sylvia," called Roaddog. She turned and looked at him. "Father Francis agrees with you, it's the fire that cleanses everything." She smiled but said nothing. They arrived at the pub and said hello to Karen.

"Sorry Roaddog, I had to give your table away, it's been a busy day," she said.

"No sweat Karen, I'm sure you'll be able to fit us in."

"I've got a couple of tables in the conservatory; we can move them together if you want?"

"That'll be great, we've never eaten in the posh outbuilding," laughed Roaddog.

"I'll get it sorted," said Karen shaking her head, "you have a drink at the bar," she waved one of the bar staff over and set off into the conservatory to organise the tables.

"What do you people want to drink?" asked Mandy. Before Mandy had pulled all the pints Karen and Liz came back into the bar.

"Your table is ready when you are," said Karen. Liz walked straight up to Jane, threw her arms around Jane's neck, and kissed her enthusiastically. Jane made no effort to get away. In a few seconds Liz broke away panting.

"What's up?" asked Jane.

"I followed your advice," whispered Liz, "we're going to hang out tomorrow afternoon, she looks weird, but she tastes great, and her name is Hannah."

"I'm so glad I could help you, how did you do it?"

"I caught her coming out of the loo, pinned her against the wall and kissed her."

"How did she react?"

"She struggled for a second or two, then surrendered, that moment felt so sweet, she just melted against me, she felt so soft and warm, she was breathing so fast, her hands grabbed my waist. I looked into her face and her eyes were closed, it was so intense."

"Sounds like a good start," said Jane.

"We didn't have time to talk, I'll let you know after tomorrow."

"Great," laughed Jane, "you can let me go now." Liz kissed her again instead, then released her.

"Remember," said Jane quietly, "don't push her too hard. Though she does seem to have a submissive side."

"I'll try, but she feels so good in my arms, I can't wait to taste her properly." Liz blushed and looked at the others all watching the interaction. Roaddog smiled and licked his lips. Liz turned her head to the ground. Jane reached out, took her chin and lifted her face.

"Never be ashamed of who you are. Enjoy your new friend, who can tell, she may be the one for you."

"I hope so." Liz looked round, shook her head briefly, before continuing, "Your table is ready please follow me." She broke away from Jane and led them all into the conservatory. When they were all seated Liz smiled and said, "I'll come back in a little while to take your orders." She turned on her heel and walked back into the main bar.

"Damn," whispered Jane, "that's one fine ass, look at it swing."

"Oh, the glories of youth," said Sylvia.

"Your ass is most fine," whispered Slowball.

"That's down to expensive jeans," laughed Sylvia.

"Not entirely," said Slowball reaching over to kiss her. Very soon Liz returned to take their food orders, it was no real surprise to her that burgers were not among the orders placed.

"No burgers then?" she asked, with a huge smile.

"I've spent most of the day cooking them, and eating the leftovers," laughed Jane, "I really don't feel like anymore, right now."

"More drinks?" asked Liz. Then she wandered off with both orders.

"So what tactics are we going to use for Melchion?" asked Bug.

"You me and Slowball will be getting in close. Hopefully the guns will mince the bastard, but if not, I've got four blessed knives. They'll definitely hurt it. I don't want you girls in too close, but I do have something you can do."

"What's that?" asked Jane.

"Well, from the Templar report they tied its legs with a chain and knocked it down before killing it. Chain we don't have, but I've got some thousand kilo test strapping we can use."

"We could tie its legs together," said Jackie, "and drag it down the road until it is dead. Tarmac will wear away anything."

"It could take too long, and the rope could wear out as well."

"We could use vehicles to tear it apart," suggested Sylvia quietly.

"That could work," said Roaddog.

"Did anyone else get a picture of the black knight from the holy grail?" asked Slowball.

"Come back, 'tis only a flesh wound," laughed Bug.

"Don't," laughed Sylvia, holding her sides and trying desperately not to cry with laughter.

"I don't understand," said Jane.

Slowball explained the black knight scene to her, and she laughed along with the others.

"That's simply a classic," said Roaddog.

"Especially as it took so many Templars to kill it last time," said Slowball.

"Well," replied Roaddog slowly, "there's only three of us and four girls, and I couldn't bear to lose any of you."

"We'll have the clergy on our side," said Bug, "and you can bet that Jake is going to be there."

"Yes," sniggered Roaddog, "he still feels he owes us."

"Doesn't he?" asked Sylvia.

"Not really, he's providing us with free ammunition, and you can guarantee he's watching those damned birds twenty-four seven." Roaddog's phone rang in his pocket and he pulled it out. "Speak of the devil," he muttered before hitting the accept button.

"Hi Jake, birds up?"

"Hi Roaddog," replied Jake, "no, all quiet, I just thought I'd let you know, I'm gonna catch a little shut eye, Mary will have my phone. Once the sun goes down, we'll have to move in closer, and I'm not having her anywhere near that place in the dark."

"I really hope it doesn't surface in the dark, I do have a plan but it does sort of depend on us being able to see the bastard."

"Plan?" Roaddog paused for a while before answering.

"Right, short version, demon's eyes flash on its target, that target is the only one that can damage it, equally any others that it hits don't get too much in the way of injury. Reports suggest it can chop an armoured knight in two pieces with one blow, if you're target get someone else to stand in the way."

"Can it be killed?"

"Head off, that usually works."

"Sounds like a plan."

"You get some rest; we may be needing you at your best."

"No worries." Jake broke the contact without any other word.

"At least they're on the case," said Slowball.

"I got another thought," said Roaddog softly, "I think I saw a camera in that church."

"There was," replied Bug, "high up on the roof, wide angle from the look."

"Was it wired?"

"I don't recall any wire at all in the place, so it's solar powered wireless and currently broadcasting."

"Can you tap it?"

"I can give it a try, when we get back to the shop, I can't do that sort of stuff with my phone."

"You need a better phone."

"They don't make one that good."

"Don't apple advertise theirs as a computer in your pocket?"

"Not as such, but they do suggest it's as good, they're wrong, there is no substitute for an optical line and multicore CPU."

"Do you think you'll be able to find it?" asked Roaddog.

"Who can tell? It may be out there, and I'm hoping it's been installed by amateurs, passwords should be easy," laughed Bug.

Conversation stopped as Liz walked in with arms full of plates.

"Is there anyone else with the sudden urge to tickle someone?" asked Jane, laughing.

"You'd end up wearing all this food," said Liz.

"In some of the places I've eaten that would have been better," laughed Jane, leaning back so that Liz could put her plate down. "Thanks," said Jane, she reached out and gently stroked Liz's backside.

"Hey," said Liz sharply, "That's almost as bad as tickling."

"Yes," said Jane, "but so much nicer."

"Agreed, and you can let go anytime you want."

Jane grinned widely, and let go of Liz, so that she could continue with serving the others. Mandy came out of the kitchen with another armful of plates, and soon everyone had their meals.

"Drinks?" asked Mandy.

"Same again," said Roaddog. Mandy nodded and went back into the main bar.

Everyone was tucking into their food when Mandy brought a tray full of drinks and departed without a word. Roaddog's phone pinged an incoming message.

"Damn, it's from Jake," he said, he opened the message expecting the worst. In a moment the others were surprised by his laughter.

"What the fuck?" asked Slowball.

"Sorry," laughed Roaddog, "it's from Mary, she's just saying thank you for saving her worthless husbands life. And she's inviting us all to lunch on Sunday."

"Tell her we'll come so long as we survive," laughed Bug.

"We may just have this whole heap of shit sorted by then," said

Slowball.

"What makes you think that this next bastard is the last one?" laughed Roaddog.

"When will we know we've stopped the last one?" asked Jane.

"When that damned gate closes," snarled Roaddog.

"Will it ever close?" whispered Jane.

"It must do, there has to be a limit, Father Francis said that the last one had five demons."

"What do you mean?" asked Jackie.

"Five demons then it closed."

"Are you sure?" asked Bug.

"The priest is sure, and that's got to be good enough for me, I need to see him tomorrow anyway."

"Why?" asked Jane, "arranging an urgent marriage?"

"I'm fairly sure that Father Francis would object to the sort of arrangement that I would like to make, but no, I have a little surprise for you both."

"I love surprises," said Jackie, smiling.

"I love some surprises," said Jane, no smile on her face, a disturbing frown though.

"Don't fret Jane," smiled Roaddog, "to be honest I've got a little tired of losing two of my blades every time there is some action in the offing, so I've ordered you two some of your very own."

"I like your black bladed stiletto's," said Jane, Jackie simply nodded.

"Don't worry, I've got each of you two that are almost identical to mine, the only difference is that the handles are shiny mother of pearl. The blades are still black, and the edges will be ground by me, before Father Francis gets to bless them for you both."

"And how do we carry them? We always know where yours are."

"Remember that I used to carry only two, until I met you two crazy bitches, now I always have the spares on the back of my belt. Well, I've got belt clips for both of you coming as well."

"Fine if we're wearing jeans, but what if we want to wear skirts for a change?" asked Jane.

"I like those tartan schoolgirl skirts that Man-Dare wears," laughed Jackie.

"Right on," muttered Bug, grinning from ear to ear. Slowball only nodded, but both got a solid punch from their respective partners.

"Wear braces with your skirts," said Roaddog, "I'm seeing rainbow striped, like Mork. The belt clip will fasten to the back of the braces and hang above the skirt, under your jackets."

"Mork?" asked Jane.

"I can't help it, I'm old," Roaddog laughed, "sitcom from the late seventies, Mork is a visiting space alien, coming to terms with Milwaukee. One of my mum's favourites, played by Robin Williams."

"I remember," said Jackie, "Good Morning Vietnam, and Mr's Doubtfire, he was awesome, didn't he kill himself?"

"Yes, he had some rare form of dementia, only discovered at the autopsy." Roaddog sighed.

"Too fucking late then," snarled Sylvia.

"Yes," Roaddog nodded, "un-treatable though, very sad."

"So, braces," said Jane.

"Rainbows," said Jackie.

"The only question," said Jane. Jackie tipped her head to the side, asking the question.

"Between the boobs or outside the boobs?" said Jane.

"You have to remember, these braces are going to be carrying a lot of weight in the back, so straight down the middle is the only way to go," Roaddog tried his level best not to smile, he was almost successful.

"I can see that," said Bug, getting another slap.

"So," said Jane slowly, "straight down the middle, right over the nipples." Slowball spit beer over his plate.

"Be aware gentlemen," said Jackie, "the first person that pings said braces will choke on his cock before he dies, are we clear?"

"Rest assured," said Slowball, the remnants of his beer dripping from his chin, "if anyone other than those around this table attempts such a thing, they will regret being born, if only briefly." His smile did little to appease the two girls.

"I don't know about you," said Jackie, "but I'm seeing a stocking top holster, a snap-out rig, you know, snatch, flick, stick."

"Lara Croft," laughed Jane, "knives not nine mills."

"That's the sort of thing," laughed Jackie.

"Oh, my god," mumbled Slowball, bracing for another slap from Sylvia. He waited a few moments before looking at her.

"Would you like me dressed like that?" she asked, leering.

"Would you do it?" he asked.

"If you want."

"My want is of no importance," he said, "if you want to do it, then I'll not argue, though I'm going to be very busy fighting off the chancers."

"Would you do that for me?"

"Of course he would," laughed Bug, "he'd die taking on the world to protect you, that's who he is."

"So are you, you ass," snarled Slowball, looking pointedly at Cherie.

"Agreed," said Bug, "but Dog's twice as crazy."

"That's without doubt," laughed Slowball.

"Jealous much?" asked Bug.

"Definitely, but could you handle that?"

"Not a chance, I'd run like a girl."

"And how do girls run?" asked Jackie.

"You bitches," replied Bug, "you don't ever run, you're scary as fuck."

"That's right, and don't you forget it," snapped Jane. Roaddog put his arms around the shoulders of both girls and pulled them in close.

"You girls are something more than special, you understand that I love you both?"

"Of course," said Jane.

"For real," said Jackie. They both reached in close to kiss his cheeks.

"Oh, my god, I am doomed," said Roaddog.

"We're all doomed," laughed Slowball.

"Classic," said Sylvia.

"You remember?" asked Slowball.

"Of course. 'Don't tell them your name, mister Mainwearing,' followed by 'Stupid boy, Pike.' Who can forget the classics?"

"Oh, you'd be surprised, so many find it so offensive that they have to go hide in a safe place."

"Is that Hyde?" laughed Sylvia.

"They have no clue where Hyde is, or what it means, they've lived nothing and nowhere, they are the original 'nowhere man' that the Beatles made famous."

"I've never been to Hyde," said Sylvia seriously.

"I hope you never go there," said Jane, her eyes dark and dangerous.

"I really can't imagine how that was," said Sylvia.

"I'm sure you've been told," whispered Jane.

"I have," said Sylvia, "but I just don't get it. I mean, how can people be so crazy?"

"Oh, they can be far more crazy than that," said Jackie, "if Bandit Queen had walked into that unit, then they'd have found out what crazy really is, damn, I love that bitch, she saved us."

"Her and Groveller," said Roaddog.

"Bastard," muttered Jane, "I'm trying to forget that shit."

"Sorry love," said Roaddog, "it's part of your life, part of your history, you can't deny it, you have to learn from it, and move on."

"I don't want to do that; it hurts too much."

"If you don't deal with the hurt, it will only grow to be far bigger than it deserves to be," said Slowball. "You survived, as did the others, that is all that counts."

"But at what price?" asked Jane.

"Would you rather have died? Or worse?" asked Jackie.

"Of course not," mumbled Jane, "but, hell, I don't know, it would have been so much better if no one had died."

"They started the killing," whispered Jackie, the others staying out of this conversation, as they knew it was important, she reached across Roaddog's body and took Jane's hand, "then they paid the price."

"But did you have to be so brutal?"

"Given time I'd have carved small pieces off them until they begged to die, but time was short, they died in fear and pain, that'll have to do for me."

"What would you have done, given time?" whispered Jane.

"I'd have made the Bandit Queen proud," smiled Jackie.

"Bitch, you're far crazier than me."

"That's as may be, but I love you, and they hurt you, they deserved to die in the worst ways, but I didn't have time."

"I'm not sure you are helping here," said Jane.

"It's your history, you were there, how would you have liked those bastards to die?"

"After the way they threatened us, I wanted them to burn, but whether I could actually watch, now that was a different matter."

"Burn, now that's a memory, tied on their knees, a car tyre around their necks, filled with petrol and set afire. How does that sound?"

"Truly horrible."

"Warranted?"

"Perhaps, they had promised us some dreadful consequences."

"Man-Dare took those for herself, and the guys rescued us, should I have taken time to burn those bastards?"

"Bitch, I could really get to hate you sometimes, but, fuck yes."

"That's good," laughed Jackie, "those bastards should have burned in their own very personal hells, so their deaths at the hands of Vera were far cleaner than they deserved?"

"I suppose," replied Jane quietly.

"Great, now stop beating yourself up about this shit, they got what they deserved, end of story, agreed?"

"Bitch, sometimes I hate you as much as I love you," mumbled Jane.

"I love you too, but you have to deal with the history that we share. And you have to handle the fact that these guys here came to rescue us."

"And let's not forget Sharpshooter," said Roaddog.

"Bastard," muttered Jane.

"He paid," mumbled Slowball.

"Cunt," snapped Jane, her eyes flashing into the big mans, though they softened in a moment, a tear rolled slowly down the right side of her nose. Liz walked into the room to ask how their meals were, she paused just inside the door, the tension around the table was clear to her, then she spotted the tear.

"Jane," she said, "are you okay?"

"I'm fine," replied Jane, looking up into the younger girls concerned eyes, "just talking about history."

"Then why are you crying?"

"It was a hard time."

"You mean these assholes are giving you a hard time?" Liz put her fists on her hips and glared at the whole table.

"Assholes," laughed Jane, "oh, they're that and more. When life is at its darkest, and you can see no hope, these assholes are riding to save you, and hell rides with them." Jane paused, she reached out and picked up her glass, held it high in the air, and whispered. "Sharpshooter." The others all raised their glasses and spoke his name.

"Ride the wind brother," said Roaddog.

"Who's Sharpshooter?" asked Liz.

"When some of us girls had been kidnapped," said Jackie slowly, "he spent his life to save ours."

"Love that mad man," said Cherie quietly. The silence in the room started to become oppressive, until Roaddog's phone bleeped, it's tone so loud it made everyone jump, Jane gasped. Then everyone started to laugh.

"You people are crazy," said Liz as she turned to leave.

"She's not wrong," said Sylvia.

"That was a text from Father Francis, he's sent us a web address, and password."

"What for?" asked Bug.

"Damned cameras in that church, he's been talking to the charity that looks after it, and convinced them to give us the cameras, guy's really on the ball. I'll forward it to Jake, so he can keep an eye on the place."

"Send it to me as well," said Bug. Roaddog sent a text message and Bug did something to the text, then there was a flurry of text messages to all the phones around the table.

"Just click the link I sent, and the camera's will appear as an icon on your phones," he said, smiling. "There are two cameras, one on the inside, and another covering the gate. If you check the gate, you'll see it is a favoured place for the birds to rest. If the birds aren't there, then the demon is out and about."

"Will it work in the dark?" asked Jackie.

"Should do," said Bug, "I suppose most of their troubles with vandals will be in the dark, so only really stupid people would put up cameras that don't work at night."

"Never underestimate the ingenuity of idiots," laughed Slowball, "one of my father's favourite sayings." The conversation faltered for a short time, after a couple of minutes of silence. Roaddog spoke.

"Hey Jane, we're assholes then?"

"Yes," said Jane slowly, "you're all assholes, but you're my assholes and I love you all."

"For a girl with so many assholes you aren't half chubby," laughed Bug.

"Thanks for that Bug," giggled Jane.

"You're very welcome," Bug bowed to her, a huge smile on his face.

"You are a bad person," said Cherie, poking Bug in the ribs.

"He's not a bad person," said Jane, "he's like the rest of you, the best people in the world."

"That's so good of you to say," replied Roaddog.

"Hey," she said, sharply, "you're taking on demons when you should simply be running away."

"Not what we do," whispered Roaddog.

"And I am so grateful for that," she said.

"I'm so glad you decided to come to see us," said Jackie.

"So am I," replied Jane. "I've missed you all so much."

"But will you stay?" asked Jackie.

"It's Monday evening, and I'm still here, I should be on my way back to go to work tomorrow."

"So should we," said Sylvia, looking at Slowball.

"I'll take you home if you really want to go, but I'm coming straight back," responded Slowball.

"I think I feel sickies coming on," laughed Sylvia.

"I think we're going to be a right poorly bunch tomorrow morning," laughed Bug.

"Probably for the whole week," said Cherie.

"I'll have to call in," said Jane.

"For how long?" whispered Jackie.

"I don't know," replied Jane, "I'm still very conflicted, I want to stay, but I'm sort of afraid."

"I can understand that" said Roaddog, "but you respond like you fit in here so well."

"What do you mean?"

"Well, when that fool interrupted our greetings, you went straight for the belt knife and threatened to stick the idiot, you moved at exactly the same speed as Jackie, it was beautiful."

"He pissed me off," muttered Jane.

"Me too," said Roaddog quietly.

"Sylvia was great," said Jackie.

"That's for sure," laughed Slowball, "it got a little nervous for a while."

"Yes," said Bug, "could have gone all sorts of badly."

"It didn't," said Roaddog, "I think Jane acted perfectly in the church as well."

"I was scared, that demon was freaky," smiled Jane.

"Freaky is the word," said Cherie, "I was more than ready to run."

"Nutter was scarier," whispered Jackie.

"Damn," said Bug, "that guy was indeed a nutter, but the guy had balls."

"But did he really need to barbeque them for us?" asked Slowball.

"He did what needed to be done," said Roaddog. "We can't ask for more."

"What do we do now?" asked Jackie.

"I think we need to get some rest," said Roaddog, "let's head back to the van, and settle in for an early night, tomorrow could get real busy real quick."

"Agreed," said Slowball, picking up his pint and emptying the last third. He was rapidly followed by the others.

"Let's roll," said Roaddog standing up from the table and leading the others out of the conservatory into the main bar.

"Can I settle up?" he asked of Mandy as he approached the shiny bar, the surface of the bar was more than a little unusual, it had been covered with copper coins embedded in clear resin. It only took Mandy a moment to present him with the bill and take his card payment. "Thanks Mandy," he said as he turned away, as he walked through the door he almost bumped into Karen.

"Leaving early?" she asked.

"Heavy day, and tomorrow could be worse," he smiled.

"I know the feeling," she laughed, "I think I'm going to sleep until Wednesday."

"I don't blame you. Are you not opening tomorrow?"

"That has not as yet been decided."

"We can always get a curry, if we have to," he replied.

"It may be late when we open, but you know how bored I get if the bar's closed," Karen laughed.

"I'm the same," said Roaddog.

"No you're not, if your place isn't open you'll be out cruising somewhere."

"I actually meant that if your place is closed we get bored."

"Oh, that's a lot better," she paused for a moment, "I'll be open by teatime."

"That's great, I just hope we're not too busy."

"You better not be, someone has to drink the beer we've got left from this weekend."

"We'll do our best, but our schedule isn't entirely under our control right now, we are dependent on other people showing, or not."

"You can always bring them with you."

"I don't think so, they're messy eaters."

"What sort of people are they?"

"They're just devils, we'll finish our business with them before we come in, hopefully."

"If you think that's for the best."

"You just want some extra customers," laughed Roaddog.

"Can't be a bad thing, as I said, lots of beer left."

"No, these would make far too much mess."

"Then why deal with them?"

"Someone has to."

"But does it have to be you?"

"No one else around, we'll sort them and come for tea as well, how's that?"

"Sounds like a fun day to me, I have another question," said Karen slowly.

"Ask away," smiled Roaddog.

"Liz is worried about Jane, apparently she was crying, what's that all about."

"Jane has been going through a bad time, we are helping her come to terms with it, it's never going to be easy."

"Poor Jane, she's such a lovely young girl." Karen glanced round to make sure that Jane was out of earshot. "You'll look after her?"

"Of course we will." He turned to follow the others who were already on their way back to the workshop. He caught up with them before they turned into the huge open carpark.

"I gotta check the hardware before we leave."

He went straight into the backroom and powered up his computer. The news wasn't as good as he had hoped, the miners hadn't hit anything, but they were running on batteries, so the work they were doing was free. A quick check showed that his order for the girls was already well on its way, having arrived at the Grimsby terminal a few hours earlier. The courier was promising early delivery in the morning. He smiled to himself and shut the computer down and went outside where everyone was waiting.

"Should we check out the church?" asked Slowball.

"No," replied Roaddog, "we got cameras now and Jake is on the case, he'll call if anything happens."

"So," said Bug, "early to bed, could be a heavy day tomorrow."

"Sounds like a plan to me," laughed Roaddog, throwing his leg over the Victory and firing up the heavy twin, before rolling it forwards into the open air. Jane waited by the door control. As the heavy door rattled down in its tracks Bug suddenly called out.

"This ain't right."

"What's up?" asked Slowball.

"I used to be the noisy one, and now I have to check my rev counter to see if the engine is actually running, you are a pair of noisy bastards."

"Now you know how we used to feel, someone would say, Bug'll be here in thirty minutes," laughed Roaddog, leaning forwards so Jane could drop onto his pillion.

Only five minutes later they were parking outside the caravan. Jackie was first inside, she filled the kettle, and switched the radio on to give a little background music, as the others trouped in and took up their places on the various seating she asked if they wanted brews. Coffee and tea were distributed and shots of bourbon to go with them, the newly opened bottle of Western Gold was half empty by the time it dropped onto the coffee table. A silence consumed the room, everyone thinking their own thoughts about the past and the future. As the light started to fade outside Roaddog spoke up.

"How's everyone feeling about tomorrow?" he asked quietly.

"Fucking scared," replied Slowball.

"Agreed," said Bug.

"It's not going to be easy," said Roaddog, "someone is going to get hurt, the odds aren't really in our favour."

"I'm just hoping that bullets will kill the damned thing," said Slowball.

"Father Francis asked me why we don't simply run away," whispered Roaddog.

"He doesn't know us, does he?" said Slowball.

"He does now," said Bug.

"He's right in a way," said Jane softly, "we could just leave it to him and his friends."

"You of all people know we don't do that sort of thing," smiled Roaddog.

"When you rode out to save us, you were coming for people you cared about and intent on killing the ones that killed your friends, these people are strangers."

"They were strangers, but now Karen at least counts as a friend. By the way she's worried about you. Jake and Mary, they're friends now, and far too close to that church. For god's sake even Father Francis and his cronies could be counted as friends right now."

"Even after you chopped that druid in half?"

"They weren't happy with him anyway; I don't know but I get the feel that he wasn't the one they were expecting."

"He did seem like an outsider in their group," offered Slowball.

"Their dynamic was definitely off," agreed Bug.

"Either way, we stay, we fight," said Roaddog, he raised his glass in a toast, the others followed his lead and then Roaddog refilled all the shot glasses, leaving an empty bottle for the recycling.

"I'll never get the chance to thank them," whispered Jane, taking half of her second shot.

"We may be able to do something about that," said Roaddog, "do you trust me?"

"Of course," replied Jane, a little unsure.

"Fine, stand up, and close your eyes." Jane looked at him for a moment, then did as he asked. Roaddog used hand signals and Bug stood up in front of Jane.

"Jane, remember Sharpshooter, his short hair, his lobsided grin, those crazy cold eyes," he paused, and she nodded.

"Fuck I can smell that cheap aftershave of his," whispered Slowball, a glare from Roaddog forced him into silence.

"Jane, Sharpshooter is in front of you, keep your eyes closed and thank him for taking those bullets to save your life." Jane reached forwards tentatively and felt Bug's arms and then she reached up and pulled his head down to kiss him, her tightly closed eyes leaking gentle tears. When she released him, her breath caught in her throat, but still she didn't open her eyes.

"Jane," said Roaddog, "turn left. Remember that giant known as Lurch, he stands in front of you now." Jane lifted her arms high, and Slowball scooped her up by the waist. They kissed for a second or two, then she broke away and whispered, "Thank you." Slowball let her down slowly.

"Jane, step right," said Roaddog, "In front of you is Bandit Queen, who held on to tell me that you had been taken." Jane threw her arms around Sylvia and kissed her enthusiastically. The chest she felt was not as impressive, and the belly lacked the circumference of the original, tears were flowing freely by the time Jane stepped away from Sylvia.

"Jane, turn round, in front of you is Man-Dare, who took all that pain so that you wouldn't have to." Jane rushed into Cherie's arms and kissed her repeatedly, half laughing, but always crying.

"Right turn," said Roaddog, "let's not forget Jackie, who finished off the last two with a certain aplomb." Jane stepped into Jackie's open arms, her eyes open now and tears rolling down her face, then she turned to Roaddog, she held him close, her tears soaking into his beard, and his falling into her hair. Gradually her breathing slowed, and she leaned away from him, looking up into his eyes, she spoke quietly.

"Dog, you are a bad man."

"Someone else used to say that quite often, she wasn't wrong." Jane looked around the room and there wasn't a dry eye to be seen, she paused for a moment.

"That's odd," she said.

"What now?" asked Roaddog.

"I think I just saw the light go off in Gladys's bedroom, then the curtains open."

"Why would they do that?" laughed Roaddog.

Chapter 10: Quiet night in.

"I wonder what they are up to?" asked Jackie.

"The only reason to do that is to be able to see out in the dark, so what are they watching?"

"You mean other than us?" asked Roaddog.

"There's not a lot going on around here this time of night," said Bug, "except for us, could they really be wanting to see what's going on in here?"

"Who can tell?" said Roaddog reaching up into one of the overhead lockers and taking down another bottle of Western gold.

"I thought you were out?" asked Slowball, smiling.

"Well, I was hoping that one of you would feel guilty at drinking all my booze and go get some, but it seems you all know me too well."

"I guessed that you had more than just the one bottle," laughed Bug. Cherie just shook her head as the shot glasses were refilled. Roaddog lifted his and spoke gently.

"Absent friends," he said. The others all raised their glasses and repeated his words before emptying the shots. Refills created another empty bottle.

"How many you got left?" asked Sylvia.

"Enough," laughed Jackie, "enough to get Slowball smashed for a week." She opened the overhead to show them all that it still held a few bottles and then opened one of the lower cupboards, it also was full.

"Why have you got so many bottles?" asked Bug, "I'm sort of worried about your liver."

"The local shop seems to have had some supply issues over the summer, the white label stuff is always available, but the black that we like so much has been unreliable, so I buy four bottles every time they have some in," laughed Roaddog, "it stacks up real quick."

"Last time we went to Lidl and they didn't have any, the manager came out with half a case when he saw us," laughed Jackie.

"It got sort of difficult to not buy any after that," laughed Roaddog.

"So, we better start drinking some then," said Slowball.

"Not too much though, we may have a call out soon," said Roaddog. Bug took his phone from his pocket and clicked the link. In seconds the church cameras opened. The video was as normal for night-time cameras, it was monochrome, the infra reds showing as pale light patches. The floor of the church was covered in small shapes, that appeared to be milling around aimlessly. The outside camera was showing no birds on the roof of the gate.

"I'm hoping that the birds are all inside the church, it certainly looks like them, but the definition on this camera is a bit crap," said Bug.

"How come they're so difficult to see?" asked Jane.

"Feathers are a damned good insulator," replied Bug, "the outside of the birds is very nearly at room temperature."

"Or tomb temperature," laughed Slowball.

"The bright spots are probably their eyes, both warm and reflecting the camera's lights straight back at them."

"So, there's plenty of birds in the church?" asked Roaddog.

"Oh yes," replied Bug, "number of eyes divided by two is still many."

"Dick," laughed Roaddog.

"No dicks," grinned Bug, "just eyes."

Roaddog sat down on a short settee, with Jackie on his right, and Jane on his lap. Jackie had one hand round his back and the other on Jane's thigh. Jane smiled as Jackie's hand moved slowly up and down the young girl's thigh. Jane turned her head and kissed Roaddog, her right arm around his neck and her left reached down to stroke the back of Jackie's hand as it, moved slowly around.

"You okay?" asked Jackie quietly.

"I don't know," replied Jane, "I feel a little better, but the image of Lurch standing in that doorway, that will never go away."

"Nor should it. It's part of your history, an important part."

"You were there, what did you see?"

"I have to admit," said Jackie shakily, "when the gunfire started, I hit the floor, rolled under a cot and had my eyes shut until that asshole dragged me out by my hair."

"You didn't seem to be as shocked as I was."

"I just got mad, I wanted to kill them all."

"And then you did," muttered Jane.

"Bastards had it coming, killing all my friends and threatening the ones still alive."

"I was just so frightened," said Jane.

"So was I," replied Jackie.

"Not on your own there," said Roaddog, "I was terrified that we would be too late, or worse going to the wrong place."

"You should have heard Man-Dare howl when you arrived, she was pissing herself laughing at them."

"I even smiled," said Jackie, "I knew that we were safe."

"They could still have killed us all," said Jane.

"They were too busy trying to stay alive, until they surrendered of course."

"There weren't so many of them left by then."

"Just enough to keep me amused for a moment or two," laughed Jackie.

"I think you enjoyed that too much," said Jane softly.

"They had it coming."

"I'm not going to argue with that," Jane smiled and reached across to kiss Roaddog.

"Thank you for saving my life and the others, it was a wonderful thing to do."

"Don't sweat it, into hell and back, you know that."

"Why?" whispered Jane.

"Because we love you, dumbo," laughed Bug.

"That and revenge on the scumbags," smiled Slowball.

"Yeah," said Roaddog, quietly, "we couldn't let them get away with that shit."

"You mean that you have a reputation to uphold?" asked Jane.

"What reputation? Dragonriders are no more, we are all that is left. Who knows what happened that day? Only those sitting in this room. We have no reputation; we are simply gone."

"And is that pissing off Hopkins?" laughed Jane, as she kissed him again.

"He been giving you a hard time?"

"Not really, he just turns up every now and again with that guy with the dodgy leg. He says that he knows that you are alive somewhere."

"And how does he know that?"

"Because Jackie here has disappeared, and her family aren't going crazy looking for her."

"Maybe you should have a word with your dad next time you ring him?"

"I'll mention it, but I don't see it doing any good, no matter how much noise they make now, it's not going to achieve anything," replied Jackie.

"What about Lewis?" asked Roaddog.

"We never see him; I think he's distanced himself from Hopkins. Hopkins has gone a little crazy."

"What do you mean?"

"He's made the link to Hyde, they've found enough DNA to say that you were there, they know that all us girls were there, but we're telling them fuck all."

"I think the investigation has been pretty much dropped," said Cherie, "the only time we see Hopkins is when he's off duty."

"How do you know that?" asked Roaddog.

"Always in his own car, no radios, and never with a partner, if you know what I mean."

"Has he been fired?"

"I don't think so, maybe suspended."

"What for?"

"Spending too much time with a dickhead whose brother was found in a drug processing plant, with his crotch and head turned to burger meat." She grinned at Jackie, "Good shot girl."

"Do you have to?" asked Jane, "makes me feel like puking, just thinking about it." Jane shivered in Roaddog's lap, he held her tighter and kissed her softly.

"So, what did you tell them about how you got home?" asked Sylvia.

"Nothing," replied Cherie, "they keep asking and they keep threatening, but they get fuck all."

"That is part of the reason I came here," whispered Jane.

"What do you mean?" asked Jackie.

"The continuous pressure was starting to get to me, I almost told the bastard a couple of times, the last time was two weeks ago, I was working in the rugby club, pulling beers and chatting to customers, a band was setting up and the bastard walked in. He flashed his warrant card at the boss and dragged me over to a table in the corner, he was laying it on real, obstruction, contempt of court, promising all sorts of dreadful things, then someone walked in. She took one look at my face and came over, she was flanked by Billy and Geronimo, she advised Hopkins in a cold voice, one that would have made Bandit Queen proud, she told him that the only thing he was going to get was dead."

"That must have made his day," laughed Slowball.

"He accused her of threatening a police officer," smiled Jane, "then she laughed in his face, she turned to the guy he had brought, 'You, I'm going to feed to the dogs, one slice at a time,' she said. Bitch is crazy, she took my hand and pulled me away from them, as we went between the two guys they closed up, Billy just glared at Hopkins, Geronimo growled. It was awesome, but I knew I would most likely break at some point."

"Are you going to stay?" asked Jackie.

"Fuck you," snapped Jane, "of course I am. I know I can't go back; he'll know I've been to see you, and he'll never let up." Jackie moved in and kissed her.

"What about Man-Dare?" asked Roaddog.

"Bitch is batshit crazy," laughed Slowball. "She's still with Billy, but she's having a great time being queen bitch of the Centurions, even the leader's old lady backs down from her, it's an insane situation, one thing for sure, Bandit Queen would be proud of her."

"What do you mean?" asked Roaddog.

"Oh my god," said Slowball, "it's almost like Bandit Queen has been reborn, she struts around like she owns the world, and will spit in the eye of anyone who challenges her."

"Risky path she walks," said Roaddog.

"She doesn't walk, she stamps. She's already stamped on more than a few toes, last month some guy pissed her off, and she challenged him, she took his knife from him and threatened, to use her words, 'to cut his fucking head off.' The leader convinced her not to kill the ass, but she kept the knife and wears it in her belt all the time."

"Fuck, what did Bandit Queen create?" asked Roaddog.

"Bandit Queen two, flyweight and deadly," laughed Bug.

"Bandit was never no flyweight," grinned Slowball.

"She's great fun to watch," said Sylvia, "there is no doubt that she is Bandit Queen two, and everyone knows it, though most of them don't know who Bandit Queen was. She's certainly enjoying life, but I don't think it's going to last long."

"Burn fast, burn bright, don't fade away," said Roaddog.

"Definitely," replied Slowball, "but she's having fun."

"Is she going to tear apart the centurions to be the leader's woman?" asked Roaddog.

"No," laughed Slowball, "to be honest, she's not picked a leader for them yet."

"Fuck," said Roaddog, "what have we created?"

"Sorry mate," said Slowball, "not us, that bitch Bandit Queen, she has created this monster, and this monster is called Mama."

"Who is Mama?" asked Jackie.

"Mama," said Bug, "Mama is the chick that took control of the hells angels when Chopper went to jail."

"Fine," said Jackie, "who is Mama?" anger clear in her voice.

"Right," laughed Roaddog, "Chopper was the leader of a hells angels' group who went to jail, Mama was his old lady, she took over when he went inside. They were both main characters in books by Peter Cave in the nineteen seventies."

"So, they don't exist?" asked Jackie.

"No," said Roaddog, "pure fiction."

"Does Man-Dare know about these books?"

"I don't think so," replied Roaddog.

"Then don't fucking tell her, she doesn't need to know. So long as she believes in who she is, she'll be fine," laughed Jackie.

"She'll be fine," said Bug, "but will the world?"

"The damned world can look after itself," said Slowball.

"It may just be damned if we don't close that portal," muttered Roaddog.

"Won't the church be able to close it?" asked Jane.

"Only if they get their asses in gear," sneered Roaddog, "and that doesn't look like it's happening."

"They set Father Francis to watch it," said Jane.

"I think they set him up to fail, could be they know more than they are telling him."

"What do you think?" asked Slowball.

"I think they have a prophecy, one that tells them the priest is going to die, but someone else will shut the thing."

"Why would they keep it secret from him?" asked Jackie.

"Back in the twelve hundreds, priests were killed for their faith all over the world, and they died willingly, I don't think that sort of belief is so common these days."

"You think he'd run away if he thought he was going to die?" asked Sylvia.

"Most likely," replied Roaddog.

"I think you do him a disservice," said Sylvia softly.

"You could be right," said Roaddog after a moment's thought. "He wasn't willing to sacrifice the children, so perhaps he'd sacrifice himself to save them, or the rest of us."

"He does strike me as more than a little old fashioned in some ways," chuckled Sylvia.

"What do you mean?" asked Bug.

"He struggles to take his eyes off Jackie's tits, and Jane's ass, but he looks embarrassed when he catches himself doing it, he even checks around to see if anyone has noticed," Sylvia laughed, "he went bright red when he caught me laughing at him."

"A guy would have to be dead not to notice those two," said Bug, getting a slap from Cherie.

"But he's not supposed to, is he?" asked Jane.

"No, he's not supposed to, but he is a guy after all," said Bug, picking up the bottle of whiskey and topping up the glasses, he glanced at the bottle meaningfully as it ran dry. "Another dead soldier," he muttered.

"More in the cupboard," said Jackie, then she turned to Jane. "Are you really going to stay?"

"I think so," whispered Jane.

"Why?"

"I've been so bored."

"That's not enough."

"I've missed you all."

"Still not enough, why?"

"Fine," said Jane reaching down and taking Jackie's hand in her own, then she looked straight into Jackie's eyes, "I love you," she whispered.

"I love you too," said Jackie, Roaddog coughed softly.

"And you, you fool," said Jane without looking into the man's eyes, she pulled Jackie in close and kissed her gently, then she turned to Roaddog and kissed him as well.

"Well, that's settled at least," whispered Jackie, watching the two kiss. Bug smiled at the scene, then turned to Cherie, just in time for her lips to intercept his. Conversation died, there was too much kissing going on for words. In only moments kissing heated up, and clothing started to be eased, then removed. With four hands working on her Jane was naked first, but not by more than a few seconds, Jackie was down to her underwear when the two of them started working on what was left of Roaddog's clothes, not that he was putting up any sort of fight. As they were pulling off his jeans Cherie muttered "Fuck" the pair looked round to see Cherie and Bug struggling with her jeans and boots.

"Jeans up, boots off, then jeans off," laughed Jackie, she glanced at Jane, then the two of them went to help Cherie with her wardrobe malfunction. Seconds was all it took for the tangled boots to be liberated and the jeans to drop on top of the pile of discarded clothing. Sylvia was moving a lot slower than the others, almost as if she was embarrassed, Slowball pulled her in close and whispered, "You okay?"

"I've never done anything like this before," she replied.

"Not even as a teenager?"

"No, religious, remember?"

"You don't have to join in, you know that?"

"Yes, but part of me wants to, and part is frightened."

"Frightened of what?"

"I'm sort of scared what they will think of me,"

Slowball pulled his mouth away from her ear, then turned her head, Sylvia was just in time to see Jane lower herself onto Roaddog, taking him completely inside, she moaned as she bottomed out against his crotch. Slowball pulled her in tight again.

"They're sort of busy, they'll not be noticing anything, you have nothing to fear from these people, they are more family than friends." They heard Cherie grunt as Bug slammed into her from behind.

"Fuck," muttered Cherie, "harder you bastard." Bug and Cherie together set up a rhythmic slapping as their bodies moved as one.

"You okay?" asked Slowball again.

"Damn it," whispered Sylvia, "fuck me big boy."

"You got it," smiled Slowball, lifting her t-shirt up over her head, and unsnapping her bra with one hand, Sylvia shook her head, and soon joined in the nakedness that was all around, Slowball was the last to be undressed, he struggled with the laces on his boots. Sylvia stretched out on the settee; her legs spread to welcome him. Jackie chuckled as Slowball gently settled on top of Sylvia, his quiet sounds made it clear that he was enjoying the sensation of her warmth. Jackie stood up and turned Jane's head so the younger girl could suck on her large nipples and her hand slid between Jackie's slightly opened legs, into the very centre of Jackie's sex.

"Fuck," said Jackie.

"You like?" asked Jane, releasing the turgid nipple.

"Yes," replied Jackie, "but not that." She turned Jane's head until Jane could see out of the front window, across the way the light was now on in Gladys' bedroom, there was Gladys, what they could see was certainly naked, she was propped up on the windowsill, looking out into the night, from the way her heavy breasts were swinging someone hidden in the dark was giving it to her hard from behind. The shockwaves in Gladys' body matched the sounds of Bug and Cherie, then drifted off frequency, then back on again.

"Looks like John is giving her a good time," laughed Jackie.

"You're not wrong," grinned Jane, then she groaned as Roaddog slammed up into her, as if he was feeling a little left out. "Look at Gladys," she said leaning back to get out of Roaddog's line of sight.

"Fuck man," muttered Roaddog, "Johns really giving her a going over."

"How do you know it's John?" asked Jane, moving in small circles on his lap.

"True," said Roaddog, "go for it Glad."

"Jesus," said Cherie, looking up, "look at those titties bounce. Hey Bug, mine could get that big once they're full of milk."

"Awesome," said Bug maintaining a steady motion, and reaching around to hold her already sizable breasts, "I can't wait."

"Squeeze them nipples you bastard," muttered Cherie. He rolled them between thumb and forefinger, quite firmly.

"That'll do it," said Cherie, slamming backwards against Bug's thrusts, then she twitched and groaned, she would have slumped forwards if it hadn't been for Bug's hands moving to a solid grip on her hips. He continued to pound into her until his own orgasm caused spastic twitching of his muscles as the pleasure took away all control. Sylvia glanced over as Bug settled back onto his haunches. 'Damn,' she thought, 'there's one part of him that's not small.' Then Slowball's heavy thrusts sent her over the edge as well, she grunted as the spasms took her. Slowball looked down into her closed eyes and slowed right down, he was nowhere near ready yet. He waited until her eyes opened again, then started to increase his speed. Bug looked across at Jackie, he could see that she was getting a little frustrated being out of the action, he watched as a smile crept onto her face. She stood up on the seat and pulled Jane's head away from Roaddog's, then stepped across their bodies, so that she was facing Jane, she pulled Jane's face into her own crotch and held it there until Jane started to lick and suck at her pussy. It didn't take Jane's experienced mouth long to give Jackie her first orgasm. No sooner had Jackie slumped into the seat beside them, Jane came on Roaddog's thrusting cock, her tight writhing set him off. Soon the only sound other than heavy breathing in the caravan was the steady beat of Slowball pounding his not inconsiderable mass into Sylvia. Cherie sat up and looked across the road.

"Looks like Gladys has finished and gone to bed, lights are off and the curtains closed," she laughed.

"Jane", said Jackie nudging the younger girl, until her eyes opened, "next time I get to ride the pony."

"I am here," interrupted Roaddog. The girls simply looked at him, it took a little while but eventually he spoke again, "Fine, in the interests of equality I'll shut the fuck up." The girls both smiled at him and moved in to kiss him.

"I do have a question though," he paused briefly before continuing, "Jackie, tasty as your ass is, how come Jane got pussy to eat?"

Cherie burst into gales of laughter.

"What's funny?" asked Roaddog, looking into the smiling faces of his girls.

"Oh, Dog," giggled Cherie, "masterful linguist that you are, no guy eats pussy better than a girl, sorry, it just doesn't happen."

"I see," replied Roaddog, slowly. Then he turned to Jackie and Jane, "you two are going to have to teach this dog some new tricks."

"We can try," laughed Jane, hugging him tightly, "but it's very much a feel thing, and guys just don't have the feel."

"You can teach me; it may take a while."

"Do we have that much time?" asked Jackie.

"I don't care," smiled Jane, "just think of all the orgasms while he learns."

"Point," whispered Jackie, "what if he gets bored?"

"We'll have to think of something to keep him interested. I'm sure we'll manage it between us." Jane reached out to stroke Jackie's breast, she cupped as much of it as she could and rolled the nipple, causing Jackie to groan, Jane wriggled, still perched on Roaddog's lap. She grinned up at him and wriggled again. She turned to Jackie, "Looks like it's pony time again," she said as she slid from his lap, allowing Jackie to take her place.

"Don't I get some say in this at least?" asked Roaddog, guiding Jackie into position slowly.

"No," whispered Jackie as she dropped slowly onto his thighs.

"Damn, you feel good," he sighed.

"Looks great from over here too," said Bug.

"Sure does," agreed Cherie, climbing onto Bug's lap, "at least I can't get any more pregnant," she laughed.

Conversation died for a while until Sylvia had another shattering orgasm, after the shuddering had subsided, she snarled at Slowball, "Either get off or get off."

"There's a reason he's called Slowball," giggled Cherie.

"You're killing me, you bastard," muttered Sylvia.

"Fine," whispered Slowball, shifting into high gear, the whole caravan shaking with the pounding of his thrusts. Sylvia achieved one more orgasm just as Slowball was spent.

"Thank fuck for that," she whispered. She reached up and pulled his sweating face down, kissed him firmly, "I love you," she mumbled. In only a few more minutes the caravan stilled as all the people stopped moving. The only sound heavy breathing. Jane filled the shot glasses again and passed them around to the ones too tired to move. A silent toast was given by Roaddog. Then the shots were refilled.

"Bug," he said, "cameras?" Bug nodded and checked his phone, in only moments he had live images from the church.

"The birds are still milling around inside; don't those bastards ever sleep?" he asked.

"They always seem to be docile when they're outside in the sun," observed Slowball.

"Any pattern to their movements?" asked Roaddog.

"Looks pretty brownian to me," smiled Bug.

"What?" asked Roaddog, loudly.

"Oh my god," said Sylvia, "I've not heard that in years, and I do mean years."

"So, what does it mean?" demanded Roaddog.

"Brownian is the term used to describe the random motion of particles in a gas," she laughed, "you remember it from school Bug?"

"No," he smiled, "Hitchhiker's guide to the Galaxy," he laughed loudly.

"You're kidding?" said Sylvia, Bug only shook his head.

"So, the birds are moving randomly in the church?" asked Roaddog, Bug and Sylvia nodded.

"Was that too hard to simply say?" demanded Roaddog.

"But nothing like as much fun," replied Bug.

"Great," said Roaddog, "I think we all need to get some sleep; tomorrow could be a heavy day and it might even start real early."

"Agreed," said Slowball, the others simply nodding or starting to prepare the beds.

Roaddog, Jackie and Jane retired to the bedroom and climbed into the bed that was definitely a little small for them all. Roaddog was in the middle with an arm around each of the girls.

"You two had a good day?" he asked.

"Yes," said Jane. Jackie only smiled.

"Worried about tomorrow?" he asked.

"Some," said Jackie, "we're going to fight a demon from hell, and I don't believe in either of those things."

"But you were there when Nutter torched Kyronatha."

"I am sorry," said Jackie slowly, "I feel horror movie monster and a hole in the ground, demons and hell do not exist."

"How can you deny them?" whispered Jane.

"Darling," smiled Jackie, "it's the only way I can maintain my sanity. Demons and hell belong to crazy people, not me."

"But you're still frightened of them?"

"I'm so scared I'm pissing in my pants."

"Are you going to run away?" whispered Jane.

"Not a chance," snapped Jackie, "the people I love are in danger, so I'm staying, we may all die, but I'll be here until the end."

"That's one of the things I love about you," smiled Jane.

"What are the other things?" asked Jackie.

"Well, there's boobies," laughed Jane.

"There's definitely boobies," said Roaddog.

"Tits, is that all you ever think about?"

"Yes," replied both simultaneously. Jackie grinned and lifted up to present the relevant articles for the others to see.

"Put those away," said Roaddog.

"Why?" asked Jane.

"If things get moving in here, then Slowball might wake up again, and Sylvia will kill us all," said Roaddog, reaching up and pulling the light cord.

Darkness filled the room.

Chapter 11: Tuesday morning.

Roaddog and his friends woke up early as they normally do to catch the sunrise over the lake, as the trees across the rippling water started to turn red with the light behind them, they were joined by two new people, John and Gladys came out of their van and leaned over the railing of their veranda.

"Oh, look," said Sylvia, "sunrise and two moons as well." They all laughed.

"It's good to see new people joining in," said Roaddog.

"They certainly ain't young anymore," observed Slowball.

"That's for sure," replied Roaddog, "but I don't think they care about that."

"Why the hell should they?" asked Slowball.

"If they're there again tomorrow, we'll take them a brew," said Sylvia, "They certainly look cold."

"Good idea, that might shake a few people up," laughed Roaddog.

"That'd be fun," said Jackie. With a sudden flush of brilliant red light, the sun shone through the trees, Gladys and John were picked out in the beam, they became silhouettes against the glare, dark shapes picked out in red.

"Fuck," said Sylvia.

"What's up?" asked Bug.

"My camera is in the bag, and the shot will be gone before I can get it."

"Maybe it'll come back tomorrow," he replied.

"You know that never happens, it'll only come back when the camera is in the bag," Sylvia laughed.

"You're probably right." Bug held up his phone and shot a couple of photos, as the day brightened before them.

"They'll not be as good as my camera," said Sylvia.

"Probably not," smiled Bug, "but they're something, I was thinking maybe a backdrop for a web page."

"With two old people's asses on it?"

"Ya could put another pic over the top there, if you really have to, personally I like the shot exactly as it is."

"Why?"

"I don't know, perhaps it shows a sort of freedom that doesn't appear to exist that much these days, especially for the older folks."

"I like your thinking," smiled Sylvia. "I'm hungry, we got anything to eat?"

"Not really," laughed Jackie, "a bunch of locusts have paid us a visit, we're sort of out."

"I'm getting tired of burgers, I have a craving for cornflakes," said Sylvia.

"Me too," replied Cherie, "all this meat and carbs is just not good for a girl in my condition."

"Here's an idea," said Roaddog, "we have another coffee, then go into the village, the co-op will be open in a little while, we can get the necessary healthy breakfast options and eat at the workshop, I need to be there early, delivery expected."

As the decision was reached, they watched as John and Gladys turned from their veranda rail and walked inside their van, both waved to the watchers.

"Damn they look a lot happier than they used to," observed Jackie.

"It's sort of sweet to see such old folks still holding hands after all those years together," said Slowball.

"You're just an old softy," said Sylvia reaching up to kiss him. The kiss only lasted a few seconds, then she pushed away.

"None of that, you randy bastard, I'm still sore from last night, and there may be a demon today, you'll need your strength. So back off."

"I can't help it love, that guy has no sense at all."

"Then put some fucking pants on and imprison the dick," Sylvia laughed.

"Oh, he's that," replied Slowball, reaching for his bag and some clean clothes.

By the time they'd all had another coffee and were going outside to start up the bikes and set off to the workshop the sun was above the trees and another beautiful day was promised. John came out of his caravan, dressed for fishing he took his trolley from the storage shed at the side of the van and pulled it slowly into the road.

"Morning guys and gals," he said cheerfully.

"Hi John," said Cherie.

"You people are a fine sight first thing in the morning."

"Not so bad yourself," laughed Cherie.

"Time and gravity have exacted a serious price," smiled John.

"But you still got the balls to stand by your rail naked."

"Balls, now there's another thing, do they really need to get tangled in the knees when I walk?"

"That's only when the weather is really warm," grinned Cherie.

"You be careful," said John.

"Why?"

"Glad has a strange feeling about today," he replied.

"What do you mean?" asked Roaddog.

"She thinks something bad is going to happen today, it was the same on Sunday, but there was nothing, today is even worse, she's like a cat on hot bricks."

"What do you mean?" asked Cherie.

"She's jumpy as hell, oh, pardon my french."

"Don't worry," laughed Cherie, she turned to Roaddog, "take heed of the old lady, she knows what she's talking about."

"I agree," said Roaddog softly, "she was right about Sunday, so it looks like we are on for today, just so long as it's not too soon." He looked around for a moment then called out, "Let's hit the road." Slowball's VW rumbled into life, followed by Roaddog's victory, Bug hunched over his petrol tank trying to hear the Pan-Euro over the noise of the others.

"I hate this," he muttered as Cherie dropped onto the pillion behind him.

"Cheer up," she said, "it could be worse."

"This damned bike's too fucking quiet."

"Rig something for it then you fool," laughed Cherie as Bug started to roll forwards after Roaddog.

"I might just do that; can you imagine how this V4 will sound with open pipes?"

"You're a bad person, make it so number one," she called loudly over the noise of Slowball's trike.

They arrived at the main road and turned right, once the smoother tarmac was under their wheels and they were far enough away from the caravan site they were able to let their motors sing without worry of causing any alarm. Bug showed his displeasure by holding the throttle open in second and letting all one hundred and twenty-five horses loose. He blew past Roaddog as if the Victory was standing still, the gentle curves of the approach to the village were somewhat of a challenge for Bug as the heavy bike really didn't do too well in the curves, as he approached the thirty mile an hour sign, he had sixty miles an hour to dump, Cherie was pressed hard against his back as the brakes hit, the front suspension compressing and the rear wheel getting light. Bug made the right at the Axe and arrived at the workshop only a few seconds ahead of the others.

After they had parked the bikes inside Roaddog asked.

"What's got your knickers in a knot mate?"

"I'm sick of the quiet, I want the noise back."

"I'm sure we can work something out for ya, how you fancy an exup?"

"Huh?"

"I'm thinking an exup type valve on the pipes, with a turn out at say five thou, might even give a power boost, but it'll stress the shit out of the motor."

"Can it be done?"

"Take some work, some custom plumbing, and some electronics, but yes we can do that."

"Deal," Bug smiled, because he knew exactly what he had just bought into.

"There is a more important question right now though," said Roaddog.

"What?" asked Slowball.

"Did anyone else see a big blue car as we hit the main road?"

"I think so," replied Slowball.

"Was it called Moya?"

"Don't know," laughed Slowball.

"There was some writing on the front wing, but it was gone too fast to be sure what it said. It was some fancy sort of script," said Sylvia.

"I thought so," said Roaddog.

"So, what does it mean?" asked Jackie.

"I think that vehicle was turning into the caravan site, I can't be sure because some bad-tempered bastard was tearing the tarmac up with his damned V-four."

"And?" asked Jane.

"I think the other Roaddog just turned up at our caravan site."

"You're kidding?" grinned Slowball.

"Either that, or he's sold his damned big car to someone who hasn't taken the decals off, I clearly remember the name of that car, white letters in a fancy script on the front wings. Smaller writing on the filler flap, it said 'powered by Roaddog's farts.'"

"That's hilarious," said Sylvia.

"Yes," said Roaddog, "I noticed it while he was kissing Man-Dare goodnight."

"You believe he's here?" asked Slowball.

"Who else would drive that damned car?"

"True, but why is he here?"

"That, my friend, is a damned fine question, maybe we'll get a chance to ask him later."

"You think it's a coincidence?" asked Slowball.

"I have no idea." Roaddog turned to Bug, "Cameras?"

Bug's phone appeared in his hand and in a moment he replied.

"Birds are all settled on the outside now, warming themselves in the sun, inside is empty," said Bug.

"Right," said Roaddog, "we're not really open for business today, I'm waiting a delivery, so we need to leave one of the doors up, Slowball take the girls to the co-op to get some cereals and milk, someone wanted a healthy last meal."

"Last?" asked Sylvia.

"Gladys seems to be some sort of sensitive, she felt Kyronatha's arrival before it happened, and she had a bad feeling about today as well. So, we go into battle today, let's just hope we get things right."

"You think Father Francis and his buddies will be able to help us?" asked Bug.

"If they take the hits while we waste the bastard, that'll do for me."

"Here's hoping," said Bug.

"Okay girls," called Slowball, "we're going to the co-op for some cereals, load up. Dog you're on coffee duty," laughed the big man as he climbed into the front seat of the heavy trike. Sylvia, Jackie and Cherie, took the three remaining seats, Jane showed no interest in going with them.

"You okay, Jane?" asked Roaddog.

"Yeah," sighed Jane, "just not too interested in breakfast."

"Worried?"

"More than a little."

"Why?"

"More real monsters to face."

"What do you mean real?"

"The monsters I've met before, and that was all courtesy of you, were at least human, now we're facing demons, and I am scared."

"You and me both, but we really can't just let these assholes loose in this neighbourhood."

"I know that, intellectually, but internally I'm terrified," whispered Jane.

"Aren't we all, but we gotta fight on one more day," he smiled and hugged her.

"One more day, what does that mean?" she asked.

"There was a time in my life, a very dark time, when I decided that there was only one way to get out this life, only one course of action for a biker."

"And that is?"

"I had it planned, I had my wall chosen, enough straight to hit that wall at more than a hundred and twenty miles an hour."

"So, what stopped you?"

"When you face your wall, and you see it just waiting for you. Then you know, while you have the strength to hold that throttle open all the way in, you also have the strength to fight on one more bastard day."

"How many times did you look at that wall?"

"I have no idea, it was a few, or many, depending on how you count these things. Then I met Bone, and Bandit Queen, they saved me, but I couldn't save them."

"You made the bastards pay, and you saved me and the others, you did them proud." She reached forwards and hugged him hard to her small breasts.

"Sometimes, that's not enough," he whispered.

"For me it is more than enough, for the others it is more than enough, and for Bandit Queen it is more than enough," her tears joined his as they held each other.

A white van pulled onto the forecourt, it had a green logo on the side, Yodel it said. The driver got out with a package in his hands.

"This is going to sound a little strange, I'm looking for Road Dog."

"That'd be me," said Roaddog, "and that's Roaddog, one word."

"Great," said the guy, handing over the parcel. "Surname?"

"Just Roaddog."

"Okay by me," said the driver, handing over the cardboard box.

"Cheers," said Roaddog.

"Catch ya later," said the driver heading back to his van.

Roaddog walked into the workshop, he opened the box, and took out the contents, a quick check showed that they were exactly what he had ordered and were in perfect condition. After a couple of minutes on the bench grinder he was finally happy with the edge. He presented the stilettos to Jane and the recently returned Jackie, along with the belt clips to hold them.

"Don't forget, as soon as we see Father Francis get him to bless them, it may just help." He helped the girls fit the belt clips and left them to practice drawing their own knives for a change. He wandered into the back room, fired up the computer and checked out the miners, no hits, but they'd been trying real hard for most of the night, the batteries were very low, but the sun was shining and they were filling up quite quickly. Bug came up behind him as he was checking the cooling systems.

"Are we planning on doing any work today?" he asked.

"I'm thinking we'll wait until we've killed another demon, before we get down to the hard work," laughed Roaddog.

"I've just checked the cameras, and all those fat lazy birds are still just sitting there."

"That's sort of good, but the damned waiting is killing me."

"The girls are having fun, but any passing cop is going to see a knife fight and stop to watch at least."

"I'll get them to come inside, we don't need busybody bizzies right now," as he turned towards the door, they came inside anyway.

"You two okay?" he asked.

"We're fine," said Jane, "just getting a little tired."

"We're not used to this sort of exercise," said Jackie.

"And we're saving ourselves for later on," said Jane.

"We're gonna mince that demon," said Jackie.

"You two keep away from the bastard, I want you to tie its feet together so it falls over, then we'll chop it into little pieces."

"So, a standard slice and dice," laughed Jane, tossing her blond hair like a famous TV star.

"I'm actually hoping some high velocity lead will sort the damned thing out, but after Kyronatha, it's unlikely."

"What did Nutter say before he set that bastard alight?" asked Bug.

"I think he said something like, salt and remember."

"He wasn't shooting lead, he was shooting salt and his gun had more effect than ours, it definitely hit harder. Every round made the demon step backwards."

"The circles were drawn in salt," observed Sylvia.

"So, shoot it with salt," said Roaddog, "but it only stuns it, no penetration, I've only got one drum, I can't load salt cartridges before we face Melchion. I'm not even sure the blowback will be enough to operate the automatic, shooting lead is close to the limit, the mech is designed for the back pressure from a solid lead slug in the barrel, I can't change to salt."

"The mac-10 won't shoot salt either, so we're stuck with lead," laughed Bug.

"Jake can reload for salt in a heartbeat," said Slowball.

"I'll call him," said Roaddog. It only took moments to make the call, Jake answered on the very first ring.

"Hi Roaddog, you okay?"

"Fine Jake, we've been talking, can you reload your shotguns for rock salt?"

"Of course, but why?"

"Salt had more effect on Kyronatha than our lead."

"No sweat, I actually already have a box full of those cartridges."

"I really don't want to ask why," laughed Roaddog, "but I can guess."

"I'll load one gun with salt and the other with solids, one or the other will knock the bastard over."

"Sounds like a plan, keep an eye on those cameras, we have information that it is almost certainly today."

"I was watching when you called."

"No change?"

"Nothing, I'm beginning to wonder what those damned birds eat, they never fucking move."

"Perhaps the energy of the portal feeds them," interrupted Sylvia.

"Could be," said Jake, "I'll call before I set out."

"Good," said Roaddog, "don't get too close, just keep the fucker contained until we get there."

"You got it mate. See ya later." Jake broke the link.

"So, we'll have one or two guns to shoot salt at the bastard," said Roaddog.

"Let's hope it's enough," replied Slowball.

"Well, we have a sort of plan, all we got to do now is wait," sighed Roaddog, looking around at his friends. He glanced towards the road and whispered "Fuck." The others all looked the same way, a car was rolling slowly from the road, it slowed to a stop and the occupants stepped down. The driver was wearing shorts, t-shirt and denim cut-off, he walked towards the group a huge smile on his face.

"Hey Roaddog," he called.

"Hey Roaddog," replied Roaddog.

"Surprised?"

"Not so much. I spotted you earlier, how did you find us?"

"Leo was surprised that I knew you."

"Of course. Damn, it's a small world."

"I was amazed when I recognised Slowball's trike," laughed Mick.

"You got a caravan on the site?"

"Yes, tourer near the small pond."

"I can't believe it," said Roaddog.

"Of all the caravan parks in the world you had to roll into mine," laughed Mick, mis-quoting an old film.

"This your holiday destination?"

"Yes, ya can't believe the peace and quiet around here," smiled Mick.

"Peace and quiet," said Slowball, "when we going to see some of that?"

"What do you mean?" asked Mick.

"It's anything but, right now," said Roaddog, his phone bleeped several times in quick succession. Roaddog checked the messages quickly. Then turned to the others.

"Birds are up, Jake and Francis are on the road. Get hot people. Mick you're going to have to leave now, we're busy." Mick watched as the bikers moved into action, Bug almost ran to his bike and pulled the Mac-10 from the pannier, shoving a magazine into it and snapping the bolt, then he checked the safety and passed the weapon to Cherie, Roaddog yanked the parts of Vera from his own bike and started the assembly while Jane was locking doors and closing the big shutters. Mick ran to his car and then yelled.

"Slowball, a hand please." He waved the big man over, as he was opening doors, by the time Slowball had got to the big blue car two seats were out and sitting on the floor.

"Put them somewhere safe please," said Mick. Slowball picked one up in each hand and carried them inside as one of the shutters closed. Another seat and a large holdall were ready by the time Slowball came back.

"Lose those as well."

"What the fuck are you up to?" yelled Roaddog, "get the fuck out of here."

"You people have no idea where you are."

"What do you mean?"

"Ambulance is fifteen minutes away. Hospital thirty. You are going to war, and I now have a six-foot flat bed, and I know where the nearest hospital is. We're in, where we going?"

"Boltoffs," snapped Roaddog.

"I know it," said Mick, "I'm last in, gives me a clear run out with any wounded."

"Condition," snarled Roaddog.

"Go," replied Mick.

"If you gotta shoot the bitch in the leg, Cherie gets out."

"No worries," laughed Mick. "You people ready to roll yet?" The bikes were rolling out into the daylight and the shutter was coming down.

Jackie hopped into the pillion seat behind Roaddog, and snatched Vera from him, Cherie did the same behind Bug, Sylvia and Jane took their places behind Slowball as the heavy trike started to roll forwards. The two bikes hit the main road without even slowing down, an old audi had to jump the brakes so as not to run into them, the driver was still making hand signals as Slowball shot out in front of him, followed in a moment by Moya. Engines were howling and tyres burning as the four vehicles tore through the village, the left turn towards Skidbrooke was taken at speed by them all, though Slowball did lose a few seconds on the two bikes, and even more as they accelerated as only motorcycles can. Moya was hanging on and working hard. The bikes shot passed the entrance to the caravan site at more than a hundred miles an hour, Slowball was losing ground all the time, the bikes hit the brakes hard as a van slowed to turn right ahead of them off the road they were using, but still slowed them down more than a little. Both bikes lit up the rear wheels as Slowball closed in on them and the van pulled out of the way. There is a small bridge over a drain under the road, it's only a small bump in the road, but still it was enough for the bikes to get both wheels off the ground at the speed they were travelling. The bikes had to slow for the left hander, Bug positioned himself to the right and turned in early, he hit the apex with full power on the Pan-Euro, as Roaddog ran wide Bug blew through on his left, the power of the Honda was far superior to the Victory, but as it hit the red band the torque of the Victory began to show, the two were side by side as they jinked through the small turns, then the right at South Farm came up, Roaddog had the inside line, though he knew he was going to run well wide at this speed, he hoped that Bug would back out, or the four of them would die in the trees beside the farm. As the pair tore through the righthander, the dust on the road making the tyres skitter and slide, a small green quad was trying to pull out, Jake stopped suddenly, Mary almost slid out of the rear seat, and flailed as she attempted, successfully to retain her position. Jake decided there was enough gap, so he gunned the little four stroke and pulled out in front of Slowball, who was still slowing down for the bend, by the time Slowball had fought the heavy trike through the righthander Jake was a good fifty yards ahead, Mick's big blue car wallowed through the bend and followed only a few feet behind Slowball. As Roaddog approached the left turn towards the church the hedges moved back from the road, giving a large grass verge, and a distant view of the church appeared, above it there was a dark cloud that circled almost like the funnel of a tornado but with none of the destructive energy, though the destruction was waiting at the base. Roaddog and Bug shot down the driveway, and parked alongside the scout bus, as they unloaded from the motorcycles Roaddog, and Bug took the guns from the girls and set off towards the lynch gate. Roaddog paused. He turned to Cherie, "If things get dicey, you run, you've got a young 'un to think about, get in Mick's car and high tail it, you hear?"

"I hear," muttered Cherie.

"For a change," said Bug, "do as you're fucking told," he leaned in and kissed her, then followed Roaddog and Jackie through the gate. Slowball reversed his trike into the parking area, but Jake left his quad in the field, Mick's heavy car rolled backwards down the drive and stopped just outside the entrance, the tailgate of the Espace lifted and from somewhere beneath the floor came a large green box. Jake and Mary walked in through the gate and caught up with the others.

"Has the demon turned up yet?" asked Roaddog, looking straight at Father Francis.

"Not yet, we're working on containment right now, we got here before the birds even knew he was coming."

"How did you manage that?"

"Courtesy of Ava," he pointed to the woman dressed in a white robe covered in strange symbols standing next to him.

"Hi Ava," said Roaddog, "maybe you should have stayed at home."

"Maybe I should have been here earlier, but no, the damned council voted for Fintan. I hear you killed him."

"I did, he wanted to sacrifice two children, that was not acceptable."

"You killed him here on consecrated ground?"

"See that column," Roaddog pointed at a column that was just in view from where they were standing, "The brown stain is his blood, I cut him in two with Vera." He lifted the thompson, so Ava would understand the word Vera.

"Fintan should never have been here," she said, "he goaded you into killing him?"

"I suppose you could look at it like that, I told him he had to earn his life, he failed, and threatened the children again."

"His arguments for being here were sort of reasonable, which is why the council went for them, but they were unaware of the sort of people that were going to be here. They'd never have sanctioned his presence if they knew hotheads such as you were going to be here."

"Lady," snarled Roaddog, "you're doing a good job of walking down his path."

"I could never walk his path," she said calmly, then she turned to the priest. "Fintan was a necromancer."

"Fuck," whispered Francis.

"Yeah," said Ava, "killed near an open portal, was the demon dead?"

"Kyronatha was dead," said Roaddog, "Fintan wanted to kill the children to close the portal."

"Was he really a necromancer?" asked Father Francis, his voice quaking.

"Yes," replied Ava, "rare as such things are, he was one. He convinced the council that his unique powers could contain the demons and close the portal."

"You sound sceptical?" asked Francis.

"Do we really have time for all this?" interrupted Roaddog.

"No," said Ava, "let's get the wards set, and see if we can contain Melchion, then we can look to taking him apart."

"That sounds like the voice of experience?" asked Roaddog.

"No, just reading between different lines from the good father."

"What can we do?" asked Roaddog.

"Stay out of the way," laughed Ava.

"Fine," smiled Roaddog, "once your barriers are up and Melchion is imprisoned can we shoot through the force fields?"

"Force fields?" laughed Ava, "I suppose not a bad analogy, yes, your bullets should go through without affecting the wards.

"What about salt?"

"No, salt would destroy the conduction properties of the wards, why salt?"

"An old friend used it to good effect against Kyronatha."

"I have heard that salt can affect demons but never actually seen it in action," said Ava.

"Well, if we can't stop Melchion with the barriers up, then you're going to find out. If we have to let him out, I want him out of this door and into the field outside, we're going to need some space to deal with him."

"Fine," said Ava, she placed her staff upright in the doorway, and whispered something, that sounded to Roaddog almost like the words from a song, one he could almost remember, but it just wouldn't come to the fore. The quartz in the head of her staff flashed deep red and streamers of red light passed slowly outwards to fill the doorway. Once the light settled in place, she removed the staff and the barrier of swirling red and pink light stayed in place.

"That is the strongest forbidding you will find anywhere; I suggest you don't touch it."

"What about the windows?" asked Roaddog, looking at the open window frames, most had no glass at all, and those that did only a fragment or two.

"We don't need to worry about the windows," said Father Francis, "Melchion is not much of a climber."

"Bastard must weigh about two tonnes," said Ava, "he's exceptionally dense."

"Do you mean stupid?" asked Roaddog.

"No, high mass in a small space."

From somewhere underground came a heavy booming sound,

"He's almost here," shouted Ava, "brace your wards." Through the opposite door of the church she could see the rabbi and the imam praying quickly, their doorway was partially obscured by blue veins of light. The Buddhist monk was bracing the wooden wall that replaced the west door of the church. The ground beneath their feet started to shake with heavy foot falls.

"How big is this mother?" demanded Roaddog, a shrug was all he got by way of reply, Father Francis was far too busy strengthening the magic holding the doorway. Roaddog turned to Jake, "you go round the other side, me and Bug will take this side, remember no salt, and watch what's in the back of your field of fire." Jake nodded and took Mary with him as he ran round the west end of the church, he took up position so that he was shooting through a very damaged window, his field of fire covered most of the church, without endangering the people by the doors. Roaddog and Bug moved to the other window beside the west door. The shaking of the ground became louder, a slow steady beat of heavy foot falls, ever nearer.

"Where is that mother?" whispered Roaddog, as he slid the safety off Vera. He could see the opening in the floor, and the narrow stairway down into the darkness beneath. Roaddog glanced to the left, he could see the Imam through the doorway, the man was sweating profusely and chanting rapidly, but his words were now inaudible, the noise of the approaching demon was so loud that nothing else could be heard. A pair of pointed horns appeared from the blackness, they were pointing straight up and about a foot apart, they were ribbed and black. With the next rising step the head of the demon appeared, almost exactly as the Minotaur that Roaddog was expecting, wide spaced, dark eyes moving slowly around, pausing for a moment when they caught Roaddog's eyes, before moving on. Another step, shoulders and upper chest came into view, pushing the stones of the floor even further apart, another booming step and narrower hips became visible, then thighs, knees, and finally the wide hooves of a heavy horse came stamping onto the uneven stones of the floor. Melchion threw back its head and roared, a deep throated howl that shook the stones of the church and made the ears of the people hurt. The deafening noise was cut short by a loud crack, a ring of smoke rolled slowly towards Melchion to be shattered by the following shot from Jakes twelve bore. The heavy solid slugs hit Melchion square in the chest, the demon took half a step backwards when the first one hit, but barely settled when the second struck only an inch away from the first. There was a pause while Jake swapped guns with Mary. Roaddog leaned hard against the Thompson, with the stock pulled into his shoulder, sighting along the barrel he let Vera loose. Aiming for the eyes he tracked the demon as it moved towards the south door, it appeared to be only slightly disturbed by the lead shot splattering its head. The red light of Ava's warding turned the demon away, as it turned towards the north Roaddog switched target, he aimed for the joint just above the hoof, the demon was disturbed by the impact of so much lead against the fetlock joint that it turned towards Roaddog, Melchion howled again. Roaddog noticed that even though its head was shaped like a bull, the teeth and mouth were much more like that of a man. It was into this screaming maw that Bug fired a whole magazine of high velocity forty-five calibre slugs. The scream choked and died, dark blood poured from the damaged mouth and the demon charged, it crashed into the wall in front of Roaddog and Bug, but the wall held, the huge sword plunged through the window seeking Roaddog's heart, Roaddog had stepped to the side and the sword couldn't reach him, Melchion reached his sword arm through the narrow window sweeping from side to side, Roaddog stayed just out of reach, and started to shoot directly at the demons eye, from such close range it was almost impossible for Roaddog to miss, blast after blast of lead shot struck the demon in the side of the head, suddenly the eye burst open, scattering sticky black ichor over the demons face, it howled and backed away, more black blood poured from its mouth. Melchion raised its sword and slashed at the four-inch-wide stone mullion, shattering it. A heavy chunk of stone caught Bug in the head as it fell, knocking him to the ground, Roaddog stepped across his fallen friend and sent another barrage of lead towards the demon's head. Slowball rushed forwards and dragged the unconscious Bug from beneath Roaddog's legs, he passed Bug over to Jackie and Jane, then recovered the magazines from his belt, Cherie helped the other two prop Bug up against a tall cross shaped headstone. The small man's eyes flickered open a few times, then finally stayed that way.

"You okay?" asked Cherie. Bug looked up into her concerned eyes, the other two girls had returned to the window where Roaddog was still spraying Melchion with the occasional burst of shotgun pellets. Slowball had a fresh clip in the Mac-10, looking for an opportunity to put it to good effect. The real problem was that the hide of the demon was as hard as a rhino's. Roaddog stepped back from the window and passed Vera to Jackie, he stepped back to the window with a stiletto in each hand. He waved a blade at the demon and saw its remaining eye flash yellow. Roaddog smiled to himself and waited, he didn't have to wait long, the demon lunged with its sword, Roaddog stepped a little to the side as the sword flashed past him and he plunged a knife into the demon's forearm. The twelve-inch blade sank into the arm all the way to the hilt. The demon froze for an instant then screamed. Roaddog looked it in the face and noticed that the eye he had destroyed was slowly recovering.

"Jackie," he shouted, "shoot that eye out again." Jackie grinned and leaned in close to the window as Roaddog pulled on the arm, holding the demon as still as he could. Jackie took careful aim and then fired four quick rounds mincing the eye again. Roaddog grinned as the demon writhed, hopefully in pain, he knew that he was going to be in real danger when he released the arm. Slowball reached across and took Melchion's wrist in his hand and pulled backwards. Roaddog nodded at his friend, then started to saw the stiletto backwards and forwards, lengthening the slit in the demon's arm, black blood started to pour from the wound, Roaddog could see the tension building up in Slowball's muscles, Melchion was pulling hard now to get away from the pain. There was a loud boom from across the church and the demon lurched to Roaddog's right as a heavy solid slug hit it in the chest. Roaddog and Slowball picked that surge of motion to release the wrist and yank the knife from the arm. Melchion staggered backwards into the church, his sword falling from his hand. Roaddog grinned as he retrieved the demon's weapon, he glanced at his own knife, covered in black steaming ichor, and dropped it.

"We need to get this bastard out in the open," he yelled. He nodded to Jackie to precede him, she moved away from the window and followed the broken path towards the south door. Father Francis stared in disbelief at the sword Roaddog was carrying.

"You're kidding," he exclaimed. Roaddog simply raised his eyebrows and smiled.

"Ava," he said, "be ready to drop the shield and run." Looking through the doorway he caught Jake's eye, "We're going to take him outside, into the open where we can work on him properly. Be ready to switch to salt, we don't want people taking those heavy slugs," he called. Jake nodded and started moving around the west end of the church.

"You two hold that door," yelled Roaddog looking at the Rabbi and the Imam, "bastard has to come this way." From the motion of the two it was difficult to see if they had heard him, until the Rabbi raised a thumb, he had no wish to disturb the prayers that were securing the door against the demon. The imam's petitions to Allah left him no freedom to respond.

"Ava," said Roaddog, "you ready?" The only answer he got was a small nod.

"Hey, Melchion," shouted Roaddog. "Look at what I got, I have your blade, you want it ass, you gotta catch me." The demon turned to him and ran hard against the barrier. Melchion bounced off and staggered backwards.

"Oh," said Roaddog, "poor pussy, can't get out?" he turned to Ava, "Go now." He whispered. Ava rolled to her feet and moved away from the doorway, the faint red traceries vanished as she moved behind the large yew tree just outside the door, she dragged Father Francis with her. Melchion stamped towards the doorway, as he approached Roaddog his surprise was obvious, he had expected a forbidding that didn't exist, he stepped into the open air with a look of astonishment.

"What's up ass?" demanded Roaddog waving the demon's sword in front of his face. "I got your blade, what you got?" Roaddog grinned stepping backwards all the time, along the path towards the lynch gate, Jackie to one side, Slowball to the other, and Jane behind him. Each step Melchion followed, a glance showed Roaddog that Bug was recovered and following, but not too close.

"Talk to me ass," said Roaddog as Jane opened the gate behind him, Melchion's hooves booming on the tarmac of the path. "You got nothing to say?" asked Roaddog.

Melchion howled, his mouth still bubbling with black blood from the damage done by the Mac-10. Black blood spewing into the air ahead of him. Roaddog held for a moment while Jackie, Jane and Slowball, went through the lynch gate ahead of him, or more accurately, behind him, as he was facing the demon. Looking over the shoulders of the demon Roaddog saw the clerics following behind, he smiled to himself, 'as normal,' he thought. Every time the demon's claws slashed at him the sword was in their way, as they stepped out into the sunlight, the swirling column of birds overhead, Roaddog pushed backwards quickly, opening some space between himself and the demon. He didn't take is eyes off Melchion for a moment, when the demon rushed forwards, he pointed the sword straight at its chest, hoping for a heart in there somewhere. The sword point slid sideways off the heavy musculature of the demon's chest, Jackie moved to her right to give herself an angle, and opened fire again, high speed lead impacting the side of the demon's head caused its rush to stall for a moment, Roaddog's backwards path opened more space between himself and the demon. Jackie had to stop shooting when Melchion moved so that Slowball was behind it. Melchion's only functional eye flashed yellow again, its new target was Jackie. A none too subtle change came over the demon, a huge phallus rose from the junction of its thighs. Roaddog took the sword in both hands, and screamed, rushing towards the monster he slashed at the head, the impact of the sword shocked both his hands and forearms, it shook the demon a little as Roaddog moved between it and the woman. Roaddog slashed at the head again, the curved horns took the blow with no discernible damage, the demons sweeping arm brushed Roaddog aside as if he were nothing, then it rushed towards Jackie, she stood her ground and raised Vera to her shoulder, Slowball dropped to the ground, and Vera started to sing her own particular song, a song of death, before Melchion closed the distance to Jackie its right eye had been destroyed, now it was blind, but still it came on, Jackie turned and ran between the hedge and the open tail gate of Mick's car, out into the open field in front of the church. Roaddog slashed at the demon's legs and caused it to stumble, though he did little damage, a shallow cut that closed as the demon regained its balance. Melchion cast around looking for its target. Almost as if by scent it turned towards Jackie, as it moved into the open Jackie stopped, thirty feet separating them, she paused to bring Vera to bear again, there was a loud boom, which caused most to duck, Melchion staggered as it took two full loads of rock salt into the back, a huge shallow wound opened in the demons back, but it was short lived, Jake had passed the shotgun off to his wife and taken the reloaded one from her, as he moved towards the demon, trying to keep an angle so that Jackie wouldn't take any harm, Mary broke the gun and reloaded it.

"Hold fire," yelled Roaddog, he had noticed Sylvia moving forwards.

"Come on asshole," shouted Jackie, "I'm here, come get me." The blind demon moved towards the sound of her voice, Sylvia threw the heavy strap she was carrying across the demon's path, Jane rushed in and picked up the other end, the two moved behind the demon and crossed quickly pulling the strap tight around it's legs, suddenly it couldn't move at all, it toppled face first onto the grass.

"Tie that off," yelled Roaddog, Jane passed her end of the strap under the other then ran away from Sylvia, the single knot raced along the strap until it met the demon's legs, with the two women pulling equally on the straps this was not going to let the demon regain its feet. Melchion was attempting to crawl towards Jackie, it's legs useless, but it's claws gouging deep grooves in the grass. Roaddog stood over the struggling demon and raised its own sword above his head, with a brutal two-handed blow he brought the sword down on the demons back, it made little impression in the bulging shoulders, a shallow cut that closed in moments.

"Now what?" asked Slowball.

"Jake," called Roaddog, "hit the bastard in the arm." Jake shrugged and fired both barrels at the demon's right arm, the rock salt stripped the skin from the upper arm and Roaddog's sword slashed into it before it could heal. The arm was severed, black blood poured sluggishly from the open wound, like hot bitumen. The shoulder healed and the bleeding stopped.

"Other shoulder," commanded Roaddog, in a moment the demon was without arms. Roaddog held the sword in both hands point down into the demons back. He glanced at Jake and nodded, both barrels boomed and the demon was momentarily obscured by smoke and dust, Roaddog drove the sword down-wards with all his weight behind it, but failed to make any sort of penetration at all, the skin grew back very quickly it seemed to be trying to envelop the sword, but Roaddog snatched it away.

"I think this is our turn now," said Father Francis moving closer. He stood over the demon, he was muttering quietly in Latin, he poured some liquid from a flask onto the demon, it writhed and smoked, it's skin dissolving, exposing twisting pink musculature underneath, Ava stepped up, and plunged her staff into the demon. The bronze heel driven straight into the centre of the demon's back. The scream from Melchion was drowned by the noise of the birds circling overhead, a plume of red fire leapt from the crystal in Ava's staff, up into the sky it tore, burning any bird unlucky enough to be within its ravening fire. The demon died, the fire from Ava's staff failed, and the sound of the bird's wings faltered, and stopped. The birds started to fall from the sky, on folded wings they dropped towards the fallen demon.

"Run," screamed Ava, dragging Father Francis away from the body. Jake looked up and automatically fired both barrels up into the flock of grey birds. The effect of the rock salt loads was minimal at best. Jackie turned Vera upwards and squeezed the trigger, the stuttering roar of the Thompson had more effect, birds were falling all around them, Roaddog stood with her, Melchion's sword ready to slash at any that managed to get too close, though none did. Soon the flock was on the ground and fighting amongst themselves for the flesh of the demon.

"Come on love," shouted Roaddog, "They're no danger to us." Jackie still held Vera on the flock of birds, the thunder of Vera's voice stopped with a final click. Jackie looked down at the gun as if it had betrayed her.

Roaddog engulfed her in his strong arms and pulled her away from the feasting birds, together they walked towards the lynch gate, where the others had gathered.

Jackie looked up into his concerned eyes, tears flowing freely down her cheeks.

"Fuck," she whispered, "I think I hate those birds more than Bug."

"Speaking of the short guy," replied Roaddog softly, before calling out, "Hey Bug, you okay?"

"Still shaky," said Bug from his seat within the lynch gate. "Knees are a bit wobbly, and my fucking head hurts."

"It didn't look like you got such a heavy hit," said Slowball.

"You go pick up that chunk of rock," snarled Cherie, "gotta be a hundred pounds."

"They don't make windows like they used to," smiled Slowball. Roaddog surveyed the survivors, as Jane came to join him and Jackie, in a gentle three-way hug.

"Well, that went better than I could have hoped," he said.

"That's for sure," replied Father Francis.

"You expected something worse?" asked Ava.

"Yes," laughed Father Francis, "these people seemed to be charmed, I can't believe that they just killed Melchion."

"We didn't kill him," snapped Roaddog, "you did."

"You'd have found a way. What was your next thought?"

"To be honest," laughed Roaddog, "given the damage caused by shooting the ass in the mouth, I'd have stuck a twelve down his throat and unloaded two barrels of salt, if that didn't work then two barrels of solids, after that, I don't know, oh yes, tie his feet to a tree and his head to a heavy vehicle, Moya looks good, drive away, end of demon."

"Any or all of those could have worked," replied Ava, "but my staff drained his power and killed many of his birds."

"That's for sure," laughed Roaddog, "and Jackie here emptied Vera, that took many more of those feathered grey bastards. Now tell me, are there any less birds here now?"

They all looked around as the birds finished their meal and took to the wing, the lynch gate was covered as were most of the gravestones in the church yard, and the roof and tower also had a good collection as well.

"Fuck, whispered Bug, "there's even more of them."

"And we've got enough feathers to make duvets for all the beds in all the caravans in Mablethorpe," laughed Roaddog, looking pointedly at the drifts of feathers collecting under the hedges around the graveyard, "but no corpses."

"I'll deal with the bones," said Father Francis, "we can't let those fall into the wrong hands."

"That's for sure," whispered Ava, following the priest as he went to collect the scattered remains. He picked them up carefully and collected them within the depression created by raising the hem of his cassock. The bones were certainly heavy, and the horns even more so, he was struggling back towards his scout bus when Jackie laughed loudly.

"Damn Francis, you've got real old man's knees."

"Thanks for that," smiled Francis, "not many get to see my legs, you are honoured."

Francis returned from the rear of his van, with his spindly legs covered, he looked to the clerics. "Everyone okay?" he asked. He got nods from all.

"I'm actually feeling very good just now," said Ava.

"Watch that," said Francis quietly, "that's stolen demon energy, don't get hooked on it."

"I'll be fine, I'm used to all sorts of power surges, from all sorts of sources," smiled Ava.

"I'm not surprised," said Francis.

"What's next?" asked Roaddog.

"I've felt no reset yet," observed Slowball.

"Well, it looks like I'm going to be busy for a while," said Jake, a small smile on his face.

"Why?" asked Roaddog.

"Am I mistaken, or did Jackie just run Vera dry?"

"That is true," laughed Jackie.

"Something I never thought would happen," said Roaddog.

"I'll get to reloading as soon as I get home," said Jake, walking out into the field again. Jackie pushed away from Roaddog and followed him, together they started to collect the spent cartridge cases. Roaddog picked up the strap that had been used to trip the demon and dropped it into his panniers. Very soon the only evidence was drifts of feathers, and a few scars in the turf of the field, along with a broken mullion on one of the church windows.

"Bug, you need a ride to hospital?" asked Mick gently.

"No man, I've had worse, no real black out, just wobbly, I'll be fine."

"Can you ride?"

"Fuck," laughed Slowball, "little bastard can ride a bike when he can't stand up."

"Up yours," grinned Bug.

"What's next?" asked Roaddog, looking straight at Father Francis.

"Still waiting for a reset," replied Francis. Then the ground flinched beneath them. Ava strode firmly into the church, leaving the others in the sunlight. When she returned her look was grim to say the least.

"What we got next?" asked Father Francis.

"Fuck," said Ava.

"Tell us," said Roaddog.

"Fintan."

Chapter 12: Tuesday

"Well, that was interesting," said Mick, "not what I expected at all."

"You didn't have to come," said Roaddog.

"But I did, this is a dangerous place to get injured, now the real question is what the fuck is going on?"

"It's sort of complicated," laughed Roaddog.

"Isn't everything?" smiled Mick.

"Michael," called Jackie, from the passenger seat of Moya, "F fifteens inbound to Donna."

"Shit," said Mick, "Sorry Roaddog, I gotta go, can't miss those."

"What the fuck are fifteens?" asked Roaddog,

"You'll hear them in a bit, you be in the workshop later?"

"Probably, or the Axe."

"Good, we'll catch up in a bit." Mick turned and ran to his car, dropping the tail gate and jumping into the driver's seat, in a moment the big blue car was driving away from the church.

"What's lit a fire under him?" asked Slowball.

"No idea, Jackie said something about fifteens into Donna, didn't mean anything to me. Let's check out the inside."

"Okay," replied Slowball, then he turned to Bug. "How you doing Bug?"

"I'm fine, just a bit wobbly," he joined them as they walked towards the lynch gate. "Fuck," he mumbled, "I hate those birds even more now."

"At least they cleaned up some of the mess," said Roaddog.

"At least they're relaxed now they've eaten a demon," pointed out Slowball.

"The bastards still give me the willies," said Bug, following the other two into the church.

Roaddog paused once he was inside to check out the opening in the floor.

"Am I mistaken or is that bigger now?" he asked.

"Could be," replied Slowball, "not much, but a little maybe."

"And Fintan is coming next?" said Roaddog, as the trio approached the boarded up west door. Embossed into the wooden surface was an image of Fintan, though it looked more than a little strange.

"He don't look entirely human," said Bug.

"He shouldn't," replied Roaddog, "I cut him in two with Vera."

"He's not going to appear in the fathers' books, is he?" asked Slowball.

"No," said Roaddog, "this one is going to be a complete surprise."

"Perhaps Ava will know something," said Bug.

"Let's find out," said Roaddog turning away from the wooden wall. When they got to the gate Jake and Mary were just about to climb onto their quad.

"You guys leaving?" asked Roaddog.

"Yes," said Jake, "I got a lot of reloading to do, I'll catch up with you later at the workshop, okay?"

"Or the Axe. Thanks for your help today, it was greatly appreciated."

"No problem, let me know if there are any special ammunition requirements for this next one," laughed Jake, swinging his leg over the quad and thumbing the starter. Mary climbed up behind him, "If you feel like something proper to drink, drop by, anytime," she said.

"We may drop in later," laughed Roaddog.

"Always welcome, just keep my man alive."

"We'll do everything we can," said Roaddog as Jake thumbed the throttle and the little four-by turned towards the church driveway.

Roaddog looked at Jackie standing there in the morning sunlight, the stock of Vera propped against her hip, her right hand ready on the trigger.

"You, okay?" he asked.

"Fine," said Jackie, then she turned to Jane, "you okay?"

"I'm getting there," smiled Jane, "not quite peeing in my pants, but feeling better about things." Roaddog looked over at the clerics all standing by the minibus, there seemed to be some sort of intense discussion going on. He walked over.

"Thanks for your help today," he said, "have you any idea how we can deal with your ex-friend."

"Not what I'd call a friend," said Father Francis.

"The council really fucked up there," said Ava, "I wonder if one of their seers had something to do with it."

"Could they do that?" asked the Buddhist Phurba.

"It's possible that the testimony of a seer may have influenced the council," said Ava.

"To what end?" asked Abraham the Rabbi.

"It could be that Fintan actually wanted to be here and wanted to die."

"What sort of person would do that?" asked Abraham.

"A necromancer," snorted Ava.

"And what does that actually mean?" asked Roaddog.

"He has power over the dead," replied Ava.

"Dead is dead," said Roaddog.

"Not always, and Fintan is coming back."

"If he comes back, what sort of physical form will he have?"

"I can't be sure, he could be something like what you would call a ghost, or he could be completely solid, or he could take another form entirely."

"You don't have a clue?"

"Not a one, I have no experience of this sort of thing, and the only one that I know of you cut in half with a shotgun," Ava said with a small smile.

"Ah," grinned Roaddog, "he had it coming. If he comes back in any sort of solid form, we have shotguns, knives and a demonic sword. We'll find some way to slice and dice the bastard, spectres I have no idea."

"Well," laughed Father Francis, "I remember something about a bell, a book and a candle."

"That's Hollywood garbage," snapped Ava.

"I thought it was based on some catholic ritual?" asked Slowball.

"And what the fuck do they know about the spectral?"

"I've no idea," replied Slowball.

"Fuck all, that's what they know, any real knowledge has been suppressed for hundreds of years. All they know is that women are witches."

"That's a little unfair," said Father Francis.

"No, it's not," said Ava, "almost all bishops and cardinals know about witches, and only a very select few, know about all the other things out there."

"That is I suppose true."

"So how is it that a simple parish priest with no real rank has been educated enough to watch this portal?" asked Ava with a wicked grin.

"This place is known to have a high incidence of strange happenings, and there are some historical references to a portal opening here."

"But why you? What special training do you have?"

"Well, none really, but I have many reference books that aren't generally available."

"So, the bishop said, 'Here's some information, go watch that place and let us know what happens.' Is that right?"

"Pretty much," replied Father Francis, with a frown.

"What do you reckon Roaddog?" asked Ava.

"They set him up to fail."

"I agree," Ava turned back to the priest. "What happened when you told the bishop that demons were appearing?"

"He said, 'do what you can and keep us informed.'"

"So, nothing?" asked Ava.

"I suppose."

"No promises of help, no mobilisation of the trained demon fighters, no suggestions of how to close this portal?"

"No, just let us know."

"What about you three?" she asked looking at the other clerics.

"I was sent to support the father," said Rabbi Abraham.

"Same for me," said Imam Mohammed, "the demons cannot prevail against the truly faithful."

"I am here to help in any way I can," said Phurba, "if I can help people along the path to enlightenment then so much the better, I believe that my next incarnation will bring me closer to nirvana."

"So, you've come here to die?" snorted Ava.

"If you see death as the end, then that is how you see it."

"Well," said Ava quietly, she glanced at Roaddog for an instant then turned to face the tower of the church, she covered her eyes with both hands, then spread her arms, hands flat and pointing upwards towards the sky, her voice was loud and firm. "I am Avalon, of the line of Avalon, if I am the last of my line then so be it. I am here to fight the demons, and close this portal, any that stand in my way will die. The line of Avalon reaches back into the mists of antiquity, and forwards into the undiscovered country, the line of Avalon will always prevail." She held the cruciform pose for a long moment, then let her arms drop to her sides. She turned to Roaddog. "Get me the fuck out of this place." Roaddog looked into her eyes and made instant decisions.

"Dragonriders roll," he shouted. Roaddog mounted his motorcycle and fired the V-twin, Jackie dropped into the pillion seat, with Vera in her right hand, stock resting on her right thigh. Cherie dropped into the seat behind Bug, the mac-10 had no stock, so it rested across her thighs. Slowball started the VW as Jane and Sylvia took their places behind him; Avalon took the centre seat in the back row. Seeing everyone mounted Roaddog snapped the throttle open, and the victory howled into the red band, Slowball's VW made a similar racket, and Bug tried his best, but the Pan-Euro was just way too civilised. Roaddog gave Father Francis a significant look then lowered the revs and slid the clutch, rolling along the driveway away from the church, followed by the almost silent Bug, and the raucous Slowball.

The return to the workshop was much more sedate than the race to the church had been earlier. As soon as they stopped Roaddog checked his phone, there was a message from Father Francis, 'keep her safe, we are going to need her.' Once the passengers were unloaded Slowball went straight to the bar and pulled out some chilled bottles of beer, he passed them around, though he specifically excluded Bug.

"What the fuck?" demanded the small man.

"No beer, not until we're sure you don't have some sort of concussion," said Jackie.

"When will that be?" asked Bug.

"How's the head?"

"Head's fine now, my neck hurts some though."

"Give it another hour," smiled Jackie, "just to be sure."

"Okay," mumbled Bug, knowing that he didn't have concussion, and equally that his friends were worried about him, so he made do with a drink of water.

"Okay Avalon," said Roaddog, "what was that display all about?"

"Sometimes the menfolk just piss me off."

"What do you mean?"

"Where are they now?"

"Presumably they'd be back at Father Francis's place by now."

"Yes, and they'll be slapping each other on the back, telling each other how they beat a demon. Do you know what would have happened if Melchion had headed for the other door?"

"No."

"He'd have walked through their barrier like it wasn't there, he'd have ripped their hearts out, and fed the rest to the birds."

"They're that weak?"

"Oh yes, Melchion simply ignored them. He knew where the biggest threat was."

"That was you?"

"No, the non-believers are the greatest threat to the demons."

"I don't understand."

"Your lack of belief gives you the strength to defeat them, believers always have the fear that they cannot win."

"Even you?"

"Even me, when Melchion came up out of the ground, I damn near wet myself," Avalon looked away.

"But you still held it together," Roaddog smiled.

"Not by so damned much, if you guys hadn't been there, I'd have been running and screaming."

"I don't believe it."

"Without the damage you did to him, my forbidding would not have held for more than a moment."

"You don't believe in your own power?"

"Sometimes no, I've never faced a demon before, almost no one alive today has."

"Could Fintan's return be even worse?"

"It's entirely possible, it very much depends on how much of him is still left."

"What do you mean?"

"He has died, as a necromancer he'll be able to hold himself together to some extent, but how much of the human will return is almost anybody's guess."

"And we don't even know if he's going to be solid enough to shoot?"

"Very true."

"But if he's a ghost, not that I believe in such things, what harm can he do?"

"Oh, you'd be surprised, even in spectral form he can affect the living, and as a necromancer, he can affect the dead."

"Graveyard, many dead," muttered Roaddog.

"Just so, whether he'll be able to raise them is another matter, most of them have been dead a long time."

"Does that make a difference?"

"Yes, they're more difficult to raise."

"Another question, how do we kill the dead?"

"One of your lovely young ladies called it, slice and dice, chop them into pieces so that they no longer can function."

"How many will he be able to raise at once?"

"I can't tell, but any raised will be solid, so shotguns should work well with them."

"Here's a plan then," smiled Roaddog, "the others take on the raised, you, the other clerics, and I take on Fintan."

"It's somewhere to start," laughed Avalon. They each raised a beer and clinked the bottles together to seal the plan.

There was a huge roaring sound that was obviously distant, but extremely loud. Roaddog snapped his head round and shouted to Bug.

"Cameras." Bug's phone was already in hand, another rumbling roar filled the air before Bug called back.

"Birds are all settled, no action at the church."

"Then what the fuck is that noise?" A new noise came to them, not the roaring but still loud, the smoother sound of jet engines working hard, the muted crackle of afterburners as they accelerated rapidly.

"Fifteens," laughed Slowball.

"Make sense," shouted Roaddog.

"F fifteens," replied Slowball as a pair of fighter jets shot over their heads at about three hundred miles an hour. "Mick's wife said something about Donna, so there's an air force bombing range nearby, and those fighters are practising."

"Do you think they'd lend us a couple?" asked Bug. "Those big canons will make a real mess of anything in the way."

"Can you fly one?" asked Jane.

"No, but I could try," laughed Bug. They all ducked as the fighters made another run at the targets.

"How far away is that range?" asked Roaddog, Bug was already looking for it.

"Less than two miles away, why?"

"I don't know, fasten a demon to the target and let the pilots finish it off."

"It's a thought," laughed Avalon, "but it's not going to be easy, and there's no certainty when or even if the pilots will fire."

"Hey," said Roaddog, "a guy is entitled to a dream."

"That would be better," said Avalon, "but you've now got a capture, transport and restrain. Far too many ways for that to go wrong."

"It does give me an idea," said Roaddog, "won't do for a spook though, maybe the next one."

"What idea?" asked Avalon.

"No, I'll need to think it through some more, maybe we'll work it out, maybe not."

"Fine, keep your secrets," she laughed.

"You're a fine one for secrets, I don't believe that Francis knew your full name."

"I have guarded the secret of my lineage quite jealously; my family goes back centuries."

"Francis was definitely shocked."

"I would have thought he actually knew, but apparently that was not so."

"How much contact does he have with your council?"

"I'm not sure, he has a sort of problem talking to us, he struggles with the fact that our religions where around long before his."

"So were so many," laughed Roaddog.

"Yes, but his book says that his god created it all, then wasn't the boss for a long time, all these other religions sprang up all over the world. This is something he struggles to get his head round, but not my problem." She smiled and looked around as two jet aircraft went overhead; the sound of the engines was so loud it almost hurt.

"Damn, they were low," declared Roaddog.

"They look like fun though," said Jane, as she walked towards the two, a stiletto in each hand.

"Did you get the father to bless those?" asked Roaddog.

"Yes, it only took him a moment, and a sprinkle of holy water."

"You comfortable with them now?"

"Sort of, they fit nicely in the hand and I'm getting quicker at the draw."

"What about Jackie?"

"She's sort of taken with Vera," laughed Jane looking across at Jackie who was sitting on one of the couches with Vera in her lap and a beer in her left hand.

"Vera's almost useless until Jake gets here with the reloads, and I don't expect that to be any time soon, there's a lot of delicate work in reloading shot gun cartridges."

"And he's got a lot to do," laughed Jane, turning away and going to where Jackie was sitting. She picked up Vera and sat in the place now empty. She kissed Jackie.

"You okay love?" asked Jane.

"I'm fine, but scared, you know, I was hoping for a sort of peaceful life here in the country, but now we got demons."

"We'll get that portal closed, and things will settle down."

"Are you thinking happily ever after time?" giggled Jackie.

"Who can tell? This seems like a nice place, nice people, well, mostly."

"Fintan wasn't nice, and demons aren't nice, but all the people we have met have been nice."

"There could be a reason for that," replied Jane quietly.

"Go on."

"Roaddog is an impressive guy, isn't he?" she glanced across at the man who was still standing talking quietly with Avalon.

"And?" Jackie frowned.

"With Slowball standing on one side of him and the psycho Bug on the other, what citizen in their right mind is going to give them grief?"

"I do see what you mean, but Jake wasn't afraid of us."

"Jake was more afraid of what was killing his cows."

"I suppose, but you mean that people are nice to us because they are frightened?"

"That's most likely how it starts, not frightened though, more likely wary. But they soon realise that we are simply people."

"Once we get this demon crap sorted out, will we be able to stay here?" asked Jackie.

"So long as too many citizens don't die, but there will be a price to pay."

"What price?"

"Once word gets out, and it will, that we sorted out the demons that were invading their little corner of tranquillity, then we are going to be expected to fix anything strange that turns up."

"Bad thing?"

"Not necessarily, but it could get complicated, especially if some fool involves the damned police."

"Never seen one," laughed Jackie, "that's not actually true, I saw one once, it went tearing through the village with its lights on, and its sirens blaring, I'm sure it was lost."

"I've an idea," said Jane quietly.

"For what?"

"If, no, when, we get this shit sorted out, we give Francis the credit."

"Why?"

"He's the sort of guy that should be dealing with this, and when other shit happens, the locals will prefer to go to him, rather than us."

"If there's shit, he can't deal with he'll still come to us."

"True, but we'll be one step away from the citizens, and that will matter to them."

"I suppose he's more of an establishment figure than we are," replied Jackie.

"Hey Roaddog," said Avalon, suddenly close to the pair on the settee, "your blondes aren't really blond, are they?"

"No, they're both sharp cookies," smiled Roaddog.

"Not the typical blond trope then?" said Avalon.

"That recurring theme is a joke at best, and a bad one at that, these girls are both wonderful, both intelligent, both loving, and both deadly. Piss them off at your own risk."

"I would never do that," grinned Avalon, "what I would do is offer them a chance to join a powerful organisation, as acolytes to start, with a view to rapid promotion as high as they can go." She paused for a moment, "Thought's girls?"

"I've never been much for organised religions," said Jackie, "I mean look at what it's done to those two kids that opened the hell mouth."

"Not for me," said Jane, "I don't want to spend the rest of my life training, when I could be having fun."

"Oh, it can be fun as well," laughed Avalon.

"Not for me," replied Jane, seriously. "I like my fun, hot naked and sweaty."

"We do some of that as well, which is why the more recent religions really don't like us. We don't have their hang ups about the more physical aspects of human life."

"And how would that have helped our current situation?" asked Jackie.

"The portal would never have been opened."

"How do you work that out?" asked Jane.

"Children would not have been sneaking off to find somewhere private to experiment."

"Please explain."

"By the time their bodies are capable of any sort of activity they already know about it, they have no need to experiment. If they really want to, they get guidance and assistance."

"You mean that people will actually help them to have sex?" demanded Jackie.

"Usually their parents, or a priest, or priestess."

"One such as you?" asked Jane.

"No, usually one of the lower orders, my skills tend to be reserved for more important matters."

"Like what's happening here?"

"Very much so."

"So how come Fintan got the first invite?" asked Jackie.

"Influential friends on the council. If they'd known what was happening here, they'd have locked him up."

"I thought they knew, that's why they sent a representative."

"It was thought to be just the usual foolishness of the locals or visiting idiots."

"You didn't think it was real?" demanded Jane.

"No, but it seems that Fintan knew, he worked quite hard to ensure that he was sent here."

"How long had he been working towards that end?" asked Roaddog as he came up behind her.

"Looking back, it appears that he's been engineering his presence for months, perhaps even a year."

"So, he knew this portal was going to open a year ago?"

"Perhaps," Avalon nodded slowly.

"So, what did he know that the rest of you didn't?"

"I'll find out," she said softly. Avalon reached inside her robe and pulled out a phone. The three listened to her side of the conversation as she told the person of Fintan's death and his impending return, she gave instructions to search his documents, to find out what and how he knew about this portal.

"And do it quick," were the last words as she hung up.

"Well, that was a little incongruous," laughed Roaddog.

"What do you mean?" replied Avalon.

"I mean look at yourself, long white robe, magic staff, too long to be a wand, crown made of flowers, and out from your pocket comes an I-phone."

"I see," she smiled back, "I could have reached out to them, but I'm going to need all the energy I can muster when Fintan returns."

"Let's hope we have a few days before he comes back," said Roaddog.

"I second that thought," replied Avalon gently. They all looked round as a large blue car rolled to a stop on the forecourt. Mick and Jackie got out and walked towards the group.

"How's everyone?" asked Mick.

"We're fine," replied Roaddog, "you?"

"Great, got some cracking shots of the F-15's, after they'd unloaded all their cannon shells, the pair of them buzzed the tower, at about eight hundred feet and only just sub-sonic, the halos they had were awesome."

"Halo?" asked Avalon.

"It's fog that forms in the decompression zone it looks gorgeous, it's like the plane is dragging its own personal cloud along with it."

"That must look very strange," said Avalon.

"It does," said Mick, "but eerie and wonderful at the same time."

"What you up to for the rest of the day?" asked Roaddog.

"Nothing in the plan, why?"

"Fancy joining us for lunch?"

Mick looked to Jackie, with his eyebrows raised, she nodded.

"Why not," laughed Mick, "I gotta get my seats back in the car, then I'm ready when you are, where we going?"

"The Axe," replied Roaddog, smiling.

"No problem, food's always good there," said Mick, he turned away and went into the workshop to pick up his car seats and reload them. In less than three minutes Mick's car was returned to its normal configuration.

"Sorry," called Mick, "I've only got three spare seats."

"We don't need them, we usually walk," said Bug.

"You okay to walk?" asked Slowball.

"I'm fine," smiled Bug, "head hurts a bit, but only from the gulls egg lump on it."

"Damn, that might just double your brain size," laughed Roaddog.

"Thanks friend," said Bug shaking his head, then immediately regretting it.

"Jackie, drop the doors," said Roaddog. Jackie chuckled and went to the internal switches to turn off the lights and drop the right-hand door. Once it had started its downward journey, she stepped outside to drop the other door.

"Hey Roaddog," said Mick, "what if there's a bike under that door as it comes down?"

"Then it gets crushed," replied Roaddog.

"Bit of a safety issue there."

"I think we have bigger problems right now, anyway there are two down switches on the inside, I want those doors coming down even if the guy with his finger on the button gets killed."

"Good enough, if a little sad that you think of it that way."

"If we'd had proper doors at the old unit, then not everybody would have been dead."

"Hey man," said Slowball softly. "Not your fault, those doors wouldn't have stopped forty-five calibre slugs."

"I know, but it still hurts." The first door closed with a crash, the second only a moment or two later. "I need beer," snarled Roaddog. The others all followed as he walked quickly towards the pub.

"What happened?" Mick asked of Slowball, leaving Roaddog a little space to cool off.

"Ass holes with machine guns killed everyone there, except the girls."

"The girls?"

"They took them away."

"And?"

"We took them back."

"All that I knew was that the Dragonriders had died, it wasn't even clear how. You have no idea how shocked I was to see your trike this morning."

"And us you, how come you weren't here for the weekend?"

"Some ass booked a gig for yesterday; it was a rally so we couldn't turn it down."

"So, what time did you hit the road to come here?"

"Drove home from the gig, unloaded the PA, loaded the suitcases and set off."

"You must be knackered?"

"Yeah, I suppose, but hey, plenty of time to rest when I'm dead." Mick laughed and followed Roaddog into the darkness of the pub.

Chapter 13: Smeg.

"Karen," called Roaddog. Karen came around the end of the bar.
"We need beer," he said.
"I'll need a little more information than that," Karen smiled widely.
"Beer Mick?" asked Roaddog. Mick moved into Karen's view.
"Hi Mick," said Karen, "You are late." She laughed, "I know what they want." She turned back to Roaddog.
"One other new one," said Roaddog, "What do you want Ava?"
"Orange, lime and water," said Avalon.
"Been a while Ava," said Karen.
"Christ," snapped Roaddog, "do you know everyone?"
"I'm sure there's a couple of guys in Louth I can't put names to, but hey, most everyone yes."
"Shit," whispered Roaddog shaking his head.
"Is that a smile I see?" asked Karen, putting a pint on the bar with the three she had already pulled.
The others came past him and went to their usual table. Jane smiled and nodded at Liz, who was sitting at the end of the bar with a girl dressed in black, the young girls smiled at Jane and went through the door to the kitchen.
"Somehow I thought you weren't local," said Roaddog to Avalon.
"I'm not, but I come this way occasionally, mainly to keep an eye on Botolph's"
"You've known about it for a while then?"
"Oh yes, but I didn't expect it to open during my lifetime."
"How long have you been waiting for it to open?"
"We've been aware of it for a couple of hundred years."
"How so?" asked Roaddog.
"An old manuscript came into our hands, and it hinted that there was something bad going on here, we sent a group to investigate, and found a gateway that was closed."
"No hints as how to close it again?"
"Not really."
"Karen, put these on a tab, we'll settle up later," he called picking up

his beer and turning towards the table where the others were waiting. Behind him he heard the door open with a crash. He turned towards the noise and a man in a black jacket, pushed a double-barrelled shotgun into his guts, Roaddog stared into the man's brown eyes, all that was visible of his face as the rest was covered by a balaclava. The man that came in with the intruder was already behind the bar, pointing another gun at Karen.

"To quote Dave Lister, how can the same smeg happen to the same guy twice?" Roaddog spoke slowly and clearly. He glanced down at the gun then looked back up into the man's eyes. "You got two shots, and it's going to take both to put me down, do you believe you can survive what happens next?" Slowball and Bug rose from their seats and moved apart from the rest of the people, Bug towards the bar and Slowball to Roaddog's left.

"Open the safe bitch," shouted the man behind the bar.

"That's not going to happen," said Roaddog, "you two assholes are going to die here today."

"Shut your face, or I'll cut you in two," snarled the man in front of Roaddog.

"Somehow I don't think so," smiled Roaddog as the man flinched but didn't move.

"That," said Roaddog, "is a Remington pump action twelve bore, pressed against the back of your neck, he's got five shots."

"No," whispered Terry, "six."

"Six, good man, hand over your guns now or die," said Roaddog. Bug started moving towards the bar, the man there turned towards Bug and took his eyes off Karen, she snatched a bottle of spirit from the back of the bar and brought it crashing down on his head, he dropped behind the bar, as Bug jumped over it. The robber in front of Roaddog took his right hand from the trigger and let the butt of the gun drop, so that it was hanging vertically in front of him. Roaddog snatched it and swung the butt upwards into the man's groin, the thief fell to the floor with both hands between his legs moaning quietly.

"You okay love?" asked Terry.

"I'm fine," replied Karen, taking her phone from her pocket and hitting a speed dial.

"Police," she said when the call was answered.

"Axe and Cleaver, North Somercotes, armed robbery." Then there was a pause.

"Two guys with shotguns."

"No, they have been subdued."

"You better hurry, they threatened people with loaded guns, I'm struggling to find reasons that they should carry on breathing." She smiled as she hung up the phone.

"Hey Terry, have you got any cable ties?" asked Roaddog. Karen reached under the bar and produced a bag of heavy cable ties and tossed it to Roaddog. The man on the ground was first bound wrist to wrist behind his back, and then his ankles were bound to the wrists. Bug dragged the other one out from behind the bar and he was treated the same. Roaddog took the double-barrelled shotgun and placed it against the man's backside.

"Can anyone think of a reason why I shouldn't shove this all the way up and give him both barrels?" He hefted some weight behind it for emphasis.

"Clean up would be a nightmare," said Terry.

"Cop's three minutes out," laughed Karen.

"Fuck," said Roaddog with a smile, "can I just blow a few bits off him?"

"I'd rather you didn't," laughed Terry, "clean up again."

"Sometimes I never get any fun," laughed Roaddog. He dropped the gun on the restrained man's back, and picked up his beer from the bar, he looked down at it and thought, 'seems like it's been there forever.' He smiled to himself and took his seat amongst his friends. There was a scream of tortured tyres outside the pub, and then the crunch of the gravel as a new car pulled up outside, this one was covered in blue and yellow squares. In a few moments two policemen came into the bar carrying AR80's. They took in the room in a heartbeat.

"I presume these are the alleged robbers?" said the elder of the two.

"Alleged?" asked Karen loudly.

"We do need to investigate you know," he replied. Then he looked at the shotgun on the bar. "Who's is this?" he asked.

"You know very well who's that is Stephen, and you know it's not real."

"It's still illegal to carry in the street."

"As you can see, I carried it in my own home, where these assholes threatened my family with real guns."

"I hope you didn't use excessive force to restrain them."

"When threatened with firearms, ultimate force is acceptable, and as you can see the bastards are still breathing," Roaddog snarled, "I'm so surprised that you guys got here so quickly, I was expecting to have to wait until tomorrow."

"We were investigating reports of machine gun fire somewhere around here."

"Get used to it," laughed Roaddog.

"What do you mean?" demanded the policeman.

"It was only a matter of time before this arrived in this out of the way place, it's been a fashion in the southeast for a couple of years now, petrol heads have got bored with the sound of their turbos, now they like to drop petrol into the exhaust causing back fires, with the press of a button your car sounds like a machine gun, look out for some hopped up turbo and you'll find your machine gunner."

"Beside the point right now," said Stephen, "back to these alleged robbers."

"He threatened to stick a gun up my ass and pull the trigger," said the trussed-up robber, his voice muffled by the carpet his face was pressed into.

"That sounds like excessive force," said Stephen slowly.

"Whose gun was it fucker?" Roaddog growled.

"Mine," mumbled the man.

"As you can see" said Roaddog quietly to the copper, "his asshole is as yet inviolate, that can wait until he gets to jail."

"That's definitely threatening behaviour," said the policeman.

"Stephen," interrupted Terry, "you have got to be joking?" The policeman simply smiled.

"Enough," snapped Avalon loudly. The policeman turned towards the sound of her voice and recognised her for the first time. All the colour drained from his face, he stuttered for a moment before getting his words sorted out.

"Er, Avalon," he almost tripped over his feet as he turned to face her, "my, er, I didn't know you were here, I'm sorry," his words tumbled over one another, his whole body twitched as some spastic impulse rushed through it. "How can I help you, erm, Avalon?" Again, the twitch shook him, his head bowed and then he looked up into her eyes.

"Get these scumbags out of here, I never want to hear of them again," her reply so slow and low, it made Stephen shake, his eyes went wide.

"Never?" he whispered.

"Never," Avalon twitched her head to get the cops moving. Stephen looked around, and finally focused on Terry.

"Terry," he asked, "you got a knife? I'm not carrying these bastards to the car."

"Girls," said Roaddog grinning. Jackie and Jane both moved together, as if by magic knives appeared in their hands and the cable ties were slashed. Leaving the thieves with their hands still fastened behind their backs but their legs now free.

"Those knives are definitely," said Stephen to be interrupted by Avalon.

"Stephen," she snapped, "we shall discuss your behaviour at a time when things are not so pressing." The policeman went pale again, then he reached down and dragged one of the thieves to his feet and pushed him out of the door, followed in a moment by his compatriot.

"What the fuck just happened?" asked Roaddog, "are you some sort of undercover cop?" Avalon smiled.

"No, Stephen is a member of a semi-secret society."

"So, you're some big muck-a-muck in the masons?"

"No, but they do understand where the real power lies, and we only allow them so much."

"So, he was struggling with your title and some sort of gesture of obedience?"

"I suppose, high priestess, and on his damned knees, and that's where he will be when I have time to deal with his insubordination, it may be time for another lesson, it's been a couple of years."

"They get out of hand, do they?" asked Roaddog.

"Yes, it's been a few years though since they needed a lesson."

"What sort of lesson?" asked Bug.

"The last time they got too big for their boots, they went medieval on some of our people in the northeast, there were witch trials and burnings."

"Your response?" asked Roaddog.

"I took a couple of my sisters to Tyneside, they were having a committee meeting to decide what to do next, or more accurately who to kill next. They'd just killed a high priest, they were celebrating. My sisters held the doors, and I put the fire to them all. The fire investigators were very confused. They probably still are, or they have nightmares."

"Maybe both," laughed Slowball.

"Brutal," smiled Bug.

"So, you could have torched Kyronatha for us?" asked Roaddog.

"Unlikely, he would have resisted my power, it would take many of us to burn him."

"But Fintan's staff was enough to set fire to him," said Sylvia.

"There must have been some other force there as well," replied Avalon.

"Nutter gave his life," whispered Roaddog.

"That'd be enough, a sacrifice like that generates a great deal of power, the sort of power that a demon can't ignore."

"Could we do the same with Fintan when he comes back?"

"Unlikely, he has more knowledge of fire than the demon, it could be turned against you."

"So, what the hell can we do?"

"I'm not sure, but there may be a chance to release the demon within and let that destroy Fintan."

"I don't understand."

"In order to make his way through the barrier, he's going to need a demon inside himself, even though the portal is nominally open, only demonic power can come this way."

"So, if we go in, we'll not be able to get back out?"

"No, you're supposed to be on this side, you'd be able to come through the barrier, so long as you do so before it closes."

"I don't think we'll bother with going inside," he replied slowly.

"That might be for the best," Avalon smiled.

"Okay Avalon," said Karen as she walked over, "a new name and what the hell frightened that copper? He can be a real pain."

"Old name and that would be me," laughed Avalon.

"He damn near wet himself when he saw you."

"So he should, he owes much to me and mine."

"I don't understand."

"Nor do you want to."

"I thought you were just one of those new age pagan nutters," she paused as Avalon smiled, "sorry, that didn't quite come out right."

"I know what you mean, and we have done nothing to change this opinion, once a person gets such a nice label, they are simply placed in the box marked 'Pagan Nutter' and forgotten about. No one pays any real attention to what we do, generally we are left pretty much alone to get on with whatever pagan stupidity we are up to," she laughed aloud.

"So, what does he owe?"

"The life of his youngest child."

"Was the child sick?"

"After a fashion."

"What was wrong with him?"

"He was struggling with something that modern medicine couldn't deal with effectively, we sorted the kid out."

"How?"

"We removed his problem and sent it back to hell."

"I don't believe that," said Karen slowly.

"He does, and that is all that matters, the child is better, and coming along nicely."

"You are a strange one Avalon."

"You're not the first to tell me that," Avalon smiled.

"How about some food Karen?" asked Roaddog.

"Sorry, sort of distracted just now, what would you like?"

Food orders were passed, and more beer ordered and brought to the table, while they were sitting waiting for the food to be delivered a rather disturbed Liz came running from the kitchen.

"What the hell did I miss?" she demanded as she stopped by their table.

"Just a typical day in the life of batshit crazy bikers," laughed Jane, "You still want in?"

"Fuck no," laughed Liz, "but I do hear that thanks are in order, it could have gone much worse if you hadn't been here." She leaned over and grabbed Roaddog by both cheeks, she turned his head towards herself and kissed him firmly on the lips.

"Thank you Dog," she whispered as she blushed and ran back to the kitchen.

"Well," said Roaddog, "that was different."

"She's a very emotional girl," replied Jane smiling broadly.

"I thought she was gay?" he asked.

"Oh, she is," said Jane, "that only shows you how much the people here mean to her."

"Well, they mean a lot to us as well," his words soft and gentle. From the kitchen came the food they had ordered, once the food was distributed the waitresses returned to the kitchen leaving Karen behind. She leaned over and whispered into Roaddog's ear.

"I damned near peed myself when I saw those guns, thank you."

"So did I," he replied in what could only be described as a stage whisper. "But did you have to hit him with a bottle of Jack Daniels?"

"It was close to hand and full, I wasn't going to get another chance, anyway your terrier Bug was on him before he hit the ground. So, a bottle of jack is a small price to pay."

"At least no one that matters was hurt," grinned Roaddog.

"I think Stephen's in for a bad time when yon woman gets him alone."

"That's for sure," said Avalon, "is he always such a dick?"

"Sometimes he can be, other times he's almost like one of the guys, just a touch sensitive about some things."

"What things?"

"I really can't tell what's going to set him off on any given day, though quite often it seems that women aren't his favourite people."

"I'll see if I can give him some pointers about that when I get the chance," Avalon's eyes sparkled as she said it.

"We all understand that he's a cop, but he doesn't have to be such an ass about it," Karen paused for a moment, "anyway, thanks for getting him and those scumbags out of here before things got any worse. I only wish it had been one of the other teams that responded, they're much nicer."

"You mean nice for cops with itchy trigger fingers?"

"None of them have that sort of reputation, not even Stephen."

"That's good to hear," interrupted Roaddog, "if they'd walked in a few minutes earlier it could definitely have gotten messy around here."

"That's for certain," replied Karen, "Thanks again," she said as she walked slowly back to the bar to serve some customers that were getting a little restless. "Sorry for your wait," she said, "we've had a bit of a robbery."

"Is everyone all right?" asked one of the women in the group.

"Oh yes, our local bikers took care of two guys with shotguns." She nodded in the direction of the group sitting in the bay around the big table.

"Local?" asked one of the men.

"Their shop is the old bus depot."

"I'd noticed something happening there, I'll have to go and have a look."

"They're doing food as well," smiled Karen.

"Food?"

"Roaddog calls it burned meat between bits of bread with sauce in two colours."

She guided them to a table and took their orders. Once she had left one of the men got up and approached Roaddog's group.

"Hi guys, my name is Geoff, I hear you've had an exciting afternoon here?"

"Sort of," said Roaddog noncommittally.

"Armed robbery is not something that happens around here much, Karen says you stopped it. Is that correct?"

"Yes, when a guy sticks a twelve bore in my guts, he better be ready to use it, and with the girls here, he wasn't going to get a re-load, he saw it our way in a very short time."

"Well done guys, and girls, and thanks from all of us."

"Don't forget," said Roaddog, "Karen took one down with a bottle of JD."

"She's definitely a one," laughed the guy as he turned away. "Hey Karen," he called on his way back to his table, "little bird tells me you put one down with a bottle of JD."

"I did, fool turned his back on me."

"Did you have to use Jack Daniels?"

"It was full and to hand, so yes."

"Well done anyway, make these guys tab ours."

"Too slow, already taken care of."

"Who?" he asked. Karen simply tipped her head to one side, "ah, stupid question I suppose."

"Karen you can't do that," said Slowball loudly, "have you any idea how much these assholes drink when they're not paying?"

"I don't care," laughed Karen.

"What the fuck Slowball?" snapped Roaddog, "you're not paying anyway, I am."

"Hey," said Slowball, smiling, "we've worked hard considering we were invited to an opening day, we're worth it."

"Of course you are, that's why I'm paying."

"No, you're not," laughed Karen, "and drink till ya fall over I don't care, the savings on insurance, more than cover anything you could drink."

Roaddog glanced at Karen, then looked around the table. He picked up his half full glass and finished it in one swallow, by the time his glass hit the table the others were all empty as well. "Beer us Karen," he laughed.

"You got it," she replied laughing.

It seems that word got around the village very quickly, they had just finished eating, when Jake came into the bar, Karen intercepted him.

"You be nice," she snapped at him.

"No problem here," he smiled back at her. He walked over to the bikers.

"I hear you've been having fun," he laughed.

"I moved here from the busy city for a quieter life, what the fuck is it about this town?" snarled Roaddog.

"Hey, stop calling this a town, we're a village and glad of it."

"Said the local idiot," said a voice.

"Wind your neck in Geoff," laughed Jake. "Karen, can we have a few shot glasses please?" he pulled a wine bottle from inside his jacket.

"You can't sell that shit in here," she called.

"Sell? This is free to the heroes of the hour," Jake smiled, his eyes twinkling in the low lighting of the dining room.

"Just this once, I suppose," smiled Karen, "you're a bad man Jake."

"I know, but you love me just the same, as do these guys."

"After the way you talked to them a few days ago?"

"That's all been sorted out, yours isn't the only life they have saved recently."

"Okay then, just this once," Karen laughed as she brought out two handfuls of short glasses.

As the golden liquor poured into the glasses Geoff called out, "What about us?"

"Not for you Geoff," laughed Jake, "only for heroes today."

"That's mean," said Geoff laughing heartily, his whole table joining the hilarity.

"You're driving Geoff," said Jake.

"So are they."

"But I have far more confidence in their tolerance than yours," laughed Jake as the shot glasses raised and clinked together then were emptied. Coughing ensued.

"Damn, that's some good stuff," said Roaddog once he had his breathing back under control.

"Hey Dog," coughed Slowball, "one thing you can be sure of, we are certainly accepted here now."

"Nothing wrong with that," said Roaddog.

Before they had finished their meals there had been more than a few visitations from locals, all of them happy that Karen had survived the robbery.

After the detritus of the meal had been cleared, they were sitting quietly drinking slowly. Suddenly Slowball said "Fuck."

"What's up?" asked Roaddog, his back was to the door, so he had no idea what Slowball was looking at.

"Ah, Roaddog," said a voice that they all recognised.

"Father Francis," sighed Roaddog, "what can we help you with?"

The father and his three friends gathered around the table and pulled up chairs where they could, not that there was a lot of space. Karen came over to take drink orders for the new arrivals, beer and scotch for the father, beer for the rabbi, water for the other two.

"Are you okay Mohammed?" asked Roaddog.

"To be honest it is difficult for me in these places, but I know that these people will meet their own gods in due course. They will make atonement for their sins then; they are not my responsibility."

"Phurba?" asked Roaddog.

"These people are each on their road to enlightenment, though most of them have a long way to go."

"They walk a different road to you," laughed Roaddog.

"All roads lead to Buddha," smiled Phurba.

"All this is of course by the by," said Father Francis.

"Indeed," said Avalon, "you have news?"

"Yes and no," smiled Francis, "yes, a returning necromancer is a first, and no, we have no clues how to deal with him."

"Nutter recommended salt as a deterrent," said Roaddog.

"Salt may help," replied Francis, "in a shotgun, but that's not a lot of use to you."

"Jake," said Roaddog, "would a multiple layer of wadding give me enough back pressure?"

"Maybe, in a standard load I use linen wadding, and that pushes the salt down the barrel, maybe three layers will give enough for your mechanism, you'll lose muzzle velocity, but you're not depending on that for impact."

"Range isn't going to be an issue either, I plan on sticking it down his throat before I pull the trigger," laughed Roaddog.

"I'll load you some for the morning, hundred do?"

"If a hundred don't do the job, then a thousand won't."

"I'll bring them early," said Jake.

"Hang on," said Roaddog pausing for a moment, "don't bother, there will be enough shotguns with the ability to fire salt at the asshole, standard lead loads for me please, I'll have the sword anyway."

"Anything else from the clerics?" asked Roaddog, looking at Francis.

"We could set up the same forbiddings as we did today," suggested Abraham.

"Ha," snorted Avalon, "he knows my power so well he'd tear mine apart in a heartbeat, yours wouldn't last half so long. Containment is not an option. We have to break his control of the demon inside."

"Of course," said Francis, "he'll have to be possessed to cross over."

"Possessed or possessor," replied Avalon gently.

"You think he's powerful enough to possess a demon?" asked Abraham.

"I think he's been planning this for a long time, it's no spur of the moment thing," said Avalon.

"You think he engineered the whole thing?" asked Father Francis.

"No, but he was ready for it when it happened, his cronies got him on the first team, and that was what he wanted, whether his death was intentional, I can't be sure, seems like something of a risk, but not something he would be averse to. The whole thing is a risk, his thirst for power is well known, but I thought it would be more subtle."

"Subtle he wasn't," replied Roaddog.

"You'd already given him the trigger he needed, he knew that if he threatened the children you'd kill him. He waited until Kyronatha was dead and then pulled the trigger, that opened his path for a return."

"But what does he plan to achieve in this return?" asked Francis.

"I have no idea," said Avalon, "and that frightens me more than anything."

"Okay," said Roaddog, "what's the worst thing he could be after?"

"Absolute worst case," said Avalon slowly, "as a returning necromancer, having beaten death for himself, he ends the power of death forever."

"Is that a bad thing?" asked Bug.

"Imagine a world where nobody dies," said Francis.

"Again," replied Bug, "bad thing?"

"Think of all those people whose lives end in pain, death is no longer a release from that pain, it goes on, maybe forever. Who would you wish that on?"

"I see," Bug swallowed and looked away. "Fuck," he whispered, "that's horrible."

"Worse still," said Avalon, "what if the only way out is with the services of the necromancer? What would you give to end the pain of your friend?"

"Anything, and everything," said Bug.

"Exactly, that's power," said Roaddog, "looks like I'm going to have to kill that bastard again."

"Are you sure you can do that?" asked Francis.

"Gonna give it a try."

"But how?"

"I was hoping that the local experts would be able to help me with that."

"We don't have much to go on," said Francis, "there are no records of necromancers coming back to the world, usually they just die."

"So, they can control the dead but not their own deaths?" asked Roaddog.

"That is right."

"So, all we know is that he'll be coming back, man shaped?"

"Most likely," said Avalon, "but there will be a demonic force in there somewhere, that's what we have to let loose."

"Why?" asked Francis.

"If we can break the demon loose, it'll tear him apart from the inside."

"I never thought of that," said Francis slowly, "he'll need a demon to get through. What sort though?"

"That's to our advantage," grinned Avalon, "it'll be something weak, something he can control, if we can break that control, we'll beat him."

"How is that control achieved?"

"You're joking surely?" asked Avalon.

"No," Francis stuttered, "faith is enough."

"Your belief will get you killed."

"I don't understand."

"Your training was good, well sort of good, for restraining a demon, at the portal, three circles and the spinning cage will work, but not for a demon that is already imprisoned inside a dead man."

"So, what can we do with that?"

"We need to break his hold on it."

"This is way outside anything I have ever even heard of," Francis mumbled.

"That does not surprise me," chuckled Avalon. "He'll be holding the demon with his mind, keeping it caged, we have to break his concentration on that cage."

"And how in all the hells do we do that?" demanded Francis.

"There is only one hell," said Mohammed.

"Yes," laughed Francis, "you got one, we got one, the Jews have one, I am unclear about the pagan religions, Avalon can you clue us in?"

"Well Francis, as far as we are concerned you have two hells, the Buddhists live in hell until they escape, the pagans have a few, but that is entirely beside the point. We need to distract him enough so that he loses control."

"How do we do that?" asked Roaddog.

"I'm not really sure," replied Avalon, slowly, "I think we just need to keep him moving, keep him surprised, somehow."

"We need to pull him out into the open and keep attacking him from different sides," Slowball said.

"The church has two doors but many windows," suggested Bug, "we can keep him guessing which way the attack is going to come from next."

"That's better," Avalon replied, "we can keep out of sight to some extent and keep hitting him in the back."

"I'm not averse to stabbing a guy in the back," Roaddog grinned, "but does your magic include any ranged weapons?"

"Oh, I can hit him from a distance," smiled Avalon.

"I can shower him in holy water," said Francis.

"Will that work?" asked Roaddog.

"It might," said Avalon.

"What about the rest of you?" Roaddog asked looking around at the other clerics.

"The word of Allah will protect us all," replied Mohammed.

"The faith of the followers of Abraham will keep the demons at bay," responded the rabbi.

Roaddog looked pointedly at Phurba.

"The road to enlightenment is never straight, we will follow the path as each of us should, sometimes death is the only way forwards."

"Well, that's sort of gloomy," laughed Slowball softly.

"As I have always said," replied Roaddog slowly, "if you're going to spend your life, then buy something worthwhile with it, or make some bastard pay heavy for it. If you can do that you will be remembered with honour."

"That makes me feel so much better," laughed Phurba.

"Bug," said Roaddog, "punch up the cameras, what are those birds up to?" In only a few seconds Bug had an answer for him.

"They seem to have finished feasting; they are just sitting around being fat."

"There must be quite a few less."

"They're certainly a little scarcer, ugly bastards."

"They're not that ugly," said Jane surprised to hear the venom in Bug's voice.

"Yes they are," snapped Bug, "they look like sweet innocent fat birds, but they are actually vultures not averse to cannibalism. They give me the creeps."

"I gotta get home," said Jake, "Mary is worried about me."

"I can understand that, keep an eye on those birds," said Roaddog.

"I'll do that, when the time comes, I'll be there."

"Thanks Jake, you're a great help."

"Hey man," said Jake, slowly, "I owe you my life."

"No sweat," smiled Roaddog, "we just did what any reasonable person would have done."

"Yeah, right," Jake shrugged, "most of the people that I know would have run away screaming."

"We don't do that shit," said Bug.

"I'd noticed," replied Jake, "anyway, gotta go." He turned on his heel and walked away.

"He's a happier chappy now," said Karen with a giggle.

"In some ways yes."

"And in others?" asked Karen.

"Not so much, life is sort of complicated right now."

"Can I help un-complicate things?"

"Probably not, we're just going to have to ride this shit until we get it sorted."

"If there's any way I can help you will let me know, won't you?"

"Of course we will."

"Karen that was a silly thing to say," observed Slowball.

"How so?" asked Karen.

"He may decide that free beer will make everything better," laughed Slowball.

"I'm not that cynical," said Roaddog.

"Yes you are," grinned Slowball, "you're just slower than me."

"Thanks brother," grunted Roaddog, "I can do without your help."

"Just glad to be of assistance."

"Don't worry Slowball," replied Karen, "I'd not fall for that shit." She laughed and returned to the bar.

"It's getting late to be lunchtime," said Roaddog.

"Are we re-opening the shop?" asked Slowball.

"Really can't be arsed," Roaddog replied, "I feel a lazy afternoon coming on, I think we should retire to the van and drink steadily."

"You got room for me?" asked Avalon.

"Sorry love," replied Roaddog, "pretty full at my caravan, I got all these visitors."

"Damn," muttered Avalon, she turned to Francis, "looks like I'm dependent on your hospitality."

"I would never turn away a person in need," smiled the father.

"Even a heathen such as myself?"

"I look on it as an opportunity to convert you to the one true faith," smiled Francis.

"I can't believe you just said that," said Mohammed.

"Nor can I," said Abraham.

"Gentlemen it was a joke," laughed Francis, "I would never attempt to convert anyone, I leave that to the fundamentalists."

"You don't class yourself as such?" asked Sylvia.

"How can I? I'm here in concert with a group of high priests of various religions and a group of heathens that believe in the gods of Harley and Davidson," he grinned widely.

"But do you think you could convert them?" asked Sylvia.

Francis paused and looked around the table, he caught the eyes of each of the bikers for a moment, none of them looked away, each challenged him in their own way, Roaddog scowled, Jackie dropped her hand to the back of her belt, Jane glowered, Slowball sneered, Bug smiled, Cherie glared, his eyes returned to Sylvia, her face blank, her eyes cold.

"Sylvia, my dear. I have to say that your friends, though they be unbelievers, fight harder than any twenty fundamentalists that I can think of. I'd much rather have them at my back in the battle that is to come than anyone else."

"Why does it feel that you're at our back?"

"Score one to the biker chick," laughed Avalon.

"I have to admit," said Father Francis, pointedly ignoring Avalon, "that all of our book learning has done little to prepare us for the realities of physical confrontation."

"And in facing the necromancer?" asked Sylvia.

"I'd say less than useless," mumbled Francis, turning away from her steady gaze.

"You really need to pick up your game, if my people die here, there will be consequences."

"What sort of consequences?" asked Francis slowly.

"You'll probably find," said Roaddog, "if she believes you haven't done enough to keep us alive, then she's going to kill you."

"You think she would?" asked Francis.

"If she doesn't" said Jackie softly, "then I will."

"And me," said Jane, her right hand behind her back.

"I'll have to do what I can to help everyone stay alive," mumbled Francis.

"That's probably for the best," laughed Avalon.

"You know Avalon," said Francis, "we've faced two demons, we were too late for the first I know, but they don't scare me as much as these young women here. There is something terribly implacable in their eyes, it drives fear into the very depths of my soul."

"Damned right," said Roaddog, "if you'd ever met Bandit Queen, you'd be pissing in your pants." He paused and looked down, then slowly raised his glass above his head and called softly, "Bandit Queen." Six other glasses raised and answered his toast. "Bandit Queen."

"Burn in hell baby, burn in hell," whispered Roaddog.

"Why would you wish that a friend burns in hell?" asked Francis.

"She went to hell, and found it was full of wimps and pussies so she torched the place, and now it burns, get it?"

"I think that I am beginning to see," said Francis.

"Hell burns because that is god's decree," said Abraham.

"Abraham," interrupted Francis, "do me a favour and shut the fuck up. I was mistaken about these people, they don't serve gods, they worship a queen."

"Maybe we worship her memory," said Roaddog, "How would she have faced Melchion?" he asked looking straight at Slowball.

"She'd have spit in his eye and beat the bastard to death," replied Slowball.

"How would she have beaten Kyronatha?" asked Roaddog, looking at Bug.

"She'd have spit in his eye and beat the bastard to death," laughed Bug.

"Common factor in these two scenarios?" asked Roaddog.

"She liked beating bastards to death," suggested Slowball.

"She was a psycho?" asked Bug.

"Wrong," said Jackie, "I only knew her a short time, but I know how she would have beaten these demons, the same way she lived her life."

"Go on," said Roaddog.

"She believed in who she was, she was absolutely certain of the power of her fists. There was no power in the universe that she wouldn't face down."

"And she always had us to back her up," replied Roaddog with a smile. He turned to Avalon. "Your barrier, when you were holding back

Melchion, did you believe in it?"

She thought for a moment or two before replying.

"I believe that my forbidding is the most powerful you will find anywhere, I wasn't sure it would contain a demon of his power."

"Could it be that your lack of belief weakened your forbidding?"

"I don't know, and I don't think there is a way to test your theory," said Avalon.

"We don't need to test it; simple observation is enough."

"Explain," said Father Francis.

"When Melchion was contained in the church, these two," he pointed at Abraham and Mohammed, "were holding one door, and crapping in their pants, the terror in their faces was unmistakable. They didn't believe that they could hold against the demon, Avalon on the other hand knew that she could hold for a little while at least."

"You're saying that belief is everything?" asked Francis.

"Strange question for one in your profession," replied Roaddog, with a smile. "But I'd say more confidence, belief in oneself."

"Self-confidence didn't keep your queen alive," said Francis. Roaddog surged to his feet, and gripped Francis by the back of the neck with his left hand, in his right twelve inches of black stiletto was resting against the priest's belly, the point concealed within two layers of cloth.

"My knife is an inch from your heart, do you know why you are not dead?"

"No," Francis' reply quaked in his throat.

"Bandit Queen used her last breath to save the lives of four people, three of whom are sitting around this table, had the fourth one been here you would already be burger meat. I'm not quite the hot head that she is, I'm going to give you the opportunity to match Bandit Queens sacrifice, do you understand?"

"I'm sorry, I meant no disrespect to your queen, she sounds like a wonderful person." Roaddog smiled, then laughed aloud and sat back down, the knife vanished as if by magic. All the bikers were laughing.

"What have I said that is suddenly so funny?" asked Francis.

"Oh, she was wonderful," said Slowball, "but not in the way that you mean."

"I've watched her feed living men to a meat grinder," said Roaddog.

"Fuck dog," said Bug, "you helped her."

"True," replied Roaddog, "but they really deserved it." He looked up at Francis again, "She'd have beaten your brains in with her bare hands."

"I have a barely related question," said Francis quietly, breathing a little easier now.

"Ask," said Roaddog.

"Your knife was more than an inch from my heart, why?"

"School boy error on your part. Hitting the heart through the ribs is not as easy as the movies make it out to be. Much better to go in under the ribs, turn the knife upwards, rips through stomach, diaphragm, aorta, and then heart. Without a diaphragm there is no scream, the only noise you make is when your dead head hits the floor."

"It's somehow scary that you know this," muttered Francis.

"British military training, the best in the world."

"A Gurkha would have just taken your head," Bug smiled.

"You are certainly a blood thirsty bunch," observed Phurba.

"You want a committee of social workers to take on a hell mouth?" asked Avalon.

"I see your point, but there is a terrible lot of killing going on, and I'm certain this is not good for my chances of improvement."

"You'll find out when the necromancer kills you," Roaddog said, "that is of course if he lets you stay dead."

"You think he might hold me here?" Phurba's fear clear in the cracking of his voice.

"That's what necromancers do," Avalon laughed.

"That's intolerable," mumbled Phurba.

"Then make sure you kill him, not the other way around," said Francis.

"So, Dog," said Slowball, "if we're not opening the shop what are we going to do for the rest of the day? Laundry?"

"Well, I don't know about the rest of you, but I feel like raising some hell."

"Don't you have enough hell going on around here?" asked Father Francis.

"I mean old fashioned biker hell. I'm looking for a large town, not city size, somewhere close. Know of anything?"

"South is Skegness, north is Grimsby," Francis replied, "Skegness is a holiday town, and Grimsby is a fishing town, thirty miles away each."

"If we go to Grimsby we may bump into Vince and his club." Slowball said.

"North it is," laughed Roaddog, then he turned to Mick, "You want to tag along? Your bus isn't exactly a bike, but you're welcome." Mick looked at Jackie for a moment then answered.

"Why not? Could be fun."

"Avalon," smiled Roaddog, "why don't you tag along with Mick, you can always crash out in his car, it's big enough."

"I'm in," said Avalon.

"Our van has enough space for you to sleep in anyway," said Mick.

"Okay Dragonriders, looks like we have a plan, let's ride."

"I'm not sure about using the old name," said Slowball, "could be tempting fate a bit."

"What do you suggest then?"

"How about Hellriders? Sort of appropriate right now."

"Movies, books, almost certainly some other club somewhere, what the hell. Who are they going to sue?" laughed Roaddog.

So, the Hellriders were born.

Chapter 14: Hell Comes to Grimsby

While they were walking back to the workshop Roaddog called Vince.

"Hey man, where you at?" he asked.

"Why?"

"We're looking for some old fashioned biker fun, you know of any around here?"

"Well we're currently at our home pub, it's a little quiet, but what can you expect after a run?"

"Send me the postcode, we're coming to party," laughed Roaddog.

"Will do, see ya in about an hour," replied Vince.

"An hour? It's only thirty miles."

"Humberside man, speed camera capital of the whole damned world."

"Fuck em, they can't get me," laughed Roaddog.

"We'll see you when you get here," laughed Vince.

"We'll be on the road in about three minutes," Roaddog punched the call cancel button and waited for the text message with the postcode. As soon as it came in, he called it out to Mick.

"You'll need that because there is no way you are going to keep up."

"Thanks Roaddog, we'll catch you up in Grimsby, just get the beers in," grinned Mick.

It only took a few minutes for the bikers to load up and leave the little village, heading north up the main coastal road. Roaddog in the lead, with Bug's whispering Honda behind, and Slowball following with Jane and Sylvia behind him. Mick followed in the big Renault, not seeming to hurry at all. Avalon spoke from the rear seat.

"Aren't you going to try and keep up?"

"No, I know this road, I'll catch them up in a little while, once they get frightened by a couple of bends that come up real quick," he laughed.

"What do you mean?"

"There's a couple of killers, that suddenly tighten up, you go in thinking you've got plenty of space to get around the bend, and then it's a surprising hairpin. A couple of those and they'll slow right down, and there's the first," he said as they left the village, a left hand bend that tightened up, but Roaddog was ready for this one he'd been caught out by it when they went to see Vince at the bike rally.

"Once we get past Marshchapel he'll be on roads he's never seen before," laughed Mick looking back at Avalon in the rear seat.

"Where are we heading?" asked Jackie.

"The Empire," laughed Mick.

"You're kidding."

"No."

"I bet you can get there first," smiled Jackie.

"I'm fairly sure we'll be on our second beer before they work their way through all the traffic lights."

"Okay for you, Avalon?" asked Jackie.

"So long as we don't die on the road."

"Have no fear, we know these roads fairly well."

"Probably better than the local cops," laughed Mick, as he followed the road that the bikers had taken, this far it was the only option. Before long they arrived at the small village called Tetney. There was a hard right turn climbing the hill, the bikers were cautious as they made the turn, immediately the road straightened out there was a turn to the left, Mick snapped into this turn.

"Here's hoping," he said as he accelerated hard along the narrow street, at the Tee junction he paused for an instant then hit the throttle again, turning right and giving the huge car all the power it had. Moya was up to the challenge, the turbo howling and the tyres scrabbling Mick powered along the short straight and blew through the give way sign in front of the Plough pub. Braking hard for the left hander he accelerated into the straight, a glance in his mirror showed the bikers coming around the left hander, Roaddog was catching up quickly as Mick piled on the brakes. Twenty miles an hour through the school zone, he twitched to the right to block Roaddog's overtaking manoeuvre. Roaddog was hard against Mick's bumper when they passed the truvelo camera, Mick smiled, thinking of the picture that camera would have taken, a clear view of Roaddog's face, no matter what the registration numbers yielded, the man's face would have been enough to damn him in the cop's eyes. Mick hit the button to open the driver's window and waved the bikers past, once the school zone was ended.

"The local cops take their school zones very seriously," he laughed as Slowball's trike shot past, the VW howling. Shortly after the village of Humberston Roaddog's satnav made the error that Mick was waiting for, it made a right turn at a roundabout, the bikes were only just in view as they made the turn, Mick laughed aloud.

"Google really have to get their maps fixed." He powered into the roundabout and carried straight on, A quick jink through the S bend and then a right at the roundabout and there was the Empire on the left. Mick pulled into the huge carpark and stopped the big diesel.

"Abandon ship," he called, the two women in the car did exactly as they were bid. The three of them were walking in through the side door as they heard the sounds of a Victory and a VW coming along the road. Mick smiled to himself as he turned to watch the others arrive.

"How the fuck did you manage that?" yelled Roaddog as he pulled up alongside Moya.

"Sat nav's don't always know the best routes, for some reason they think that the S bend back there is two roads that don't actually meet, so they take you the long way round, with all those traffic lights."

"Well," replied Roaddog, as the motors around him quieted, "let's get some beer and see what's happening inside." Crash helmets were deposited in Slowball's lock box. As they walked into the darkness it took a few seconds for their eyes to become accustomed to the gloom. Roaddog spotted Vince and some of his riders at the end of the long bar. Roaddog bought the beers, and they went to sit with Vince and his people.

"What's happening?" asked Roaddog.

"Not much," replied Vince, "usual Tuesday stuff, but a bit quieter after the weekends run."

"Never been in a place that has bands on Tuesdays before," said Roaddog, waving his hand in the direction of the stage at the other end of the long room.

"They're in here every Tuesday, it's a rehearsal not a gig."

"That'll make a change," said Mick, as he wandered to the other end of the room to watch what was happening on the stage, Jackie went with him, but Avalon stayed with the rest.

"Who's the not so new girl?" asked Vince.

"This is Avalon," replied Roaddog.

"Hey Avalon, why the fancy walking stick?" Vince asked with a puzzled look.

"It's sort of necessary to my work," she grinned.

"What work is that?"

"Well," interrupted Roaddog, "she used the staff to contain a demon in the church until we were ready to kill the mother."

"For real?" stuttered Vince.

"For truth," Avalon smiled.

"What are you?" asked Horse.

"I'm a simple country girl."

"Bull," snapped Vince.

"Okay, high priestess of the local druids, that do for you?"

"Wow, druids are actually real?" asked Vince.

"And real powerful," smiled Roaddog.

"Never been one for religion," said Vince.

"Me either," laughed Roaddog, "not much choice right now, they're the only real source of information that we have."

"They actually help?"

"Of course we do," interrupted Avalon, "my barrier held Melchion inside the church until our friends were ready to take him on. The gunfire was hurting him, but not enough to kill him."

"I have a semi serious question," said Vince slowly.

"Ask." Roaddog's quiet reply.

"How did you come by the squirt gun?"

"Bug took it from the dead hands of some drug dealers."

"You went up against a guy with a mac-10?"

"Three actually, I wasn't even aware that Bug had taken the gun, or the magazines, until he came here."

"That took some balls," observed Horse.

"We had extreme motivation."

"Explain please?" said Vince.

"They'd killed all our friends and taken some girls."

"That'd do it," grinned Vince, "any survivors?"

"The only one left alive was in hospital having a broken leg fixed. He was a wimp anyway."

"Would he know where they got the guns?"

"If he turns up here, you better ask him fast, he doesn't have much in the way of life expectancy."

"Special hatred there?"

"Damned right, his lies got everyone killed."

"Lies?"

"He said he was attacked by all of us, he didn't admit that his leg had been broken by a girl, Jackie trapped his leg in his car door, Man-Dare kicked a couple of them and threatened to cut the balls off another. I confiscated all the 'insurance' money that they had collected. All in all, they weren't having a good day with the girls."

"You plan on hunting the liar down?"

"Nah, he stays away, he stays alive. He seems to have a police escort much of the time."

"Where the fuck is this crazy place you come from?"

"Lancashire, only a hundred miles or so away."

"Yeah, but it's the wrong side of the Pennines."

"You do know the war of the roses has been over for a few years?"

"So what?"

"You don't exactly look like the typical Yorkshire man."

"Leeds, born and bred, you've got to go back four generations to find immigrants from India in my past. Yorkshire as they come, by gum," Vince laughed. "My grandfather was a miner, when we still had mines. My father a steel worker, when we still had steel. Me, I'm the black sheep."

"Do they still have sheep in Yorkshire?" asked Roaddog.

"The only place in the world with more sheep than Yorkshire is New Zealand."

"It's a crazy world."

"Do you think the liar will turn up here?" asked Vince.

"It's a possibility, but that bastard cop will have to be with him, he wouldn't have the balls to come here on his own."

"Will you kill him with a cop as a witness?"

"I'll kill him and the cop if the cop gets in the way."

"Can I ask a favour?" said Vince gently.

"You can ask."

"Please don't kill him until I've had the chance to question him."

"I can't promise that," replied Roaddog, "I may not even be the biggest risk to his life."

"What do you mean?"

"Girls, how do you feel about the lying scumbag?" Jackie and Jane stood up and in a moment there were stilettos in each of their hands, four black blades ready to kill.

"And I'll stick the ten up his ass and empty it," said Cherie.

"If Man-Dare is here, then they'll all be too slow, she'll tear him apart with her bare hands," said Roaddog. Vince looked around as the girls returned the knives to their belts and sat down again. He waved to the barman who had his phone in his hands, to indicate that everything was fine.

"You got some good people here," said Vince, he thought for a moment before going on. "Tell you what, if a cop shows up with a guy with a gammy leg, looking for you, I'll hold them and call ya, okay?"

"Why would they come here?"

"Looking for desperados, go where desperados hang out."

"You're that well known?"

"The local plod seem to think we are involved in guns and drugs and all sorts of criminal activities."

"They got any evidence?" asked Roaddog.

"They got Jack and shit, and Jack's left town," laughed Vince.

"Like some of their cops," said Horse.

"They tend to get cross when you kill cops," Roaddog said.

"I've never killed a cop," smiled Vince.

"No," Horse said, "but they are struggling to get cops to accept promotions around here."

"What do you mean?"

"Well," said Horse, "there was that DCI who was caught smuggling five kilos of heroin in a car he bought from Spain."

"Let's not forget the DI that went to jail for rape, you really can't beat that DNA evidence," laughed Vince.

"Then there was the Deputy chief constable, his bank accounts were a complete mess, payments coming in from all over the world, and going out to criminals all over the county. So sad when a good man goes bad."

"I've always wanted to screw with someone's bank account like that," said Bug, "but never really had the incentive."

"Could you do it without getting caught?" asked Roaddog. Bug frowned for a moment before answering.

"Probably, there must be someone here that knows how to do it."

"Hang on," said Vince, "I never said that we were involved."

"Sorry Vince, you don't come across as the sort of guy that would claim someone else's victories."

"Damn," laughed Vince, "just too honest, that's me."

"That's good, tell Bug how to scramble the lying scumbags bank accounts, if you can mix him up with that bastard Hopkins, that should help muddy any evidence he can bring to a court, especially after his death." Roaddog smiled, and Vince shook his head, but still he called "Felix, get your ass over here." A young biker stood up from another table and walked over slowly.

"Yes Vince?" he asked.

"Can you show Bug here how to crack someone's bank account?"

"Hey Bug," said Felix, "I can do that, you are going to need some very specific information though, let's go somewhere quiet and talk." As the pair walked away Roaddog started to laugh out loud, so much so that he almost spilled his beer.

"What's so funny?" asked Jackie.

"Felix," spluttered Roaddog between giggles.

"I don't understand," said Jackie.

"I'm not surprised," said Vince, "but I am surprised that Dog gets it, he's too young."

"Sign of a mis-spent youth, I just loved those old cartoons, they were so funny, and so illegal these days."

"What cartoon?" asked Jackie.

"Felix the cat, he was a small black cat that had a magic bag, this bag always had everything he needed, I've seen a long extension ladder come out of that bag, one rung at a time, and then go back the same way."

"So what's the connection to Felix?"

"The bag he has slung over his shoulder is just like the one in the cartoon. Vince, does he understand his name?"

"Oh yes, it took some explaining, and his original bag was a little different and more colourful."

"So he changed it to match the cartoon?"

"Yeah," laughed Vince.

"That's simply wonderful."

"It's his own fault, he always has that bag, unlike the cat it doesn't have an extension ladder, or at least not one we've ever seen."

"Will he be able to help Bug?"

"I couldn't say, that sort of thing is illegal," laughed Vince.

"Thanks anyway," grinned Roaddog.

The conversation turned the way these things do, crazy stunts, drunken parties, and great rallies. Some time later Roaddog's phone rang. He took it out of his pocket and frowned. Not only was it a number he didn't recognise, there was no number at all. He hit the accept button and spoke softly.

"Yeah."

"Hi Dog," was the reply.

"Billy?"

"Ya got it, how's tricks?"

"I'm okay, you?"

"I'm good, but you're not going to be."

"What do you mean?"

"The bastard Hopkins says that he knows where you are, Man-Dare damned near killed the twat, I had to drag her off."

"Did she get a good piece of him?"

"No, but we think you are in danger."

"If he turns up here I'll kill the dick."

"He says he has a tracker on you."

"Maybe he was just fishing?"

"I don't think so, I wish Bug was here, we'd have cloned his damned phone, I can't do that shit, I need to learn from Bug."

"You're good enough at the legit stuff, could he have a tracker on me?"

"He can't have your phone number, there's only me here that has it, all the others are already with you."

"Could he have a tracker on them?"

"No, Bug's been very serious about phone security, none of us have even mis-placed our phones in months."

"What about Man-Dare?"

"Her phone doesn't have your number, she knows how careless she is."

"What if it's not a phone he's following?"

"You think he may have tagged one of the vehicles?"

"Airtag?"

"Could be," Billy paused, "not on Bugs bike, too difficult to hide, if he has tagged anything it'll be Slowball's trike, plenty of heavy steel under there for a magnetic tag."

"Thanks for the heads up," said Roaddog, "we'll check out the trike once it gets light."

"You be careful," said Billy.

"Cheers man," replied Roaddog, "look after that crazy bitch."

"Thanks for that, that's a task and a half."

"But it's worth it?"

"Fuck yes, the rate she's going I'll die with a hard on."

"You need some blue pills?"

"Shit no, bitch can suck start a leaf blower," laughed Billy.

"Well, don't die too soon, I got shit going on I can't leave even for your funeral."

"Do you want me to bring her to you?"

"I'm not sure the locals could deal with her, they're a tad straight laced."

"Didn't you tell me, 'I don't worry about what people think, they don't do it often.' I'm sure that's what you said," laughed Billy.

"Give us a second Billy," said Roaddog, then he called, "Hey Roaddog."

"What to want Roaddog?" asked Mick from the other end of the room.

"Can we billet a couple of crazy bikers with you for a few days?"

"Sure," replied Mick, "I can put two on the inside and four in the awning, if they bring air beds."

"Thanks friend," said then he put the phone to his ear again. "Okay Billy, you and Man-Dare can come down we got a comfy billet for ya."

"How longs that ride?" asked Billy.

"Three and a half, unless you really hammer it."

"Fine, we'll be with you tomorrow morning, but not too fucking early," Billy laughed as he broke the connection.

"Tell me you didn't just invite Man-Dare and Billy?" asked Jackie.

"I did," he laughed.

"Fuck," muttered Jackie, "this could get crazy."

"What do you mean?" asked Vince.

"Man-Dare is plain crazy."

"You're going to have to explain that at least a little."

Jackie looked at Jane and Cherie, she got nods from both.

"Fine," she paused for a moment before continuing. "Some months ago there was a disagreement with a group of drug dealers from Hyde, they turned up at the Dragonriders club house, armed with machine guns, they killed everyone except for four of us girls. Three of us were terrified almost out of our minds, Man-Dare was not. She yelled at them, she called them limp dick bastards, she told them that Roaddog was coming for them. She told them that today is their last day on this earth. They beat her and still she yelled at them, she kicked one of them in the nuts, and we all got taped up, unable to move. Still she called them pussies. They told us that they were going to get us hooked on heroin then sell us to whore houses in Pakistan. Man-Dare spat in their faces and called them girls. She was tied spreadeagled on a table, the rest of us in chairs. They ripped off most of her clothes and set about raping her, she laughed at them and called them gay boys, pufters and ladyboys."

"Bitch has got balls," laughed Vince.

"And some," agreed Jackie. "These guys weren't in the least bit bothered by sloppy seconds or thirds. They fucked her one after the other, the rest of us just had to suck cocks to get them hard again. Not my favourite thing, but she kept screaming and they kept fucking her. It seemed like it was forever, then we heard a screaming engine and one of the men tucked his cock back in his jeans and went towards the front door. Then there was a loud crash from one of the other rooms, and the howl of a motor that suddenly died. "They're here," screamed Man-Dare, "all you bastards are dead." The men stuffed their cocks back in their pants and went off to see what was happening. One went out of the side door, and the rest into the room where the crash had come from, I couldn't hear their guns, but I heard Bug's sawn off, and Sharpshooters pump action, and of course the rattle of Roaddog's Thompson. Then there was silence. Man-Dare screamed, "where the fuck have you lot been?" as Dog walked into the back room with two of the drug dealers. I cannot describe the relief that I felt when I saw his face, Bug checked out of the back door, and returned to say that Sharpshooter was dead. Once the rest of us were safe Man-Dare passed out."

"She'd only goaded them because she knew that the rest of us couldn't take the treatment that was to come," said Jane, "she told us so in the van ride home. I was so glad to see this madman," she nodded at Roaddog, "I just can't describe it."

"Not what you said in the van," said Roaddog.

"I was still too frightened then, given a couple of weeks I was kicking myself for not coming with you, then worrying about what you'd say, then frightened you might not want me, then terrified you might actually want me, then, fuck, I don't know what," Jane looked down as Jackie wrapped her in her arms and kissed her cheek.

"You're going to bring this crazy Man-Dare to our side of the country?" asked Vince

"That could be fun," smiled Roaddog, "she fought with Bandit Queen for the leadership of the Dragonriders, she lost, but she learned. She's looking for a new club to take over."

"She'll have no luck here," laughed Vince.

"Probably not, but you never can tell, she's learned that going after the leader is risky, perhaps she'll hit one of your lieutenants, then engineer a coup."

"You think she's capable of that sort of thing?" asked Slowball.

"From the conversations I've had with Billy, she's pretty much managed it, without actually having to shag the leader." There was a moments silence as people around the table considered his words.

"I have a question," said Cherie.

"Ask," replied Vince.

"It's not entirely relevant, but, cars are crashing into the building, and those ass-holes waste time tucking their cocks away, why? They're going to war, what difference does it make?" Roaddog and Vince exchanged looks then started laughing.

"It's just something you do," replied Bug, "you'd tuck your tits away wouldn't ya?"

"No, while you're staring at the tits, I'd but a bullet in your head."

"Damn woman," said Bug, "that's cold, you'd kill the father of your unborn?"

"Only if he really pisses me off."

"That's you told," observed Vince, "It wouldn't work for Horse though."

"Why?" asked Cherie.

"He'd trip over the thing," Vince howled with laughter and reached out to take Horse's hand.

"Thanks mate," Horse said sarcastically.

"You know I don't mean it," he turned to Roaddog, "you gotta bring the Man-Dare here, I wanna see how good her gaydar is."

"That's wicked," Jane said.

"That's cruel," agreed Jackie.

"She'll fucking kill you when she works it out," Sylvia said quietly.

"But it's gotta be worth a giggle, no one tell her, it'll be a blast," said Roaddog.

"On your head, and your's alone," replied Bug, "I'm not taking the flack for this shit."

"You lot are making this woman interesting," Vince said slowly, "she wants to be leader, but doesn't actually need to be in the leaders bed."

"Not having a clear leader for the women has been known to cause us some issues," said Horse.

"It does raise a little friction now and again," replied Vince, he paused for a moment, "I definitely want to meet this bitch with balls."

"Billy says they'll be here tomorrow early, I don't know what we've got on, but I'll let you know when we're going to come this way," Roaddog said.

"That would be good," said Vince, just as Roaddog's phone rang. Roaddog looked at his phone and saw that Jake was calling.

"Fuck," he said, "Bug, cameras." He answered the phone, "What's up Jake?"

"Nothing much," said Jake, "just wondering where the fuck you lot are, I figured you'd be at the church by now?" Roaddog looked at Bug.

"Birds are down, nothing happening," whispered Bug.

"We're actually in Grimsby, but we'll be coming home fairly soon."

"That's quite a way off. The birds are down, but you're still half an hour away."

"I figured we'd have a few days before the damned necromancer comes back. Why you looking for us?"

"The damned clerics are crawling all over the church, fuck knows what they're up to."

Roaddog looked to Bug again, "Inside camera's," he snapped.

"Hang on Jake, checking now."

"They're in there," said Bug, he turned the phone so that Avalon could see it. She looked intently at the grainy black and white images of the infra-red camera.

"They're up to something," she said slowly, "looks like they're trying to set up a forbidding across the whole of the portal, I don't think they have the power to do that sort of thing."

"Why not?" asked Roaddog.

"It's never been done, or even tried as far as I am aware, it's not the sort of thing the clerics generally do."

"So what do they normally do?"

"You really want to know?"

"Yeah."

"Fine, under normal circumstances they turn up after the event, clear up whatever mess is left, then find someone to blame, and burn a few witches."

"That's callous."

"It's how they operate."

"Could they know about the thing in the northeast?"

"It's possible."

"So they know that you have better control of fire than they do?"

"That is also possible, but we'll just have to ask them."

"This is all getting too complicated for a simple man like me."

"Fuck off," snapped Avalon.

"How you doing for energy now?" asked Roaddog.

Avalon frowned at him then looked up at the crystal in the top of her staff, it flashed briefly through the rainbow up to indigo, not quite violet.

"Doing fine," she said, "almost full even, been a long time since I held this much power."

"Where you getting this power from?" demanded Vince, looking round at his people.

"All around," she said quietly, "all of your people have very strong, and powerful emotions, it is that I am tapping into, I'm only taking a little from each, they will be more relaxed, a little quieter maybe, but completely unharmed."

Vince looked at Horse.

"We've been drinking steadily for three hours on a boring Tuesday night, and we've not had to break up one fight yet" said the master at arms.

"That is indeed unusual," said Vince. "Could you pop down on a Friday night when things get rowdy?"

"No," said Avalon, "they don't notice being a little relaxed on a Tuesday, but I'm sure that the tensions on a Friday night would be so much greater, I'd not be able to cope with all that energy."

"How do you normally charge your, er, wand?" asked Vince.

"I'd call it a staff, and I would normally have a large group of acolytes chanting and specifically feeding me their energy."

"They actually send it to you?"

"Yes, but their energy is not as intense, not as powerful as the strong emotions here tonight."

"Still sounds like a good way to control dangerous situations?"

"Perhaps, but sometimes there is a price to pay."

"Reminds me of a song," interrupted Horse.

"What song?" asked Vince.

"The Wizard, by Sabbath, how's it go? 'Never talking, just keeps walking, weaving his magic.' That's what you do, making people happy."

"It's what I try, by taking the top out of strong or violent emotions people can get happier."

"But you've gotta keep walking?" asked Horse.

"Yes, it's like any system of energy, when you take some away, the system generates more to make up for the loss."

"And when you take away the drain the energy in the system spikes?" asked Vince.

"It can happen, I have been very gentle today, I knew that your people would provide more than enough and I was in no hurry."

"So the spike when you leave will be small?"

"Hopefully none existent, bar one."

"Who?"

"The guy over there," she nodded in the direction of the table with the highest tension, "he thinks his girl is cheating, and really can't understand why he hasn't slapped her yet, he's been winding himself up all night, he'll blow when I shut down the field."

"Give it ten seconds, then shut it down," said Vince, "Horse go sit on Jingo." Avalon waited until Horse was standing behind Jingo and put her hand over the crystal in her staff and smiled as the closed the hungry eye in it. Jingo shook his head and jumped to his feet, as his right hand pulled backwards it fell into Horse's grip. From there that fist had nowhere to go. As Jingo pulled the fist forwards his body pressed backwards against Horse, and Horse's left hand came around Jingo's waist holding him firmly.

"Problem Jingo?" asked Vince.

"Er, yes, er no, I don't know, I'm very angry right now."

"Your girl has not cheated on you, but she probably should leave you if you slap her about again, are you going to slap her?"

"No boss." Jingo's quiet reply.

"Good," said Vince, and he nodded towards the back door. Horse picked Jingo up and carried him out of the back door.

"What is Horse going to do?" asked Roaddog.

"Keep him outside until he has calmed down enough to be with real people, maybe threaten him a bit, definitely intimidate him a lot."

"And if he won't calm down?"

"They all calm down, always."

"How come?"

"You really want to know?"

"I asked."

"If Jingo really gets stroppy, then Horse will put him over a picnic table. And pull his jeans down, by the time that monster is pressed against Jingo's asshole he'll calm the fuck down."

"That's brutal," said Roaddog.

"But you love it, don't you?" asked Sylvia.

"There aren't many people with my capacity," smiled Vince.

"Sounds like a match made in heaven," Sylvia smiled.

"Oh, it is." Vince grinned.

"Fear of rape is not the way to control a club," said Roaddog.

"I agree," replied Vince as Jingo and Horse returned to the bar, the later with a prominent bulge in his jeans.

"Jingo," called Vince. The scruffy biker stopped and looked towards Vince. "Final warning," said Vince, "next time you're out. This is the last boozer in town that we can drink in, you're not ruining that for us." Jingo nodded and returned to the table where his girl was waiting, quiet words were exchanged as he took his seat next to her and reached out to take her hand.

"He's a lot calmer now," observed Avalon.

"Horse has a calming effect on everyone," smiled Vince.

"Except you," said Sylvia.

"Oh, fuck," replied Vince, "he excites the hell out of me."

"You said the last boozer?" asked Roaddog.

"Yeah, we've had problems in the past, they get pissed about the least little fight, then they kick us out, then they burn down and we got to find a new place."

"Seems like a hard life for you guys?" Bug asked.

"We all have our crosses to bear," Vince sighed with a grin.

"We better get moving, Jake is nervous with us so far away," said Roaddog.

"So am I," agreed Avalon.

"Mick," called Roaddog, he continued when Mick looked round, "we gotta get moving, you take Avalon back to yours, okay?"

"No sweat," replied Mick, as he and Jackie came away from their places by the stage and dropped their empty glasses on the bar.

"You ready Avalon?" asked Mick. She nodded and got to her feet.

"See you later," she said to Roaddog, "keep in touch."

"I got your number; I'll call you if anything comes up."

"Anything?"

"Well, obviously not anything," laughed Roaddog. "Slowball, Bug, ready to roll." He turned to Vince. "Thank you for all your hospitality and your help, if we survive it will be in some way down to you and yours."

"Not a problem," said Vince, "I really want that mac ten, and don't forget to bring Man-Dare to see us."

"No worries." Then they all stood up. "Hellriders," said Roaddog, "let's ride." He waved to Vince and headed for the door. By the time he got to the door Moya was already leaving the car park.

Chapter 15: Late Tuesday at Botolph's

Roaddog followed Mick and the big Renault as they left Grimsby, once on the open roads the bikes and the trike blew past Moya, the speed differential was so great that the wind of Slowballs trike passing caused the heavy car to twitch to the right. Riding the winding country roads gave Roaddog time to think, the high torquing twin needed few gear changes and little actual attention as it rolled smoothly through the bends and opened up on the straights. Before he was halfway back to the caravan site, he had decided that he wasn't going to wait until morning to find out what the clerics were up to. He blew past the turn into the site and went straight on towards the church, the others simply followed. As they made the right-hander at South Farm Roaddog was surprised to see Jake in the driveway on his quad, when Roaddog slowed to make the left-hander towards the church he spotted the two little headlights behind Slowball's trike. The four new arrivals parked up alongside Father Francis' minibus. As soon as Roaddog dismounted he pulled his phone from his jacket. And punched up a number. The phone only rang once before it was answered.

"Yeah," said Mick.

"Do us a favour, bring Avalon to the church, we need to know what these guys have been up to."

"I'm just entering the village, three minutes."

"Cheers," Roaddog closed the call and turned to Jake.

"Anything happening?"

"Nothing that I can see, the damned cameras can't make their minds up, day or night, they keep switching it's very confusing."

"At least the birds are down."

"That doesn't make me feel any better, I just want to take a shotgun to the lot of them."

"We already have the cops sniffing around looking for machine guns."

"Bastards should be dealing with this crap, not us."

"By the time they stop bitching about whose job it is the whole world will be on fire."

"Speaking of fire," smiled Jake pulling a large flask from inside his jacket, he passed it to Roaddog who returned the smile and took a small sip, before passing it back. Jake passed the flask to the others; none turned it down. Before Jake returned the flask to his jacket a car turned into the driveway, almost immediately followed by another one. Mick parked Moya alongside Jakes little quad and the other car stopped in the entranceway, effectively blocking it. Jake stepped over to his quad, pulled a shotgun from the holster on the side, draped it over his arm and broke it open in the approved manner, but he didn't remove the cartridges. The man in the car waited until he saw Avalon get out of the blue car, he walked quickly towards Avalon, Bug and Roaddog moved to intercept but Avalon waved them off. The man stopped six feet from Avalon and threw himself face down on the ground.

"High priestess Avalon I apologise for my behaviour, I really didn't know that you were there, this is not the sort of company I would have ever expected to find you in. Please mistress, please forgive me."

"Stephen you owe enough for the favours we have already done you, now you ask for more?"

"Mistress, please don't withdraw your grace, I will do anything, anything at all."

Roaddog smiled at the grin on Avalon's face.

"Fine Stephen, we do have need of some good strong hands, especially ones that can shoot a rifle."

"Surely you don't want me to kill someone?"

"We're not killing people here, only demons, can you deal with killing demons?"

"You mean actual demons?"

"Yes, Stephen, real honest to goodness demons, these fine people have taken out three demons already, and we have at least one more due someday soon."

"I cannot refuse to help you, you and yours have been so good to me."

"I'm glad you see the reality of the situation, there is something else you have to be aware of," she paused while Stephen looked up, fear in his eyes, "our local demon killers tend to use methods that are frowned on by your employers, you will forget what you see, and be thankful that they will protect your back as well as their own, do you understand?"

"Let me guess, there are machine guns involved," Stephen smiled.

"Damned right," laughed Roaddog, "though currently out of

ammunition."

"No you're not," said Jake going back to his quad to pick up a heavy bag, "here you go mate." He handed the bag to Roaddog. "Sorry, hard lead, I don't have the soft stuff you like yet."

"Thanks Jake," said Roaddog, "Jackie, you emptied the damned thing, you can fill it up." He passed the bag to Jackie, and she went to his bike, retrieving the Thompson, she turned to him.

"Explain how this works," He took a few moments to show her how to reload the drum and check the mechanism. Quickly she was loading the cartridges into the drum.

"Petrolheads," snorted Stephen.

"You believed it until just now," laughed Roaddog.

"Only because it sounded legit."

"Oh, it is legit."

"You mean that we can actually look forwards to cars that sound like machine guns?"

"Oh yes, and more."

"More?"

"With careful tuning an exhaust pipe can turn into a flame thrower."

"They already do that," replied Stephen.

"No, real flame thrower, sets fire to the paint and overheats your radiator so your car blows up."

"You're kidding?"

"No, be careful who you get too close to."

"Somehow I think this job is getting too dangerous for a simple copper."

"You're here with us now, we're dealing with demons, not criminals. Perhaps you'll understand what danger really is," laughed Roaddog.

"Let's go inside and see what the others have been up to," said Avalon, her tall staff beating a regular tattoo on the tarmac of the path, she walked through the lynch gate and towards the south door. The others followed in her wake, except for Jackie, who was still reloading the thompson machine gun's drum. Roaddog was at Avalon's shoulder as she stepped through the door,

"What have you lot been up to?" she called, looking at the clerics who were scattered about the nave of the church.

"We're trying to at least slow down the next demon, maybe we can separate it from Fintan, before he gets through, that may just kill him, and seal the breach."

"So, what have you actually done?" she demanded, her right foot tapping impatiently on the tiles of the floor.

"Avalon," said Phurba softly, "what have you done? I've never seen anyone carrying that much power."

"I decided I'd most likely need some power, so I loaded up, I'm not entirely maxed out, but I am close."

"You're carrying so much power that you glow."

"Only to those that are sensitive."

"I'm such a one, and you are seriously hot."

"Most of the energy is within the staff, I show as energetic because I am in contact with the staff, it is after all mine."

"Well a demon will sense it, and target you accordingly."

"There is nothing to be gained from hiding from this fight, it could be that the fate of the world is in our hands."

"You think it could be that important?" asked Father Francis.

"With one demon to hold the gate open, who's to say how many can come through. While we hold them back there can only be one at a time."

"I think we need more help," said Francis timidly.

"The powers that be have decided that we are all there is," she smiled at the fear in his eyes.

"Well, I'm going to call the bishop," snapped Francis.

"I'm betting he says 'you're it, deal with it.'"

In a heartbeat the other clerics agreed to call their own superiors, Roaddog laughed loudly.

"You are wasting your time," he laughed, "they already have plausible deniability, I can hear their words now. 'We sent the ones who said they were the best suited for this task, we had no idea what they would face, all we knew was that they said they were the best.' And you'll all be dead, so no come back."

"Surely they understand that if we fail, then they are ultimately responsible?" asked Abraham.

"They're politicians, they can't be held responsible, and they have documentation to prove that they did everything they could reasonably be expected to do, other than putting their own lives on the line, but they are far too important for that, aren't they?"

"Ever felt like a goat of the scape variety?" asked Mohammed.

"Today more than ever," muttered Francis.

"So, how has the work gone?" asked Avalon.

"We have woven a restriction around the portal, so the demon will be slowed and hopefully we'll be able to kill it, before it can come through properly and then all we have to deal with is Fintan, without demonic support."

"I can feel it," said Avalon gently, "you have certainly created a powerful spell."

"Spell?" said Abraham.

"What else could you call it, you have woven a magic barrier, using words and symbols, powders and potions, thoughts and belief. This is magic."

"Magic is not something we are ever involved with," said Mohammed, "magic is the realm of Allah."

"Well," laughed Avalon, "your barrier will work to some extent, I can feel its power even now, when it is dormant. It may even slow the demon down enough for us to get here before it breaks through. Then we will be able to support the barrier and end the demon."

"But," interrupted Roaddog, "the demon as displayed by the notice board over there is Fintan himself."

"That is true," replied Avalon, she thought for a moment or two, looking round at the others, as if after some sort of hint. "Could it be that he is a demon?" she asked.

"No," said Francis, "he can't be a demon, or more accurately, he can't have been a demon when he was working with us, we would have been able to feel it." He looked round and the other clerics agreed with him. "So, he is a demon now, maybe he's been promoted."

"Is that possible?" asked Roaddog.

"Oh yes," replied Avalon, "the problem generally is that when people work towards getting promoted they fail to take into consideration the fact that the demon takes over, they are just gone and a demon takes up residence."

"Can you be sure of that?" asked Roaddog.

"Actually no," smiled Avalon, "looking back at the records anyone who became a demon seems to have fallen quite easily to the power of the local clergy, and ultimately the fire."

"Sounds like more bullshit," said Roaddog.

"Could be," replied Avalon, "here's another thought, what if the demons we have already faced here are others who have been promoted?"

"Looks like the job selection process is seriously flawed, only one managed to leave the church grounds, and that's because only the children knew about him."

"Here's another thought for you," smiled Francis, "what if we are the job selection process?"

"You mean that we are the interview body that decides if these are worthy to be demons?" asked Avalon.

"It could be so," said Mohammed.

"So how come the demons have a history?" asked Roaddog.

"Perhaps," replied Abraham slowly, "the challenge is to take a known set of properties, and face the selection committee, and stay alive."

"That gives them three failures in a row, and the next has no history, at least not a demonic one," said Roaddog.

"This one is definitely out of the ordinary," said Francis.

"Is any of this ordinary to you?" demanded Roaddog.

"Actually no, none of it is, this is not what any of us expected to happen here."

"So, what did you expect?"

"To be honest, none of us were sure what would happen, I expected our first attempt to seal the portal, the threefold spinning barrier should have worked to hold and kill the first demon, though it was actually the second. I wasn't expecting someone to have to jump inside and set the demon afire."

"Well that failed, and Nutter set him on fire, so why didn't you try the barrier again?"

"It failed once, and we couldn't actually trust it again."

"Belief is everything, without confidence in it you knew that it could fail and knowing that it certainly would."

"Pretty much," said Francis quietly.

"So, what about the barriers you have been working on for the last hour?"

"We expect them to hold the demon, while the more physical methods deal with Fintan, if we can kill him, then the demon should return to hell."

"But the portal won't be closed?"

"Not likely, that's going to take something more drastic."

"Well I have a plan for that, but it's going to take some work."

"What sort of plan?" asked Francis.

"You really don't want to know, you magicians get one more chance, then I'm going to shut the thing forever."

"I'm not sure I like the finality of your thought," said Francis.

"Worst of all you're going to be in the eye of the storm when it hits, along with the rest of us."

"You got a plan?" asked Bug.

"Yes, surprising the thoughts that rattle through your head when your body is riding, and your mind is floating free."

"You want to share?"

"Not when the civilians are around, later brother."

Bug turned to Slowball saying, "This is going to be fun, I just know it."

"I have every confidence in Dog coming up with something that will work," smiled Slowball.

"Belief is everything," laughed Roaddog.

"Just what are you planning?" asked Avalon.

"You'll find out if sending Fintan back to hell doesn't close the thing, if another demon appears on that wall, then we are going to end this."

Avalon turned to her fellow clerics, "Anyone else get a shiver from this scary biker's words?"

"I fucking did," said the cop.

"Me too," added Francis, "the guy has a level of certainty that cannot be denied."

"You've already made it clear that belief is everything," said Roaddog, "I believe I can shut this thing for good, it'll take a few days, but I can do it. Can you?"

"We," replied Francis, "actually have no real idea, we have no belief, we have no faith in our actions, if you have these things then you cannot fail."

"Confidence is everything," said Roaddog, "you and yours are going to have to come up with a story for the rest of the world, but those of us that survive, we will be the only ones that know the truth."

"By all the gods," laughed Avalon as she fell to the ground, sitting on the hard tiles of the floor she howled in laughter.

"What's so funny heathen?" demanded Francis loudly.

"Don't you see it?" asked Avalon, "With all our beliefs and all our religions, we are not as pure in our intentions as this man and his brothers."

"Hey." Snapped Jackie as she walked in through the south door.

"And sisters," smiled Avalon. "Jackie is that gun ready?"

"Nearly," replied Jackie.

"Please make it ready." Jackie looked to Roaddog, and received his nod. She pulled the bolt and pushed the safety into the off position.

"Locked and loaded, she's called Vera, and she's hungry," said Jackie, with a smile as she swept the church for a target, before settling the stock on her hip, with the barrel pointed at the ceiling.

"Good," said Avalon with a wicked grin, "now, all my religious colleagues, I have a serious question for you all, who here is not prepared to believe with all his heart in the power of Roaddog and his cabal of followers? Be aware we can not allow any un-belief within our ranks, any such would destroy the purity of his intentions, anyone not prepared to believe completely in the power of Roaddog and his cohort speak now."

"You cannot be serious?" demanded Francis. Avalon glanced at Jackie, Vera spoke twice, then Jackie lowered the gun to point directly at Francis, as dust fell from the damaged rafters, and bats took to the air.

"Francis, I am more serious than you can imagine, I have no superiors, you do, and yours have abandoned you. Your choice is simple, back the biker heathens or die. Your leaders have no clue what to do here, they have no idea how to stop this, they are simply going to blame you and walk away as they always do." While this conversation was going on Stephen dropped briefly to his knees and pulled a thirty-eight revolver from an ankle holster, he came up pointing it at Jackie, and shouting.

"Put the gun down, and surrender."

"For fuck's sake Stephen, have you learned nothing today? The knife at your throat is Jane's, but the one you can't feel is Roaddog's, it's set to plunge between your skull and your C1 vertebra, you will not be able to move anything at all as Jane's blade severs your carotid arteries and your brain dies slowly of lack of oxygen. The question you need to ask is why hasn't he already killed me? The answer is that he is waiting for clearance from me. Should I tell him to end you?"

"She's threatening a clergyman's life," said Stephen, shakily.

"And if you're lucky, you'll get to watch him die before your brain dies."

"You'll let her kill him?"

"I'll kill them all if they don't actively support the biker religion, and this may surprise you, I'll kill you as well." Roaddog reached forwards and took the thirty-eight from Stephen's shaking hand. The knives moved away from his neck.

"You're that serious?" asked Abraham.

"Yes," replied Avalon, "belief is everything, will you believe?"

"I believe that The Lord works through many peoples, and perhaps even the heathen bikers are part of his will, so I will follow them as they seem to have some idea what to do with this portal."

"The followers of Allah can believe in the bikers and their strange ways; they may break so many of the rules but their power can only come from Allah."

"Phurba?" asked Avalon.

"The ways of the cosmos are manifold, progress is normally made through passive acceptance, there are times when the path of passivity involves fighting for one's life, this could easily be one of those situations, I will follow."

"Father?" asked Avalon.

"Given the thoughts of everybody else, how can I go against the majority?"

"Fool," spat Avalon, "you think this is a committee? You believe this to be a democracy? No, this is a theocracy, I'm fairly sure you understand the term, and within the normal tactics of a theocracy, believe or die, is the rule. Can you believe?"

"I have seen what these people can do, so yes I can believe, is that good enough for you Avalon?"

"Why was that so hard? These others saw the necessity, why couldn't you?"

"Of course I saw it, but I didn't want these brothers to think there was only one voice."

"You took a great risk."

"I knew you wouldn't kill me out of hand, you'd have to give me another chance, we've known each other too long."

"Agreed, however, your people have persecuted mine for generations, that could certainly have affected my choice."

"No, you're far too intelligent to let something like that take a potential ally out of the game. You know I can be of some use to you, even if it's only to foul a demon's sword with my belly while you burn his life away."

"Francis, you know I could never use you like that," smiled Avalon.

"But you could use me like that," whispered Stephen.

"Don't fret it mate," laughed Roaddog, "so could I, but I have a problem with cops."

"I have an observation to make," said Bug.

"Speak Bug," said Avalon.

"Well, the sun's gone down and the night is closing in, I'm reliably told that this is not a place to be after dark."

"I agree," replied Avalon, "let's repair to our beds and attack this thing in the morning, or whenever that damned necromancer deems to show his face."

"I can go for that," said Roaddog, "we don't have much in the way of food in, and it's a bit late to be dropping on Karen, suggestions?"

"I got a gas-powered barbecue and a freezer full of steaks and burgers, some cracking sausages, a couple of cases of wine, and some grass to sit on," said Mick.

"You got buns for that?" asked Roaddog.

"No, but I don't generally serve steaks on bread."

"First time for everything," smiled Roaddog, "we'll swing by the workshop and pick some up."

"So, who's coming back to mine?" asked Mick.

"I will be," said Avalon quickly, "Stephen you're with me."

"I think that the rest of us will be going to the rectory to meditate in more peaceful surroundings," said Father Francis, he gathered the others up and walked through the deepening gloom towards the car park.

"Looks like we got a party," said Bug, taking Cherie's hand and walking out of the church after the clerics.

"You wanna come?" asked Roaddog of Jake.

"I'll ask the misses and catch y'all up, or not." He followed after the clerics, the rest only a step behind him.

As they were approaching the lynch gate Avalon spoke up.

"Stephen move your damned car and follow Mick, you're having a party with the bikers," laughed Avalon.

Stephen ran to his car, started it and drove into the car park, clearing the exit for the others. Jake's little quad left first, followed in a moment by the minibus, then both bikes and the trike peeled out, finally Moya rolled serenely down the drive with Stephen's car immediately behind it.

When Roaddog pulled into the front of the workshop he sent Jackie inside to get a couple of packs of frozen buns.

"Are you sure that party is what we should be doing right now?" asked Slowball.

"The clerics need to meditate to recharge their batteries, Avalon has already done that, what do we do? We party and when the time comes we fuel up on corrosive coffee and face all the demons of heaven and hell, we spit in their eyes and call them pussies as we kill them," said Roaddog.

"He's not wrong," agreed Bug, as Jackie came out of the door and tossed two packs to Sylvia, she closed the door and walked over to mount up behind Roaddog.

"Let's party," shouted Roaddog as engines started and Jackie dropped into the seat behind him.

The peace of the village was shattered by racing motorcycle engines, as the three set off towards the Axe, by the time they made the left at the Axe, Mick was parked behind his caravan with Stephen's car behind his. As he climbed down from Moya he looked at Avalon.

"Sounds like the guys are on their way," he laughed, the rumble of the Victory and the howl of the VW unmistakable in the quiet of the countryside.

"There should be a law against that sort of racket," observed Stephen.

"There is," laughed Mick, "go arrest them." He walked into the awning at the side of his caravan and rolled the barbecue out into the open between the awning and the car. He unlocked the caravan door and lifted a portable speaker out from under one of the benches, he placed it on the ground in the awning and plugged it into the mains power that was there. He fired up the barbecue and set it to low, he didn't want to heat the frozen food too quickly. They only had two chairs, so Avalon and Jackie took those. The motorcycle engines slowed down and made the turn into the lane, the soft burble of the Victory and the gentle rumble of the VW showed that they were being considerate to the neighbours, now that they'd woken everyone up. Mick smiled and shook his head as he pulled a case of wine from one of his lockers and put it on the floor inside the awning, he took a bottle of red from the case and passed it to Avalon.

"Chilean Cabernet Sauvignon, a cheeky wine with a kick like a mule, and an explosion of berries in the mouth."

"Glass?" asked Avalon.

"Washing up?"

"Erm?" muttered Avalon.

"We're going to war against demons and your worried about a few germs?"

Avalon giggled, unscrewed the top, threw it on the ground and took a hefty swig, then passed the bottle to Stephen, he took a hit and passed the bottle to Mick. Mick took a gulp and said, "Here's to a long life."

"I don't believe you," said Avalon, "by your own admission you're going to war, and you toast for a long life, it makes no sense."

"You expect him to make sense?" asked Jackie, pouring her coke into a pint glass.

"I would have hoped for sanity at least," replied Avalon.

"Ha," laughed Jackie.

"You married him," said Avalon.

"Not fucking boring," said Jackie with a grin.

Avalon shook her head briefly and asked Mick, "Explain long life?"

"That's easy, you're top of the heap in your particular heap, you've achieved a lot, big cheese, number one, what you got left to do?"

"There is still much to do, closing that damned portal would be good."

"But only a step along the way, I've lived, I've loved," he glanced at Jackie, "I've danced with Stacia, and sung with Suzie Q, I've raised children that I would die for, and kill for. It's been a long life."

"You're ready to die?"

"Just because I'm ready, don't mean it's gonna be easy."

"Buy something worthwhile, or make some bastard pay heavy," said Roaddog from beside the barbecue.

"Right on brother," said Mick as a square bottle with a black label flew through the air towards him. He snatched it mid-flight, spun the top off and took a swig.

"Smooth," he sighed.

"Lidl's finest," said Roaddog, as Jackie dropped the packs of buns beside the barbecue.

Mick passed the bottle back to Roaddog and opened the chest freezer, he started pulling out packs of steaks and burgers and two packs of frozen sausages. These he took to the barbecue and placed them on top to defrost.

"This is going to take a while I'm afraid, I usually plan a barbecue a couple of days in advance," said Mick.

"No sweat," replied Roaddog, "we got nothing urgent to do yet, or have we? Bug, cameras?"

In only a moment Bug had the cameras up and his report was much as normal.

"Birds are down, nothing happening."

"Inside?" asked Roaddog.

"Inside is clear as well." Roaddog's phone rang. He answered it in a heartbeat.

"Yes," said Roaddog.

"Where you at?" asked Jake.

"Jake wants to know where we at?" said Roaddog.

"Tell him, small lake, caravan called Britannic," laughed Mick.

"He heard," said Roaddog, "Why Britannic?"

"She wanted Titanic because of the size of the thing, I pointed out that it sank on its first trip, I wasn't towing something called Titanic, then she wanted Britannica, encyclopaedias, no thanks, we settled on Britannic, sister to Titanic, but she lasted a while before she got sunk by a mine."

The distant rumble of a quad told them that Jake was near, sure enough he came around the small lake and parked in front of the caravan, Mary dismounted first, a heavy jug in one hand, a broken shotgun in the other.

"Hi guys," said Jake, "someone said there was a party."

"Always welcome," said Roaddog, "but we've been drinking all afternoon, so we'll not need much of that lovely stuff."

"You're welcome anyway," said Mary as she dropped the jug alongside the cases of wine, and four bottles of Western Gold black label. "There seems to be a shortage of chairs around here," she said.

"I'm sorry my dear," said Mick, "we don't usually entertain, it's generally just the two of us."

"No problem there's plenty of grass to sit on," Mary smiled, "it's nice to get out of the house for a while, we don't get to do it that often."

"I'm sorry love," said Jake, "we have animals that need seeing to."

"I know all that, I'm not complaining really, I just wished we got out more."

Mick turned on the caravans outside lights, the van and the awning were surrounded by a pool of light, that pushed the encroaching darkness back, the remains of the sunset were fading fast, Mick's speaker started to throb with a classic rock radio station, all at such a low level that conversation was still possible at barely more than a whisper. It wasn't long before the meat was defrosted, and Mick set to cooking it. Stephen was having a hard time, he really didn't know these people, all he did know was that they didn't like him. Roaddog came and stood beside him, and offered him a bottle of Western Gold, Stephen took a swig, then passed the bottle back with a nod of thanks.

"Here," said Roaddog, passing the thirty-eight to him. "You point that at me and mine again and I won't be waiting for permission, do you understand?"

"I don't really understand what is going on here at all."

"Well, it's simple really, hell mouth, demons, fight for survival. Basically, the plot of a Stephen King horror story."

"But it's real?" he asked.

"Very, and very dangerous, we've done very well so far, we've only lost one man, and he came even knowing he was going to die."

"Still he came?"

"Yes, he'd been waiting a long time for this portal to open, I think we'd have really struggled without him, but we took the next one out without too much difficulty, and with no losses. We learned a lot from Nutter."

"Hello," called a voice from the darkness. Mary's shotgun snapped shut, Jake snatched one from the holster on his quad, and pulled the hammers back.

"Hi Leo," called Mick, "come in, you're safe here."

"Safe, I'm not sure about that, armed people on my land, pointing guns at me."

"Sorry about that, we've been having a bad few days, I can explain, well sort of."

"And a cop with a pistol?" asked Leo.

"Even that," laughed Mick, as Stephen pushed the pistol into his belt. "Notice that the people with guns are all locals."

"You're all locals, for god's sake," said Leo, "the crazy bikers live just across the way, and you are as much a local here as you are in your other home town on the wrong side of the Pennines, and the two with the shotguns are farmers from down the road. Hi Jake, what the fuck is going on?"

"Sorry Leo, surprises coming out of the dark are not things we really need right now, you're welcome to get your own guns and join the hunt, you know?"

"Hunt for what? I heard about the armed robbers at the Axe, but what else are you lot hunting?"

"You wouldn't believe me if I told you," laughed Jake. Leo raised his eyebrows by way a question.

"We're hunting demons," said Jake slowly.

"Bollocks," laughed Leo.

"God's honest truth, Roaddog and Bug, here," he waved in the direction of the two, "came into my milking parlour and shot one to pieces, they saved my life."

"I'd heard about your crazy stories, I just thought it was a bad batch of your home brew," Leo glanced at Stephen then looked back at Jake, wondering if he had put his foot in it.

"Come on Leo, which is more likely, dinosaurs rising from the slime in the bottom of your lakes, demons breaking out of Botolph's church, or me making a bad batch of shine?"

"I suppose," said Leo quietly, "so what gauge do I need for hunting dinosaurs?"

"Sorry Leo," said Roaddog, "we're hunting demons, but a two gauge would certainly help."

"Sorry Dog, I don't have a punt gun, and I certainly wouldn't want to fire one when there were friendlies in the area, know what I mean?"

"I do Leo, I do, what do you have ferreted away?"

Leo looked pointedly at Stephen.

"Don't worry about him," said Avalon, "he knows he's going to see things he's not allowed to act on during this mission, or after."

"Avalon," said Leo, "I didn't see you there."

"We'll talk about that later Avalon," said Roaddog, "it seems to happen a lot. Go on Leo, what you got that the cops don't know about?"

"I picked up a six bore, single barrel, it's a breech loader, and I've got shot and solids already loaded, but not many, it's not a gun with a good rate of fire, but generally when I hit something it stays down," Leo laughed, thinking about a telegraph pole he hit by accident last time he tried the thing with a solid.

"Damn," said Roaddog, "that's a one inch bore, you're in if you want, but this shit has its risks, if you don't want in you could lend us the six?"

"You're too tall, thin and light, that gun would break your spine. I'm in, what do I need to know?"

"Jake you fill him in with everything that has happened, Stephen, you go listen as well, you might find it interesting, or maybe you'll pee in your pants. I need to talk to Avalon." Roaddog went into Mick's awning and knelt at Avalon's feet, looking out of the window he could see Jake, Leo and Stephen in a huddle talking earnestly. He turned to Jane, "It's a party, get it happening." Jane nodded and snagged Jackie by the arm, together they started passing drinks around, wine and spirits went round the group freely from their hands.

"Okay Avalon, dearest, what the fuck is going on?" asked Roaddog.

"What do you mean?" replied Avalon, trying her best to look innocent.

"I walk into a boozer, with a middle aged chick on my arm, she's wearing a long white robe, covered in black and silver symbols, she's carrying a five foot long wooden staff with a glowing crystal in the top, and no one sees her, not even people who know her, no one, how do you manage that?"

"What do you mean?"

"I've seen it now, three times, in the Axe, Stephen didn't see you until you spoke, if anyone should have seen you that was him, I put it down to a complex and intense situation. Then, we went to Grimsby, we walked into a biker bar, and no one even commented on your attire, no one, it's like they didn't see you, even when you spoke it was quiet and intended for the table we were sitting at, and still no one saw you. Just moments ago, you were sitting in plain view, even sitting in the lights and Leo didn't see you until you spoke, and he even said so. Don't be coy, what is going on here?"

"Fine, being who I am, and how recognisable I am, it is better that people don't actually see me, so I make that happen."

"You make yourself invisible?"

"No, I just make it so that people see me, then ignore me, like I'm not important enough to register, they know I am there, no one will try and sit in a chair I already occupy, but I am of no consequence at all, it's far better that way."

"Sounds like a perfect system."

"Not always, occasionally, and I do mean very occasionally, certain minds take the ignore me instruction too far, I actually have had people sit on me, then I ramp up the aversion to the place and they run away, they'd rather cut their own throats than sit on that chair ever again, but they have no idea about the person sitting there at all."

"Sounds like a useful skill," said Roaddog, smiling.

"When you have an existence as covert as mine, certainly."

"Could you teach me this?"

"Only in about a hundred years."

"What do you mean?"

"Come on Dog, you walk into a room and your very presence says 'look at me', you cannot do that if you want to be ignored, and you, don't want to be ignored, not ever."

"I suppose you're right there. Still, it would be a useful talent on those occasions when you want to walk into the den of the enemy and kill them all before they know you are there."

"Yes, but not for your character, and you can never work against your character."

"That's a tad depressing, but no surprise really."

"I spend most of my life hiding who I am," said Avalon, "I'm used to being a ghost that walks through other people's lives, you are no way the same."

"I stamp through people's lives with hobnailed boots," laughed Roaddog.

"Exactly," smiled Avalon.

"I can't argue with that sentiment. I really can't hide who I am."

"Not really, you are who you are."

"So are you, but no one knows who you are."

Avalon smiled but said nothing more.

"I'm hoping most of us survive this shit, but I'm not betting on it," said Roaddog as he got to his feet and went outside. "Hey Leo," he said, "you understand the shit we are in now?"

"I see what's happening, and I can't be doing with demons wandering around in my neighbourhood, I'm in."

"Good man," smiled Roaddog, "Bug put the cameras on his phone and send his phone number to everyone."

"I don't understand," said Leo even as he handed his phone to Bug.

"There are cameras in the church, and they show us the birds, when the birds are resting the demons are nowhere near, when the birds are in the air, the demons are on their way. If someone calls you and says the birds are up, I want you on the road with your six immediately, I expect you to be at the church the same time we are, if by some chance you are there first, do not get involved on your own, back off and track the demon, call someone, and advise the situation, rest assured we are on the way as fast as we can, but don't take on one of these demons on your own. Your six gauge may take down an elephant, but there is no saying it's going to take out one of the demons we have already faced."

"You mean they'd survive a hit from a one-inch solid slug at sixteen hundred feet per second?"

"To be honest we don't even know if they have vital organs as such."

"That's not exactly helpful," said Leo.

"I know," said Roaddog, "we know that salt hurts them, we know that holy water hurts them, we know that shotguns can tear some of them to pieces, but to take one on your own would be foolish, track it and wait for backup."

"Do we even know what these things look like?" asked Leo.

"Surprisingly enough we do, the church has a sort of notice board, it shows us who is next, and the next act on stage is a human necromancer that I killed a few days ago, I cut him in half with Vera, and now the bastard is coming back."

"Vera?"

"Given your fascination with firearms, you're going to love Vera," laughed Stephen.

"You'll have to explain," said Leo.

"Fine," replied Roaddog, "Thompson machine gun, converted to full auto four-ten shotgun." Leo's eyebrows raised, and then he frowned.

"Damn it," he whispered, "some machine work, but certainly not impossible. I think I could do it, not with the machinery I have in my shop, but I know a man who'll let me into his."

"Oh fuck," muttered Stephen, then he turned to Roaddog, "now look what you've done, that's another machine gun I'm going to have to look out for."

"Only for rabbits, right Leo?" asked Roaddog,

"And rats," replied Leo.

"And damned revenuers," laughed Jake.

"You guys aren't making me feel any better about this," said Stephen glumly.

"Don't fret Stephen," smiled Roaddog, "we'll try to keep you alive."

"But will she?" Stephen nodded in the direction of Avalon.

"Well, you have been a bit of a dick recently, she'll probably not waste your life."

"But she may expect me to die."

"For your kid."

"Price worth paying, Avalon, if this shit kills me, you'll make sure my kid stays healthy, won't you?"

"Of course, your child was never in danger, only you are in any danger here, and that only as much as the rest of us."

"I've been a dick again, you could never harm a child, fuck," muttered Stephen.

"What do you mean?" asked Roaddog.

"Part of her religion," said Stephen.

"Is the same true for the damned necromancer?" snapped Roaddog, glaring at Avalon.

"Definitely not," said Avalon slowly, "he'd gut them to see which way their entrails dropped, if it suited his purpose."

"And you let necromancers live?"

"They can be very powerful and often useful, though this policy is going to be under review as soon as I can call a meeting of the council."

"Fuck," mumbled Stephen, "just what we need a war amongst the pagans."

"I don't think it will amount to a war," replied Avalon, "just some curtailment of their activities."

"And if they resist?"

"An example or two is usually enough."

"More corpses for us to find," said Stephen.

"Somehow Stephen, I don't think there's going to be that much left," laughed Roaddog.

"You're not helping," replied Stephen.

"So how did this shit start?" asked Leo.

Roaddog gave him a quick rundown of the activities so far while Mick was distributing food and drinks.

"That damned church has always been creepy, and I've lived here all my life."

"Looking at some of the more modern gravestones, you know the ones in the outer yard, it's still in use occasionally?"

"Yes it is," interrupted Stephen, "for locals with an historical link to the church, but there can't be many of them left, so many have moved away, there just isn't the work round here anymore."

"You mean, no one wants to do the work anymore," snapped Leo, "they want to sit at desks for thirty hours a week and take home forty thousand a year, no one wants to graft any more, no one wants to get their hands dirty anymore, that's why the machines are taking over, and they're not fit for grafters anymore, bastards."

"What's up Leo?" asked Roaddog.

"Typical case for you, I've got an excavator, you've seen it, I don't use it much, I got it cheap, I got it cheap because it needs a bearing replaced. A simple bearing replacement makes it beyond economical repair."

"We may be able to help you with that, I don't have presses yet, but they're on the purchase plan."

"That won't do any good, the bearing in question is probably only about ten quid, but it's buried inside an assembly, and the assembly is available from the manufacturer only."

"Break it down and change the bearing, but I'm sure you've thought of that."

"I have and it's impossible, the assembly is welded, to break it down you'd have to cut it with a gas axe, and then you'd never get it back together, you've got to buy the assembly from Taiwan."

"Grandma and sucking eggs, scrapyard?" asked Roaddog.

"The part that governs the life of these machines is that bearing, and the amount of crap it's spent its life running in. Buy the assembly from Taiwan."

"They're not making this easy, are they?"

"No."

"How easy is it to get the assembly off?"

"Heavy lifting and three or four hours, why?"

"How easy if the machine in question has sort of fallen over?"

"Two guys an hour, why?"

"Find one, knock it over, that's easy enough, it's a powerful piece of kit, take the assembly off, load it in your van and drive away."

Stephen looked from one to the other, shook his head, stuck his fingers in his ears and walked away, saying, "La, la, la, la."

"I have actually considered that," laughed Leo, "the nearest one is in a yard in Lincoln, and they've got some real mean dogs."

"Dogs can be easily dealt with."

"I'm not prepared to kill somebodies' dogs just for a part for an excavator."

"Here's another thought, can you get me the technical drawings for the assembly?"

"I should be able to, why?"

"Off the wall idea for ya," smiled Roaddog, "we find a way to re-engineer the assembly, your mate with the machine shop, he has NC, doesn't he?"

"Yes, all singing all dancing."

"We'll have to cut him in, re-engineer the assembly, machine the assembly to dismantle it, replace some parts and especially the bearing, if we sell the new assembly for twice the price of the Taiwanese part, and the customers get an assembly with a replaceable bearing. We can retrofit every one of those excavators that are currently in the UK, we could even offer a world wide service. How many are we talking?"

"There's a thousand registered for road use currently, another thousand SORNed, god knows how many in scrap yards waiting to be chopped up."

"So that's two thousand for those currently on the road, another two thousand for those currently off the road, and say another four for those waiting scrapping. It's not going to be a big market, but for a cottage industry in Lincolnshire it'll make some of us a few quid. Be aware the street value of your excavator just crashed," Roaddog laughed.

"The damned Taiwanese are going to have a fit."

"Any bet's they come up with a replacement to put us out of business in less than a year?"

"We better make it a good year then," laughed Leo.

"We might find another one of their scams to deal with by then," said

Roaddog.

"Not a chance," said Leo, "once the chancers catch on to our deal there will be thousands of them after that market."

"We just gotta be sure we can make some money off it, here's a crazy idea, sell the idea to the Taiwanese, and they take over our market, for a price of course."

"I have an issue," said Leo, "those bastards have engineered this problem deliberately, why should they profit, fuck 'em."

"I agree, fuck 'em, get me the drawings, and we'll see what we can do about helping out a few people who have bought their machines," laughed Roaddog, he reached out a hand, for Leo to shake.

"Shit," said Leo, "that's not something I see much these days."

"A gentleman's agreement, can you handle that?"

"Of course I can, it's just not de-rigueur these days."

"I would have thought many of the off the books deals that farmers make are a simple handshake."

"Ha," laughed Jake, "that used to be true, but nowadays so many places are owned and run by conglomerates that the traditions have all but died out."

"Your farm run by one of those?" asked Roaddog.

"No, they keep trying, but so far we are still hanging on, so many of the old fashioned suppliers are gone as well, no credit on the strength of a handshake any more, no 'I'll pay you when my customers pay me', no 'give us a couple of months to get things sorted.' All they want is a credit agreement, usually backed by one of the major credit card companies, and they're on thirty percent interest. It's hard for us independents to stay in business these days."

"Have you thought of forming some sort of credit union?" asked Roaddog.

"No one has the capital for that sort of thing," replied Jake.

"Actually capital isn't really the issue, what you need is members and monthly subscriptions."

"There hasn't been a proper farmers union around here for thirty years," said Leo.

"Perhaps you should get the remaining independents together and form one," said Roaddog.

"That'd be difficult," laughed Leo, "the remaining independents are all stubborn ornery bastards, they don't play well with others."

"You mean like you and me?" asked Jake.

"Sort of," said Leo, shaking his head.

"Well, if you get it sorted out, I may be in a position to put some capital in, some of my investments are really flying right now, no idea when the bubble will burst, but when it does, I can't lose more than half."

"How can you not be worried about losing half?" asked Jake.

"It's investment," shrugged Roaddog, "no effort, or very little, a bit of capital in, and regular returns, sometimes massive returns, let's just say that these last couple of weeks have been amazing."

"That's not the shop you're talking about, is it?" asked Leo. Roaddog just shook his head.

"Just let me know if you need some sort of cash investment to get things started, now, I'm not talking hundreds, but if things keep spiralling, maybe fifty."

"I've got more than fifty in me pocket," sneered Leo.

"Thousands," sighed Roaddog.

"Oh," said Leo, "really?"

"Yeah, in the last two weeks I've hit thirty, and pulled twenty out, can't pull too much or the prices will crash, gotta be subtle."

"Don't believe him," said Slowball, "he wouldn't know subtle if it bit him on his fat ass."

"Hey," laughed Jane, "his ass ain't fat."

"Merely an expression," laughed Slowball. Jane looked down at Slowball's ass. "Okay, maybe one I shouldn't use." Roaddog turned to Leo.

"You got a minute; I need some local colour?" Leo nodded and Roaddog indicated the darkness towards the hedge at the side of the lane and set off in that direction. Once they were far enough from the rest not to be overheard, he turned to Leo again, finding Slowball standing next to him. Roaddog glared at Slowball for a moment and spoke harshly, "Fuck off."

Chapter 16: Wednesday and off to the workshop.

Jane woke to sounds that she immediately recognised, that wet slurping noise and a deeply resonant groan, these were unmistakable.

"Bitch," she whispered looking down at Jackie making a meal of Roaddog. After only a heartbeat she moved up in the bed and straddled Roaddog's head, settling into place and making her own groaning noises as his tongue went to work. Jackie giggled as she felt him tense underneath her ministrations. She sat up and then settled into a different configuration, reaching forwards she grabbed Jane's breasts from behind and eased her backwards, not enough to break contact with the hardworking oral digit, but enough so that they could share a morning kiss.

"Morning love," said Jackie as their lips separated.

"Morning darling," replied Jane as she pushed down on Roaddog's face.

"How you feeling today?" asked Jackie.

"Fine, head's a bit thick, but hey, that was some party last night."

"Wasn't it though, I can't believe how Jake and Mary left."

"That was amazing," said Jane, "do you think they got dressed before they got to the road?"

"Probably not, they were wasted," replied Jackie, grunting as Roaddog thrust upwards into her.

"I hope they made it home," said Jane, "can you imagine the headlines, 'Two naked people and quad bike found in ditch, two shotguns recovered from the scene, confused police looking for witnesses.'" She reached down and pulled Roaddog's head harder into her crotch, she grunted at the pleasure his tongue brought.

"The cops around here are always confused," laughed Jackie, she increased the speed of her hip movements, and the commensurate noises.

"What are they going to make of whatever happens next at that fucking church?" asked Jane.

"That's the advantage, whatever Stephen tells them, they have to believe him, oh, that feels good."

"Do you think that Avalon has full control of him?"

"More than enough, he can't risk his child turning back into whatever sort of devil he was."

"I hope this next asshole is no problem for us."

"Hope is good, but we're doing so good so far, I'm worried that things are going to go badly."

"Why this time?"

Roaddog pulled away from Jane's grip.

"Hey, I am here you know," he said.

"We know," said Jane, "now shut up and keep doing what you're supposed to," she pulled harder on his hair and turned to Jackie, "men, they really don't know when to shut up, do they?"

"He'll learn," laughed Jackie, as she moved faster against his manhood. "We've just done too well, no losses, it's only a matter of time until we start losing people we care about."

"I could lose the cop with no problem," laughed Jane, as she wriggled on Roaddog's face.

"Or any of those damned clerics," said Jackie.

"Agreed what the fuck use are they?"

"Not much, though their barriers have done something to hold the demons in place while we kill them."

"But does that really count for much?"

"Holy water does count for something, surely?"

"Not too sure about that, to quote their own words, belief is everything. What if all that matters is that the demons believe the water will hurt them?" said Jane.

"The bottle says 'Holy Water,' so they think it will hurt them and it does?"

"Belief is everything," laughed Jane, as she clenched her thighs against Roaddog's head, "I believe I am coming."

"To quote a common hashtag, #metoo," said Jackie, "and so would he, if he had any voice in this at all," she spluttered as her whole body clenched and she fell to her right, liberating him from herself.

"Hey," said Roaddog, "I'm not in anyway sure I'm getting the best of this deal."

"Shut the fuck up bitch," called Slowball, "and deal with it you cunt, before the rest of us get jealous and beat you to death."

"I do believe the wonderfulness of his situation has just been explained to him," laughed Jackie.

"But is he intelligent enough to understand? asked Jane.

"That is by no means sure," laughed Jackie.

"Do you understand Roaddog?" asked Jane.

"I'm fairly sure I understand," said Roaddog, "just get off my face so I can breathe."

"There he goes," shouted Bug, "bitching about needing to breathe."

"What's that shit about?" asked Slowball, "who needs to breathe? When there's a pussy on his dick, and another on his face, guys just a limp fuck."

"Hey guys," said Roaddog, "I hope you never find out how hard this is."

"I hope we never find out how hard this isn't," laughed Bug.

"Bastards," muttered Roaddog.

"Poor Roaddog," laughed Jane as she rolled away from him.

"Don't worry love," said Jackie, "they're just jealous." as she settled alongside his sweaty body.

"What do they know?" asked Jane as she dropped against his other side and kissed him.

"Why do I feel like a fifth wheel here?" asked Roaddog.

"Not fifth," replied Jackie, "you are the one we love, and that should be more than enough for you, you are our everything, as we should be for you. What do you say?"

"I'm more than happy to say that you are my everything, but we have shit to do today, let's get rolling."

"What we got to do today?" asked Jane.

"If nothing else we have to prepare for the arrival of Man Dare and Billy,"

"Fuck," called Bug from the other room, "we better get the workshop up to her standards before she gets here, any idea when that's going to be?"

"Not a clue, but I don't see Billy on the road before eight o'clock, do you?"

"So, we've got until lunchtime really," said Slowball.

"Cameras are clear, the birds are still resting," said Bug.

"That's something we don't need to surprise her with," said Roaddog.

"Personally, I can't wait to see her slapping a demon around for disturbing her day," laughed Bug.

"We'll have to try and keep that crazy bitch alive," Slowball said.

"That may not be easy," said Sylvia.

"You're not fucking wrong," agreed Cherie, she coughed gently, then spoke quickly, "clear the way." She rolled out of bed and ran towards the bathroom. Sounds of coughing and retching filled the caravan, Jane rolled out of bed and went to the kitchen to make at least one cup of tea, knowing that there would be many more to make, by the time she got there Bug already had the kettle on and was collecting cups.

"You know what you should do?" said Jane.

"What?" he asked.

"Go keep her hair out of the water and stroke her back for her."

"I don't want to be that close, she has a tendency to lash out."

"Are you a man or a mouse?"

"Squeak fucking squeak," he laughed going into the bathroom, to console the woman carrying their baby.

Roaddog came out of the bedroom to help with the morning coffees, he was rinsing cups and there was a slap from the bathroom, followed by a groan.

"Hey Dog," said Slowball, "don't you ever wear clothes?"

"Not until I have to man," laughed Roaddog.

"We like him that way," said Jackie as she came into the living area of the van.

"Now you being naked is not an issue," observed Slowball, there was another slap and a groan from Slowball as Sylvia left a hand print on his heavy shoulder.

"Nakedness is never an issue," said Roaddog.

"Only in the rest of the world," observed Slowball.

"Far too many put too much importance in the status symbols of their clothes," said Roaddog.

"So do we," smiled Slowball.

"Hey I'm naked here, please explain."

"So am I, but still in bed as yet, talking of status symbols and clothing, what about your cut?"

"My cut no longer carries the Dragonrider's patches, but I still have the Master at Arms, and to be honest DILLIGAF sort of explains it all. I agree that these are status symbols for us, and they always will be, but these are earned, not bought."

"But we still view them as status symbols, as do the assholes in the armarni suits."

"Any asshole can buy an armarni suit, or steal one, give me a second." He went into the bedroom and returned moments later wearing his cut. "That better?" he asked.

"That's better," laughed Slowball, "just what the well dressed man in the street is wearing, we need to sort out Hellriders rockers, while there are still a few of us left."

"Is it really worth it?" asked Bug, "I mean, we know who we are, do we actually care what the rest of the world thinks?"

"I suppose not, but it would be nice to die with our colours on," observed Roaddog.

"Gloomy much," said Sylvia.

"Maybe," replied Slowball, "but he does have a point."

"Once we get to the shop, I'll start looking for some patches," said Jane, "but they'll have to be generic if you want them quickly."

"That's sounds like a plan," smiled Roaddog, he reached over to kiss her.

"When are we going to the workshop?" asked Slowball.

"Soon as possible, we need to get things sorted out."

"What about Avalon?" asked Bug.

"She'll most likely have her cop taxi driver," laughed Slowball.

"We still got to check for airtags," said Roaddog.

"I've got an app for that," laughed Bug, he came from the bathroom, picked up his phone and started up the appropriate application, after only a moment or two Bug spoke again. "Definitely something nearby," he went out of the door, and returned in only a few seconds.

"There's an airtag on the tail of Jane's car. It's too close to the hedge for me to get in to find it,"

"You could have put some clothes on," laughed Jane.

"Have you seen the size of the thorns on that damned hedge, I'd not go in there in full leathers."

"So that bastard Hopkins tagged Jane's car, I think we'll have to have words with him," said Roaddog. Dressing and drinking coffees took little time, and once they'd moved Jane's car forwards a couple of feet Bug found the magnetic tag in only a few seconds, it was fixed to the inside of the rear bumper. He showed it to Roaddog.

"If you can spare me for an hour or so I'll find one of those foreign trucks bound for Immingham, that should get the fucker off our trail."

"That's fine, but surely the thing will show a track, so he'll know where it has been?"

"I suppose, if he can work out how to read the thing."

"He's not that stupid."

"Perhaps, we'll see if he turns up," said Bug.

"Let's hope he doesn't come mob handed."

"If they do then they're in for a surprise," Bug smiled as he thought of the mess the mac-ten would make of a policeman or two.

"Damn it Bug," snarled Roaddog, "we don't want any of the girls hurt, and you've got a kid to think of now."

"Hey," said Jane, "we're good enough to be demon fodder, but not to take on a few wimpy cops?"

"Yeah," said Jackie, "Man-Dare is on her way, you see her backing down from any fight?"

"That's one of the things that worries me," replied Roaddog, "she doesn't have the sense to run away."

"Then you'd better drag her away," laughed Cherie, "now that's something I'd like to see you try."

"Fuck that bitch is going to get us all killed," muttered Slowball.

"Or keep us all alive," said Sylvia, gently.

"All this is pretty much pointless anyway," Roaddog said, "let's get to the workshop, there's some things I need to sort out, and we have to hope that the god botherers find some way to deal with Fintan. Bug you and Cherie go find a truck for that tag; it'll be easier to place with a pillion on board. Let's move." In moments the bikes and Slowball's trike were leaving the site and heading to their separate destinations.

Slowball and Roaddog pulled up in front of the workshop and Jackie jumped off the Victory to open the door. The two machines rolled backwards into the parking area, the silence as the motors stopped was almost oppressive, but not something the group were unaccustomed to. Roaddog looked around the place and decided that it wasn't as bad as he had first thought, he realised that he hadn't been paying too much attention to the place with everything else that was going on at the moment.

"When do you think that Billy will get here?" asked Jane.

"Who can tell," he shrugged, "depends on how much she wants to be here."

"That's for sure," said Slowball, "she's never been much of an early riser."

"That's going to have to change," laughed Sylvia.

"That'll make her happy," said Roaddog, "let's get this place tidied up a bit, eh?"

"You really care that much how she sees the place?" asked Jackie.

"It's crazy, I know, but, I know it's Man-Dare on the way, but, it feels like Bandit Queen is coming," he shook his head slowly.

"I know what you mean," mumble Slowball, as he turned on the coffee machine and started to straighten up the counters.

"Hey Dog," said Jackie, "how long since you checked the miners?"

"Fuck," he was shocked into stillness. "It's gotta be too long." He went into the back room and fired up the computers. It only took moments to get the details up on his screens, he made an instant decision, transferring almost all of his takings into sterling, he went to his favoured on-line supplier and purchased another forty solar panels and two battery packs. Further searching didn't find him any miners that were of a suitable price, so he didn't actually buy any of those. He went into the front as the others were sitting down with coffees, he grabbed himself a cup and looked at his friends.

"Well guys," he said loudly, "if you want to stay here I have more than a few weeks work for ya, I've just bought some more solars and some batteries, mining is doing really well right now, so I want to stay on top of it. We'll build a lean-to along the side and that should increase our free power by at least half, miners are too expensive right now, but I'll keep an eye on the prices and buy some if they come down, or maybe just because we hit another thirty thousand overnight."

"How much did you make in these last two days?" asked Sylvia.

"We made fifty, you'll all be seeing your shares in the bank later, it's going crazy, and the value of bitcoin is still rising, it's going to crash, but I don't know when. I'm shifting more into sterling, that way a crash won't hurt as much."

"Sounds like fun," said Slowball, "providing we survive this demon thing."

"That is the plan," laughed Roaddog.

"I'm in and I'm sure Bug will be," replied Slowball, he looked at Sylvia, hoping for some indication of approval, he only got a raised eyebrow, he knew they'd talk later. Less than an hour later they were sitting waiting for the first customers to arrive, when Bug returned.

"How'd it go?" asked Roaddog.

"Tag's on a truck bound for Romania, well it had Romanian plates on it, I'm sure that bastard Hopkins will have fun chasing that one."

"He's probably already on his way here, but a little misdirection can't be bad."

"Anything happening here?" asked Bug.

"Yes," said Slowball, "more cash in the bank from Dog's miners, and an offer of a few weeks work increasing his solar power."

"Sounds like fun," smiled Bug, as he took Cherie's hand, "we're in." Bug glanced at her then went to get them both coffees.

"I'm getting a strange feeling," said Roaddog quietly, "Bug punch the cameras up on the big monitor." Bug raised his eyebrows briefly then did as he was asked. The large monitor on the back wall stopped its cycling advertising images and switched to the live images from the church. Split screen showing both inside and out at the same time. The lynch gate was covered in birds, the floor of the knave the same, the inside birds seemed to be milling around, not a settled as the ones in the filtered light of the rising sun.

"Are those bastards dancing?" asked Slowball.

"Could be," laughed Bug, "don't think it's likely to be the next craze in the disco though."

A shaft of sunlight cut through the trees and streamed through the shattered east window, illuminating almost the entirety of the knave. The camera shifted to colour, showing the yellow of the sunlight and the black of the shadows of the mullions, bars of light and dark across the floor, picking out the birds and their slow strolling dance. The increased light helped to resolve the pattern of their motions, three circles, rotating in alternating directions, as they watched birds walked their slow circles, moving from one circle to the next and changing direction. The ever changing pattern was hypnotic, the people struggled to look away, then a cloud covered the sun and the lowered light level shifted the camera back into its night time mode, the pattern dissolved into almost complete randomness.

"Something is going on there," whispered Roaddog.

"Looks like we could be in for a visitor today," said a female voice and they all looked to see Avalon standing just outside the main door.

"More than one," laughed Bug as a heavy Harley rolled in behind her, one they'd never seen before. The rider was instantly recognisable, his long beard stuffed into the front of his jacket. His cut identified him simply as "Billy", behind him his pillion stood up on the foot boards, she stepped off the bike and handed him her helmet, shaking her long, straight black hair loose. She walked towards the workshop with a stately strut, she dismissed Avalon with a glance and strode straight up to Roaddog, she threw her arms around his neck and pulled his head down for a hot and meaningful kiss. When the kiss ended she spoke softly.

"Fuck I've missed you."

"How you doing Man-Dare?" he asked.

"Centurions aren't anything like as much fun as Dragonriders," she turned to Jackie and hugged her, Roaddog saw the full range of patches on her back, it surprised him for only a moment, then he smiled. Man-Dare hugged everyone and returned to Roaddog, Billy just sat on his bike smiling.

"Dog," she said, "I know you've gone country, but why you got video of your chicken shed on the wall? And who's the pagan bitch?" she nodded in the direction of Avalon.

"Them's ain't chickens, and witch is more appropriate," laughed Roaddog.

"Explain asshole," snapped Man-Dare.

"We got demon problems, there's a sort of infestation we need to deal with, and the chickens tell us when the demons are near, and the witch is the most powerful in the country, or so she tells us."

"Less boring already," smiled Man-Dare, "demons eh? Sounds like a worthy opponent for a change."

"Oh, they are that," said Avalon, "they'll eat you alive, little girl." Man-Dare turned at these words, she stared at Avalon for a moment, she looked Avalon insolently up and down.

"You got no cut, you got no patch, you no one," snarled Man-Dare turning her back on Avalon.

"Damn Roaddog," said Avalon loudly, "this bitch has got more front than Brighton, she'll do nicely."

"What do you mean, cow?" snapped Man-Dare turning to face Avalon, her fists clenched.

"Bait, my dear," smiled Avalon, "you're ten times the bait of the others, so strong, so certain, so dead. The demons won't be able to resist you."

"Ladies plcase," called Roaddog loudly, "we are all on the same side here, we have a common enemy, we really don't need to fight amongst ourselves." Slowball and Bug moved into empty space, though not sure what they were going to do with it. Jackie and Jane fell in behind Roaddog, hands on their belts, but knives still in their holsters. Sylvia and Cherie moved to the back of the workshop out of the way.

"You side with the witch?" demanded Man-Dare, turning towards Roaddog and moving closer, legs spread, weight balanced, not quite within striking distance.

"Listen Man-Dare," snarled Roaddog, "we got enough shit going on here, and we don't need you competing for top-dog. Is that clear?" Man-Dare glared at him for only an instant, then she spun in low and fast, her right leg rising quickly to strike him in the ribcage, he blocked the strike with both arms, then hooked the leg lifting it high, Man-Dare being so much shorter had no chance, as the leg rose, she lost contact with the ground and so any traction that she had. Pushing down on her right thigh she lifted her whole weight and drove her left knee towards Roaddog's head. He felt the change in weight and released her right leg completely. Man-Dare fell to the ground her left knee strike aborted from lack of leverage. Roaddog followed her down and forced her chest down with a large hand, her shoulders pinned to the ground, and his other hand at her throat.

"You really want to do this?" he snarled, his fist clenching on her neck, threatening to cut off both air and blood to her brain.

"I thought you'd gone soft or crazy, dealing with fucking pagans," her voice choked by the constriction of his fingers, "all this for real?"

"More real than you can imagine, you in or dead?"

"In, I thought you'd gone nuts."

"I wish, how do I wish that this was actually crazy, and some time in a rubber room, stoned out of my mind on Thorazine is the cure. This is real, and you gotta understand that."

"I feel you," whispered Man-Dare. Roaddog glared into her eyes for a long moment then released her. He stood up and reached down with one hand to help her to her feet, she rose slowly with his assistance.

"You're trying too hard to be Bandit Queen," he said gently, "you've a long way to go before you have her strength or weight."

"Was she really that strong?"

"She knocked you out with one punch," he smiled. She rubbed her left breast remembering. "Did you ever see her working out?" he asked.

"No, why?"

"I have, I've been in the gym, holding the heavy bag for her to hit, and I know exactly how much force she could have hit you with, take my word for it, she pulled that blow. Remember the mess she made of that gypsy boy."

"I'll never forget that fight," whispered Man-Dare.

"You've got a way to go but try not to get too close to these damned demons, they really do hit hard."

"How hard?"

"One knocked part of a window frame out and dropped it on Bug, damned near killed the guy."

"Hey," called Bug, "not even close to dead."

"You were basically unconscious, if the bastard could have followed through, you'd be in that damned graveyard now."

"I suppose," mumbled Bug.

"When I say window frame I mean four inch square section of stone five feet long," said Roaddog looking seriously at Man-Dare.

"Fuck," she whispered.

"So yeah, they hit real hard."

"So, what are the plans for the next one?" asked Man-Dare.

"That's sort of up in the air right now, we're hoping that heavy firepower will do the next one in, but perhaps the clerics will be able to control the thing while we finish it off."

"You're relying on church people?"

"And pagans."

"You're kidding?" she snapped.

"You've not seen them work, they're very useful."

"I'll believe that when I see it."

"Let's hope it's not too soon," smiled Roaddog, "but the way those birds are behaving, I don't think we've got long to wait." They all turned to the large monitor and the sun was streaming in through the east window again. The full colour and sharp images from the inside camera looking down from the high roof of the nave, showed the birds moving in a more organise pattern, three circles clearly visible, the outer and inner turning anti-clockwise, the middle one clockwise. "What do you think?" asked Roaddog looking at Avalon.

"Something is certainly happening, notice how the birds change circles only at the cardinal points, and each circle is actually made of three circles all walking the same way."

"Should we get ready?" he asked, as his phone rang. He hit the call accept button.

"Hey Jake," he said.

"Hey Roaddog, you seen those crazy birds?"

"We're watching now, looks like they're up to something, you want to get in there early?"

"Waiting till the birds are up has meant we're arriving into something that's already happening, I say get there first," said Jake.

"I agree, you hit Father Francis, and I'll phone Leo."

"Done," said Jake breaking the call.

"Gear up people," said Roaddog loudly, "we're going to war again." He punched a few buttons on his phone.

"Hi Leo," he said.

"Hello Roaddog," was the answer.

"You ready to kill some demons?"

"Sure," laughed Leo.

"Well, we'll be coming passed yours very shortly, tag on the back of the convoy, don't go in on your own."

"No problem, I'll wait at the end of the lane."

"See ya soon," said Roaddog as he hung up. He looked up to hear Avalon speaking loudly into her own phone.

"I don't give a fuck, you get your ass here, I need a ride." There was silence for a short time.

"You know how important this shit is, and you fuck off shopping, asshole." Small sound from the phone.

"You got ten minutes if you're not at the church in ten, then all agreements are off, and your soul burns forever." She stuffed the phone into a pocket, "I need a ride," she said.

"I can take another one, but it's going to be friendly, three across the back of the trike," replied Slowball.

"Good enough," said Roaddog, "Lock and load, let's hit the road." Jackie and Jane were already shutting things down and ready to close the doors as the bikes rolled out onto the forecourt. Jane dropped onto the back of the victory, Man-Dare was already sitting behind Billy, their helmets were touching as they exchanged quiet words. Sylvia was behind Slowball with Avalon to her left, enough space left for Jackie once the doors were down. 'It is a good job that none of us are too big,' thought Sylvia as she pulled up hard behind Slowball, the centre seat being much like a motorcycle seat, leaving just a fraction more space for Jackie. Roaddog rolled forwards to the edge of the road, Bug took up station to his right, Slowball waved Billy into the next slot and then joined the back just as Roaddog threw out the clutch and set off into the road, the roar of the v-twin had school children scampering to safety as they approached the gates. Followed by Bug's almost silent Pan-Euro, and Billy's Road Glide, its big bore pipes adding to the thunder, then the four cylinders of Slowball's trike joined in the racket of departure. All eyes were turned as the four tore up the road towards the Axe. Less than thirty seconds later the small convoy passed the lane from the caravan site, waiting at the end Roaddog saw a green Landrover, not the quad he was expecting. As they passed the Landrover it added its own noise to that of the bikes, heavy plumes of black smoke pouring from the exhaust stacks as the heavy four-by took off after them, Slowball was surprise how fast it caught up to them. As they made the right hander at South farm another quad joined the convoy, this one with two passengers, which surprised Roaddog so much that he shook his head for a moment as he accelerated out of the corner. Hard on the brakes for the left turn, and the right into the driveway, this surface not solid enough for any real power, nor smooth enough really. Turning into the grassed parking area he turned the bike around before parking it and stopping the motor. All the vehicles parked in a short time, passengers unloaded and weapons started to be assembled.

"Hi, Edward," said Roaddog to the young man who had accompanied Leo, "I wasn't expecting you."

"Dad told me what you said, and I wasn't missing out," replied Edward as he pulled a pump action twelve bore from behind his driver's seat, Leo lifted the heavy six bore from the back of the Landrover.

"Fuck," muttered Jake, "that's a cannon."

"That's the idea," laughed Leo.

"Sorry Bug," said Slowball, "your bikes too quiet and your gun looks like a toy."

"Thanks mate, I'm gonna put turnouts on the Honda and wake up the whole county."

Roaddog cocked Vera, clicked the safety on and passed it to Jackie.

"That's the fucking Thompson," said Leo.

"It is," laughed Roaddog, taking Melchion's demon sword from the bungie cords that held it to the side of his bike. Jake and Mary joined the group, three shotguns and three bandoliers between them,

"I wasn't expecting you to be here," said Roaddog to Mary.

"If you're going to put him in danger then I'm going to be here, is that a problem," she snapped, her shotgun levelling at his guts.

"The more the merrier," he laughed then looked along the driveway as a mini bus came off the main road followed closely by a police car. "Looks like everyone is here." The minibus parked alongside Jake's quad, with the police car beside it. Father Francis led the other clerics over to where the rest had gathered, Stephen went to the boot of his car and took a rifle from it, snapping a magazine into it and pulling the bolt, he walked towards Avalon and fell to his knees.

"Please forgive me High Priestess, I really wasn't expecting any action so soon. Are we sure the demon is coming now?"

"The birds are acting strangely; it certainly looks like we are going to see a necromancer today."

"I have seen the birds," interrupted Phurba, "I know that pattern, it is part of a ritual to open a portal, though the dancers are normally human."

"You think the birds are the cause?" asked Roaddog.

"Not directly, but their numbers are still climbing, despite the terrible toll we took only yesterday there are even more here now."

"Where are they coming from?" demanded Roaddog.

"Who knows," smiled Phurba, "no one knows, they just turn up for these events, maybe they hide as something else where there is no demonic energy to feed on."

"Will wiping them out stop the demons getting through?" asked Jake.

"No, they'll still make their way through the portal, but maybe a little slower," replied Phurba, "their dance is making the portal wider, the demons will pass through easier."

"You mean they have to work to get through?" asked Roaddog. Phurba only nodded.

"Can we make the portal narrower?" asked Bug.

"If we disturb their dance the portal will get narrower, but not enough to keep the demons on the other side."

"Especially not this demon," said Avalon, "he has planned his return, I just wish I knew what his intentions are."

"What can he want?" asked Roaddog, "All these demons are destined to return to hell, someone is going to beat them eventually."

"Perhaps he's simply after a promotion, to the upper ranks of the demon world," said Francis.

"How can he do that?" asked Roaddog.

"If he collects enough souls, then perhaps Satan will look favourably on him," replied Francis uncertainly.

"So, these portals are a testing ground for demons?" asked Stephen.

"No one knows for sure," replied Francis, "the demons aren't that talkative, and the portals don't open like this very often."

"How do demons normally get through?" asked Roaddog.

"They have to be summoned."

"Occasionally one will sneak through the cracks," said Mohammed.

"This is more than a crack, this is something that has been planned for a while, and Fintan has certainly messed with whatever was planned," said Roaddog.

"There was one that sneaked through, or was summoned, it's not clear, it was a few years ago, this one killed seven hundred before it was eventually overcome."

"When was this?" asked Francis,

"Ten years ago."

"Why have we not heard of it?"

"The west doesn't get to hear all the news out of Iran, I'm afraid."

"How could they cover up that many deaths?" asked Roaddog.

"It was at a very large mosque and passed off as a gas explosion."

"So how was that demon beaten?" asked Francis.

"It was a gas explosion, but most of the people were already dead."

"Most?" asked Roaddog.

"Most, but not all, some had to be there to hold the demon in place while the explosion was set up."

"Volunteers I hope," said Francis.

"Of course, and guaranteed their places in the afterlife."

"Surprising what people will do when they're promised paradise," said Roaddog.

"Only for the true believers of course," replied Mohammed.

"How many true believers here today?"

"Only me," laughed Mohammed, "the rest of you heathens are already doomed."

"But you're the only one that believes in your particular heaven, so it's meaningless to the rest of us."

"If I get killed fighting one of Satan's minions, then I am assured of a place in paradise."

"Even if you are standing with a catholic and a Jew and surrounded by women?"

"I'll still be killed by a demon; my future is secure."

"Well do us a favour."

"What?"

"Don't give in too easily, we may need you in the coming days."

"I shall fight as hard as I can, of that you can be certain, but I have nothing to fear."

"Fear is the thing that keeps you sharp."

"Fear also turns a man's guts to water and makes him freeze."

"This is equally true, but not around here," snapped Roaddog, then he turned to Francis, "Can you bless this blade?"

"It's a demon sword, but I can give it a try." Father Francis poured holy water along the length of the sword and whispered a blessing for it, he seemed a little surprised when it didn't simply dissolve.

"Dog," said Man-Dare, "I didn't bring any weapons, I usually find that my fists are enough."

"Not round here they aren't." He passed her a stiletto from his belt and tossed another one to Billy. "Don't worry they've already been blessed by the good father." He looked round at the people gathered outside the churchyard.

"Everybody ready?" he asked not waiting for an answer, "Let's go and disturb the dancing birds, and make things as difficult as we can for Fintan's return." He led the way through the lynch gate and across the graveyard, one of the fat grey birds walked across the path in front of him and the sword slashed at it, the bird fell dead.

"Wow," said Roaddog, "that felt really good."

"Careful Dog," said Avalon, "no one knows what a demonic sword can do in human hands."

"I didn't mean to kill the bird, I just thought about it, and the rush of energy is just amazing."

"Be careful it doesn't burn you out."

"I'll be fine, this is fun," his huge grin, as he strode purposefully toward the church entrance, though his purpose had subtly changed. As he approached the doorway a blue grey streak came out of the yew tree and hit the bird he was following into the church. After a moment of noise, the bird was dead and carried up into the trees by a bird with short but wide wings.

"What the fuck was that?" snapped Roaddog.

"A sparrowhawk, I think," laughed Francis. "A male, because the females are darker underneath, oh, like that one there." A larger bird dived in and snatched another of the grey harbingers.

Once inside the church Roaddog stepped right up to the dancing birds and started cutting them down, as a scythe does wheat, corpses scattered around the church as he danced through them a manic grin on his face and a laugh on his lips.

"Avalon," said Phurba, "he's carrying an awful lot of power now, and gathering more by the moment, let's hope the demon comes quickly, before he runs out of birds."

"Why?" asked Avalon.

"That sort of power is bound to be addictive to someone new to it, you and I are used to these sudden influxes of energy, Roaddog has no experience."

"You think he'll try to kill us when he runs out of birds?"

"I wouldn't be at all surprised."

"I would, there are people here he loves beyond life, you and I not so much," she laughed as Roaddog waded through a drift of dead birds, their dance completely destroyed, more birds were flying in all the time, so it didn't look as if he would run out. Suddenly a pounding of heavy hooves drowned out even Roaddog's insane laughter.

"He comes," yelled Avalon, as she felt the portal stretching to allow something through.

The clerics spread themselves out around the portal, not in any real pattern, just to cover any path that Fintan could take. The birds took to the air, no longer would they fall prey to Roaddog's demon sword. Roaddog ran to a point where he could look into the portal down the stairs that had been used before. The sound of hooves grew louder and he saw a man coming through the opening, riding a red horse, the horse had bat like wings folded along it's flanks, it burst into the open, and reared on its back legs, howling more like a wolf than a horse.

"By all the gods," yelled Avalon, "he's come riding Saratoga."

Chapter 17: Fintan returns.

There was a moment of stunned inaction before Roaddog finally got to grips with what he was looking at.

"Leo," he shouted, "hit the guy." Leo shouldered the heavy shotgun and fired, the boom was deafening, and the massive slug hit Fintan in the centre of his chest, the effect was not all that Roaddog had hoped for, the bullet managed no penetration but did knock Fintan from his horse. As Fintan lay dazed on the ground Roaddog approached him quickly thinking that the sword may end this with a minimum of risk, he spared no glance or thought for the horse, holding the sword high above his head he brought it flashing down, six inches short of the necromancer's chest the sword stopped, it howled in anger and bounced upwards turning Roaddog's wrists as it came back towards him, he staggered backwards with the force of the rebound.

"Phurba, Mohammed, Abraham, you support Roaddog," yelled Father Francis, "Avalon, with me on that horse." Stephen went with the three clerics to help Roaddog, his SLR barking as seven point six two millimetre rounds flashed towards Fintan. As per his training Stephen was aiming for centre mass, five shots had almost no affect, Stephen switched target, this time going for head shots. Again to little affect, though Fintan was definitely more distracted by these, more impact made it through his protective shield, but not enough to make any real difference other than to slow his rise to his feet. Stephen dropped to a knee and picked an even more difficult target, this one was smaller and moving more quickly. His first shot was a miss and the bullet buried itself in the heavy wooden beams of the ceiling, the next hit, the head of Fintan's staff twitched appreciably moving out of alignment with its target. Fintan glared at the policeman for a moment, from his position on his knees, then with a wave of his staff an unseen force swept Stephen from his knees and rolled him across the tiled floor, until he came to rest against one of the stone columns. Roaddog spared him the merest of glances and hoped that he was still alive.

"That's no horse," replied Avalon, as the two stepped between the mount and Fintan, forcing it to move away, it became clear to Francis that she was correct, though horse shaped with wide heavy hooves, the thing was equipped with teeth that would put a wolf to shame, and claws on its legs that a tiger would be proud of, clawed fingers that retracted around the hooves, one of these limbs came flashing towards Francis, he struck it aside with a fist wrapped in the beads of his rosary. Avalon slashed at the knee of the other front leg with her staff, and caused the horse to rear, its front legs flailing in the air, as it attempted to reach the two. The stuttering roar of Vera filled the air as Jackie drew a bead on Fintan, he was climbing slowly to his feet as Roaddog moved to strike again. The auto-shotgun was causing him little in the way of difficulties, it appeared that the shot was being stopped before it could reach its target, though some of the impact was passed on to the necromancer, though not enough to knock him over. As Roaddog watched the hole that Leo's first shot had made in Fintan's robe healed. Before his death his robe had been much as Avalon's is, white with cabalistic symbols in silver and gold, now his robe was so black that it shed the eye that focused on it, and the symbols were now the glowing red of iron from the forge, waiting for the blacksmith's hammer. The pale white of the necromancers' skin disappeared behind the black robe as the hole closed up.

"You will be mine," howled Fintan as he turned his staff towards Roaddog, a roaring red flame shot towards Roaddog, and engulfed his upper body, and he fell to his knees, Jackie screamed and ran towards the fallen man. Avalon turned at the sound and brought her staff to bear, a stream of argent light flooded from the crystal in the end of her staff, it intercepted the red fire and stopped it in its tracks. The red fire and the white light fought for dominance as an undamaged Roaddog climbed to his feet, and quickly closed the distance to the necromancer. Jake saw that Francis was basically on his own against the horse shaped demon, so he stepped up to the thing and struck it hard on the snout with the butt of his shotgun, when it reared again, he put two solid slugs into its conveniently exposed belly. Saratoga howled and attempted to stamp the farmer to death, but he was already moving, running slowly towards the south door, reloading as he went. Mary fired both barrels into the horse's flank as it passed, they did little damage to the horse, but managed to tear the wing membranes to shreds. Leo's heavy gun boomed again, and a one-inch solid slug hit the wing root on the other side of Saratoga, the wing fell to the ground and dark red blood poured sluggishly from the wound. Saratoga briefly paused as he came up against the barrier the clerics had erected, with a wriggling and a tensing of his huge hindquarters he forced his way through the south door and out into the open air, looking round for the man Saratoga failed to find him, and turned towards the lynch gate.

"Chase him into the open," shouted Leo's son Edward as he followed Mary out of the church, his own shotgun discharging twice in rapid succession and catching the demon in the back of its head, causing it to duck slightly. It crashed through the lynch gate smashing both the gates to tinder, then passed under the roof section without actually knocking it down, only a few of the precarious slates slid to the ground one to smash on the tarmac the rest to stick edge on into the soft earth. Mary knelt behind the demon as it moved into the car park area, she was waiting for the right moment, the demon's almost prehensile tail swished to her right, the bodily orifice that she was expecting to see wasn't there, so she gave the demon both barrels.

"That should give it an asshole," she muttered, "where's that damned husband of mine?" she asked of no one in particular.

The sudden impact below the demon's tail made it jump forwards then turn to face Mary, it screamed its defiance at her.

"Duck," yelled Leo from behind Mary, she dropped to the ground, Leo gave her a second to be sure she wasn't going to get up again, and then his heavy shotgun boomed for the third time. The energetic slug tore into Saratoga's mouth, almost destroying the lower jaw. The demon turned and fled through the carpark out into the open. Edward ran over to his car and jumped in. A plume of black smoke from its stacks showed that it was running, no one could actually hear it though, Leo's gun had done a real job of taking away peoples hearing. Edward's landrover lurched as it took off, tearing clods of grass from the carpark's surface. By the time he caught up with Saratoga he was doing forty miles an hour, he hit the demon from behind and three tonnes of metal bounced over the demon's haunches, driving it down into the hard ground and causing considerable damage. It's front legs still worked, and Edward came around for another pass, this time going for the demon's head. Saratoga tried to bite the bars on the front of the car but having only an upper jaw this was never going to work, even if the car hadn't been doing thirty miles an hour when it hit. The demons head twisted around and folded back along it's body. Edward slowly reversed so that the main weight of the landrover was resting on the demon's neck. It wasn't dead, but it was seriously damaged, its legs twitching fitfully trying to lift the vehicle, or slash at anyone that came within range. Man-Dare and Jane were the ones closest, putting their knives to good use, it looked as if the priest's blessing gave the knives the ability to cut into the demon's flesh, as if it was water. Saratoga was losing a lot of blood and getting weaker by the second.

"How do we kill this bastard?" demanded Man-Dare, slashing another gaping wound in its side. Something about the demon changed, as her blade left the demons flank the wound started to close.

"It's pulling energy from somewhere, and healing itself," said Francis, he took his flask from inside his jacket. "Cut it again," he commanded. She cut as deep as she could into the demon and Francis poured holy water into the wound, the wound smoked, and the demon twitched spastically. In only a few seconds it stopped moving completely, blood flow from its wounds slowed and stopped.

"Is it dead?" asked Man-Dare.

"It's as dead as a demon can be," Francis smiled at the young woman, then he turned to Edward, "Leave the truck on it for a while just to be sure."

"Where's that jackass husband of mine?" asked Mary as they went back towards the church.

Jake, having left the church by the south door, turned left and squeezed between the tall yew tree and the wall, running quickly around the eastern end and up to the north door. As he stepped through the open door, he was directly behind Fintan, he dropped to his knees and raised his gun. Avalon's silvery light sputtered and failed, she dropped to the ground, utterly exhausted. Fintan turned his red fire on Roaddog again, the tall biker dropped to the ground, the sword of Melchion dropped onto Fintan's elbow and slid slowly towards the ground. Jackie aimed for Fintan's head, and the stuttering roar of Vera filled the air, it caused little damage to Fintan, but some distraction, for an instant the red fire swept Jackie against the wall and the gun fell from her hand into silence. Jake noticed that the sword not only cut the necromancers robe, but also left a stripe of blood in the crook of the man's arm. Jake changed his target, he aimed at the black robed upper arm directly in front of him. He fired the first barrel and then almost immediately the second. The first was salt, something he knew to be effective against these demons, the second a solid two-ounce lump of lead. The salt disrupted whatever was protecting the necromancer if only for a moment, that moment was enough for the slug to tear through the protection and then through the upper arm bone of the man. The arm was almost completely severed, and the staff fell to the ground, its fire extinguished. Roaddog staggered to his feet, the weight of the sword seemed to be too much for him to lift, though the grip was in his hand the tip was dragging along the tiles of the floor. Fintan was lying on his back, where he had fallen, Roaddog grinned at the look of horror on the necromancer's face, was it the pain of losing his arm, or the shock of losing his staff. Avalon staggered forwards and kicked Fintan's legs together then sat on his ankles, Jake pulled his remaining arm hard above Fintan's head, making sure he was going nowhere. Roaddog stood astride the fallen man, he dragged the sword so its point was resting on the man's chest.

"Wait," called Avalon, "I need to be sure." She reached forwards with her staff and slowly pressed the crystal against the blade of the sword. "Now you can kill him," she said.

Roaddog looked at her a little confused but slowly he pushed the sword downwards into the necromancer's chest, there was some resistance but not enough to stop the demon forged blade. As the point reached into Fintan's heart there was an enormous surge of energy, it rushed into Roaddog, replacing all that the necromancer had stolen and much, much more. Roaddog screamed in exultation, Fintan's scream was more desperate.

"My soul," he howled, "not my soul."

"Avalon," yelled Phurba, "you can't."

"I can and will," replied Avalon softly, "this soul has been to hell and returned, it cannot be allowed to continue."

"That's wicked," muttered Phurba as the sound of Fintan's voice slowly faded, and then he was dead, again. "Now he can never reach nirvana," whispered Phurba.

"He was never getting there anyway," replied Avalon, "even if he'd been trying."

"Now that was a rush," laughed Roaddog, looking around, he noticed Jackie by the wall, unmoving. He shouted and ran over to her. He rolled her quickly over onto her back and felt for a pulse at her neck, finding none he started compressing her chest with both hands.

"Help here," he yelled, Jane came sprinting over and slid to a stop alongside Jackie's head and fell to her knees and started mouth to mouth. While Jane was breathing for Jackie Roaddog called out, "Slowball get here." When the big man arrived Roaddog spoke softly to Jane.

"Let him in, bigger lungs." Jane moved aside and placed a hand on Jackie's neck, she shook her head as Roaddog pumped her chest again. Avalon moved closer and placed the crystal in her staff against Jackie's belly.

"Dog," she said, "you have to hurry, the spark is failing."

"How? I can't lose her."

"You need the sword." He stared at her for a moment.

"Jane, take over," he said and ran to get the sword from where he had dropped it.

"What do I do with it?" he snapped.

"This is not going to be easy," said Avalon, "it's going to resist, but it is the only available conduit."

"Just fucking tell me," snarled Roaddog.

"Her shirt is in the way," said Avalon softly. Roaddog grabbed a fist full of Jackie's shirt and in a heartbeat the whole thing was shredded, and gone.

"Place the tip of the sword against her belly, above the belly button." He pressed the point gently against her soft white flesh.

"Inch higher," said Avalon, the sword moved and Roaddog glared.

"Now for the hard bit, take all your love for the girl and force it through the sword into her, all your energy, all your life, with everything that you feel for her, you can bring her back." Roaddog tried with all his heart to do as Avalon said, the sword blocked him, it cared nothing for love or life, the man pushed harder, forcing the sword to his will, demanding the life of his love. Avalon's staff touched the blade of the sword, and her power was added to the struggle, then Jane turned and put both hands around the blade, adding her love for Jackie to the fight for the girl's life. In a battle of wills that seemed to last for an eternity the sword finally gave way, energy, power and love flowed into Jackie, hot fire filled her, she drew her first breath in many minutes and screamed. Roaddog threw the sword away again, and picked her up, Jane joined in the three-way hug, all three were crying unashamedly. Avalon looked around at the assembled group, there were more tears to be seen, her own included.

"Well, that was more than a little surprising," said Francis.

"You could have been of more help," observed Avalon, "but you stood around like a wet weekend in Scarborough."

"I had no idea how to help in this, it's not part of our training, resurrecting the dead is sort of frowned on by the church." Roaddog separated himself from the two girls and picked up the sword.

"Damn, it feels empty now," he muttered. "Avalon, that damned red fire of his was just draining my life away, but the energy the sword gave me when he died was amazing."

"And you only got some of it," said Avalon, "I took some as well."

"It felt so great, but it's all gone now," grinned Roaddog.

"That's why it's so dangerous," said Avalon gently. "That sort of power is utterly addictive, and only attained at the cost of lives."

"Where have the birds gone?" asked Jackie, looking around the church for the first time.

"Jake," shouted Mary, now that the emergency was over, "where the hell did you run off to?"

"Sorry love," he replied with a smile, "I had to sneak up behind the bad man and blow his arm off."

"Well, is that it then?" she asked, "Is all this shit over?"

"Sadly no," said Avalon, "the gateway is still open, but the wall is now empty."

"So, we've no idea who is going to be next?" asked Jake.

"We've got to wait for the reset," said Roaddog, "we don't generally have to wait too long. In the meantime, there's some clean up to do." He looked at the remains of Fintan lying on the ground, there was little blood despite the hole in his chest.

"Slowball, help me with this, there's a small stream along the eastern edge of the church yard, and a compost heap in the north-east corner, we'll drop him in the stream and cover him in compost, we only need him to stay hidden for a couple of days."

"Okay," said Slowball.

"Here," said Roaddog handing the sword to Jackie.

"No," yelled Avalon, "that damned sword is yours now, it could easily kill anyone else that handles it."

"How is that possible?" demanded Roaddog.

"It's attuned to you, you have killed a demon with it, and given life to a lover, it knows you and won't like anyone else. Though a powerful demon may be able to take it over, so don't lose it when the next one comes."

"So, what the fuck do I do with it?"

"Just leave it on the ground, and no one will touch it."

"Fine," muttered Roaddog, as he knelt down, he slowly placed the sword on the ground. "It doesn't want me to let go," he said, "I'm trying but it's very hard."

"You must put it down," said Avalon clearly, "remember when you threw it away only minutes ago? Feel the same for it again. At some point you're going to have to give it up for good, it has to get used to being away from your hand."

"Done," said Roaddog as he very deliberately opened his fist, the sword fell to the ground with a clatter. "Damn that was hard," he muttered.

"And it will get harder the more you use it," said Avalon.

"Why is that?"

"It's a demon blade and it just loves to kill, it can't do that on its own, it needs a hand to hold it and an arm to wield it."

"Even its own kind?"

"It doesn't care, it feeds on life, in whatever form."

"So how come it didn't kill me when I first picked it up?"

"You had made Melchion drop it, he'd given it up, so it passed to you, beware of it's allegiance, it's more often a traitor than anything else."

"Why didn't you tell me at the time?"

"You might not have taken the sword, without it Fintan would have been much more difficult to kill."

"We'll talk about this again," snapped Roaddog, he waved to Slowball to help him with the remains of Fintan. Between them they picked up the body and were surprised by just how light it was.

"Give it to me," said Slowball quietly, he knew that he could easily carry this weight all on his own, Roaddog lifted the necromancer's shoulders until he was almost upright. Slowball hoisted the body upwards and draped it over his shoulder. When they got to the eastern perimeter of the graveyard Roaddog held the tree branches out of the way so that Slowball could throw the body down into the stream.

"More of a ditch than anything," observed Slowball, as he turned back towards the church.

"Wait," said Roaddog, "I have a task for you, when we get back, I want you to take the van and go find either a building suppliers or a building site, I want enough heras fencing to cover all the damned windows and doors on this church."

"No problem, but why?"

"The next demon ain't getting out and I'm going to bring the whole damned thing down around its head."

"How you going to do that?"

"There is a plan, one or two things to steal first."

"Like what?"

"Don't you worry about it, just get the fences to block off those windows and doors."

"Okay boss, just let me know what you need."

"I will, your job is easy, Bug's got the harder task."

"Give me his then."

"I can't, you can't drive an artic."

"Neither can Bug," laughed Slowball.

"Legally no, but he has done it in the past, so he can again, without breaking it too much."

"Fine," said Slowball, "let's get back inside before they come looking for us."

"Agreed," Roaddog slapped Slowball on his back as the two turned towards the church's north door, just in time to see Avalon come out into the daylight.

"Thought you two had run off," she smiled.

"Nah," replied Roaddog, "shit to sort out, plans within plans, you know."

"No I don't, tell me."

"Not until I'm sure I can get all the things together in one place at the one time, and we're going to be running on a tight schedule."

"Still no news on who's next," she said slowly.

"I'm actually hoping that the damned portal just gives up."

"It's a good dream to have," said Avalon.

"But it's not going to happen, is it."

"No, I don't think so."

"It's just been too easy so far."

"I wouldn't call any of it easy," said Slowball, looking to Avalon for confirmation.

"I would," said Avalon, "you've beaten four demons, and the only losses have been a guy who gave his life willingly, and that damned necromancer."

"Don't forget some of Jake's cows," laughed Roaddog.

"Sorry, they don't count," replied Avalon.

"Well, I'm planning on no losses at all," snapped Roaddog, "I just need a couple of days to get things organised."

"We may be that lucky," smiled Avalon, by the time they returned to the church the other clerics were already resetting their barriers.

"Can you add anything to our wards?" asked Father Francis.

"Not really," answered Avalon, "when I set up a forbidding, I have to be there to maintain it." Francis nodded and turned back to the south doorway. "And you'd probably be better waiting a while until you're not so tired," she continued.

"We were marginally affective against that demon, so we're going to keep coming back and reinforcing the wards through the day, and night if necessary."

"Repeated reinforcement may help, but that very much depends on who is coming next." They all heard the deep bell like sound and felt the ground tremble beneath their feet. All eyes turned to the wooden wall that blocked the west door. Avalon walked slowly towards the wall, as if dreading what she would find there. The embossed image in the wood was difficult for her to see, Roaddog brought his phone to the wall and shone the light from the side. Avalon gasped.

"By all that is holy," she whispered, "I'm not ready for this."

"What is it?" asked Francis.

"Heralth."

"It can't be," muttered Francis.

"You come look, you tell me that's not her symbol," snapped Avalon angrily. Francis approached cautiously and stared for only a moment.

"She'll bring her hoard with her, she always does," he said.

"You better put in a call to the big guy, we need some archangels, three or four might just be enough."

"I'm not sure he'll be listening right now," mumbled Francis.

"What are you worrying about?" asked Avalon, "How many times can you die?"

Francis glared at her for a moment then pointed to the small pool of blood left behind by Fintan.

"Ah, I see what you mean," laughed Avalon. "I wouldn't worry about it though Heralth doesn't generally take prisoners."

"Just souls."

"True, talk to the big guy, a heavenly host would be just the thing when she turns up."

"I'll certainly give it a try, but you have to remember that I was sent here to guard this place, I'm most likely all we get."

"Assigned by god's representative here on earth?"

"Sort of, by an indirect route."

"Let's hope there is something in that, because we are going to need all the help we can get." Avalon looked for a moment at the blood on the ground.

"Hey Roaddog," she called, "anyone get Fintan's blood on them?"

"I did," said Slowball, "why?"

"Be careful, demon blood is very powerful, even once the demon is dead, it has a great corrupting influence."

"I got some on my jacket, and some on my hands."

"Get clean as soon as you can, and definitely before you eat."

"You mean the bastard can come back again, resurrected from his blood?"

"Perhaps, more likely it will be another demon, I shredded Fintan's soul, he ain't coming back ever."

"So," said Slowball, "ingesting demon blood could give the demons a chance to take a person over?"

"That is correct."

"Hey Dog, can you think of anyone we'd like to be taken over by a demon?"

"I can think of a couple right now, you?"

"Probably the same two, Hopkins and the bastard?"

"That's the ones," laughed Roaddog.

"That is not funny," said Avalon, "we've got enough problems with demons as it is, we don't need any strays just turning up."

"Don't worry," replied Slowball, "it was more of a joke than anything serious."

"Not funny," said Avalon sternly.

"That depends on your sense of humour," said Slowball.

"I have no humour when demons are involved."

"I can understand that, but we don't have your experience, yet," smiled Slowball.

"I pray you don't, I've heard too many horror stories."

"But have you actually experienced them?" asked Roaddog.

"Well, no, demon incursions are very rare, I haven't actually witnessed one before."

"You have said that this is your first."

"Yes, but I have read many reports of others, we've been fighting these demons for generations."

"So how are we doing so far?" asked Slowball.

"Astoundingly well, I am so surprised that you haven't taken more loses."

"Well, we're not your run of the mill citizens," said Roaddog.

"Nor the run of the mill clergy, they tend to hide behind their crosses and pray, which is generally not very effective."

"Not what Francis is doing then?"

"No, which is a surprise. What are we going to do while we're waiting for Heralth to show?"

"I have some things to set in motion," said Roaddog, "let's get back to the shop."

"I'll see you there, I've got to make sure that Stephen is fit to drive, he took one hell of a hit."

"He did, but what did Fintan hit him with?"

"Simple projection of his staff."

"You mean the staff got longer without us being able to see it?"

"No, it was only partially in his hand, it's physical presence was projected to coincide with Stephens body."

"But we couldn't see it."

"It was sort of half in both places."

"That's nuts."

"And quite simple to achieve."

"You people are crazy," laughed Roaddog, "Let's get moving." He walked into the darkness of the church, Jane and Jackie were standing together arms around each other, Jackie with Vera hanging loosely from her right hand, Avalon went to help Stephen who was still a little groggy from his confrontation with Fintan.

"Damn that bastard hits hard," he whispered to Avalon as she placed an arm around his waist.

"How are you doing?" she asked.

"I'll be okay, I've taken harder knocks at Grimsby town matches," he smiled wanly.

"We're going back to the workshop, if you can drive?"

"I'm fine," he said, "the flack jacket took most of the impact, or spread it out more," he chuckled.

"He came a lot closer to killing Roaddog than he did you," she said as the bikers walked from the church into the sunlight.

"I don't understand."

"Neither does Roaddog, that red fire of Fintan's, it was draining his life, a few more seconds and he would have been dead, then under the control of Fintan. Think of that, an undead wielding a demon sword. That would have been so dangerous for us all."

"Should we tell him?" asked Stephen.

"I don't think so, he really doesn't need to know how close he came."

"What about this next demon, it seems to have both you and the good father rattled?"

"She's definitely a force to be reckoned with, and she brings her children along, normally in numbers around the hundred mark."

"And what are these children like?"

"Well, I'm sure you've seen the representation of cherubs, well her children are pink, and there the similarity ends, they're more like small winged dogs, with teeth and claws to match, sort of a dog version of a griffon, and pink."

"We've got enough shotguns for flying vermin," grinned Stephen.

"I'm not at all sure how effective they will be."

"Well, let's catch up with the others, I want to know what Roaddog is planning."

By the time the pair got into the carpark the bikers were long gone. They climbed into Stephens police car and set off to the workshop, as they left the carpark area, Stephen said, "Where'd that damned horse go?"

"I've no idea," replied Avalon, "they chased it out here and killed it somehow."

"There's a patch of bare ground over there," said Stephen pointing.

"Saratoga must have died there."

"What do you mean?"

"Some dissolve when they are dead, or have been killed, some don't. Saratoga was an incidental here, so it dissolved into the ground, not much will grow there for a few years."

Stephen set off along the drive, being careful to avoid what bumps he could, every pothole made his ribs hurt all over again.

They were both surprised when they arrived at the workshop, and it was all shut up. Avalon took out her phone and called Roaddog.

"Hey Dog," she said when he answered, "where you at?"

"We're on the road, we got some things to do and having Stephen around would make things very difficult for him, and this shit is going to get hard enough. We've dropped Sylvia and Cherie with Mick, you could tag with them until the axe opens, and we'll meet you there. Okay?"

"So, you're not going to tell us what you're up to?"

"Not until it's done."

"Okay," replied Avalon, "we'll catch up later." She turned to Stephen, "Back to the caravan site, it looks like the bad boys have gone out to do naughty things, and they didn't want to compromise you."

"So, what are we doing?" he asked.

"Just chilling, until the axe opens, then we'll go and get some beers. Sounds like a fun day to me."

"At least nothing is trying to kill us right now," laughed Stephen, as he pulled out of the workshop forecourt and headed towards Leo's caravan site. When they got there Stephen went to Roaddog's caravan and saw that Roaddog's Victory, and Bug's Pan-Euro were parked outside but Jane's car was gone. So, he slowly rolled round to the small lake and parked alongside Moya. Avalon climbed out of the car and walked into Mick's awning.

"Hey Mick," she said, "any chance of a cup of tea?"

"Of course, come on in, I'll put the kettle on."

She went into the caravan with Stephen behind her, she saw Sylvia, Cherie, and Jackie chatting and sat down with them.

"Looks like me and you are banished to the awning," said Mick to Stephen.

"Best place," laughed Stephen, "if the womenfolk are going to start talking about childbearing and whatnot."

"It's the whatnot that really gets to me," replied Mick, pouring water into two cups and then milk. "Sugar?" he asked.

"Not for me," said Avalon, Stephen just shook his head. Mick passed out the cups of tea and then followed Stephen out into the awning.

Avalon waited until she was sure Stephen was far enough away before she spoke.

"Do you know what the guys are up to?"

"Not with any accuracy," whispered Sylvia, "but we do know it involves some sort of heavy articulated truck."

"They don't have any heavy trucks," said Avalon.

"They will do in a little while," giggled Cherie.

"Trucks full of what?" asked Avalon.

"There's a gas terminal nearby, and an oil refinery, so I'm betting on some sort of fuel," said Cherie.

"You think they're planning on setting fire to the whole church?"

"I think it's going to be something bigger than that."

"Dog's not short on imagination," said Sylvia.

"Or engineering skills," agreed Cherie.

"But what the hell are they making?" asked Avalon.

"We'll find out in due course," said Sylvia, "so don't worry about it."

"I'm not worried, who am I kidding?" said Avalon, "of course I'm worried, but I'm happier knowing that they have a plan, no matter how crazy."

"Oh, it's going to be crazy, of that you can be certain," laughed Sylvia.

"Where's Billy and Man-Dare?" asked Avalon, "his bike wasn't at the caravan."

"Can't get six in Jane's car," observed Cherie, "and there is no way she'd be left behind."

"Is she really as crazy as she makes out?" asked Avalon.

"Crazier," laughed Sylvia, "she'll certainly be of use if there's a truck driver they need to distract."

"I don't understand," said Avalon.

"She can be quite a distraction," laughed Cherie.

"Remember the Railway?" asked Sylvia. "Should we?"

"Yeah," smiled Cherie, glancing out of the window to make sure that Stephen was still seated in the awning.

"Some time ago we were involved in an armed robbery at a pub," said Sylvia.

"That was only yesterday and I was there," replied Avalon.

"No, it was some time ago," said Sylvia, "three guys armed with a shot gun, Man-Dare distracted the guys by lifting her skirt and playing with herself, she was at that time without underwear. While the guys were watching her masturbatory activities they were overcome by their intended victims. The day did not go well for them."

"That's why Roaddog mentioned the same thing twice," smiled Avalon.

"Yeap," said Cherie.

"He was so damned cool when that guy stuck a gun in his stomach."

"In the railway it was Bandit Queen with the gun in her guts."

"Was she cool?"

"Deadly."

"Did you hand the robbers over to the cops like yesterday?"

"No, and if you mention this anywhere else we will deny all knowledge, as there is no evidence that it even happened," said Sylvia quietly.

"So," said Avalon almost a whisper, "Roaddog and Bandit Queen disappeared the robbers?"

"No comment," replied Sylvia with a smile.

"Remember there was a robbery in the Axe yesterday?" asked Avalon.

"Of course, we were there," replied Sylvia looking confused.

"Have you seen the reporters from the TV and the newspapers?"

"No."

"CID follow up investigations?"

"No."

"What did I tell Stephen?"

"I'm not sure," said Sylvia slowly.

"I told him I never wanted to hear of them again."

"You mean that he's disappeared two armed robbers simply on your command?"

"No comment," smiled Avalon.

"But he sounded so upset that you might want him to kill someone?" asked Cherie.

"No comment," shrugged Avalon.

"Fuck, bitch, you're as crazy as Man-Dare," snapped Cherie.

"And a shit load more powerful," replied Avalon, with a huge grin.

"Fuck," whispered Sylvia.

"Yeah," replied Cherie.

"What's wrong?" asked Jackie.

"If it turns into a competition for the title of Queen Bitch, there's going to be blood," said Cherie.

"That won't be a problem," said Avalon.

"I wouldn't bet on that," said Sylvia, "she'll find a way to get to you."

"We'll cross that bridge when we get to it," said Avalon.

"Watch out that she doesn't burn it under you," said Cherie.

"I have nothing to worry about," smiled Avalon.

"Let's hope that is true," said Cherie.

"What about this next demon?" asked Sylvia.

"Heralth is one of the princes of hell, I suppose we should call her a princess, but that generates far too nice an image, she always comes along with a hoard of her children, and they're mean savage little bastards."

"Like how mean?"

"They're like winged dogs, only not as nice," said Avalon, "and the more Heralth gets to eat the more children she gives birth to, and damned quick at that."

"How quick?" asked Cherie.

"I'm not sure, the last time she was here there weren't clocks as such. We could be looking at a couple of minutes or less. Not many survivors and none too literate either."

"How long ago was this?" asked Sylvia.

"Mid thirteen hundreds, but there may have been more recent appearances, just not documented."

"So, she's been beaten before?"

"Perhaps, but by humans, who can tell?"

"Who beat her last time?" asked Cherie.

"The report tells of a white light and lightning, it could have been a natural phenomenon, or maybe an archangel."

"Angels exist?" snorted Cherie.

"You've been fighting demons, but you doubt the existence of angels?"

"Let's just say they've been fuck all use to us," snapped Cherie.

"That's for sure," agreed Sylvia.

"Your feelings about them do seem to be echoed quite a lot by the rest of the world," laughed Avalon.

"Does Francis know how to summon them?" asked Cherie.

"If there are procedures to summon angels then these are closely guarded secrets, only the Vatican knows, and they're telling no one."

"They're useless as well."

"I'm not arguing with that statement," laughed Avalon, "they're too concerned with keeping the power to themselves, perhaps if Heralth and her children came storming through the gates of Vatican City, maybe then they'd actually do something, but by then it would be far too late, it always is with them."

"So, we're on our own," said Sylvia.

"Most likely, yes," said Avalon with a grim nod.

"Listening to everything you've been saying, I'm having a problem with my husband being involved in all this," said Jackie quietly.

"I wouldn't worry," said Sylvia, "I think that Roaddog's plan won't include you two, at least not until it's all over."

"What do you mean?" asked Jackie.

"You'll probably get the call to pick up the survivors, if there are any."

"You think people are going to die?"

"Yes, it's a distinct possibility."

"And still you go?"

"Slowball will be there, and so will I," replied Sylvia softly.

"Me too," said Cherie.

"You better keep moving," smiled Sylvia, "given your condition Dog is likely to handcuff you to a tree."

"Fuck him, I'll be standing by my man when the shit hits the fan."

"What condition?" asked Jackie.

"Cherie is expecting," said Sylvia.

"You happy about that?" asked Jackie.

"It was a hell of a surprise, but I've got used to the idea, and am looking forward to it, I'll be a damned sight better mother than I had."

"What do you mean?"

"My mother was a junkie and I ended up in care, but that's ancient history."

"I'm sure you will be fine."

"You got any kids?" asked Sylvia,

"Yes," replied Jackie, "all growed up and kids of their own now."

"You don't look old enough to be a grandma."

"Well I am, living with that asshole keeps a person young," she nodded her head in the direction of the awning, "he's as mad as a bucket of frogs."

"He seems like a nice guy," said Cherie.

"I suppose, but bat shit and crazy come to mind."

"How do you mean?"

"All that music, and bands, late nights, early mornings, I'm just surprised the old fool hasn't died already."

"He must enjoy it," said Cherie.

"He does, and so do I, but it gets wearing when there are three gig weekends, followed by a rehearsal. I'm sure the booze will kill him eventually."

"Until then you can enjoy yourselves."

"We have fun, and sometimes too much of it."

"That's what life is for," laughed Sylvia.

"That's for sure," said Cherie.

"Hey Dog," called Jackie, "what you two talking about?"

"Just shooting the breeze, my love, chatting about music, and ancient history."

"Yeah," called Stephen, "I can't believe he met Suzi Quatro."

"He did that," laughed Jackie, "and he got her to sing with his band."

"That was a great night, so many of the punters thought she was a look-a-like," laughed Mick, "we still had a great gig, and drank too much."

"That's always the case with you," smiled Jackie, "damned piss head."

"Hey, not drinking now."

"It's early yet, the damned pub's not open."

"Karen will be open soon."

"Time for another brew," said Jackie.

"Yes dear," replied Mick with a smile.

"Bastard," muttered Jackie as Mick came into the caravan and filled the kettle.

"Bastard, why?" asked Sylvia.

"It's not three little words that make a marriage last, it's two. He made this very clear at both of our daughter's weddings, and every time he uses them, I call him a bastard."

"Is that because he is right?" asked Cherie.

"Don't you hate it when they are right?" asked Jackie, finally smiling a little.

"Avalon," said Cherie, "are you married?"

"No, never really had the time, and to be frank, not the inclination either."

"Why is that?"

"In my line of business, the men I meet are always after something."

"What business is that?"

"High priestess."

"But you've not always been high priestess, you must have started lower down the order?"

"Yes, but I was totally focused on being the best."

"Are you?"

"Yes, I am."

"You've not left it too late, you could still have children if you wanted."

"How old do you think I am?" asked Avalon.

"Mid-forties," replied Cherie.

"Try sixty some," laughed Avalon, "perhaps it's not having kids that has kept me so young."

"They can be a real strain," said Jackie.

"Worth it?" asked Sylvia,

"Jury's still out on that," laughed Jackie.

"Well, it's far too late for me now," said Avalon, "but I have enough that look to me, I don't need blood relations."

"I know what you mean," said Jackie, "we've got plenty that regard us as parent backups."

"It must be wonderful to have so many depending on you," said Cherie.

"Damned tiring," smiled Jackie, "but we tend to be more help to the parents than the kids."

"What do you mean?" asked Sylvia,

"We've made all the mistakes, so we know where they are, I explain to the children, and tell them how they can tell the parents, most of the time the errors can be avoided, but there always the times when someone is too certain to take advice."

"I suppose parents can get upset at someone outside telling them they are wrong," said Cherie.

"Not just the parents, children don't like to be told that their parents are right."

"How do they take it?" asked Sylvia.

"Badly, generally. Usually they come around, but that can take a while, sometimes they see it the right way when they are having the same problems with their own children," laughed Jackie.

"What time is it?" called Mick from the awning.

"Can't you tell the time?" asked Jackie.

"My phone's in there, and I don't want to disturb your vital conversations."

"It's quarter past twelve, fool," laughed Jackie.

"Damn, the pubs been open for fifteen minutes. Come on people, let's go get some beer." Mick came into the van carrying two cups.

"Come on ladies, you're burning opening time."

"It's definitely beer o'clock," laughed Cherie.

"Should you really be drinking?" asked Jackie.

"I look at it this way," said Cherie, "there's a very small chance that me having a couple of beers is going to affect the kids brain, whereas there's a fifty-fifty chance that it's going to be a hoody wearing chav, be it dumbo or genius."

"That is of course one way to look at it, though some would say 'why take the chance?'"

"Currently the chances aren't that good that any of us survive," whispered Cherie.

"You really believe that?" asked Jackie.

"I do, either the next demon will kill us, or the one after, the only thing that is certain is that everybody dies."

"But not today or tomorrow," said Jackie.

"Who can tell?" said Cherie.

"Bright side," said Sylvia, "pub's open."

"Beer o'clock will do for me," laughed Cherie, standing up. "We've got no wheels, who's gonna take us to the pub?" she asked loudly.

"Stephen will," said Avalon, then she turned to Jackie, "you can catch up if you wish, thanks for the tea."

"We'll be along in a little while, I need to have some serious words with my husband."

"I understand," said Sylvia as she went out of the door and followed Stephen to his car. In a few moments they were rolling slowly through the caravan site, heading for the Axe.

"I wonder what she wants to talk to Mick about in private?" asked Cherie.

"She wants him to stay alive," said Avalon, "this shit is getting too real for her."

"She's right," said Sylvia, "but we don't really have a choice, I don't see any of the guys backing off now, do you?"

"Not a chance," laughed Cherie.

"How about you Stephen?" asked Avalon.

"I'd love to walk away, or better still arrest the whole damned bunch and lock them up so they stay alive, just give me the nod."

"I'm not going to do that," said Avalon, "we need them, the others don't stand a chance of stopping this thing, whereas I believe in Roaddog, and whatever it is he is planning."

"I hope that you are right," said Stephen softly.

"So do I, so do I," whispered Avalon, as Stephen turned into the car park at the Axe.

The four trooped into the Axe and greeted Karen, who looked behind them for the others.

"Where's the rest?" she asked.

"They'll be along presently," replied Avalon, "they have things to do." Before Stephen had ordered the drinks the heavy rumble of a harley could be heard pulling up outside.

"What can I get you?" asked Stephen as Billy and Man-Dare walked in, if Billy was smiling his beard did a damned good job of hiding it, Man-Dare in no way hid her grin.

"Two pints and two large Jacks," said Man-Dare giggling.

"Successful trip out?" asked Stephen.

"Oh yes," said Man-Dare, "but I really shouldn't tell you about it. You're a cop after all."

"I don't see how it really matters," said Stephen, "Jackie uses a thompson automatic shotgun, Bug has a mac-ten stuffed in the back of his pants, Roaddog is swinging a four-foot demonic sword, I'm driving around with an illegal SLR in my boot, and you're worried about me finding out they've been stealing trucks?"

"Okay," laughed Man-Dare, "they've been stealing trucks, Bug's got two and a half thousand gallons of unleaded, and Roaddog's got a truck full of gas bottles, and Slowball's robing fences from somewhere, I have no idea what is going on."

"He's going to fill the church full of petrol and burn all the demons," said Stephen.

"That should do the trick," replied Avalon.

"It's going to make one hell of a mess," said Stephen.

"I really don't care that much," said Avalon, "the thought of Heralth and her hoard out in the world is simply terrifying."

"Sometimes I feel the same about Roaddog," whispered Stephen.

"With reason," said Man-Dare quietly.

"How are we going to explain a burned out church, and stolen trucks."

"We're not," laughed Avalon, "imagine the fun the tabloids will have with all that, not to mention all those crazy conspiracy theorists. By the end of next week it'll be aliens and incendiary ghosts."

"At least we'll be in the clear," smiled Stephen. The conversation died for a little while before Stephen finally spoke again.

"What the fuck does he want gas bottles for?"

"Easier than finding a pump for the fuel," said Billy, "tankers usually feed by gravity into the petrol stations, no pumps required."

"Perhaps he knows what he is doing," said Stephen.

"I wouldn't go that far," laughed Man-Dare, "he's most likely just winging it."

"What makes you say that?" asked Stephen.

"Number one I know him, number two, why has he sent Jackie into Louth for three fishing poles?"

"Fishing poles?"

"Yes, fishing poles."

"I think he's lost it," laughed Cherie.

"The strain has finally got to him," agreed Sylvia.

"It was bound to happen," smiled Avalon.

"I'm saying nothing," said Billy.

"You know what he is planning?" asked Stephen.

"Maybe, but if he doesn't want to tell, then I'm not guessing."

"What is it?" asked Avalon.

"Fucking scary is what it is," replied Billy, quietly.

"So, what is it?" demanded Stephen.

"I'm not saying, I hope I'm wrong, but if he tells you to run, then fucking run, because your life depends on it."

"If it's that dangerous, why do we have to be so close?" asked Cherie.

"Bait, what else?"

"You think Roaddog will use us as bait?" asked Sylvia.

"Don't forget, he'll be standing with you, bait himself."

"Now I am getting frightened," said Cherie.

"Bug's going to be there as well," said Sylvia.

"Frightened, but by his side," whispered Cherie.

"Do you really think it's going to be that bad?" asked Stephen, looking straight at Avalon.

"Heralth is coming, the only way it could be worse is if Satan turned up."

"Is that likely?" he whispered.

"No, he almost never comes out of hell."

"Almost," spluttered Sylvia.

"No records exist, but who is to say," smiled Avalon.

"That's not exactly re-assuring," replied Stephen.

"I'm sure the guys will need our help once they get back from wherever they are," said Avalon, "until then it's a waiting game, but I hope they don't need too much time to set this thing up."

"You think Heralth is going to show soon?"

"Maybe, so far we've had a couple of days between demons, let's just hope that this one is the same."

Sylvia glanced at her phone. "The birds are still milling around aimlessly, so it's not soon."

"Don't you worry about Slowball?" asked Cherie.

"Of course, but it does no good, he's going to do what needs to be done, I'm just hoping he will survive."

"So, you're not worrying about yourself?"

"Not especially, I'm absolutely certain that he will find a way to ensure I have a chance to run."

"But will you take it?" asked Avalon.

"That is a question that will have to wait until the moment is upon me," Sylvia smiled softly.

"Looks like it's going to be all or none," muttered Stephen.

"You in or out?" asked Avalon.

"In, how can I be anything else."

"Good man," said Avalon.

"Not bad for a cop," observed Man-Dare.

"Thanks bitch," laughed Stephen.

"That's Queen Bitch," laughed Man-Dare.

"You've decided on your new name then?" asked Cherie. "What would Bandit Queen say?"

"I've no idea," mumbled Man-Dare, "I think I'll stick with the current one, after all, imagine how much bitchier I'd have to get to make the guys actually use it," she howled with laughter at the thought. She turned to Billy, "You're a bit quiet, you okay?"

"I wasn't exactly expecting something this exciting, you know, a few beers, a bit of a party then fuck off back home. This is a whole other thing."

"I know, but it's fun," laughed Man-Dare.

"I'm not so sure about that, I didn't come here to die."

"You came here for some excitement; it was getting boring in Lancashire."

"No, I came here to be with you, and you came for the excitement."

"You beginning to regret coming?" she asked softly.

"No, of course not, but a big red horse shaped fucker and an already dead dude, does give one pause for thought."

"Well," she smiled, "the fuckers only get one more chance, cos our Dog is going to shut their asses down good." She leaned forwards and kissed Billy, long and hard.

"Damn, woman," he mumbled as she broke away. "What the fuck am I going to do with you?"

"Anything you damned well want," she whispered as she stroked the front of his jeans with one hand. She kissed him again, then turned away. Liz came up to the table and asked.

"Anyone wanting more drinks or food?"

"Beer would be good," said Man-Dare looking hard into Liz's eyes. Liz glanced down for a moment, then returned her gaze with a smile.

"Same again?" asked Liz, holding Man-Dare's eyes.

"That'd be great, but no jacks, we've got a long day," said Man-Dare softly, then she smiled as Liz walked slowly away.

"Damn she's gorgeous," she whispered to Billy.

"Not wrong," replied the bearded man.

"And gay," laughed Cherie, "Jane's already convinced her to stay away from crazy bikers, and that was before you turned up."

"So why did she give me those super-hot eyes?" asked Man-Dare.

"Maybe to sound you out," said Sylvia.

"Damn, she's got me hot," whispered Man-Dare.

"That don't take much," laughed Cherie, "you thinking of switching teams?"

"Not exactly," replied Man-Dare slowly, "but I could bat for both sides, the thought of those eyes looking up from between my thighs is giving me a squishy, what colour are those damned eyes?"

"Again, that don't take much," smiled Billy.

"Her eyes are a sort of amethyst colour," said Cherie, "and very pretty."

"Careful dick," muttered Man-Dare, prodding Billy with one finger, "I might just jump your bones right here."

"I'm sure the locals would have something to say about that," he laughed.

"They can wait their damned turn," Man-Dare laughed loudly.

"Turn for what?" asked Liz as she walked up to the table with a tray of drinks.

"Turn for me," smiled Man-Dare, "turn for me, are you up for a go?"

"Leave her alone," said Jackie walking up behind Liz, "she's just starting a new relationship and definitely doesn't need a psycho bitch like you getting involved."

"Who you calling bitch?" laughed Man-Dare.

"Two more lagers please," said Jane to Liz as she steered the young girl towards the bar.

"Is she really psycho?" whispered Liz.

"Certainly, and generally horny as hell," laughed Jane. The two got to the bar just as Jane asked a question, "Should you be serving drinks?"

"Not really, but what the hell, there's no one else available right now," Liz went behind the bar and started to pull two more pints. Jane reached in her pocket for her wallet.

"Forget it," laughed Liz, "it's going on Roaddog's tab, I'm sure he'll be in later to settle up."

"Does he know about this?"

"Not as such," Liz chuckled gently, "you going to be eating?"

"I'm not sure about that, I think the plan is to wait for the guys to get back from their chores."

"Any idea when that will be?"

"Not a clue, but we've just dropped off three fishing poles at the workshop, so they could be a while."

"Roaddog, Bug and Slowball, fishing, somehow that doesn't ring true."

"We got what he asked for then left them in the workshop, maybe he's putting a Wi-Fi extender twenty metres up in the air, we should be able to use the workshop network from the caravan," Jane laughed as she walked away from the bar towards the table where the others were gathered. As Jane passed one of the pints to Jackie some more people entered the bar. Father Francis went to the bar and ordered the drinks for the four clerics. The four approached those already gathered, Jackie got up and went to the bar.

"Avalon," said Francis, "I need your help with something."

"What do you need?" replied Avalon.

"I need the ingredients for this ritual," he passed her a paper.

"Where did you get this?" she asked.

"I talked to the bishop this morning and advised him as to who was coming to our little church next, he went very quiet for a while then told me to check my e-mail, and there was this."

"Well, I have most of what you need, Saint John's Wort, I have, Sage, I have, sadly Hemp I don't, it's illegal you know."

"Do you have connections that can get some?"

"We might," laughed Cherie, "Vince should be able to help us with that."

"That's good," said Avalon then she turned back to Francis, "If I was to perform this ritual, then you'd have me fastened to a pole and set the fire around my feet."

"I know, it seemed more than a little strange to me, but the bishop says it is fine for me to perform."

"Typical double standards, I'd even go so far as to say that this is one of our spells that your lot have stolen, looking at the language, three hundred years ago."

"You can read the old latin?" asked Francis.

"Yes, and I can translate it into a more modern version, or even English if you wish," she laughed.

"Think I'll stick with it as it is, wouldn't want to upset the bishop."

"Why not? The guy's a dick anyway."

"What do you mean?"

"He only pays lip service at best to the church, he's an avaricious bastard who'd steal pennies from orphans, he's the worst sort of sexual predator who has his very own dungeon, pray you never get to see it. You might want to see to his retirement once this crap is all over."

"You think he's that bad?"

"I know, I've had to repair the bodies and minds that he has broken."

"How does he get away with it?"

"How do they ever get away with it, someone helps them hide who they are, and everyone believes the face that they show. It's up to you to put an end to his activities."

"How do I find out about them?"

"You need to find out how he is protected, and then break that protection, that should give you something interesting to do, if we live through this, and if you live through that summoning."

"What do you mean?"

"There is always some sort of price for such a thing, and I don't believe that he has told you what it is going to be."

"What do you mean?"

"There's always a price, blood of virgin, the life of a volunteer, or your own life, these are the usual things."

"You're joking surely?"

"No, there's always a price."

"This is supposed to bring an angel to help us."

"Even your god expects a token before he grants favours."

"The blood of a virgin isn't a token."

"And very difficult to find around here," laughed Man-Dare.

"It was the blood of a virgin that opened this damned thing," said Francis, "does it have to be all the blood of a virgin, or will just a little do?"

"I've no idea," laughed Avalon, "your god."

"Well, if it wants blood, it can have mine," he whispered.

"Just that sort of sacrifice will generally do the job," Avalon said.

"How do you know all this, and I don't?" asked Francis.

"Because she's done it before," said Billy, "and you didn't even know it was possible. What does that tell you?"

"Fucking bishops," muttered Francis.

"That's what he likes," laughed Avalon, "and he doesn't care much what."

"What do you mean by that?"

"Girls, boys, donkeys, I've even heard that he summons his own personal demons when the mood takes him."

"Maybe he should be the damned sacrifice," Francis snarled.

"I'm not going to argue with that, but he's a powerful man, with many protectors."

"If we survive this thing, will you help me bring him down?"

"Yes, but be aware, there are cardinals above him."

"Will you help me bring the whole damned cabal down?"

"Yes, it's time someone from inside the church stood up to these assholes."

"It seems your church is quite a corrupt organisation," said Abraham.

"Yours isn't a great deal better," smiled Avalon.

"What do you mean?"

"The people that seek the power, use it and want to keep on doing so, the power hungry are the same all over."

"And your pagan religions?" asked Mohammed.

"Fintan as an example," smiled Avalon, "but I have no delusions."

"Are you one of the power hungry?" asked Phurba.

"Maybe," laughed Avalon, "but I do prefer to help people, not just myself."

"Does that make you a good person?"

"Not necessarily, I don't shy away from the hard decisions."

"Would you have killed Fintan before his return?"

"If I had known of his plan, he'd never have made it here, he'd have been dead long ago."

"You'd not have tried to convince him to stop his plan?"

"No, sadly I couldn't have trusted his word, far too much for him to gain."

"So, you'd have just stabbed him in the back?"

"No, we'd have been face to face."

"One on one?"

"Definitely not, he was too powerful, I'd have needed the backing of a few sisters, together we'd have stopped him."

"Sisters?" asked Francis.

"Yes, sisters. It's a function of the underlying genes, necromancers are always male, or almost always, there have been three females in the last three thousand years."

"Your history goes back that far?" asked Francis.

"Might be even older, the oral history isn't exactly linear, it can tend to skip about a bit, but three thousand is the most likely limit of our knowledge."

"That's always the problem with oral traditions, it depends very much on which stories are popular at any one time," Francis smiled.

"Yours is no exception."

"I agree, it was many years as an oral tradition before anything was actually written down. There was a time when even having a Christian text would get a person killed."

"That is still true in some places in this world."

"Sadly."

"It appears to be the nature of religion to persecute others," said Phurba.

"Even yours?" asked Avalon.

"Even mine," agreed Phurba, "when a belief comes up against

serious opposition then conflict is often the only way things can be solved."

"The problem," said Avalon, "is that conflict only removes one of the combatants, it doesn't actually resolve anything."

"Some things cannot be resolved," said Mohammed.

"Yet here we are," smiled Avalon, "the five of us, fighting side by side, maybe even dying side by side."

"You think it will come to that?" asked Abraham.

"If Roaddog doesn't come up with something really powerful, we are going to be taking on Heralth and her children, which is certain to be no fun."

"Don't forget the summoning, working together we should be able to bring a powerful force to help us," said Francis.

"Enough to take on one of the highest-ranking demons?" asked Avalon.

"Faith is everything," said Francis softly.

"Our faith is the cornerstone of all our lives," said Mohammed.

"Well, that is going to be tested and soon," smiled Avalon.

"It should be an interesting challenge," said Abraham.

"I hope that we have enough time for Roaddog to complete his plans, whatever they are," said Francis.

"I feel the need for some solitude," said Phurba.

"I agree," said Abraham, "I need to find a synagogue, and spend some time alone."

"That's a great idea," said Francis, "I'll take you all back to your cars and we can each go to find our own renewal."

"I'll just go hug a tree," laughed Avalon.

"What do you mean?" asked Francis.

"Well, that's what you all think about when paganism is mentioned, isn't it?"

"The stereotype is quite firmly ingrained," laughed Francis, before continuing, "so how will you commune with your gods?"

"There may be tree hugging," laughed Avalon, "I find a peaceful glade and commune with the power of the earth, and the sky."

"I actually feel a but coming on," chuckled Francis.

"But," smiled Avalon, "I may just wander through the grounds of the local secondary school, and suck up all that teenage angst, I should be recharged in about ten minutes."

"That quick?"

"You'd be surprised just how much energy is generated by horny teenagers," laughed Avalon.

"Isn't there enough horny round here?" asked Billy, looking straight at Man-Dare.

"Adult horniness has a specific target, normally, so isn't so much broadcast, as aimed. Teens on the other hand have so many targets that they simply keep on missing."

"What effect will your vampiric feeding have on the children?" asked Francis.

"A light touch will give the school in general a more peaceful than normal afternoon. No harm to the children at all."

"Another but?" asked Francis.

"Any horny teachers might just suffer a libido crash, but that's not a bad thing."

"I'll agree with that," laughed Francis, "nothing wrong with curtailing the libidinous thoughts of teachers." He turned to the other clerics, "Come on gentlemen, let's go our separate ways and commune with our gods, to cleanse our souls and prepare for the battle to come." He led them out of the door, Man-Dare followed them with her eyes.

"They just give me the creeps," she whispered.

"Why?" asked Billy.

"They just do, they put so much faith in something that doesn't exist."

"Are you sure about that?" asked Jackie.

"What do you mean?" frowned Man-Dare.

"Well, three weeks ago I'd have said that their faith was complete bollocks, and now we are fighting demons, so if demons are real," she let the sentence die and left the question un-asked.

"I see what you mean," replied Man-Dare slowly, "but they still give me the creeps."

"What about the demons?" asked Jackie.

"They just give me a target," Man-Dare smiled.

"Well, we're going to get some more sometime soon, hopefully not before the guys are ready."

"What are they up to?"

"I'm not entirely sure," laughed Jackie, "but it's going to be big."

"Let's hope it's big enough," said Avalon, standing up. "It's lunch time at the school, I'm going for a little walk." She smiled and looked at Stephen, he got up to go with her.

"What should we do?" asked Jackie, looking at the others.

"Beer or down to the workshop?" asked Man-Dare.

"The guys should be back by now," said Jackie, "but I'm not sure if they want to be disturbed."

"Will Roaddog want help with whatever it is he is doing?" asked Billy, "or is it secret?"

"The more hands there are the quicker the work will be done," said Jackie.

"Workshop it is then," Man-Dare said, finishing her beer and standing up. The rest followed her example.

"Karen," called Jackie, the landlady looked across the bar at her, "we'll be back later, we have some work to do."

"Okay," replied Karen, "see you all later."

Chapter 18: Workshop days

Jane parked her car alongside the workshop, and Billy rolled his bike to a stop by one of the big shutter doors. Jackie was surprised that the doors were both shut as the lights showed that there was someone inside. She turned her key in the lock and the door started to rise. Once it was high enough she ducked inside to find the place empty, Billy rolled his bike inside and stopped the engine, now they could hear sounds from the back of the building. Jane opened the door to the back room and was confronted with the tail end of a huge tanker.

"How the fuck did they get that in there?" she asked.

"Not easy," laughed Roaddog, "but fuck that bastard Bug can drive."

"Hey," said Slowball, "it took him two attempts."

"Fuck you," shouted Bug from somewhere on top of the tanker, "You'd never have managed it."

"That's for sure," replied Slowball.

"Is there something we can help with?" asked Billy.

"Actually there is," said Roaddog as he came towards them along the side of the tanker. "Out back there is a small flatbed, get the tall black gas bottles off and bring them inside, they're heavy and full so be careful not to drop them."

"Full of what?" asked Billy,

"Carbon dioxide and nitrogen at eight hundred pounds a square inch."

"How many do you need?"

"I've no idea, as many as we can hang on the side of this damned tank."

"Don't forget it's still got to get out of that door," said Bug from the darkness above.

"We may have to strap them on top as well," said Roaddog.

"How are we going to fix them on?" asked Billy.

"Ratchet straps, they've only got to get from here to the church," said Roaddog.

"I'm assuming you've thought about the plumbing?" asked Billy.

"Don't worry about that just get the bottles in, we need to lose that flatbed, someone might get curious, and it won't fit in here with the tanker."

"Come on girls let's see if we can be bottled gas movers," laughed Billy.

"Hi," said a small voice from the open doorway. Billy turned to see two school children standing in the opening.

"Hello," said Jackie, "how are you two doing?"

"We're okay, I suppose," replied Joshua, "the only time we are allowed out is for school, it's a real pain."

"I hate it," added Linda. "It's not fair."

"At least you get to be together at school," smiled Jackie.

"That's just not the same," said Joshua.

"Nothing will ever be the same again," said Jackie.

"We know," said Linda, "have you managed to close the thing yet?"

"No, but we are working on a plan, in the next few days it'll be closed for good."

"I can't believe how much trouble we have caused," said Joshua.

"We are sorry, you know," whispered Linda.

"We know," replied Jane, "don't worry, it should be sorted out real soon."

"I wish we could go back and stop it happening," said Joshua softly.

"I know," said Jane, "sadly that is not an option open to us, unless it's something that Avalon can do." Jane looked at Jackie, her eyebrows raised in a questioning manner.

"I don't think so," said Jackie slowly, "if she could do that it would have been the very first option."

"That depends very much on the price to be paid," said Jane.

"I suppose time travel comes at a high price," said Jackie.

"Nutter gave his life to stop one demon," said Jane, "how many lives to go back and stop it all from happening?"

"We'll have to ask Avalon about that," said Jackie.

"Is there anything we can help with?" asked Joshua.

"I don't think so," smiled Jackie, "most of it is heavy engineering right now."

"There is something you can do," said Roaddog from the darkness on top of the tanker.

"What's that?"

"When shit and fan finally do come together, just stay away. We are going to be struggling to keep ourselves alive, and we don't want to have to worry about you, do you understand?"

"I get it, but we do want to help," said Joshua.

"Stay away, it's going to get very loud, and very messy, if you come too close, you'll get hurt, and we don't want that."

"What about the rest of you?" asked Linda.

"We're big enough and ugly enough to look after ourselves," replied Man-Dare, smiling broadly.

"You are in no way ugly," whispered Joshua.

"And you young man are a silver tongued devil, I can see why she fell for your line of chat."

"I think that may have been more of Fintan's work actually," said Avalon as she walked into the building.

"What do you mean?" asked Jackie.

"His damned grubby fingerprints are all over that school."

"He set this whole thing up?" demanded Roaddog loudly.

"Could be," said Avalon slowly, "his psychic influence is obvious all over that place, it fair stinks of necromancer."

"Can we bring him back so I can kill him again?" snarled Roaddog.

"No, his essence was shredded, he can never come back."

"I still want to hurt the bastard some more."

"Tough, save that hate for Heralth."

"Fine," said Roaddog gently, "I've had another crazy thought, but it needs some work."

"Explain," said Avalon.

"Not yet," grinned Roaddog, "still got a few things to get straight in my head, maybe I'll let you know, maybe I'll just surprise you."

"I don't want surprises when there are demons coming," said Avalon.

"Don't worry, it'll be a nice surprise."

"Why does your smile not fill me with confidence?" asked Avalon shaking her head.

"Just your lucky day," laughed Roaddog. "Can you clean the school of his influence?"

"Yes, but not today, it'll fade without his reinforcement, but I really can't afford the energy just now."

"Soon as you can then," he replied gently, Avalon nodded, "if we survive," she whispered.

"I plan on all of us surviving," said Roaddog.

"Is that possible?" asked Jackie.

"Yes, if things go somewhere near to the plan, then we will, maybe not without injury, but without deaths."

"What do we need to do?" asked Jane uncertainly.

"When you're told, run like a bastard."

"That simple?" asked Man-Dare.

"That simple, I don't know how long I'll be able to hold off, but I will give you all as much time as I can."

"I don't like that," said Jackie.

"I'll be running as well, but I'll have other shit to do at the same time."

"We're feeling really useless here," said Joshua.

"Fine," laughed Roaddog, "you two are promoted to barman, get the beers flowing, bars in the corner."

"Great," Joshua smiled, and stood behind the corner bar, getting beers out and popping the tops off the bottles.

"Tea, for me," said Sylvia.

"Coffee," said Avalon.

"On it," said Linda as she turned to the coffee machine and the kettle, both were running by the time Joshua made his first run around those present with four bottles of beer in each hand.

"Thank you, kind sir," said Man-Dare as he passed her a bottle, her smile almost caused him to stumble as he lost control of his knees.

"Leave the boy alone," laughed Billy, "he's way too young for you."

"And you're too old," she said smiling broadly.

"Ignore her Joshua, she's just a crazy horny bitch."

"You're not helping," laughed Linda, as she turned back to the kettle.

"Hey Linda," said Man-Dare, "you not feeling a little jealous?"

"Of you? No."

"I think I'm a little offended by that, how can you not see me as a threat to your relationship?"

"Billy's right, you're way too old for him, I know you're only winding him up, your eyes give you away."

"What do you mean?"

"I ain't stupid."

"I don't understand?" asked Man-Dare.

"Your eyes tell the whole world that you love the old man with the beard."

"You could be right there kid," smiled Man-Dare, "we got work to do." She turned to Billy, "Let's get those bottles in here." Billy nodded and followed her out through the back door, and together they started unchaining the tall black bottles. Slowball and Sylvia came out to help them, in very few minutes all the gas bottles were loose and rolled to the tail-lift. When the lift went down it also carried the hand truck that had been chained up in the back.

"That'll make moving the bottles easier," said Slowball, as he loaded two heavy bottles on to it and together with Billy started to push it into the back of the workshop. They unloaded the two bottles and propped them against the tanker.

"One at a time," said Billy to Sylvia, "two will be too heavy for you." Sylvia smiled and took the hand truck back outside.

"You know that Man-Dare will see that as a challenge," said Slowball.

"Yeah, that's the plan, we strap them to the side of the trailer, and they go fetch them," laughed Billy, he tipped one of the bottles over and Slowball caught the top as it came towards him, between them they lifted the heavy container up and placed it against the uprights on the trailer. Its length was just enough to bridge the gap between the uprights.

"Can you hold it while I get the straps around it?" asked Billy. Slowball nodded, then moved to the middle of the bottle and pressed it into place with his wide chest. Billy grabbed the straps from the box on the floor and threw three turns around the bottle and the upright, before snapping the ratchet up tight. A quick repeat on the other end and the first bottle was locked in place.

"That was heavy," said Slowball breathing hard.

"Now we've got somewhere to pile the rest up," smiled Billy.

"Should make it a little easier," laughed Slowball, "except that we've got to lift them higher."

"You only got one in place?" asked Man-Dare, as she and Sylvia were slowly pushing the hand truck towards the two men, with two bottles on it. Billy laughed, and then with agility that belied his age climbed up onto the trailer. He stepped over the bottle that was already in position.

"Can you pass up another one? I'll hold it in place, and you can strap it down."

"We can give it a try," he turned to Man-Dare and Sylvia. "Can you two lift one end of these?"

"Of course we can," laughed Man-Dare, though Sylvia looked a little dubious.

Slowball rolled the bottle that was propped against the trailer, until it was far enough away from the wheels. He tilted it slowly downwards until he was taking most of the weight. Man-Dare bent down to pick up the bottom of the bottle.

"No," said Slowball, "you two come here and take this end, I'll pick the rest up." The two women did as he asked and took the weight of the top end. He smiled as they strained slightly, then he got both hands around the bottle and picked it up in a single smooth action.

"Right girls," he said, "on three it goes up and drops on top of the one that is already there."

"Easy," grinned Man-Dare. Sylvia raised her eyebrows.

"Ok," Slowball paused, "one, two, three." The three of them pushed the bottle upwards and it took its place above the first one without an issue. Billy held it in place while Slowball fastened two straps around it.

"Next," said Billy.

"Right," said Slowball, "this one is only more difficult because it's got to go a little higher, okay?"

"Easy," said Man-Dare, Sylvia just shook her head. The process was the same, but the extra height made the girls struggle a little, Man-Dare and Sylvia were both breathing hard by the time the bottle fell into place on the top of the stack.

"One more for this location," said Billy.

"New plan for the lift," said Slowball. "Billy throw straps round the uprights and we'll use them to pull the tank up into position." Billy nodded and did as he was asked, once the straps were in place Slowball dropped the next bottle on to the ground and rolled it into position so the straps went underneath it. He ran the straps through the ratchets but didn't close them. He passed one to the girls and took the other himself.

"Right," he said, "we pull on the straps and lift the bottle up into position, once it's there we can place the straps properly, much safer this way."

"Great," said Billy, "just be sure the straps don't slip off the ends of the bottle."

"Okay girls?" asked Slowball. He got nods from both and he smiled. "Take up the strain, just until it starts to lift." He was pulling the strap hand over hand whereas the women were walking slowly backwards away from the truck, the bottle rolled up to the wheel of the truck and then started to slowly rise. "Slowly, nice and easy," said Slowball.

"This is so much easier," said Man-Dare.

"Careful," said Slowball, "slowly, slowly." Gradually the bottle rose until it was almost level with the top one. The straps were now so short that the leverage was lessening quickly.

"Damn," said Man-Dare, "this is getting harder, like the weight has doubled."

"We've lost some of the advantages," said Slowball, "Can you hold it on your own?" Man-Dare looked at Sylvia, and the older woman reduced her pull on the strap, until Man-Dare was holding on her own.

"Easy," said Man-Dare.

"Liar," whispered Sylvia.

"Sylvia," said Slowball, "come get this one, you've only got to hold it for a few seconds." Sylvia slowly took the strain up on the strap Slowball was holding, as soon as she was taking the weight, he stepped up to the tank that was now just above his head height. He placed his large hands against the tank and pushed upwards, he lifted it clear up on to the top of the stack and Billy grabbed it pulling up against the uprights and locking it into place. Slowball swarmed up the side of the trailer, and took the strap that Sylvia had been holding, in moments it had three turns around the tank and the upright, then he cranked it up tight. Billy stepped around the upright and took the strap from Man-Dare. Quickly the fourth tank was fixed to the top of the stack.

"Strap all four together, and this stack is done," said Billy, two more ratchet straps and the stack was locked in place.

"Hey Roaddog," called Slowball, "How many tanks do we need?"

"How many are there on the truck?"

"I don't know."

"I have no idea how many we need to empty this thing, so all of them is what I want."

"Fine, we got four in this stack, and we can get another stack on this side, so if there's another twelve on the truck we can use them all, beyond that it's going to get difficult."

"Sixteen should be enough, or if sixteen ain't enough we're fucked anyway," laughed Roaddog.

"Hey Dog," said Bug, "how you doing with that spray head?"

"Nearly done Bug, you?"

"Getting there, this one is being a bit of a bitch, get yours finished then you start running the gas, I'll do the third."

"Hey Dog," said Billy, "you thinking common rail for the gas?"

"That'd be easiest."

"Gas fails the whole thing dies," said Billy, "three tanks, three gas manifolds, one fails, two still fire."

"That's more work," replied Roaddog.

"Agreed."

"Three manifolds it is, more likely to work to some extent."

"Don't forget Boyle," said Billy.

"Fuck," said Roaddog, "That could be a problem, suggestions?"

"Nothing that comes to mind, we got enough clerics, they can pray for a minor suspension of the laws of physics."

"Bastard, now you're just taking the piss."

"Only a little, we should get enough expansion before it gets too cold."

"It's nitrogen and carbon dioxide, it'll have to get damned cold before it loses pressure."

"I'd be more worried about water in the gas, that could easily freeze in the valves."

"What the hell are you two yammering on about?" shouted Bug.

"Physics," said Roaddog, "once we open those valves the tanks are going to cool, if they get cold enough, they lose pressure, and everything stops moving."

"And what can we do to stop that happening?" asked Bug.

"Realistically," Roaddog paused, "fuck all, it works, or it don't."

"So, stop bitching and get on with it," snapped Bug.

"That's us told," laughed Roaddog, snapping the lid shut on the vent plate he was working on. "I'm done with this one, I'll start on the plumbing. Billy you okay to carry on with the tank loading."

"Yes," said Billy, "shouldn't take us long to get these installed now we know what we are doing. What bore pipe you using for the gas?"

"I'm using twenty five mill nylon."

"Is that capable of eight hundred pounds per square inch?"

"I don't actually know, I was just guessing, I went to twenty five to get maximum gas flow and ease of install."

"Set one up and test it, you got enough valves to control it all properly?"

"Yes, well I think so, three master valves, one for each of the tanks on the tanker, manual, no electrics."

"So, someone has to turn them on by hand?"

"Yes, but there is other manual stuff that needs to be done as well, I'd rather not have electrics involved, danger of premature ignition."

"Well, no one wants to go off prematurely," laughed Billy.

"Agreed," replied Roaddog, "it's all sort of guess work, so let's just hope and pray."

"I'll do what praying I can, and I'm sure the others will as well," said Avalon.

"Oh," said Roaddog, "you're going to be particularly busy, that's for certain."

"What have you planned?"

"Well, you'll be taking part in the clerics summoning, we're going to need their angels."

"Is that all?"

"Maybe."

"I begin to worry about this whole thing," said Avalon.

"You'll have doors and windows to hold, until the angels turn up to hold them, then we'll be able to run away, or so I hope."

"We still have no idea what price we will need to pay to summon the angels," said Avalon.

"I have faith that something will come up," smiled Roaddog.

"Sometimes I don't know if you are taking the piss," grinned Avalon.

"Don't fret," said Roaddog, "I'm sure it'll all turn out okay."

Slowball and Billy fastened the first bottle to the second stack, and Roaddog attached a short section of his nylon pipe to the first bottle in the first stack, then he attached the main valve to that. Checking that the main valve was closed he opened the valve on the cylinder, there was some whistling from one of the joints, so he closed the cylinder valve.

"Try Vaseline on the O-ring in the connector," said Billy.

"Lithium grease do instead?" asked Roaddog.

"Should do, it's a bit heavy though."

"It's what I've got," said Roaddog, as he dismantled the snap connectors and smeared a little grease on the pipes, then snapped them back into place. This time there was no leakage. He smiled, then opened the main valve a cold blast of gas shot from the valve, filling the air with a thick fog.

"Looks like it'll work at full pressure," said Billy.

"Yes, if we can get fifteen bottles on the truck, that'll be five per tank, it'll work or not."

"Get with your plumbing," said Billy.

"I've finished on the front tank," called Bug, "moving on to the middle one now."

Slowball and Billy, with Sylvia and Man-Dare working as a very effective team were installing the gas bottles on the side, with Jackie and Jane bringing them from the back of the workshop one at a time. By the time they had the second stack of four bottles strapped to the side of the tanker Roaddog had finished the plumbing of the gas on the rear tank.

"Is there any way to test it without actually killing ourselves?" asked

Billy.

"I can give it a short squirt at minimum pressure," said Roaddog, "but that is all. Certainly, can't test it in here at full pressure."

"Go for it," laughed Billy. "Bug, get your ass down off there. Everyone else out of the way."

"Everyone as far away from the tanker as possible," said Roaddog. He went through the five gas bottles connected to the last tank, one by one he opened the valves on the bottles, checking for leaks at every stage. Finally, the pipework was pressurised, he glanced round to make sure that everyone was out of the way, then opened the main valve to about a quarter and snapped it shut, a small fountain of petrol spewed from the top of the tank, and dropped back to run down the sides of the tank, filling the air with the stench of fuel.

"That looks good," said Billy.

"It'll do," agreed Roaddog. "Right, no smoking in here until the stink has gone."

"You're the only one that smokes," laughed Jackie.

"Man-Dare does steam occasionally," said Slowball.

"Only when I'm desperate for a jump," laughed Man-Dare.

"Can I get back to work?" asked Bug.

"Go for it," said Roaddog, "be careful of sparks up there until that fuel has evaporated properly." Roaddog carried on with the plumbing, the front tank was ready soon after Bug had finished the work on the middle one. All the gas bottles were attached to the tanker.

"We need to get rid of the gas truck," said Bug.

"Right," said Roaddog, "Bug you drive it, take it to Grainthorpe, there's a disused pub there, it used to be the Black Horse, you can park it there, there's a place in the car park where it should be invisible from the road. Jane follow him and bring him back." Both simply nodded and left. Joshua came into the back room, handing out bottles of beer, Linda carrying cups, coffee for Avalon, and tea for Sylvia, these were accepted with a smile.

"We're going to have to leave," said Joshua, "our parents will be coming to collect us from school very soon."

"Won't school have missed you this afternoon?" asked Sylvia.

"We really can't express how much we don't care," laughed Linda, "we've had more time to talk today than we have since all this shit began. We're going to be having some serious words with the parents, time they backed the fuck off."

"Good luck with that," smiled Sylvia, "try not to burn any bridges."

"We understand," laughed Joshua, "they just need pushing the right way."

"Pushing?"

"Okay, nudging gently, until they see things our way, I'm sure that the Father will help us."

"He better had," said Linda.

"Go easy," said Sylvia, "remember these people love you."

"Yes," grinned Linda, "and that's what gives us the leverage we need."

"Damn, you're growing up quick."

"Causing the end of the world, it'll do that," said Joshua.

"Don't push too hard until we've got the thing shut down," said Billy.

"I know what you are planning with that tanker," smiled Joshua, "I just hope that they are home when that thing cuts loose, it's going to be mega."

"That's what I'm hoping for," said Roaddog.

"We gotta go," said Joshua, taking Linda by the hand and walking out into the street, they crossed the road towards the school just as Jane came on to the forecourt with Bug in her car.

"Damn those two are so much more grown up," observed Jane.

"Let's just hope they aren't right about the end of the world thing though," said Jackie.

"That's why we are working so hard," said Roaddog, "I want to secure the doors and windows of the church, but that can wait until tomorrow. I feel a good meal at the Axe coming on, then a few beers back at the caravan."

"I wonder what has happened to Mick?" asked Jackie.

"I think his Jackie doesn't like his chances of staying alive," replied Roaddog.

"What are your plans for this final, well, I hope final, battle?" asked Avalon.

"Dragonriders and clerics, everyone else off the field."

"You'll never get Jake to agree with that," laughed Jackie.

"That's true," said Avalon, "I want Stephen by my side."

"Only if he volunteers," snapped Roaddog, "this shit cannot be a punishment detail."

"No problem," said Stephen, "I've heard so much about the power of these damned witches, might be good to see it in action for a change."

"They do tend to leave no survivors," suggested Roaddog.

"It'll give me a grand tale to tell the grandchildren," laughed Stephen.

"You think they'll believe you?"

"They'll most likely think I'm a crazy old fool, but I'll know it's the truth."

"The truth is written by the winners," laughed Billy.

"Then we better make sure we win," said Avalon.

"Agreed," said Roaddog, "today has gone far better than I thought it would, let's go get some beer and food, and we can see to fencing the church off in the morning."

"Oh, there's something that no one has mentioned," said Jackie, "you've already got a tab at the Axe."

"No problem," he smiled, "oh, that reminds me, I haven't checked the miners recently."

"I thought that had to be every day?" asked Jackie.

"Well, I've been sort of busy," he laughed and sat down at his computer station. Only a few moments later, he exclaimed, "fuck."

"What's up?" asked Jane.

"Nothing really, maybe the networks faster around here than it was back in Leyland, I've hit a couple of good scores in the last two hours, you're in for a share of course."

"How big a share?" asked Sylvia.

"Split between us all, a couple of grand."

"Wow," said Jackie, "that's just what we need right now."

"I'm not sure I want our good luck spent on cash," said Roaddog.

"I agree," said Avalon, "I'd prefer good luck in the coming battle."

"That's for tomorrow, or hopefully never," said Roaddog, "let's go get some food." They loaded into the two cars and Billy's bike, only seconds later they were pulling up in the small car park at the Axe. They walked in, it was still a little early for the evening rush, or even the after-work visitors.

"Hi Karen," called Roaddog, "how's it going?"

"Fine," said Karen as she came around the centre island of the bar, "better now that we have some real drinkers in." She glanced at one of the guys sitting in the pool room.

"Hey," he said, "payday is next week, I'm broke."

"I know where you're coming from," said Roaddog, "we've all been there or worse. Karen get him a beer on us," The others started shouting out drink orders, Karen had no problem keeping up, she was already fairly certain as to what they would be drinking.

"Our usual table available?" asked Roaddog.

"Yes," replied Karen, "is this everyone?"

"Of that we can't be at all sure," laughed Roaddog. "We'll be okay with the big table for now, it's going to be friendly, but we're used to that."

"Have you any idea if others are going to show?" asked Karen.

"No," he smiled, "the clerics might turn up, Mick and Jackie, could show, Jake and Mary, they are a possible, Leo, he might be at a loose end."

"Is this going to turn into a party?"

"Who can tell? Last blow out for the condemned."

"Is it that bad?" asked Karen quietly.

"It could easily be that bad."

"Well, we've not got many booked in," she went to the end of the bar where the 'book' was kept, she looked at it carefully for a minute. "Change of plan," she said, "you can have the conservatory, I'll seat everyone in here, I'm sure you don't want too many listening to your conversations."

"That is a great idea. Thanks for that. Come on people we're living the high life in the conservatory." He laughed and led the way passed the toilets and the door to the kitchen, into the glass walled extension. It took a short time for the tables to be re-arranged, the small tables were aligned into two long ones, one that had enough for the current group and the other for the overflow.

"I think we need a war council," said Roaddog.

"I agree," said Slowball, Bug just nodded.

"Avalon," said Roaddog, "do we need the clerics?"

"Up to you, they could be a little miffed if they get left out." She smiled. Roaddog took his own phone out, and made a few calls, Francis said he'd collect the others and be there as soon as he could, Jake and Mary would be on the road very soon, Mick and Jackie were at Donna Nook, only a few minutes away, Leo didn't answer his phone, 'I'll talk to him later' thought Roaddog.

"I've just remembered something," said Avalon, "we need some hemp, for the clerics summoning."

"I'll call Vince," said Roaddog, "what sort do you need?"

"Well, this is supposed to be an ancient spell, so simple leaf will do."

"That might make things difficult these days," laughed Roaddog, taking out his phone again. He selected a number from his contacts and held the phone to his ear.

"Hi Vince," he said. His conversation was quite short, there was some laughter, but a deal was made.

"You're in luck," he said to Avalon, "there are still a few old fashioned guys who like weed in its original format."

"How do we get it?"

"Vince is on his way, and quite close to start with, he'll be here in less than half an hour."

"How many is he bringing?" asked Slowball.

"Three bikes, so four people max," replied Roaddog.

"Hi guys," said a new voice, and they all looked up to see Mick and Jackie walking into the conservatory.

"Hi Mick," said Roaddog.

"What's happening?" asked Mick.

"All sorts of shit, it's going to get real messy, and real soon."

"What do you need from me?"

"What I need from you is quite simple, just stay the fuck away, it would be real good if your car was standing by at south farm, there may be injured."

"I'm sure I can manage that," said Mick.

"Thanks for that," said Jackie, "I was worried he was going to get his stupid self killed."

"There may still be some of that, but I'd prefer a fast exit for survivors."

"How will we know that it is time to come and pick them up?" asked Mick.

"You'll know, and leave your car windows open."

"Why?" asked Mick.

"They may just survive if there is somewhere for the pressure wave to go," Roaddog smiled.

"What the fuck have you done?" whispered Mick.

"I'll tell the whole tale, or plan, once everyone is here, we're still waiting for the clerics and Vince."

"Vince?" asked Mick.

"He's only bringing some ingredients for the clerics and Avalon."

"Hey Roaddog," came a new voice.

"Hi Jake, come in, get a beer, take a seat, there are some plans to make, and you're included."

Jake and Mary took seats on the second table, the first one being almost full.

"How's it going Mick?" asked Jake quietly.

"Okay, seems I'm going to be stationed at your farm when the crap goes down, survivor recovery duties."

"Dog's actually expecting survivors?"

"Well, he's planning on there being some, or someone there to ferry out the injured."

"My quad can pull a large trailer if needed," said Jake,

"But it's as slow as shit," laughed Mary.

"True," said Jake, "it's no good for running away."

"Hopefully my car should be enough for the injured," said Mick quietly.

"What's he got planned?"

"Not a clue, but it's going to be big."

"He's not a guy to go lightly."

"In one way I'm hoping there are no injured," said Mick.

"Why?"

"First off these are good people and I don't want them hurt, second answer the question, how did this happen? Damned doctors are going to want to know."

"Don't you think that they'll believe that we were fighting demons?" There was the unmistakable sound of heavy motorcycles pulling into the car park. As Roaddog watched the entrance to the conservatory it seemed like forever until Vince strode into view, followed by the huge figure that was Horse, and behind him came Jingo and Maggie.

"Hi Man," said Roaddog.

"Hey Dog, I got what you asked for, this has turned out to be quite a meeting?"

"Yes, there are things to discuss, you're welcome to stay and enjoy the food and the beer."

"That's very kind of you," said Vince passing a bag of leaves to Roaddog, "That'll be fifty."

"Bit steep brother," smiled Roaddog.

"Supply and demand, I had to confiscate it from the only guy that I know that smokes it, you should have heard him cry."

"Francis," said Roaddog, "I'll split that cost with you fifty fifty." The clerics had just walked in behind Vince.

"Well," smiled the father, "I'd love to, but I don't actually carry that much cash around these days."

"Ain't it always the way with priests," laughed Roaddog, fishing his wallet out of his jeans and handing the cash to Vince.

"What do you need it for?" asked Vince.

"It's part of a summoning, the clerics are going to bring us some angels to help out."

"The angels you've got not enough?"

"Different sort of angel," laughed Roaddog.

"You mean harps and wings and shit?"

"Exactly."

"Good luck with that."

"Can I borrow a couple of your people for a few minutes?"

"Of course," grinned Vince.

"Jingo, Maggie, can you please secure that door, we don't want strangers just wandering in."

"Sure," said Jingo, getting to his feet and taking Maggie to guard the door.

"Thanks," said Roaddog. "My plan is sort of simple, tomorrow me and the guys are going to go to the church and secure all the doors and windows, they're going to be covered with heras fencing, bolted to the stonework. It should be enough to keep all the demons inside, if only for a little while. Once the perimeter is held by the angels, I'm going to open the valves and blow the contents of the tanker up into the air, as soon as there is enough petrol in the air, I'm going to set fire to it. That should be the end of the demons and the church. The only issue is our survival, there is a deep drain about one hundred yards north of the church, it's going to be a hell of a run, with the devil himself on our tails. Slowball, you better set off early. The ditch is deep enough to get us all out of the blast. Questions?"

"Who's going to be there?" asked Vince.

"Us three guys, all our girls and the clerics. Jake and Mick will be at South Farm, coming in for survivor pick ups."

"How much warning will you get?" asked Vince.

"Maybe an hour, the birds start a silly dance thing when the demon is on its way."

"My club will be on notice, if you can give us an hour we will be waiting at south farm and loaded for bear."

"Thanks Vince, I'm hoping there will be no stragglers, but mop up would be appreciated."

The fire door opened and a large dark shape walked into the conservatory, Jingo started to move to intercept.

"It's okay Jingo," said Roaddog loudly.

"What the hell makes you think you can keep me out of this party?" demanded Leo as he approached Roaddog.

"I don't want too many getting hurt," said Roaddog, "anyway how did you know we were here?"

"Karen rang me, she said that she didn't know what my bikers were up to, but it certainly is something big."

"She's not wrong, it's going to be big, and noisy, it looks like Vince and his crew are going to be there for any mop up that is needed, you could join in if you want, but I'd rather you waited with the others as South Farm. Are you okay with that?"

"Yes, sure," said Leo, "you better include me in the warnings."

"I will, Vince, don't let any of your guys get in front of Leo's six, that thing makes a mess."

"What do you mean six?" asked Vince.

"Damned six bore," laughed Roaddog, "don't get in front of it."

"Fuck," whispered Vince, nodding.

"Leo, a flat bed of some variety would be good if there are any injured,"

"I can do that," Leo smiled.

"Jake," Roaddog said, "I'd move your cattle as far away as you can, once this thing goes off, they'll start running, and they won't stop until they get to Denmark."

"You're kidding?"

"No, I said big, and I mean it." He passed the bag of cannabis leaves to Avalon, "That be enough?" he asked.

"More than enough," she replied.

"Don't use it all, there is a plan B."

"What is that?" she asked.

"I'd rather not say, I'd much rather not need it, but if I call for it, please don't ask questions, we really won't have the time."

"That sounds particularly desperate."

"Desperate and hopeful at the same time."

"There is power in the paradox."

"This sort of paradox I don't want to invoke, an old quotation comes to mind, with a single word he can save or damn the whole world."

"Who do you know with that much power?"

"Need to know, and you don't," he whispered.

"It's going to be all or nothing, isn't it?"

"I think so, but there are so many ways it can all turn to shit, we need a massive dose of luck."

"You've kept your mechanisms as simple as possible?"

"Oh yes, push and shove come together, and I'll light the damned thing with a zippo." He pulled such an item from his cut off inside pocket.

"That's not survivable though, is it?" asked Jane, her voice shaking.

"No, my love, it's definitely not, only in extremis."

"How about a flare gun?" asked Leo.

"Range?" demanded Roaddog.

"Hundred yards at best," replied Leo.

"Hundred yards and above ground, you're dead. I've got the drone, and the zippo, they'll have to do."

"You need something like a flare gun?" asked Avalon.

"Yes."

"If I've got some juice left, will a simple fireball do the job? If not it wouldn't be the first time I've used an Afriit."

"How far can you throw a fireball?"

"Line of sight."

"If the drone doesn't work then you get your chance to bring hell to that hellmouth."

"That would be a real honour."

"Suddenly I'm feeling so much better," laughed Roaddog. "Ignition was the part that was worrying me, now I'm thinking we have a real chance of ending this thing." He paused for a moment, then continued. "Any one any questions, if not we can settle down to eating and drinking, well?"

"I've nothing that comes to mind," said Vince, "sounds like it's going to be a real mind snapper."

"Yeah," replied Roaddog, "but we're not going to have long to get the hell out of dodge, there's going to be cops coming in fast. There's going to be a huge mushroom growing over our heads, not something we can hide."

"We'll be coming in on the returning blast wave, have no fear."

"It would be nice if you left a few of those bad guys for us," Leo laughed.

"I would much rather that we got them all in the one hit, but any stragglers you can have, gladly. Anyone else?" No one voiced any questions.

"Jingo," said Roaddog, "you can open the door, not that we are likely to get too many civilians coming in here." Jingo and Maggie left their stations by the doorway and sat down near Vince and Horse. "I'll go and tell Karen that we are ready to order some drinks and then food." He went into the bar and returned in only moments with Liz on his tail, she went straight to Jane.

"What the fuck is going on?" whispered Liz.

"Nothing for you to worry about," Jane smiled.

"It's not me I'm worried about."

"There are plans in place to put an end to a major problem, but we should all live through it."

"That is not helping."

"That's all I can tell you, the less you know the better."

"You will come and tell me when it's all over, won't you?"

"Of course, we'll tell you when it is safe to go back in the water," Jane laughed, and Jackie had a confused expression.

"When will all this happen?"

"Soon, couple of days, maybe three, but no more."

"I'll be worried until you let me know."

"Don't fret, we'll sort things out, I have every confidence in Roaddog."

"I better get some drinks orders," Liz leaned in and kissed Jane on the cheek before starting her way around the room taking orders. Soon she vanished through the doorway into the bar. While the group were chatting Mandy came into the conservatory carrying a heavy tray full of drinks, her skills as a waitress meant that she handed the drinks to the people that had ordered them, luckily some of them were wearing name tags, and the others she knew personally.

Roaddog turned to Leo, "Are you staying to eat?" he asked.

"No, I better get home, I'll be expected."

"I understand, you could always invite her."

"No, I'd rather she didn't know what was happening until it is too late."

"She'd not want you involved in anything risky?"

"You know what women are like," Leo observed.

"In stereo," laughed Roaddog.

"I have no idea how you cope with that arrangement, but maybe we can talk about it when this shit is sorted."

"No worries, other than the fact that once this shit is sorted there's bound to be something else coming along behind it."

"I have some words from a song for you, 'a curse always drags a blessing behind it."

"Let's just hope that is true," laughed Roaddog.

"We'll just have to wait and see," smiled Leo, as he turned and walked slowly out of the fire door, closing it behind himself.

"He's a strange guy," said Jackie.

"He's one of the good ones though," replied Roaddog.

"That he is, I'd have thought he'd have run a mile once he found out what was going to be happening."

"Same with Vince, I never for a moment expected him to call his club in to back us up."

"That was a surprise. The more the merrier," Jackie smiled.

"Just how dangerous is this going to be?" whispered Jane, as she snaked one arm around Jackie's waist.

"Much less now that Avalon can set it off by remote."

"All we got to do is be in the damned ditch when it goes," said Jackie.

"There is no saying how much shrapnel is going to be falling into that ditch. There are some large piles of road waste that should throw the blast upwards, that can only help."

"So long as the blast isn't strong enough to move those piles."

"That's right, look on the bright side," Roaddog smiled.

"There's a bright side?" asked Jane, her grin even bigger than his.

"The fire will start high up in the air above the church, so the blast wave will, mainly be traveling downwards, with enough force to flatten the church completely, then it will turn outwards. The trees will be blown to pieces and scattered along the blast front, I'm hoping the gravestones will simply fall over, but that is by no means certain."

"So, the trees are going to be the shrapnel? Wont the fire burn them up?"

"By the time it gets to the trees there will be no fire, it'll be an explosion."

"I've seen explosions," said Jane, "there's always fire."

"That's Hollywood for you, real explosions are almost invisible, not what they want in the movies."

"So, what will we see?" asked Jackie.

"You'll be at the bottom of that ditch staring at the water, maybe even in the water, with your mouths open and your ears covered, and your eyes shut."

"And what about you?" asked Jane.

"Once the fire starts, I'm going to be falling down that bank towards you, praying I get deep enough before the blast wave arrives, I reckon I should be good for maybe three seconds, it'll take the fire a while to get moving, but once it breaks the sound barrier then all hell will be let loose."

"I thought hell let loose is what we want to prevent?" Jackie smiled.

"This'll be my hell, not theirs."

"If it doesn't work?" asked Jane.

"Only a nuke is more powerful."

"I mean what if it doesn't burn like you expect."

"Basically we're fucked. Hell comes crawling out of that church to eat us all."

"Can it go wrong?" asked Jackie.

"Anything can go wrong, we could all die of monoxide poisoning in the van tonight."

"I mean with your bomb?"

"It's so simple, it shouldn't fail. There's no electrics, no electronics, it's all mechanical, so long as the gas gets into the tanker, then the petrol is coming out, that is all we need, If the fishing rods fail, then rather than a spray, we get a fountain. Petrol in the air is all we need. The roman candle under the drone will set it off, or Avalon can hit it with a fireball, once it starts to burn, everything in the area is history."

"But we'll be in the area," whispered Jane.

"And we've got the sense to get somewhere safe."

"How safe?"

"Safer than being in that church."

"Hey Roaddog," called Karen from the doorway, he looked into her eyes.

"What's up?" he asked, slowly.

"Have you any idea how big your tab is right now?"

"No more than I care," he laughed. "Are you ready to take food orders?"

"You're going to feed all these people as well?"

"Why not? Last hearty meal for the condemned."

"I'll send the girls in to take orders, you do understand that this lot," she waved a hand to encompass the room, "isn't going to come out all at once?"

"No problem, we're going to be here a while yet."

"I might just shut the doors," she smiled.

"Don't do that, and don't piss off any of your regulars to feed us, we're in no rush, we got nothing much to do today, tomorrow is another thing entirely."

"What's happening?" Karen whispered moving in close.

"If I told you, you wouldn't believe me, it's better that you don't know."

"Just look around the room," she paused for a moment, "you've got a high priestess of the pagan sect, leading figures of most of the major religions, you've got an off-duty cop, a local farmer, crazy gay bikers from Grimsby, about the only thing you're missing is someone from the army with his tank. So something big is going down, are we going to be safe?"

"You'll be safe here, and Leo is bringing the heavy artillery, it might be better if you forget about anything that you see."

"And hear?"

"And hear, if it works, you'll know it's happened."

"And if it doesn't?"

"We'll most likely all be dead."

"Can't you pass this over to the authorities?"

"They'd never believe, and people will die before they get their asses in gear. We know what we are dealing with and there will be no more dicking about, we're going to finish it this time."

"Please don't get killed, I'll miss all you crazy people."

"Don't worry Karen," said Jackie, "if things go well, it'll be over in a heartbeat, if it goes badly, it'll be down to hand to hand, but the god squad have promised us angels." Jackie grinned.

"They're good with the promises," muttered Karen.

"They'll be in the hand to hand as well, so they better bring the back up."

"You got any other back up if they fail?"

"I think Dog has a plan, but he's keeping it close to his chest as yet."

"Well I hope that you all survive, you're good people. No matter what some thought when you first showed."

"Now they've got to know us, they like us a little better?" asked Jane.

"Oh yes, some of the people round here are more than a little frightened of change, but you lot seem to have brought a breath of fresh air through the whole village."

"Let's just hope we can keep them all alive," said Roaddog.

"Could that actually be a problem?" whispered Karen.

"If the shit that is coming gets out, it could eat the whole world."

"Then you must stop it," her eyes locked into his and started to fill with tears, for the first time she started to feel afraid.

"I'm going to burn the bastards down," he smiled gently, hoping to allay some of her fears.

"When will this happen?"

"Soon, maybe a day, maybe two, but it's not going to be four."

"Do you need any more help?"

"No," he smiled, "if my plan fails, only nukes can hit them harder, and no one is going to get them launched in time to do any good. What we could do with is an alibi."

"Fuck, you were all here, all the staff will stand up for that one, and most of the locals. If Avalon and the father put the word out, then no one will ever know that you were somewhere else."

"Consider that done."

"Looks like we are going to be having an end of the world party whenever it happens," Karen smiled and went to help in the kitchen. Roaddog went to talk to Vince.

"Hey man," he said, "when the shit has been sorted we need to get here as soon as we can, Karen is having a party for us all, and it started half an hour before the church blew up, understand?"

"No sweat," smiled Vince, "by the time the cops show we'll all have been here an hour drinking to whatever we want."

"That's a sort of plan," Roaddog smiled. Roaddog went around the room, spreading the good news wherever he could, and making sure that everyone was up to speed on the tasks that they had been assigned, finally he returned to the place where Jackie and Jane were sitting side by side, and holding hands.

"You two okay?" he asked.

"Scared," said Jackie.

"But we'll work through that," Jane completed the sentence and smiled.

"That's good, because I really need you to be there. There is something important that you have to do."

"What is it?" asked Jane.

"Not telling," he smiled, "but you'll love it."

"Why the secrecy?" asked Jackie.

"I don't want her to have time to react," he nodded in the direction of Avalon.

"She going to be pissed?" asked Jane.

"Oh yes, but they'll all be too busy to do anything about it."

"I don't trust that crazy smile of yours," muttered Jackie.

"Don't worry, it'll all turn out in the end, if it fails we'll all be dead anyway."

"If we fail," said Jackie softly, "then Heralth gets loose, and people die, lots of people."

"Then we better not fail."

"I wonder how long we've got?" whispered Jane.

"We'll know when those damned birds start to dance," replied

Roaddog.

"I hope we have a couple of days," said Jackie, "it'll take a while to secure the church, and the birds aren't going to like it."

"We'll leave them the south door, we'll gate it but leave it open, that way they can come and go as they please until we close the gate once the dancing starts."

"If we wait until the dance starts then we can trap all the birds on the inside as well," said Jane, with a smile.

"That's definitely part of the plan," said Roaddog.

"What's the rest?" asked Jackie.

"Still not saying, you'll know when the time comes."

"You're planning on setting off an explosion that is only just short of nuclear, and you're unwilling to tell us in advance of plan B?" asked Jackie.

"Plan B must be really scary," whispered Jane.

"Plan B depends much on the success that the clerics have, if they are un-successful, then plan B could be a problem. I'm hoping they do well, if they do, then plan B could change the world."

"For the better?" asked Jackie.

"That very much depends on your point of view, personally, I think it'll be great."

"In the meantime," said Jane, "beer."

"Fine," laughed Roaddog, going into the bar, and getting them some more beer, and asking Karen to send the waitresses in to take orders for drinks.

Once the meals had all been consumed Roaddog went from table to table thanking everyone for the help they had been and assistance they had promised for the upcoming battle. Finally, he moved to the centre of the room and spoke loudly.

"Okay people," he paused until everyone was looking his way, "Thank you again for all your help, we need to get some rest, we've got a busy day tomorrow, turning that church into a prison for demons, if only for a short time. So, we're going to leave you, any drinks you get are your own responsibility, I look forwards to a 'we saved the world party' with you all. Dragonriders, let's move."

"Who?" asked Bug.

"Sorry, I forgot the change, Hellriders on the road." He left the conservatory knowing that the others would be right behind him. He had a brief chat with Karen while paying the considerable tab, the outcome of which was that she had the web address for the church's cameras.

"That way you can get to see some of the action," he whispered, "once the birds start to dance you know the shit is on its way."

"Just how dangerous is this thing?" asked Karen.

"End of the world party may be accurate; you should have seen the look on Francis's face when he found out which demon was next."

"If the father is scared, then we all should be."

"You'll hear it when it goes, and the cameras will go dead."

"How will we know if anyone is hurt?"

"We'll turn up here, then you'll know," Roaddog smiled, and led the others out of the door. When they arrived back at the caravan it took some juggling of vehicles to get the car to the back and the bikes to the front, evening was coming on quickly as the sun approached the tree line in the distance.

Coffee and jacks were distributed with tea for Sylvia, conversation was slow and light, though Bugs phone was in his hand and showing the cameras from the church.

"Don't sweat," said Roaddog, "it's always been at least a day in the past."

"I worry about them turning up before we've got the fences up," replied Bug, "we really need them penned in before the bomb goes off."

"We'll start early tomorrow, we should be able to get the whole place secured in a couple of hours."

"Anchoring fence panels to that old stone is not going to be easy."

"I know, but I've got the gear that will do the job."

"What's that?" asked Bug, eyebrows raised.

"Someone has invented self-tapping screws for concrete."

"You're kidding?"

"No, drill a twelve mill hole with a mason drill, then drive in one of these special bolts and it ain't ever coming out."

"Is that really the plan?"

"Yes, we only need to hold them for a little while, and with angels keeping them penned in, we'll be just fine."

"So long as the main bitch doesn't get loose."

"We'll manage that as well," said Roaddog as his phone pinged. He glanced at it, then turned to Man-Dare, "Your bed is ready when you are. Mick and Jackie are putting you up for the night."

"That's good," replied Billy, "I'm too old to be sleeping under a hedge."

"Bollocks," said Man-Dare, "You're more than young enough for that sort of thing."

"Maybe, but I'd much rather not, shall we go and meet our hosts?"

"Why not, early start in the morning," she smiled and turned to Roaddog, "can you spare a bottle of jacks? Wouldn't want to go empty handed."

"Sure." Replied Roaddog, taking a bottle down from one of the overhead lockers. "We're going to have to get some more before very long, you lot are drinking us out of house and home." Man-Dare took the bottle from him and followed Billy out of the door.

Bug glanced out of the window, he watched Man-Dare and Billy walking through the gloom, hand in hand. "Damn it goes dark quick round here," he observed.

"No city lights," said Roaddog, "we get proper dark here, you should see the stars on a clear night, way more than in Lancashire."

"No light pollution I suppose."

"That's right, but don't go for a walk in the dark without a torch, you'll end up falling in the lake," laughed Roaddog.

"I'll try and remember that," smiled Bug.

"I feel like an evening stroll," said Jackie, taking Jane's hand.

"Come on Dog," said Jane, "you too." Roaddog followed the two out of the door, snagging a bottle on his way, once on the main road Jackie turned right and walked towards the back of the lake.

"What's down here?" asked Jane.

"No idea, we've never even looked this way, we've been too busy getting the workshop ready," she turned to Roaddog, "remember the first night we met?"

"How could I ever forget," he smiled as they turned the corner at the end of the road, and the path became a grassy track, the turn put the last caravan between them and the security lights, the sudden darkness was so intense that Jane gasped.

"Don't worry my love, there's nothing here to harm you," said Jackie. "Hey Dog, if we met the same three guys would you still tell me to run?"

"Fuck no, I'd step back and let you gut the bastards."

"You believe I could?"

"You've learned a lot, but you'd not be fighting alone." They passed the caravans, and the security light came into view again, flashing off the windblown ripples of the lake, only a few of the caravans showed the lights of occupancy, most were dark.

"It's sure a lovely place," said Jane, "so peaceful."

"And it will be again, once we shut that church down for good," said Roaddog.

"Are we planning on staying here?" asked Jane.

"Yes," replied Roaddog, "I want to make money from mining, and run a motorcycle business on the side, maybe live here, or over the shop, but I want both of my favourite girls with me, what about you?"

"What would we do for a living?" asked Jane.

"Other than looking pretty, you need do nothing else, but if you really want to work, I'm sure Karen wouldn't mind a couple of good-looking waitresses with stilettos in their belts."

"Damned robbers will be too busy looking at the tits to notice that someone had taken their eyes," laughed Jackie.

"Local cops might get a bit pissed if your body count gets too high," laughed Roaddog, his voice soft and gentle, the darkness around the lake, was deep but not complete, there was enough light from the half moon and the stars, to pick out the path and shimmering water.

"It's so damned quiet round here," whispered Jane.

"But it's beautiful," replied Jackie, her voice equally quiet. They turned the corner at the back of the lake and the peace was shattered by the noise of many ducks, they had been sleeping on the bank, disturbed by the humans they took flight, their stubby wings clattering and moments later their feet skidding through the water, destroying the calm of the surface. The frenzied quacking settled down in moments, and peace descended again.

"It'd have to be a damned fast fox to get near those noisy buggers," observed Roaddog as they continued their stroll along the bank of the lake, they neared the next turn in the bank and expected another flurry of ducks to take to the air, but a different sound came to them, the gentle slapping as of waves against the hull of a boat, but the lake was mirror still again. Roaddog looked around, attempting to find the source of the noise, they walked quietly along the bank, until they came to an opening in the hedge. Glancing through the hedge he saw the reason for the noise, in a puddle of moonlight were a pair of not inconsiderable buttocks rising slowly to fall and slap against the person below.

"Looks like Gladys and John are having fun," he whispered as he put an arm around each of the girls and walked slowly through the opening in the hedge, soundlessly they approached the rampant pair. Gladys' motions became more erratic as they neared, she shook and groaned as ecstasy took her. She slumped forwards onto John, her breathing ragged.

"That looks like fun," said Roaddog, loud enough to be heard. Gladys looked over her shoulder.

"Damn it Dog, for a big guy you aren't half a sneaky bastard," she said.

"Can't a guy get a quiet shag in peace these days?" asked John.

"Shut up fool," said Gladys, as she rose from her place, John's penis glistening in the moonlight but only for a moment before it was engulfed in Gladys' mouth, her right hand working the shaft rapidly, John lasted only seconds before his own orgasm had him grunting in pleasure.

"Damn," whispered Jane, "that's so hot."

"We ain't anything like as pretty as you young things," replied John, as Gladys lifted off him swallowing noisily.

"It's just good to see people enjoying themselves," said Jane.

"Even at our age?" asked Gladys.

"Especially at your age," laughed Jackie.

"You kids are crazy," laughed John, as Gladys rose slowly to her feet and picked up the dress that was lying on the grass, she dropped it over her head and wriggled whilst pulling it down. In seconds she was dressed to be walking down the main street, only the unfettered hang of her heavy bosom showed the lack of a bra.

"It's not fair," said John, "you gals get it too easy," he was struggling to pull up his jeans whilst looking for his boots.

"You could wear a kilt," said Gladys with a grin.

"Round here, that'd go down a treat."

"It'd be a treat for me," she laughed.

"Damn it Roaddog, what have you done to my wife?"

"Nothing, well, nothing much, you need some viagra?"

"No, ordered it yesterday, delivered today, they say the effects can last up to five hours, but my knees only last ten minutes."

"Your knees were doing just fine five minutes ago," said Gladys, reaching down to help him to his feet.

"Remind me to go into town tomorrow and check that my funeral insurance is up to date."

"You'll have to pay a premium for the extra tall coffin to get that dick in."

"I thought you were having the cock stuffed, you know, just to remember me by."

"I have found a taxidermist but can't find a funeral director to cut the bastard off," Gladys laughed loudly, and took John's hand, "come on let's leave the field to the youngsters and go get some sleep, your five hours isn't up for a while yet."

"See ya," said John, while Gladys just smiled, the pair walked out of the field the way that Roaddog had come in.

"Watching the old people has got me real horny," whispered Jackie.

"I don't know," replied Jane, "it's a bit like catching your grandparents at it."

"They were certainly enjoying themselves," said Roaddog.

"Come on," said Jackie, "let's go home, I fancy a bed far more than the coarse grass of a field."

"But look at the stars," said Jane pointing upwards. The cloud cover was light and high, there were far more stars visible than there ever were in Lancashire, where they were standing, out of range of the security lights, the stars were much brighter than they were used to. As they looked up a white shape floated over the trees, soundlessly it drifted over the field and hung motionless for a moment over the ditch at the other end of the field. Its wings folded and it dropped like a stone, the wings flared briefly as it dropped into the long grass, there was a barely audible squeak, then the barn owl took to the air, its talons clenched around its prey, silently it drifted into the dark.

"Wasn't that beautiful?" whispered Jackie.

"Awesome," replied Roaddog.

"Not for the mouse," smiled Jane.

"Not for the mouse," agreed Jackie.

"That owl probably has youngsters to feed," said Roaddog.

"Surely they'll be feeding themselves by this time of year?" asked Jane.

"Could be second brood," said Jackie, "there's certainly no shortage of food around here."

"There's definitely more than enough rats to keep them fed," laughed Roaddog.

"Come on," said Jane, "let's go home to bed." She took Jackie by the hand and turned towards the lake again. Once through the hedge Jane turned right and followed the path around the lake, the dark under the trees was almost complete, only the occasional glimmer from the security lights cut through the branches, Jane pulled her phone out and turned on its light. Roaddog followed closely behind them, as they turned the final corner towards the caravans a dog came to greet them, it didn't bark, or growl, it just wandered up and had a quick sniff, before returning to the decking of the caravan where it obviously lived. They crossed the grass and walked onto the road that led between the houses and towards the main caravan park, in the full glare of the security lights, the harsh white casting their shadows as deepest black.

They slowly moved from the influence of one light, and onto the next, as they turned to walk up the steps at their own caravan they were suddenly standing in darkness, the light hadn't gone out, they'd just stepped into the shadow of the caravan next door.

"Damn," said Jane looking upwards, "the stars really pop out of the sky when we're standing in the dark."

"Yes," replied Jackie, "we never see stars like this in Lancashire."

"It's beautiful," whispered Roaddog, "let's hope we can still see them in a few days."

"We'll be okay," Jackie said softly, reaching out to take his hand, their conversation was disturbed by the muffled sounds from inside the van.

"That sounds like Cherie on her way to the moon," laughed Jane.

"Looks like they started without us," smiled Jackie, she opened the door and led the other two inside.

Chapter 19: Securing the church.

    The morning ritual changed slightly, Roaddog was up before sunrise and making coffee, he opened the curtains to let in the pre-dawn light and was surprised by what he saw. He smiled and took two coffees into the bedroom to wake up the young women. He shook them gently into consciousness and passed them each a coffee.

    "Up and at 'em," he said gently, "it's nearly sunrise and time for a change."

    "What do you mean?" asked Jackie.

    "On your feet and get some shoes on, let's go meet the neighbours," he chuckled, jamming his feet into his boots and yanking the zips up. Jane raised her eyebrows and grinned at Jackie as she put her trainers on. Jackie shrugged and followed suit.

    "Bring your coffee," said Roaddog, and he collected his own from the kitchen, the others were still sleeping, so he left them to it. He opened the rear door of the caravan and stepped out onto the veranda.

    "Should we be doing this?" whispered Jane.

    "Don't worry, we're not alone," replied Roaddog and he went down the stairs, he crossed the road without even looking and the girls followed him. He walked down the side of Glady's caravan and arrived at the lakeside, there they found Gladys and John sitting in folding chairs dressed exactly the same as they were.

    "Morning," said Roaddog quietly.

    "What brings you out so early?" asked John.

    "Same as you, sunrise."

    "It's really a great time of day," said Gladys, "the light is coming up, the mist is rising from the water, the birds are warming up, soon it's going to get noisy."

    "What have you got planned for the day?" asked Roaddog.

    "He'll fuck off fishing, and I'll relax with a book, or maybe the TV, who can tell?"

    "Sounds like a nice way to chill," observed Jackie.

    "What about you?" asked Gladys.

    "We've got work to do, a bit of building stuff, and some preparation, we'll probably be busy most of the day. Perhaps into the night," suggested Roaddog.

"You know what they say about all work," smiled Gladys.

"It's really not something we can put off, far too many people are depending on us."

"Well, you remember to keep some time for fun."

"We know about fun," said Jane.

"I bet you do," smirked John.

"Behave, you dirty old man," laughed Gladys, "didn't you get enough last night?"

"Most certainly my love, I'm not sure my knees and back will ever be the same."

"So the Viagra works for you?" asked Roaddog.

"Damned right it does," interrupted Gladys, "but he's having none today, this old girl needs a rest. I'm well out of practice."

"Me too," whispered John, reaching out to take her hand, "me too."

"You're not out of practice, are you?" asked Gladys looking directly at Roaddog's tumescent manhood.

"Oh, he gets plenty of practice," laughed Jane, "we may just have to trade him in for something younger if his performance slips." She reached across and stroked him a few times.

"How to give a guy performance anxiety," smiled Roaddog.

"You've got years left in you," said John, "even without the pills." A sudden increase in bird noises prompted them to look across the lake to see the sunlight streaming through the trees as the huge red ball climbed slowly into the sky. All five were bathed in the red light of dawn, they watched as the sun rose, the light turned from red to orange, then the reflections off the lake scattered ripples of colour across them, the mist was burned away in a heartbeat, and the air temperature started to rise rapidly.

"Feels like it's going to be a hot one," said John.

"Fuck it," said Gladys, "I ain't getting dressed."

"We don't have that option," replied Roaddog, "we got work to do."

"Hey Gladys," came a new voice, "these crazy bikers aren't causing any trouble, are they?"

"No Leo," laughed Gladys. "They're definitely great to look at."

"Well I ain't turning this place into a naturist camp site, mother would have a heart attack."

"It looks like it's already clothing optional," laughed John.

"You people are all nuts," said Leo, and he continued his walk along the road, shaking his head slowly.

They all turned to watch the sun come up over the trees, the light turning from red through orange to yellow, warming all the time.

"Hey John," said Gladys softly, looking at the backs of the three younger people, "I remember when you looked that slim and fit,"

"I was never that tall, but I remember when you looked almost exactly as Jackie does now, I'll never forget the first time I saw you naked, you were gorgeous, and still are," replied John.

"You smooth talking bastard," giggled Gladys.

"I'm not at all sure about the affect our presence is having on you," smiled Roaddog.

"We certainly have more fun now," laughed Gladys.

"Is that enough?" asked Roaddog.

"Time for some fun in the twilight of our lives," said John.

"You've got to be good for another twenty years or so," said Jackie.

"Who can tell?" replied John. "Last winter we lost two residents, they just didn't wake up one morning."

"Don't you dare do that to me," said Gladys, slapping him on the arm.

"It would definitely not be my choice," he smiled slowly, "though I wouldn't mind going in my sleep like my dad did, not like the passengers on his bus."

"You old fool," laughed Gladys, "that joke is older than you are."

"The old ones are the old ones."

"You people are definitely crazy," said Jane.

"And what is wrong with that? We've spent most of our lives being sensible, it's time to cut loose before we die," said Gladys.

"What would your family think if they could see you right now?" asked Jackie.

"The son would laugh and maybe join in, the daughters would have an attack of the vapours," John said, "far too tightly wound."

"The son's wife would probably join in as well, she used to be somewhat of a wild child, until she had children of her own," he continued.

"What of the daughter's husbands?" asked Jackie.

"They'd be in the vapour club as well," laughed John.

"I don't think so," said Gladys, "they'd hide their faces but peek through their fingers."

"That is the guy way," said Roaddog.

"Trying not to get caught sneaking a peek," laughed John, "certainly the guy way."

"Well if you're going to spend much more time in the sun, you better get some sun block on the white bits, especially the dangly white bits."

"I'm looking for a volunteer to cream me up," said John, a huge grin on his face.

"Any more talk like that," said Gladys sharply, "and I'll cream you with the damned frying pan."

"Yes dear," said John, his grin lessening in no way.

"Well," said Roaddog, "we got shit to do and the world to save, we'll catch ya tomorrow." He nodded to the old folks and turned to walk away.

"You be careful," said Gladys softly, "I had a dream of the flying monkeys from the Wizard of Oz last night."

"It's not flying monkeys we're watching out for," replied Roaddog.

"Whatever they are douse them good with water."

"It's not going to be water, but they're definitely going to be melted."

Gladys got up from her chair and stepped in front of Roaddog, she hugged him firmly, he held her with only one hand, the other had his coffee in it.

"I've no idea what you crazy people are up to, but come back to us," she whispered, kissing him gently on the cheek.

Roaddog and the girls crossed the road to return to their caravan.

"She's not been wrong yet," whispered Jane.

"Looks like it's today," said Roaddog.

"Let's get things moving then," said Jackie.

"Do we need to tell the others?" asked Roaddog.

"No," said Jackie, "just keep pushing along like we've got all the time in the world. They don't need to be as frightened as I am right now."

"Agreed, let's get today moving as quickly as we can."

Once inside he set about making more coffee, this time for everyone, before the kettle had boiled Cherie rolled out of bed and rushed to the bathroom, morning sickness making itself both felt and heard. When Cherie returned to the main room Jane took her in a fierce hug and held her tightly.

"You're really starting to show," whispered Jane, as their naked bellies rubbed together.

"I don't care about that, but I could do without the puking."

"Are your tits getting bigger?" asked Jane.

"Up from C to D, I dread to think what they are going to look like when they are full of milk."

"You'll still be gorgeous," smiled Jane.

"I don't feel it."

"Who's going to tell you that you're not gorgeous?"

"Who can tell?"

"Only the bastard's tired of breathing," interrupted Jackie.

"Fucking right," said Bug from the darkness of his bed. He rolled to his feet and walked towards them.

"Is that for me?" asked Cherie, pointing at his rampant manhood.

"Maybe later my love, right now it's cos I need a pee, big time." He eased past them and disappeared into the bathroom.

"Why do guys always make so much noise?" asked Jane, "Do they really need to groan like that when they pee?" She released Cherie, and then snagged herself one of the coffees from the countertop.

"It's more of a happy sigh," laughed Cherie, "but they all do it."

"Slowball," called Roaddog, "on your feet, we got a busy day, Sylvia, I've made you a tea."

"How can such a nice guy be such a bastard, it's still dark," replied Sylvia.

"It's not dark, the sun has been up for twenty minutes," laughed Roaddog, as Slowball groaned and rolled out of bed.

"What are we doing today?" asked Slowball.

"I want all the windows and doors covered with fencing," said Roaddog, "the upper story windows should be easy, the doors and the side windows much the same, it's that tall east window that's going to be difficult."

"You've got ladders in the workshop?" asked Bug.

"Yes, they should do, but it's not going to be easy lifting fence and fastening it to the stonework."

"What do we do if the neighbours get nosey?" asked Slowball.

"We're men in hi-vis, driving a white van, we're working for the charity that runs the place, securing the place to keep the vandals out, until proper repairs can be made."

"I've never seen a building crew with more women than men," laughed Sylvia.

"Call it affirmative action," smiled Bug.

"We'll look more like a community service crew," said Slowball.

"Hopefully no one will turn up," said Roaddog.

"It would be better for us if the father was there," said Jackie, "you know, sort of overseer."

"Now that's a great idea," said Roaddog, "anyone been checking the cameras?"

"I have just had a look," replied Bug, "the damned place is full of birds, and I do mean full. I've never seen so many; they know that something is coming."

"The something that is coming is us," snarled Roaddog, "they may think that they are ready, but they're in for a surprise."

"If there's so many birds, we had better leave them a way in and out," said Slowball.

"We'll put a gate on the south door, one that can be locked quickly," said Roaddog.

"I don't expect Heras fencing can hold a demon back for long," Slowball said.

"No," replied Roaddog, "but I'm hoping we'll have some heavy assistance by then."

"You think the clerics are going to come through?"

"If they don't, they'll be defending those fences until the fire hits."

"And so will we?"

"Yeah."

"I'd rather not die."

"Me too, my friend, me too."

"Right," said Slowball, "let's get this shit on the road, people we got a lot to do." He started to pull his clothes on as the others around him did the same. Roaddog paused for a moment, and called Billy.

"Fuck off," was Billy's reply as soon as the connection was made.

"Come on man, we got lots to do, and we need all the hands we can get."

"Do you know what time it is?"

"Of course, we've been up since before the sun, get your asses in gear."

"Dog," came a different voice, "get stuffed."

"Sorry Man-Dare, no rest for the wicked."

"You're definitely a bad man."

"And you're definitely wicked, get that scrawny ass moving."

"Bastard," muttered Man-Dare.

"We'll be on the road soon," said Billy, "where we meeting?"

"We'll be heading to the workshop in a few minutes, then on to the church, join us anywhere along the road."

"We'll see ya soon," replied Billy breaking the connection.

Roaddog punched another number and waited for a reply.

"Hi father," he said. "Can you come to the church as soon as you have a minute? We may need someone sort of official, if visitors turn up while we are securing the place."

"We'll be there," was the short reply, before the connection was terminated by the priest. Roaddog stared for a moment at his phone and then shrugged.

"That was strange," he observed to no one in particular.

"What's up?" asked Jane.

"Francis was a little more sharp than usual, I'd say brusque."

"Someone has got his back up then."

"But who?"

"Maybe he'll be more talkative once we meet him," Jane shrugged.

"I think we can look forwards to a whole bunch of bitching," laughed Roaddog.

"So long as he does his part, I don't give a fuck," said Jane.

"Me too," he paused for a moment, "Jane, you take your car, we'll leave the bikes at the workshop, a repair crew that turn up on motorcycles is certain to cause questions if visitors arrive, even with the good father running interference. I'd like to get the work done today, so we can get some sort of rest before the demon shows up."

"By rest you mean boozing time?" asked Slowball.

"I suppose, but we can't get too wasted, that bastard could turn up any time."

"So far they've been during the day, and in the morning."

"That's why I want that church secured today, questions anyone?"

"What about breakfast?" asked Slowball.

"Once the work is underway, then the girls can make a butty run, any other questions?"

None were forthcoming, so they all loaded up the motorcycles and left the caravan site as quietly as they could. Roaddog waved to John as he walked slowly up the lane, dressed for fishing. Roaddog smiled at Gladys, though she couldn't see him, she was still sitting in her chair watching the rapidly climbing sun, and bathing in its warming glow. He chuckled softly to himself, wondering what Gladys was going to say to the first person to complain about her lack of clothing.

They arrived at the workshop almost completely un-witnessed, it was still far too early for people to be around, as they rolled the bikes backwards into the workshop Roaddog saw a flatbed truck go quietly up the street, he smiled and thought, 'Damn, we're early, the milkman is still out delivering.' Once the bikes were stowed Slowball rolled the van out onto the forecourt and started to load it with the tools, they were going to need for the day ahead. Heavy impact drivers, boxes of plates and bolts, a rucksack full of batteries.

"What are we going to do about batteries that die?" he asked.

"Butty run can wait until we've got some batteries to charge," laughed Roaddog.

"Damn," muttered Bug, "breakfast could become lunch at that rate."

"You frightened you might starve to death?" asked Cherie.

"Not really, starving to death would involve surviving the next few days."

"Don't fret my love," she hugged him firmly. "We'll keep you alive and fed."

While Roaddog and Slowball were putting the long ladders on the top of the van, Slowball asked, "Will this be enough fencing?"

"The van is full, we can't get any more in," replied Roaddog, "where did you get it from?"

"There's one of those developments near the old airfield at North Coates, you know the ones, where the developers fence off three square miles of fields and then sell enough houses to cover their costs before they actually start building anything, it could be six months before they notice the gap in their fence."

"I presume there's plenty of fence left?"

"Loads, and it's so much easier when we don't need the heavy feet."

"Did you collect the connectors?"

"Yeah, they'll be great for fastening the panels to the walls."

"That's the idea," Roaddog paused for a moment. "Right," he called loudly, "let's get this show on the road." He climbed into the driving seat of the van. Jane and Jackie only a moment behind, the others set off towards Jane's car.

"Someone's going to have to shut the door," said Roaddog.

"That's you," laughed Jane. Roaddog got out of the van and walked to the main door, as Jane's car pulled out with Sylvia driving. By the time the heavy door was closed the car was gone, and Roaddog followed in the van, but didn't actually catch up until they arrived at the church.

"Some bastard has locked the gate," said Bug as he pulled up, something they hadn't actually seen before, the gate had always been open. Bug went to the back of the van and opened the rear door. The battery powered angle grinder made short work of the padlock, and Bug opened the gate with a huge grin. Before he could walk back to the van Roaddog shouted.

"Cut the hasp off, we don't want to have to waste time when we come back." Bug nodded and set to work, cutting off the mounting point for the padlock took longer than simply cutting the lock, but at least someone would have to bring out a heavy welding plant to fix it. Bug sat on the back of the van as they rolled slowly down the drive, pulling into the parking area they saw that the area had been mowed, and the graveyard the same.

"At least the ground crew aren't going to be coming back," said Roaddog as they got out of the van, he was parked tail in to the lynch gate, just to make the fence panels easier to carry.

Jackie and Jane were quite surprised just how light the fence panels were, they could easily carry three between them, very quickly they were all propped up beside the south door.

"We'll do the upper floor first," said Roaddog, "watch out for that slate roof, it could be both unstable and slippery. He stationed the long ladder against the wall and climbed up onto the roof. With him standing on the edge of the almost flat roof and Slowball half way up the ladder fence panels were hoisted up in rapid succession. Quickly the tools followed and the three men between them started to fasten the panels over the windows. The masonry drills and anchor bolts working far better than anything that was available when the church was originally built. In less than half an hour the seven panels were in place and the three men climbed down, they moved over to the roof on the other side, while they were installing the next set of fences the girls had lined up the other panels in front of the windows they were going to cover. It was clear that the large east window was going to be a problem, not only was it far too large to bridge with one panel, they didn't have enough panels for it anyway.

"We're going to need more fence," said Jackie as the men came down from the roof.

"I'll go get some more," offered Slowball, "want to help?" he asked of Sylvia, who simply nodded. Slowball turned to Roaddog, "Be about an hour." Roaddog nodded. The two went and got in the van, as they turned out of the driveway a motorcycle and a minibus came in. Billy and Father Francis parked their vehicles alongside Jane's car. Billy and Man-Dare went into the church yard to see how things were going, the clerics from the bus were more than a little slower, their number was increased by one. Roaddog and Billy were discussing the placement of the panels over the windows on the north side, these were slightly smaller than the south side and would be easier, when they noticed the clerics inside the church. There was a new face that Roaddog didn't recognise, though he did recognise the surprise on the man's face when Francis stepped down into the opening in the floor. Roaddog walked into the church flanked by Billy and Bug.

"Please help me," said the new face, "these men have kidnapped me, I am sure they mean me harm."

"Who are you?" asked Roaddog.

"I'm Bishop Forsythe, you must help me."

"You the bishop that put Francis in charge of this place, and left him so woefully un-prepared?"

"No," replied Forsythe after a moment of thought, "he is in charge of this parish and has enough information to deal with its issues."

"Well, that's a lie," laughed Roaddog, "I'd have thought a bishop would be better at lying, though I suppose you get out of practice when you're too powerful to fear the consequences."

"What do you mean?" asked Forsythe.

"You're normally protected by powerful men above and sycophants below, now you've been yanked out of your cosy little world."

"And?" queried Forsythe.

"Now you're in a world of demons and angels, nothing is cosy and nowhere is safe."

"You remember the one that Nutter killed?" asked Francis.

"Not personally but I know the sort of man you mean," said Roaddog.

"This one is one of that man's proteges."

"Another one with a fancy for little boys?"

"Yes."

"That is no business of yours, and you have no proof," snapped Forsythe, he failed to notice Man-Dare and the other girls approaching through the south door.

"Another damned priest that likes to fuck little boys in the ass?" demanded Man-Dare loudly. Forsythe turned to the new presence. She looked him coldly in the eyes and spoke clearly, "Dog, blade me." She snatched the knife out of the air, and with a flick of the wrist the long stiletto locked open. "Seems to be endemic amongst your kind," she whispered.

"Now," said Roaddog, Forsythe turned back to the man, "You thought the clerics were the biggest threat you faced, wrong again." Forsythe twitched as he felt the cold of black steel press against his neck, "as a victim of rape on at least two occasions Man-Dare here has a certain appreciation for the niceties."

"You can't threaten me," stuttered Forsythe.

"Wrong again," smiled Roaddog, "luckily for you the summoning that you gave to Francis," he paused and looked at the Father, who nodded, "it requires some sort of blood sacrifice, you live until we need your blood, do you understand?" Forsythe nodded with the only part of his body that he could move, his eyes.

"I'm sure that Man-Dare will take some pleasure in bleeding you dry," Roaddog smiled, and Forsythe's eyes grew wider than ever. Roaddog turned to Cherie, "you got the heavy cuffs?" he asked.

"Nah, travelled light" replied Cherie, "I got cable ties though."

"I won't ask, but see to his bishopness."

"The correct form," said Father Francis, "is his excellency."

"Fine," smiled Roaddog, as Cherie gathered Forsythe's arms behind him, "his excellency, the blood bag."

"Seems sort of appropriate to me," replied Francis, "he's often treated people as his own personal playthings, I wonder if he finds this as pleasing as terrifying choirboys?"

"You," said Forsythe for his words to be stopped by the large soft rubber ball that Cherie pushed into his open mouth.

"Yes, we can treat you like this, and we will," said Francis, "I'd like to know about your prophecy, but I really don't care that much, you knew this was happening sometime soon, and you set me up to fail, while maintaining that most political of positions, plausible deniability. Be aware, if it costs me my soul, I will bleed you to bring the aid we need."

"Let's just hope your angels are enough," said Roaddog.

"If they're not?"

"There is a plan B, but you're going to hate it."

"What is it?"

"It doesn't matter what it is, if need be, it is happening, and may your god have mercy on us all."

Francis stared open mouthed for a moment then turned to the bishop.

"You see, your excellency," he spat, "these are the people I am dealing with, they don't believe, but still ask for mercy, and they plan something too terrible to speak of, while you hide in your chambers dreaming of little boys' bottoms." He turned to Cherie, "fasten him up at the west door, no one will be able to see him from there, and we'll know where he is when we need him." Cherie grinned as she dragged the bishop into the dark under the tower, his ankles fastened with heavy cable ties, and them fastened to the ones at his wrists.

"You kneel there in the dark and think on your sins, they are all coming home to roost," said Francis once the bishop was restrained in the gloom.

"Well, your problem of your sacrifice is solved," said Roaddog to Francis.

"There was some resistance amongst the brethren, but equally no volunteers."

"There'd be no volunteers amongst my people either, but they'll all go down fighting."

"Let's hope that isn't necessary."

"Agreed, I've still got more windows to seal."

"This fence doesn't look too strong," observed Francis.

"It should be strong enough, it doesn't have to last long."

"If it's not strong enough?"

"Then we'll die defending these windows and doors, those demons cannot be allowed to get loose in the world."

"There is no nobler cause than to die for one's fellow man," said Francis slowly.

"I'd rather not, if that's all right with you."

"We'll be standing beside you."

"Enough chatter, more work," declared Roaddog loudly. Bug helped him to haul a fence panel up in front of a window and held it in place while the holes were drilled in the stonework, as the last of the four bolts was driven into the hard stone the drill started to slow down. A quick check and it was clear that the battery was almost flat.

"Jackie," he called, the young woman turned to him, "take the batteries to the workshop and bring back the charged ones." She smiled and collected the batteries from the power tools.

"Food as well?"

"Yes, for everyone, and beer," laughed Roaddog.

"Might take a little while," replied Jackie.

"Then leave me one battery, I'll get a couple more panels up before it dies completely, Bug can always wind the bolts in by hand."

"Thanks mate," said Bug, he knew the impact drivers weren't actually necessary to drive the bolts in, just a whole lot easier.

"Jane," said Jackie, "with me, we got to feed all these hungry men." Jane nodded and followed Jackie out to her own car, the two left the site moments later, the dust of their departure blew slowly into the church yard, but it didn't disturb the birds shuffling around the place.

It was almost an hour later when the car returned, followed almost immediately by the van. While Roaddog and Slowball were unloading the van Jackie and Jane set about passing out the food and drinks to the people around the church.

"I'm sorry I cannot eat that," said Mohammed as Jackie handed him a large bun with three hot dogs in it.

"The sausages are made from chicken, so yes you can."

"Have you the same for me?" asked Abraham.

"Of course," smiled Jackie.

"And for me?" asked Phurba.

"How does bean burger sound?"

"Absolutely perfect," he laughed as he took the burger from her.

"There's water and beer, in the chiller," said Jane, "with bourbon for the real men."

"No bourbon," said Roaddog, "until that east window is covered, I don't want drunks falling off ladders."

"How are you going to do that?" asked Francis, pointing at the extensive east window.

"I think we'll fasten up a big panel on the grass then prop it up against the wall, someone holds it in place while the others fasten it to the stonework. It's going to be tricky until we've a few bolt points in, but it should be possible."

"The lift is going to be the hard part," said Slowball.

"You and me will manage," Roaddog said, "a couple of large clerics can hold the top in place with the long ladder while Bug gets the bolts into the wall."

"Where you going to find them?" asked Francis, with a huge smile.

"I don't know," said Roaddog staring at Mohammed and Abraham who were sitting on a grave eating and drinking water. "They're getting along better than I would have expected," he whispered, conspiratorially.

"They aren't the most extreme members of their faiths, and they recognise that they actually have much in common, they're good people."

"I hope we can keep them alive."

"If necessary, they will give their lives to hold the demons inside while you run off and burn the place to the ground."

"Ouch," said Roaddog softly, "I'm hoping that the angels will be able to hold the demons, and we'll all be able to run away."

"If they can't?"

"Then the demons will have to do their work for them."

"How are you going to accomplish that?"

"You really don't need to know, and more so, don't want to."

"Is the plan likely to succeed?"

"We're fighting demons we didn't believe in two weeks ago, aided by angels we still don't believe in, assisted by various religions that we have always considered to be power hungry organisations for controlling the masses, and a pagan high priestess that we always thought of as complete nutters."

"Thanks for that vote of confidence," said Avalon from behind Francis.

"Have you any idea what the best outcome for me would be?"

"Other than living through this, I've no idea," replied Avalon.

"I'd like to see that shimmering scene from the movies, when a guy wakes up and finds out that it has all been an hallucination caused by a really bad batch of acid."

"But where would you be waking up?" asked Avalon.

"Is there anywhere that could be worse than what we have coming here?"

"It's your nightmare," said Avalon with a smile.

"I'm locked in a coma in a hospital in Lancashire, sole survivor of the attack on the Dragonriders."

"That would be worse, because that dream never ends," said Avalon.

"I believe this to be the real world, I have no other way of dealing with it, I'm going to try to keep as many of my friends alive as I can," he said slowly, as Jane and Jackie came over to present him with a bacon and sausage barm cake, and a cold beer.

"Damn," he muttered, "I miss those dustbin lids that Andy used to make."

"They were bad for your figure," said Jane, as she kissed him gently.

"And we've got to watch that," smiled Jackie moving in for a kiss of her own.

"It's worth watching," said Jane before she kissed Jackie.

"Isn't that every man's dream?" asked Francis as the two girls walked away.

"That nightmare was already in place before the attack on the Dragonriders."

"Nightmare?"

"Definitely, a nightmare of insecurity, and anxiety."

"But you love them both?"

"Yes, there is no life without them."

"And they you?"

"How to ramp up the anxiety, thanks Father," the sharpness in his voice brought the girls back, hand in hand they approached Francis.

"If you make our man feel guilty enough to leave us," said Jackie, a stiletto appeared in her hand.

"We will end you," finished Jane, an identical blade in her free hand.

"We are the three who are one," declared Jackie, "there is nothing that can stop us."

"Together we can end your world," said Jane.

"Together we stay," said Roaddog.

"Suddenly," said Francis, "I feel both hopeful, and terrified."

Two mother of pearl handled stilettos folded and returned to the belts of the young women. They walked out of the church and perched on a tomb near Mohammed and Abraham, listening to their quiet conversation. Much of it was meaningless to the women, but the men had become good friends in the straights they found themselves. They joined each other in round condemnation of the secrecy of the catholic church.

"Your own churches are not exactly forthcoming with information about this, and they both knew, they had you ready to come here, didn't they?" asked Jackie.

"Yes," replied Abraham softly, while Mohammed just nodded. "We were aware of the potential of this place and have been trained in some of the mysteries that the leaders thought might be required."

"For mysteries, read magics," laughed Jane.

"That could be the case," smiled Mohammed, "but we could never admit it."

"Do you have the strength to hold those windows and doors while the demons are trying to get out?" asked Jane.

"We can only try, this sort of thing has never been tested by us, there is no way to test it."

"But we do have faith," said Mohammed.

"I have faith in the fire," replied Jackie, "the fire that we will bring."

"Between us, that must be enough," said Abraham.

"If not," said Jackie, "we will be here holding them back as the fire comes."

"Remember when you left Preston," whispered Jane.

"I do, you stayed," replied Jackie taking both her hands in her own.

"I was frightened, so very frightened, and now," she paused for a long time, Jackie wanted to ask, but didn't.

"Now," said Jane much louder, "now we could be facing our deaths, and I'm frightened, but excited at the same time, how can this be?"

"The fear is real, as is the risk, back in Lancashire the fear was more internal, more personal, more immediate," smiled Jackie.

"Now I've got my friends around me, two good knives in my belt, a whole bunch of priests fighting on our side, and a bishop tied up in a corner. Can you think of anything more insane?"

"It's only mad if you look at it from the outside, here in the midst of it all, we really have no choice, we have to fight or die, or maybe, fight and die. We can't let those demons out of here, and I wouldn't want to live in a world where we did."

"If we fail, do your churches have a plan B?" asked Jane, looking at both the men sitting before them.

"I have no idea," replied Abraham, "but I also feel that they don't, as you say looking at this from the outside, it's certainly crazy. My feeling is that the elders of the church believe this to be entirely a hoax, nothing more than a complex joke."

"Much as I feel," said Mohammed gently.

"You think the bishop on his knees isn't afraid of what is coming?" asked Jackie.

"Oh, he's afraid, he thinks he's fallen in with madmen."

"Do you think we are mad?" asked Jane.

"No," said Abraham, "we have seen the things that have happened here, and much as we would like to deny them, we cannot. If we survive, then our reports are going to cause us a great deal of difficulty, especially if we tell the truth of what we have seen and done."

"It's certainly going to ruffle a few feathers," laughed Mohammed.

"Should we tell them the truth? Could they take it?"

"I don't think so, they've always considered this, shall we call it mission, a bit of a joke."

"But they had you trained and ready," said Jane.

"Jealousy," said Abraham.

"Why jealousy?" asked Jackie.

"What if the tales are true? What if the catholic church saves the world? How would that reflect on us? They just couldn't take the risk, it costs almost nothing to prepare a few renegades to save as much face as possible," said Abraham.

"I think they would be quite happy if we failed," said Mohammed, "the blame scattered across enough religions, they'll be pointing fingers for ever, though I'm not at all happy about the term renegade." Mohammed looked quite sternly at Abraham.

"You have to agree that we aren't their favourite people, now are we?"

"True, far too modern, far too permissive, far too relaxed."

"But only about the things that don't really matter anymore."

"Not the way they see it."

"They're just too desperate to maintain their power over the people, it's going to bring them down eventually."

"Again, not the way they see it. The power is absolute, and they're not for letting go."

"So where are they with their absolute power? Hiding in their cellars, refusing to believe what we have seen."

"Could it be that this is when it all changes?" smiled Mohammed.

"It is the twenty-first century," interrupted Roaddog from behind them.

"It is indeed," laughed Abraham, "wouldn't it really piss them all off if a gay writer from Wales was the one that was right?"

"They'd have apoplexy," grinned Mohammed.

"No they wouldn't," said Roaddog, "they'll find some obscure text from eight hundred years ago and show that they had it right all along. I'd even bet that they have two or three ready even now, just waiting for the outcome."

"I think that is more than a little cynical," said Mohammed.

"Power," said Roaddog, "they've hung on to it for a long time now, and that wasn't by accident."

"So even if we survive this coming apocalypse," said Abraham, "they'll see to it that our reports are buried?"

"And maybe us," muttered Mohammed.

"That is quite likely," said Francis.

"You carry the same risk," said Mohammed.

"I do."

"So why do we fight?"

"Because it is the right thing to do."

"It is," agreed Abraham.

"If we survive," smiled Mohammed, "we are going to stuff our victory down their throats until they choke on it."

"Right," said Francis.

"Good," said Abraham, "let's get back to work, we have to be ready."

"Or as ready as we can be," said Mohammed, "let's get the fences that are up as braced as we can, come on, brothers. To work." Mohammed climbed slowly to his feet, and turned to the girls, "thank you for the food and water ladies, it was most welcome."

"We'll need a ladder," said Abraham to Roaddog.

"Take the long one," was the reply as Roaddog, Bug and Slowball started to assemble the fences for the lower story windows and the north door. Jackie smiled as she watched the clerics climb up onto the sloping roof, they needed to be close enough to the window coverings to bless them in the names of their various gods, hoping that this would slow the demons down a little at least. Leaving them to their work she and Jane went to help the others lifting the heavier panels up and holding them in place while the guys wielded the power tools.

"What is it about men and their tools?" asked Jane, as she stood holding one side of a panel while Jackie held the other.

"Perhaps they just feel better with a tool in their hands," replied Jackie with a huge grin.

"Is it something to do with all that throbbing power?"

"Maybe it's the boring vibration as they drive their bits into the freshly made holes."

"The way they are shaking, it looks like they could do with a little lubrication," smiled Jane.

"Could be that their tools aren't powerful enough," laughed Jackie.

"They need something bigger."

"Something with more ooumph."

"Come on girls," said Roaddog from the top of the ladder, "these stones are old and hard."

"And you're just old and soft," laughed Man-Dare from her place at the foot of the ladder. Slowball laughed loudly from his place at the foot of the other ladder where Bug was drilling another hole.

"And you could barely lift the thing, let alone drill a straight hole with it," grunted Roaddog.

"Why would I? That's what we keep the menfolk for, and I think there's something else as well, but I forget what."

"You've a damned short memory," laughed Billy, who was holding the ladder that the clerics were climbing down.

Francis looked at Avalon who was sitting on a tomb. "Aren't you going to help with the windows?"

"No," she replied quickly, "I'll take the doors, that's where the most pressure is going to be generated, you focus on the windows."

"But the doors are on opposite sides."

"The north door will be firmly blocked with fencing, and I'm going to lay a heavy chain of yew on it. The south door is going to be an actual door, I'm going to have to close and lock it at the relevant time."

"I don't understand, chain of you?"

"I'm going to use the power of the yew tree to hold that door, have you never wondered why there is always yew in church yards?"

"I had no idea it had any sort of power; are you sure you can do all that?"

"I'm sure you can't."

"That's not really an answer, is it?"

"No, but it's the best you're going to get."

"We'll concentrate on the upper windows for now, I don't suppose Heralth is likely to try that way?"

"No, she does fly, but not that well. Her children will, they do fly."

"Just how dangerous are these children?"

"I'm not entirely sure but look on them as cherubs with claws and teeth."

"Even those are going to be hard work."

"Don't forget you're going to be summoning angels to help out."

"Yes, I know."

"Do I detect a lack of confidence?"

"Maybe."

"In the summoning, or the power of the angels themselves?"

"Yes."

"Confidence is everything, you know that you have to believe in the summoning and in the angels."

"It is very difficult to believe in the magic or the angels, one is always the work of Satan, and the other almost never witnessed."

"Believe or you fail, and failing you die, is that clear enough for you?"

"You believe?"

"I told you, that spell is one of ours."

"Please don't call it a spell, that makes things even more difficult," grumbled Francis.

"Give it any name you feel comfortable with, but belief is all that counts."

"We will try."

"Do that, I need to gather some power from the trees," Avalon turned abruptly away and went up to the largest tree in the churchyard, her arms could barely reach around half of its wide bole, but she held on to it tightly as it started to tremble in her grip. The grey birds that had been resting in its branches took flight in a clattering of wings and a screeching of avian voices. One or two tried to enter the church only to find that the upper windows were all blocked. As were some of the lower ones. They flew around very briefly before settling on gravestones and other trees. After a few minutes Avalon moved on to another tree.

"Damn that tree looks sad," said Man-Dare, "have you killed it?"

"No, just drained it. It'll recover in a day or two," replied the pagan as another tree gave up its energy, and more birds flew around the graveyard. Man-Dare watched them and noticed that they didn't return to the tree Avalon had already visited.

"Why don't the birds go back to the first tree?" she asked.

"It's hungry, it'll feed on them, rather than the other way around."

"I thought trees fed on the soil amongst their roots."

"That's true to some extent," smiled Avalon, "but haven't you noticed that when you lie under a tree you start to feel relaxed and sleepy?"

"I thought that was just peace and quiet."

"It's that and a bit more, trees don't take much, but they don't need much, however they can carry quite a reservoir of power."

"What do they need that power for?"

"They use it mainly to resist the wind, they strengthen their weak points, and firm up the ground around their roots. After a good storm they're pretty much depleted."

"So, you are weakening these trees, isn't that going to harm them?"

"Really I should be taking everything they have, the storm that is coming is not survivable."

"So why aren't you taking it all?"

"Because, though the trees won't survive, their offspring may, every splinter that is scattered by the fire has a chance of growing again, I leave them something so their chances are better."

"How much better are their chances?"

"Not much, the only parts that might survive are the fragments that are blown away on the blast front, anything that doesn't simply blow away is going to burn."

"You think that Roaddog's fire is going to be that hot?"

"It has to be, if it's not then none of us will survive, the demons will get out, and the world will change."

"So why aren't the churches doing more?"

"That's entirely down to faith."

"I don't understand," Man-Dare replied so quietly that Avalon almost didn't hear.

"Some have faith that god will defend them, some have faith that these things are simply the hallucinations of crazy people, and some have faith that the measures they have taken are enough."

"Which group do you put yourself in?"

"None, I don't even have faith in my own power to hold them back."

"But you're still going to fight?"

"Of course, what else is there to do," smiled Avalon.

"Aren't you frightened?"

"Certainly, but like these other clerics, I have to be here, I have to help, I may even have to die."

"You are the last line of defence?"

"Actually no, that's not the way I see it, the final line isn't religious at all, it's a group of crazy bikers, and they're planning to blow up the world," she laughed.

"You think he'll blow up the world?"

"Not really, but from the look of things, he's going to have a damned good try."

"Let's hope we can get out from under before the world ends," laughed Man-Dare.

"That's what Roaddog is planning on, but I think he has something else in mind as well."

"There may be something, but only in the most desperate circumstances."

"What do you know?" demanded Avalon.

"Nothing precise, all that I know is, when he makes the call, don't ask questions, it's already too late for that."

"Now I'm feeling a little scared again."

"He's planning on keeping as many alive as he can, so just go with the flow."

"Easy for you to say, you've trusted him for a long time."

"Not really, but I have trusted him with my life, and he didn't let me down, I don't believe he will ever."

"Faith again."

"If you want to call it that, it's as good a word as any."

"It could be that the fate of the world rests in his hands," Avalon muttered.

"If that is true, then he'll not back down."

"He aligns himself with the angels of hell, perhaps he is sent to open the portal,"

"If you turn against him now, be aware the sisters will end you." Man-Dare opened the stiletto with a flick of the wrist, Avalon suddenly aware that the knife had not been returned to Roaddog, looking over Man-Dare's shoulder she saw the other women approaching, Jane and Jackie each with knives in both hands, no doubt attracted by the tension in Man-Dares stance.

Avalon's shoulder dropped as she increased her grip on her staff.

"Can you kill us all, before you die?" whispered Man-Dare. Jackie stepped up to her right and Jane to her left, each giving themselves enough room to manoeuvre.

"What's happening?" asked Jane quietly.

"Avalon has a life or death decision to make," replied Man-Dare, not taking her eyes from the priestesses.

"We really don't have time for fannying around," whispered Jackie.

"If you can kill us all," said Man-Dare coldly, "imagine the rage of Roaddog, it will be without limit, without restraint, he may even tear that portal open and invite all the demons to join the party."

"I have actually considered that, but he'd have done it by now, his hatred for Fintan was plain for all to see, but once the necromancer was dead, then he could have opened the portal, there was little to stop him."

"Wrong," snapped Jackie, before going on much more quietly, "there was everything to stop him, his dead wife and child, his second family all murdered, yet still there is love in this world, he'll never let the demons loose, at least not until he is sure that all love has fled."

"By love you mean you two?"

"Maybe, but it could be Man-Dare's love for life, or Bug's for Cherie, it could be all that keeps him sane," Jackie replied.

"You think him sane?" asked Avalon incredulously.

"Perhaps not by the definitions that the rest of the world uses, but by his own he is certainly sane, are you going to stand against him?" the question the merest of whispers.

Avalon stared into each of their eyes for a long moment, before speaking slowly.

"We have invested far too much into the path he is leading us down, I cannot see another road that has the slightest chance of success at this late day, I have to stand with him and hope that he doesn't betray the whole world."

"The only sensible choice," said Jackie as she turned away.

"The only choice that keeps you alive," sneered Man-Dare, as she moved to follow Jackie and Jane. Jackie stopped and glanced back at Avalon.

"Where the fuck have all the birds gone?"

Chapter 20: Happy returns.

Avalon ran to the south door as the last of the grey birds walked slowly through it, the whole floor of the church was a seething mass of grey feathers. Birds walking on each other's backs and flapping their soft wings as they were walked over. She turned to Jackie.

"Get that bishop out of there, before those bastards eat him."

"Won't they eat us?"

"Stamp on a few, there are far too many here anyway." Avalon ran to the east window, where the men were lifting the huge panel that was to seal the window.

"You better hurry up, the birds have started dancing," she almost shouted.

Roaddog looked in through the window and saw Man-Dare kicking a path through the mass of birds, with Jackie and Jane dragging the restrained bishop behind her. As he watched the pattern started to form within the mass, there were five circles this time, the outer one turning counter clockwise, the next clockwise, until the inner one was turning counter clockwise, the birds strutting around the circles and suddenly changing direction to move inside or out, each circle appeared to be between three and six birds wide, the clear patch of ground was about six feet in diameter, centred on the shattered opening in the tiles of the floor.

"How long were the birds dancing last time?" he shouted, looking around for an answer.

"Between us noticing and Fintan's arrival was about an hour I think," said Bug.

"But we have no idea how long the birds had been dancing before we noticed," said Roaddog. "Let's hope we've got more than an hour, Bug take the van back to the workshop and bring the truck, don't forget the weapons box. Jane take your car, and come back with the truck, Bug, park it on the south side and hope the wind doesn't change. Francis, move your van out onto the road, don't forget that Bug has to get a large truck in through that narrow gate, so don't block his access. Billy get your bike out of here as well. Right people," he shouted, "move like we have a plan, and we know what we are doing." Jane, Bug and Billy ran to their respective vehicles, with Father Francis lagging behind, not in quite the same rush.

"Do we know what we are doing?" asked Avalon.

"Sort of, get that north door blocked."

Avalon nodded and turned towards the south door, as she passed the huge yew tree, she yanked a few of the smaller branches from it. She ran around the church and up to the north door, into the fencing she wove the twigs of yew. Stepping back from the door she sat upon the ground, cross legged, with her staff planted in the grass and held upright, it towered above her head. She started to chant softly, a slow and steady sound, but not of words, it was something older than words. As her plainsong grew so did the yew, the twigs wove themselves into the fencing, over and over growing as they did, tendrils reached down to the gravel path and drove downwards into the sweet soil beneath. Green power flowed and the yew grew, the doorway became a mass of solid green, laced around the steel, with roots buried in the ground and in the stonework. Avalon smiled as she ended the song, more than happy with the barrier she had erected.

"Fuck," whispered Jackie finally breaking her silence, "Will that hold?"

"Satan himself cannot break the power of the yew, it is far older than him."

"Couldn't you wrap the whole place in it?"

"With a hundred sisters and a month or two, probably, but there are only five sisters that can control this power, and only one other in this country, though her people consider their island nation to be separate from the United Kingdom."

"Who are they?"

"The people of the Orkneys, they've always been more than a little insular."

"Why is that?"

"They're celts, much as we are, but the isolation of Orkney has bred into them a massive independence, they're powerful, but they don't travel far from home."

"Will you be strong enough to hold the south door now?"

"I've got that huge yew tree standing by, it's roots run deep, its power is accessible to those of us with the knowledge."

"You should have some time to recharge," said Jackie, Avalon just nodded and went round the east side of the church, the final panels were up and being secured, Roaddog was giving no thought to the longevity of the power tools, the bolts were being driven home as fast as possible. While one of the heavy bolts was being driven into the old stone he called out above the racket of the impact driver. "Jackie." He waited until she appeared at his side. He dropped his phone into her hands and said, "Text the guys, Vince, Jake, and Karen, tell them the shit is coming soon." She took the phone and sent the relevant text messages, only a few minutes later the last bolt chattered into place, Roaddog came down off the ladder, giving the fence over the east window a last yank, to make sure it wasn't just going to fall off. He walked round to the south door and checked over the fence that was installed there, the door he had created looked secure and strong, once the bar was in place it would hold the whole door closed. He smiled to himself and tossed the impact driver out into the graveyard; its purpose served it was disposable.

"You going to be okay on this gate?" he asked of Avalon as she sat upon the ground one hand on the thick trunk of the yew tree, the other on her staff.

"I'll be fine, two chances, I'll hold, or I'll die," her quiet reply.

"I'd much rather no one else died here," said Roaddog slowly, "there are enough corpses piled up in this place."

"I'll agree with that," said Francis from behind him, then he looked at the bound bishop, "well maybe one more." The high-ranking cleric just glared, there was no sound he could make past the ball gag.

"Isn't there something about sins and first stones in the book?" asked Avalon.

"There is, but he's got enough sin already, he really needs to meet God, and discover his punishment."

"You think he's in for punishment?" Avalon removed the gag. "Are you in for a punishment?" she asked.

"I'm a bishop, why should I be punished?" replied Forsythe, his voice hoarse after so long struggling against the ball gag.

"Of course, he's used the church for his own pleasures and aggrandisement, he's got to be in for something special, something really special," laughed Francis.

"He's already in for something special, you're going to bleed him to summon the angels," smiled Avalon. Forsythe stared at the ground.

"Yes, but that won't cause him too much pain, it should be quick."

"If you really want to cause him some pain before he goes, then let Man-Dare bleed him. She has a lot of experience of pain, both giving and receiving, she'll make him hurt before he dies."

"I'd rather not do that, my part in this is dubious enough as it is, to cause extra pain, would possibly put me in a bad place as far as God is concerned."

"How can you be in a bad place?" asked Roaddog with a grin, "you've been following the instructions of your leader, you know, the one tied up and gagged, or not gagged."

"There is that, but I'm sure there are rules about the restraint and gagging of bishops," laughed Francis.

"Even when they deserve it?"

"Yes, the Pope is regarded as Christ's vicar, as he decrees on earth, so it is true in heaven."

"So, he decides the rules God works to?"

"Yes, pretty much."

"But Popes are all old, seriously old guys, with little contact with the real world."

"Thanks for that, you just turned my entire life to the whims of geriatric old men, mother thanks you."

"I haven't heard that saying in more years than I care to acknowledge," laughed Roaddog. A heavy rumble announced the arrival of Bug and his tanker. Roaddog stepped backwards until he could see along the path from the road, behind the truck came a Ford Fiesta, a heavy landrover, and a small four by four all-terrain vehicle.

"Who the fuck is that?" he asked of no one in particular.

"The landrover is Leo and Edward, the quad is Jake, but no Mary, the ford I've no idea," replied Jackie standing beside him.

The truck turned off the path and went around the parking area, struggling a little in the soft ground of the field full of tall corn, but the truck did make it to the south side of the church yard before it became completely bogged down. Jane jumped down carrying a heavy box, Bug climbed up on top of the tanker and started to raise the fishing poles into position. Jane wriggled through the trees on the south side and bought the box to Roaddog, he opened it and passed Vera to Jackie, he gave the mac-10 to Jane, and took the longsword for himself, the rush of energy as his hand touched the hilt made him gasp a little.

Walking toward him came Leo and Edward, the first with the six gauge on his shoulder and a bandolier across his chest, Edward the same but a pump action twelve for him. Behind then came Jake, another pump and two bandoliers.

"I thought I told you lot to wait outside and come in when it was all over," Roaddog snapped, not taking his eyes off the Fiesta.

"Tough shit," replied Leo. "We're not missing out on this."

"Well get your damned vehicles out on the road, they'll be blown to shit where they are."

"Stuff that," said Jake as Edward went to move his landrover, "I can walk home from here and I've got three spares in the shed." Roaddog heard both machine guns cock, and he looked up to see the passengers from the Ford.

"For fucks sake," he shouted, hefting the sword, "Detective inspector fucking Hopkins, how the fuck can you be so stupid as to bring that lying bastard here?"

"I have to know what happened, I just cannot live with not knowing," replied Hopkins his arms wide.

Jackie squeezed Vera's trigger and three shots rang out, three smoking holes appeared in the grass in front of the new arrivals.

"Don't kill them," said Roaddog, "looks like the bishop just got a reprieve." Jackie and Jane looked at him with huge smiles. "Yes, my darlings you can bleed the lying bastard when the time is right."

"Well, that's one mystery solved, full auto shotgun, very effective," said Hopkins, his hands raised.

"If he's DI then he can't be allowed to live," said Stephen, raising his own gun, "no witnesses."

"Hang on," snapped Roaddog, "let's throw him in the church so that Heralth and her children can eat the bastard?"

"That sounds like a plan," smiled Stephen.

"What the fuck is going on here?" asked Hopkins, more than a little nervously.

"How can I explain this in terms that you will understand, given that we don't have a lot of time. We have a hell mouth that is spitting demons out, demons that eat people and want to take over the world. I'm going to blow the whole damned place all the way back to hell. Is that clear enough for you?"

"That sounds like a script from Buffy," replied Hopkins.

"Don't it?" said Roaddog. Hopkins looked around, at the truck, at the churchyard where he saw Francis scattering holy water over the fences that blocked the windows, to Mohammed, on his knees, bowing his forehead to the ground and chanting in Arabic, he turned his gaze to Stephen's gun, the small black hole in the end pointing straight at his head. Slowly he looked back at Roaddog, "You're for real?"

"Real as hell come to town."

"That reminds me," said Jackie, "the queen asked about her dream, Roaddog rides to war with hell at his back, why aren't I at his side?"

"Well now hell stands before us," smiled Roaddog, "and it will fall."

"Fuck," Hopkins whispered, "how many dead so far?"

"We've managed to keep the mortalities down to two, and they both volunteered, might be three if you count the necromancer that came back from the dead. He's a bit of a grey area, he volunteered, or maybe engineered his first death, then we killed his ass again."

"The green man would have got me," said Jake, "if these guys hadn't turned up with the heavy artillery."

"Jake," said Roaddog, "what the fuck are you doing here, you were told to wait outside and only come in as clean-up crew."

"You think I'm going to let you get all the glory?"

"What glory? No one can know what happens here, we'll all end up in the loony bin."

"You think you can keep this secret?" asked Leo.

"I can damned well try."

"Well, you'll fail, the cops may have no clue what happened to this church, but the people will know."

"How?"

"Cos we'll tell them."

"Won't they tell the cops?"

"Oh, they'll tell them. There will be a thousand theories as to what happened here before the day is out, the conspiracy nuts will have a field day, one of the stories may even be the truth, but ask yourself. When the choice is alien lander crushed the church, then took off again, or hairy hells angels blew up the church to save the world, which one is more likely?"

"The smart money is on those alien bastards," laughed Stephen.

"You were supposed to be on the outside as well," said Roaddog, looking straight at Leo.

"Hey, I don't get many chances to fire the big gun, you want to watch it cut a DI in half?"

"I'm trying to keep the death toll down."

"But not for Martyn here," interrupted Hopkins.

"Do you have any idea what the lying bastard did?"

"Not with any certainty." Martyn flinched, and the two machine guns jumped back onto target, Martyn froze.

"Well, DI Hopkins," said Roaddog slowly, "this scumbag was extracting protection money from people on our industrial estate, and I caught his heavies swinging a baseball bat at our friend Andy, we stopped them."

"Was that Andy with the butty van?" asked Hopkins.

"Yes."

"I wondered why he suddenly disappeared, go on."

"We stopped them, myself Jackie and Jane, then Man-Dare turned up and help with the clean-up. The four-man crew couldn't admit to being beaten by a guy and three girls, so they told the leaders that there were twenty of us and they got out with their lives," he turned to Martyn, "correct?"

"Actually, I said ten," was the soft reply.

"Makes no odds," he turned back to Hopkins, "they came to Dragonriders home with three Mac-tens, they killed everyone except for the girls, and they took them back to Hyde, for some serious raping. I got Vera out of storage and took the girls back."

"You make it sound so simple."

"It was, rescue our people or die trying, far too difficult for you to understand."

"No, I understand okay, I just never thought you'd do it."

"You do realise there are three guns currently pointed at you?" There was a resounding clack.

"Four," said Leo.

"What the fuck is that?" asked Hopkins staring down the maw of Leo's gun.

"Six gauge," smiled Leo, "there won't be much left if I pull this trigger."

"Not enough to bury," said Edward, jacking the slide on his Remington, "five."

"Ladies and gentlemen," said Hopkins, "let's get one thing clear shall we? If killing me was your intention, then I would already be dead."

"Killing you is still an option," said Roaddog, "the liar is already dead."

"I'd rather you didn't do that," said Hopkins.

"Then you shouldn't have brought him, should you?"

"I needed to know the truth, and no one was saying anything."

"Now you know the truth, and you understand why he must die?"

"No, he should face trial and spend time in prison."

"What can you charge him with, mugging, or maybe conspiracy, but all the conspirators are dead. Some pansy judge is going to give him a bender, no our justice is sure and swift."

"So why is he still alive?"

"He was supposed to live out the rest of his life in fear."

"Well, he's crapping in his pants now."

"Not for much longer."

"Roaddog," called Avalon from the south door of the church, "the birds are getting very excited, Heralth approaches."

"Clerics," yelled Roaddog, "come to me, time to earn your keep." He stepped towards Hopkins and his companion, burying the sword a foot into the grass, he took the younger man by the chin and spun him around, Roaddog held the liar against his chest with his left hand, and a stiletto appeared in the right. His lips against the young man's right ear. "Your lies brought death to everyone that I loved, I gave you your life, I didn't come to find you, you came to me, and now we have need of your blood." The clerics were running towards the tableau, Avalon was removing her robe as she ran, revealing her naked body adorned with many tattoos generally of cabalistic designs, with one exception, a small blue dolphin just above her sparse pubic hair.

"You can't do this," snapped Hopkins, only to have Vera shoved into his guts, Jackie's look forced him into silence.

"Your final act may just save the world," whispered Roaddog as the knife sliced through the man's neck, blood fountained from the carotid arteries, spraying high in the air, the clerics arrived and collected as much of the blood as they could in their hands, and started their chant.

"Release me," shouted the bishop, desperately. "Release me, I can help." Roaddog dropped the dead body he was holding and cut the bishop free.

"You run and we'll take your legs and feed you to the demons, do you understand?" he said as he cut the bishops bonds. Forsythe nodded and ran to the fallen body. He covered his hands with the blood from the young man's sodden hair, he joined in the chanting. The clerics collected in a group and formed a circle each holding hands with two others, the chant doubled, then doubled again, a glowing ball of light formed in the centre of the circle, it expanded until it filled all the space within the circle, the light was hard and white, but somehow not blinding, it was possible to stare into this effulgence without the usual burns on the retinas. Quickly the light coalesced into five discrete shapes. Each shape went to one of the clerics, three were as men, short, bearded of olive complexion. One went to Francis, Francis bowed, one to Abraham, one to Mohammed. The other male was large and asian, he went to Phurba, the only female, the only one armed, went to Avalon, her bow in her left hand.

"You know your stations people. Take your angels where they need to be," shouted Roaddog. Francis and Forsythe went to the eastern end of the church, they had the huge windows to cover. Mohammed and Abraham went to the north side, they didn't have so much to cover, but it was on two stories. Phurba and his fat asian angel took the west, only two windows for them to cover. Naked Avalon and her amazon took the south side, with lots of windows on two floors and the only working door.

"Right spread out," said Roaddog to those armed with guns, "watch for anything getting through the fences, kill them as they get through, but try not to damage the fences any, okay?" Roaddog Bug and Slowball went to the south side, they watched as Avalon and the amazon walked the length of the south side, touching the fences as they went.

"Who's this?" asked Roaddog as the pair returned to the door.

"This is Diana, or Hecate, or Artemis, she has many names, but she is the goddess that I serve."

"Diana," said Roaddog, "we thank you for your aid, the hardest of tasks is going to be yours."

"What do you need from me?" her soft voice seemed to fill his mind, but not his ears, the noise of the birds was starting to get so loud as to be almost unbearable.

"We need you to hold this side of the building while we run away and send the fire to burn the evil out forever, can you do that?"

"I can, but you need to look to the weaklings."

"I know, that's why you have the hardest job."

Diana looked through the door and an arrow appeared at her bow, pull, release, faster than it can be said, the arrow sailed through the barriers and then on through three of the grey birds, instantly dead.

"I am more than capable," snap and three more dead birds fall from the dance. "Look to the others." An opening appeared in the inner circle of birds; they were forced out from the stairway from the depths. An almost cat like head came up through dancing birds, a heavy clawed hand swept a group of birds into the open mouth, sharp teeth closed, and the birds vanished in a moment. Wide shoulders next, long arms held high in the air. The sleek fur of her chest showed her many nipples, at which three were suckling. They were pink and smooth, though shaped like wolves with wings, a little smaller than wolves, but not by much. As Roaddog watched one broke free from the nipple and flew straight towards the door. Diana nocked an arrow and let loose, the arrow passed through the gate and then through the flying wolf, it fell to the ground to be food for the birds. The death of this wolf caused the others to break loose and many more to follow, suddenly the fences were attacked on all sides by winged wolves, the angels and the clerics were hard pressed to defend the barriers. Even as the wolves died more were born, each came fully prepared for battle from the darkness beneath Heralth. Each wave stressed the barriers eve further. Francis was killing one as his angel took out two. Mohammed and Mohammed tended one side of the north door, while Abraham and Abraham tended the other, they had one batch of lower windows each and the upper story shared, wolves were smashing into these every second, to be repelled and to return in moments. Avalon's staff was continuously turning, flashing hot white light against the barriers forcing the flying wolves back.

Roaddog took the whole situation into consideration for more than a moment, and yelled above the noise.

"Avalon stand off for a moment, girls it is time. Time for reinforcements. Time to make the call." Avalon, Jackie, Jane, Man-Dare, Cherie, and Sylvia came together with Avalon.

"I'm not sure what he wants," said Avalon, "but we don't need someone to die, just a token of blood will do, if each of us cut our palms and add some blood to the summoning that will be enough."

"We know what we are to do," replied Jackie over the noise of the wolves and the birds, she drew one of her knives and locked it open, with a careful move she slid the knife through the skin of her left palm, blood oozed from the shallow cut, and filled her palm. The others quickly followed suit, Cherie and Sylvia were loaned knives to perform the minor acts of self-mutilation.

"Circle," said Avalon, each took one dry hand in one bloodied hand and the circle formed, a circle tied together with the blood of its members. "I'll start the summoning," said Avalon, "but you'll all have to make the final call, I've no idea who you will be calling on, but I can tell from your grins that you have someone in mind." The old latin fell from Avalon's lips as the chant grew within the circle, she started the women moving in a counter clockwise direction, as they reached the third revolution of the circle and Avalon returned to her position in front of the south door, the crisis was reached, the moment of power was attained, and all the women screamed one name, the only one that could possibly help them in this most dreadful of situations.

"Bandit Queen," they shouted.

"Bandit Queen," they yelled.

"Bandit Queen," they howled.

Avalon broke the circle, but it was too late, the deed was done, the call was made, and worse still it was answered.

"What have you done"? demanded Avalon.

"We've called the only one that can help now," laughed Jackie as she wiped her hand on her jeans and recovered Vera.

"The Queen comes," said Jane taking the mac-10 from where she had dropped it.

"Shit and fan," laughed Man-Dare, her face a smile of pure glee.

"Avalon," called Roaddog, "back on this door."

"What have you done?" demanded the nude pagan.

"Called on help that no one else would ever dare, and I can tell that she has answered. The queen comes." His grin did nothing other than strike fear into Avalon's heart.

Heralth's hips forced their way through the opening, and she leapt into the air, her wings filled and flight was only moments away, she howled as her wings came downwards and she failed to move. Her wings thrashed and beat but very little progress was made. Flapping hard she lifted slowly from the ground, Heralth's legs gradually came into view, around the ankle of the left leg was a large hand. This hand came slowly through the opening in the floor, followed by an almost human head. As the shoulders of the woman came through the hole in the ground, her right hand snatched one of the wolves out of the air and stuffed its head into her mouth, the jaws snapped shut and the wolf died. Heralth glanced down at the force holding her in place and howled, she slashed downwards with one clawed hand, to no affect, Bandit Queen's hand held firm on her ankle, another of her children was born in a moment, and snapped up by the woman shape, more fuel for Bandit Queen.

"Bandit Queen," yelled Roaddog, the face turned towards him and smiled a grin full of terrible teeth, she nodded to her still living friend.

"Hold," shouted Roaddog, another nod, and a smile. A right hand snatched a flying wolf out of the air and stuffed it straight into her mouth, a fountain of blood squirted from her lips as the wolf was swallowed. Roaddog turned to Avalon, "hold this door, but don't lock it yet." He pointed to Jackie and Jane, and then to the door as he ran to the eastern end of the church, where Forsythe and Francis were holding the windows with their angel. Roaddog approached the angel with a smile on his face.

"You're Jesus, aren't you?" he asked, only eliciting a nod. Jesus reached out with a glowing rod of power and thrust a wolf shape from the fence.

"You seem to be a little restricted on this plane," observed Roaddog, "you can talk up a storm, but when in the storm, you seem to be a little out matched." Francis spared Roaddog a harsh glare but had no time for much else.

"My demon is holding Heralth, and you can't even hold back her little children." Over his words and the howls of the airborne wolves could be heard the brief chatter of Vera. It was Jesus turn to scowl at Roaddog's smile.

"I have a deal for you," said Roaddog loudly, "my queen holds Heralth until the fire comes and destroys this whole place, but only on the condition that you take her to your home afterwards, otherwise she releases Heralth, and the fire doesn't come."

"You will all die," said Jesus, his voice more resonant than Roaddog expected.

"Us and so many more, the choice is yours, save the people again, and take Bandit Queen home to meet daddy." Father Francis looked at Roaddog in utter disbelief.

"It shall be as you request," said Jesus.

"That's good, I'll go set things up, once things start happening, I'm going to pull all the people out of here, you and the other angels are going to have to hold these fences alone, but it won't be for more than a couple of minutes, once I have all the people out of here, I'm going to bring the fire to cleanse this place. Do you understand?"

"I understand, and we will all hold."

"Thank you," said Roaddog with a bow, then a smile for Francis, he went back to the south door just in time to watch Jackie blast a load of wolves from the gate, Jane slammed the gate shut as Jackie stepped back.

"Jane," he shouted, "open the gate". She glanced at him for a moment then complied, she stood to his right the mac-ten at the ready, Jackie to his left Vera targeted and braced. Vera spat twice and a wolf fell out of the air.

"Bandit Queen my love," yelled Roaddog, the demon shape turned to him, she looked a little like the Bandit Queen they all remembered, but equally very different. He threw the sword towards her and watched as her right hand snatched it out of the air. "Hold my love," he shouted, "hold until the fire comes to destroy this place, then you'll be free." Bandit Queen looked at Roaddog, a strange light in her eyes.

"Freedom," she howled as she plunged the sword into another of

Heralth's children even as it was being born. The wolf shape slid down the sword to the hilt and she bit off its head, then with a flick of the wrist tossed the body to the other side of the church. Roaddog stepped back.

"Lock this gate," he said to Avalon, then he turned to Bug. "Open the valves and get that unleaded in the air." Bug ran through the trees and around the truck. Roaddog turned to Slowball, "Once you see the fuel going out into the air, go round the church and get the humans moving, we're going to have to leave it to the angels for a short time, you know where we are going?"

"I got it, out of the gate turn right and run like a bastard, till we hit the ditch."

Roaddog took the drone from its box and made sure it was operational, the link to his phone worked perfectly. By the time he looked up he could already smell petrol in the air, and plumes were blowing from the tanker towards the church, looking a little like heat haze rising from a hot road, the light breeze did little to disperse the vapours. Slowball set off around the church telling each of the people to start moving, when he got to the eastern window Forsythe was on his knees and Francis was giving him a rapid blessing while Jesus did his level best to keep the wolves from breaking through the fences.

"Time to move," yelled Slowball as he went by, he knew that he was going to be one of the slower ones making his way to the safety of the drain. Bug came back through the trees.

"It's going okay, but damn are those gas bottles getting cold," he said to Roaddog,

"So long as they have enough pressure to get most of the petrol out, that's all we need, get moving mate."

"Avalon," he called almost choking on the thick air. "Come on, let's get out of here."

Avalon turned to Diana, "Will you manage to hold?"

"I shall hold, have no fear."

"The fire that comes is unlike any fire you have experienced; how will you survive?"

"While you believe I will return."

"I will always believe," said Avalon, bowing deeply then turning towards the lynch gate. Roaddog hurried her along, though she spent a few seconds collecting her robe from where she had dropped it. They were the last of the people to leave the church yard. Running through a field of barley was not an easy task the ground was soft despite the lack of rain; they were both breathing really hard by the time they caught up with Leo.

"I'm too old for this crap," said Leo, each word separated by a panted breath.

"Come on, old man," said Roaddog, "not far to go, fifty yards to the road, then ten to the dyke."

"Just let me die here."

"No way, run or I'll kick you all the way there."

"Bastard," mumbled Leo as he pressed on, the six gauge weighing heavily in his arms.

Roaddog arrived at the edge of the dyke just as a stranger appeared from below.

Inside the church, the battle to escape was getting desperate, Heralth was giving birth faster than Bandit Queen could kill the little demons, though the effort was rapidly reducing Heralth's power. A cluster of them attacked Bandit Queen simultaneously, Melchion's sword killed many on the first strike and the rest on the backstroke.

"You'll not escape me," howled Bandit Queen, her voice somehow distorted by the shape of the throat, more raucous than her human voice had ever been, but no less menacing.

"Fly my children," said Heralth, "fly, find these humans and end their miserable lives." Her voice smooth and soft like the purr of a contented cat, but louder than the fiercest thunderclap. Her children gave up attacking Bandit Queen and raced to the upper windows on the northside. Resilient and defended as the heras fence panels were, they were not designed to withstand the teeth of demonic dogs. The other children kept attacking the other windows and the south door, simply to stop the angels moving to defend the northside. Heralth was birthing children as fast as she could, each birth diminished her, but added to her chances of survival.

"Why have you not killed me?" screamed Heralth.

"I was told by my son to hold," replied Bandit Queen, "and hold I shall."

"Release me and together we can ravage this world."

"Never, you will die here in my hand, by the hand of my son, he has assured me that freedom will be mine."

"You trust the word of a human?"

"Until the end of time, and your end is very near now."

"My children are loose and they will end him."

"The fire comes I can smell it in the air," laughed Bandit Queen.

An elderly man dressed in camouflage confronted Roaddog.
"What are you crazy people doing?" snarled the old man.
"That depends very much on who you are," grinned Roaddog.
"My name is Alan, but people call me Mark, I came here for a quiet day's fishing, and now you people are making so much noise there'll be no fish today," answered the old man.
"You have no idea about noise," smiled Roaddog, "Slowball, save this old fools life." Slowball stepped up behind Mark and picked him up in a bear hug, walked him to the edge of the dyke and dropped him. Mark slid down the steep bank quite quickly until his feet caught on the small flat section on the edge of the water, however his forward momentum was just too great, on stiff legs he rose from the bank and fell forwards into the water.
"Drones up," yelled Roaddog. He turned to Avalon, "be ready if it doesn't fire, if it does, then get down into the cut." Avalon nodded and raised her staff; a sparkling of red light came from the crystal in the end.
"I have flying dogs coming this way," he shouted trying not to look away from the display, he heard the sound of a shotgun being broken, and still he didn't look, there was the clack of the same gun being closed, then the unmistakeable boom of the six gauge, and the flying wolves vanished into a pink haze.
"Fuck you," snarled Leo as he broke the six open and reloaded.
Roaddog made sure the drone was far above the altitude of the flying wolves, he heard the six close and fire again, a smaller shotgun firing alongside it.
"Firing," said Roaddog, the radio signal was sent, the firework under the drone lit and started to spit small balls of fire down into the cloud of vapour. A curtain of blue fire started to fall towards the church spreading sideways as it did. Roaddog turned and swept Avalon from her feet and fell down the steep bank, not caring where they ended up. Leo had already dropped the six and preceded them down the bank with Edward only and instant behind. No one saw the wave front of flame gather speed and pressure, until it was travelling so fast that the air couldn't get out of the way quick enough, two hundred feet above the church the blast front exceeded the speed of sound, it became a hammer blow of heat and pressure. The fire front hit the church at three times the speed of sound, and thousands of pounds per square inch, far more than any building could have withstood, the church collapsed, the

timbers and stones shattered into splinters and gravel, these buried themselves in the ground. Everything within fifty yards of the church was flattened, the fields of barley and corn were stripped in the blast, almost as if they had been cut by the combines of harvest time.

Roaddog felt the ground pitch beneath him, as he rolled off Avalon, he had covered her body with his own as they came to rest.

"Wait," he yelled at the top of his lungs, hoping that some still had hearing left. Debris started to fall all around them, thankfully all of it small and slow moving. Slowly he raised his head above the edge of the dyke, once he was sure there wasn't anything dangerous coming their way he stood up and looked around.

"Hey," he shouted, "where's the bishop and Phurba?

"They stayed," said Francis.

"What the fuck did they do that for?"

"Forsythe made a fast confession and announced his own penance. He stayed, I'm assuming Phurba decided to take the next step on the road to enlightenment."

"I didn't want any more deaths."

"They made their own decisions; you can't deny that they died well."

"True, but I'd have preferred that they survived." The post explosion silence was filled with the rumble of many motorcycles. With them came a blue people carrier called Moya. The motorcycles picked their way slowly through the remains of trees and the stones from the graveyard wall, Vince and Horse pulled up alongside Roaddog.

"Well man," said Vince, "you definitely fucked that up."

"Permanently I hope," replied Roaddog.

"Injured?" asked Vince.

"None, three dead."

"Any clean up needed?"

"No, they were at the church."

"What church?" asked Vince, laughing loudly.

"Slowball," Roaddog called, "fetch the fisherman."

"Well, Alan called Mark, how does that rank as loud?" asked Roaddog.

"What have you done, there used to be a church there?"

"Well, to be honest, it is very important to us that we weren't here, can you understand that?"

"I suppose, but there are so many people that know you are here."

"I trust almost all of them," he let the sentence hang.

"But you don't know me," answered Mark slowly.

"True, and there is another, detective inspector Hopkins," Roaddog spun Mark around until he was facing Hopkins, with Roaddog standing behind him. In a heartbeat Roaddog had Marks head pinned against his own shoulder and a stiletto at his throat.

"Mark, don't move, the cold you can feel is a knife, if it takes your life, it won't be the first today, the important question isn't really for you Mark, it's for Hopkins. Well DI, do I tie up the loose ends?" To emphasise Roaddog's words guns started to zero in on Hopkins, Bug, who was standing behind Hopkins dived down into the ditch, only just managing to stop before he hit the water.

"Mark," said Hopkins, "my chances of survival here are very limited, yours however are different, promise to say nothing and Dog will let you live. Is that true Dog?"

"Yes."

"I will say nothing, I was not here, though any investigation is going to show my car as being over there somewhere," said Hopkins.

"For truth?" asked Roaddog.

"Yes, upon my honour."

"You would trust a copper?" demanded Vince.

"This one yes, he's more than a little crazy," replied Roaddog.

"Your funeral."

"Mark, do you understand?" asked Roaddog softly.

"You were never here," said Mark.

"Good man, gather your gear, we've got a party to go to, and you're coming too." He took out his phone and dialled a number.

"Hi Karen, yes that was us, open the bar, we're coming for a party." He disconnected the call. "Right people, let's get the hell out of this place before the local plod realise that wasn't some typhoon going supersonic."

"Francis," he said, "a word." The others were separating to get rides in whatever vehicles were available.

Man-Dare nudged Jackie as they walked towards Mick's car.

"Did Bandit Queen look any more frightening than she did when she was alive?"

"Not so much, the face we saw today was simply hidden beneath her skin, she always was a scary bitch," smiled Jackie as she opened the rear door, and waved Man-Dare in.

"She didn't hide it very well," laughed Man-Dare.

"Would you really have killed that man?" asked Francis.

"Of course not, but Hopkins didn't need to know that."
"You do know you're mad?"
"Not the only one though."
"What do you mean?"
"You heard my bargain with Jesus?"
"I did."
"So right now, Jesus has taken Bandit Queen to heaven."
"I suppose, and your point is?"
"She's going to burn that place down as well, your god's a bit of a dick."

The End.

Afterword.

It's Easter weekend, well almost, Thursday morning to be precise. Cherie is sitting in one of the sofas, her child Christopher sucking strongly on her left breast, over her right shoulder Roaddog, Bug and Slowball are working on a Harley, they're struggling with the nut on the end of the crankshaft, they need to get the primary drive off and it's being a bitch.

"Hey guys," said Cherie, "I'd prefer it that my kids first word was not fuck."

"Sorry love," called Bug.

Cherie looked up to see Linda and Josh walking towards her.

"Hi kids, how you doing?" she asked.

"We're fine," said Linda.

"Great," said Josh, his eyes locked on the white expanse of Cherie's exposed left breast.

"How's Chris doing?" asked Linda, giving Josh a nudge in the ribs.

"Bastard is always hungry; he's killing my nipples."

"He's growing fast," said Linda.

"He's putting on weight like a good 'un." replied Cherie, then she looked at Joshua, "You can take your eyes off my tit any time you know."

"Sorry," replied Josh, "I've just never seen, sorry," his voice stumbled to a halt, and he finally looked up into Cherie's eyes. She laughed and

Linda joined in.

"How are things with you two now?" asked Cherie.

"Most of the restrictions have faded away," said Linda, "we're spending a fair bit of time together now."

"That's good, or is it?"

"Oh yeah," said Joshua, "it's a lot better now."

"You two are still too young," said Cherie.

"Yeah," said Linda, "but we've done it now, so what the fuck."

"Your parents are okay with this?"

"Better than sneaking off to the church," laughed Joshua.

"What church?" asked Linda with a smile.

"That's for sure," smiled Cherie, "you are okay though?"

"Yes, we're fine, and getting used to being together," said Linda, "we fight occasionally, but that's to be expected. If he stares at your tits much more, I'm going to smack him."

"Sometimes that's all they understand," replied Cherie.

"You still have to slap Bug?" asked Linda.

"Yes, sometimes, but he likes it." laughed Cherie. "Shouldn't you be in school?"

"Last day," said Joshua, "can't be arsed. Anyway, how is everyone?"

"We're doing okay, things are looking fine for us, we're making enough money to live on, and nothing major has turned up for us," she glanced into the carpark as a car pulled up. "Fuck, that could be changing." She looked over her shoulder and called "Dog." Roaddog glanced at the car and said "Break, five." He stood up from his place beside the injured Harley and wiped his hands on a rag. Walking to the front of the store, he met the people from the car.

"Detective inspector fucking Hopkins, and DS Stephen, what are you after today?"

"Hi Roaddog," said Hopkins, Stephen only nodded.

"What the fuck is going on?" demanded Roaddog.

"Well," said Hopkins, he paused, "I've had word from Avalon."

"What does she want now?" demanded Roaddog.

"She's got a situation, and she might need your firepower."

"You're kidding me," snapped Roaddog, "can't you guys deal with it?"

"Fuck, the guys in charge won't even believe, you know what it's like."

"So," Roaddog said, "which one of you two is Scully?"

"What do you mean?" asked Hopkins.

"The X files, you get all the crazy shit, and then you bring it to me."

"It's what you are good at."

"What about the Father?"

"He's already there and struggling."

"So, what do you want from us?"

"You know, the girls and Vera, and, you know."

"Where is she at?"

"She's in Scotland, a creepy castle, north side of Loch Ness."

"That'll be Urquhart, how desperate is she?"

"No one's been killed yet, but there have been some injuries. Sooner the better really."

"What's the opposition?"

"It's a nest of flying snake demons, she's got the whole crew there, and they're holding, but they can't get inside the nest to get to the queen."

"A queen, that's what she wants?" whispered Roaddog.

Hopkins glanced at the ground for a moment then continued, "yes, 'fraid so."

"So, every time shit and fan come together, she calls in a 52 strike?"

"Hey man," said Stephen, "that's not fair, she takes a lot of shit on by herself, how many times has she actually called you?"

"Okay, it's been twice since Botolph's, and neither time we needed to call on the Queen."

"We'll be coming with," said Hopkins, "and we'll be bringing our own firepower."

"Usual rates," snapped Roaddog.

"Come on man," sighed Hopkins, "that cash is killing my departments budget."

"Your department is standing here, and if I didn't make you pay, we'd be on the road every fucking day."

"Agreed," mumbled Hopkins. Roaddog smiled and turned towards the shop.

"Hellriders," he shouted, "we have a job, Avalon needs our hairy arses in Scotland, get hot." He turned to Cherie and Chris, he stroked the baby's head gently, "you, you little shit head, you're staying here." Cherie nodded and spoke softly, "Look after my man."

"I will," he said.

In three minutes the Hellriders were ready, Bug fired up the Pan-Euro and the howl of its exhaust filled the village.

"Fuck," muttered Stephen, "did he really need to do those mods to that exhaust?"

"Try and keep up coppers," yelled Roaddog as the victory shot off the forecourt and into the road, followed by Bug's Pan-Euro and Slowball's trike.

About the author.

My name is Mick, some call me Roaddog, I appear in this novel, basically in my true form. I came to the writing thing late in life, or maybe early, the first novel took twenty years to publish, this one only two. To my fans that read these things in three days, I hate you with a passion, but still hope that you enjoy my ramblings. I think that this is the end for the Hellriders, though I have left it open for a revisit at some future date. Now to the next, switching to sci-fi, title as yet undiscovered, follow the antics of Joens the lonely pilot and his search for love, or something, in the immensity of space.

All the best, Mick Porter, Roaddog

Printed in Great Britain
by Amazon